IN CASE WE'RE MADE INTO COATS

•THE EXOTIC SHAPESHIFTER•

BOOK ONE

BOOK ONE

TESSA CHARLEIGH

ILLUSTRATED BY

SOPHIA LOGAN-BARRÉ

ABOUT THE AUTHOR

Tessa Charleigh currently resides in Indianapolis, Indiana. She comes from a family line of doctors in varying medical fields and broke that line to become a writer. Tessa was raised in her mother's exotic veterinary clinic, gaining her unique life experiences and knowledge that she likes to integrate into her novels. Her series, In Case We're Made into Coats, was inspired by the desire to humanize shapeshifters as a species, as well as to explore their position on matters such as health and habitual life.

incaseweremadeintocoats.com

Sophia Logan-Barré's drawings are linked to her passion for the natural world. She spends much of her time walking and keenly observing life in the woods of Maine and New Hampshire. She has a particular interest in birds, studying plumage and identifying individual calls and songs. Sophia's drawings encompass both reflections of what she observes in nature and her interest in fantasy and pure invention.

sophialoganbarre.com

ABOUT THE WRITER

Chase Wagner was born in Jackson, Mississippi, and is once again homeless. (Donations not expected, but always appreciated.) He enjoys writing and sleeping. Dislikes running and shapeshifting.

Sorry, *no interviews.*

No, this book is not sponsored by any of the snack-food brands raved about in its contents, I was probably just hungry.

IN CASE WE'RE MADE INTO COATS

•THE EXOTIC SHAPESHIFTER•

BY CHASE WAGNER & ANGELA TALLON

PREFACE

My name is Chase Wagner. I'm a sixteen-year-old shapeshifter, writing this in case I die here in Louisiana and no one knows what me and my friends have been through. Today's date is May 8, 2019, but I'm sure it'll take me more than a couple days to write all of this down.

However, before I get into all the madness that happened this past week, you probably need some background information, and when and if I get to see her again, I'm going to ask my friend Angela to write in some of the parts of our story—where I may not have been present or conscious before I send this out for some kind of publication.

I'm gonna try and speed through most of this "past" stuff, because there's a ton to explain and quite frankly, I've blocked a lot of it out. That being said, I think I'll start by going back a couple years to the day I lost my freedom.

I was fourteen at the time and probably gave off the overall appearance of a crazy homeless teenager, with my once brightly colored (now faded) shorts and worn black jacket. I was living by myself at an unspecified hotel on the west side of Jackson, Mississippi. Well, unspecified to me at least. It wasn't worth bothering to remember the name of the place, considering how much I moved around. Just the week before, I had been sleeping behind the large burnt-out W of a Walmart sign. Man, times have changed. I still haven't decided whether it was for better or worse, but I was pulled away from my life of living alone when I was forced to go to the drugstore in search of more bandages.

Just getting to the store was a victory in itself. My legs were hurting horribly, and I knew at least one of our traffic-patrol officers at the hotel had a gun. As irrational as it sounds to be afraid of someone just because they were armed, I think my fear was justified by past experiences.

Shapeshifters don't have it easy. I wish I'd learned that lesson earlier. We're constantly being pursued by a group of people commonly referred to as huntsmen—psychopathic killers hell-bent on capturing shapeshifters at any

cost, and at the time I didn't know why. Come to think of it, I didn't even know what they were called.

Apart from huntsmen, I didn't think anyone else was aware of our existence. People who *do* know about us probably never talk about their encounters openly. I'm sure the very idea of a teenager suddenly turning into a pheasant and flying away is enough to make anybody sound crazy. It's not like we can risk befriending too many "normal" people, either. Talking to strangers is dangerous, and usually got me chased out of whatever temporary accommodations I had by some madman with a gun.

Because of an incident that happened when I was twelve, something I don't care to go into detail about right now, my arms and legs pretty much have never stopped hurting. But since I had no idea what was wrong at the time, I had to come up with my own solution so I could walk. I found that wrapping my limbs in cloth bandages was the most effective way to stop the pain. Which was pretty inconvenient, considering almost every time I was confronted with a huntsman, I had to shift into some large animal in order to get away and the wraps would rip from my body, just like my clothes. Then the pain would return, and, let me tell you, it was excruciating.

So every week I would make a trip to the closest drug-store to buy more bandages and food, because while the hotel supplied me with free breakfast and clothes from the lost and found, they didn't offer any other meals. I had a deal with the hotel. I'd work there, and in exchange they'd let me stay in one of their rooms. Which was more than generous, but I knew it'd only be a matter of time before someone found me and I had to leave.

It was around this time that huntsmen started becoming more and more of a "thing." Don't get me wrong, they've apparently been around since forever, but for whatever reason, 2017 was the year they started showing up wherever I went without fail.

As far as I know, huntsmen have no real way to track shapeshifters. They just follow social cues. For example, if they see someone who looks like they've got something to hide, from my experiences, they'll usually follow that person or animal around for a while in case something interesting happens. That's not to say if you're a shapeshifter you shouldn't try to keep a low profile. Huntsmen are everywhere, and the more experienced ones can tell what you are just by the look on your face, especially if you aren't

human-born, but that's a whole 'nother ballgame that we won't even attempt to go into right now.

Anyway, that's probably enough context for now. On to our narrative.

1: CHASE

Jackson, Mississippi

May 2017

I walked into the drugstore with my hoodie over my head. There weren't too many people there, but I didn't want to risk someone recognizing me from one of the many public scenes I've caused by merely existing, and someone trying to shoot me. The impaired bones in my arms and legs kept jerking out of place, pondering what form I was in and which of my appendages didn't belong. Without

my bandages, nothing was holding them together on the inside, and I was on the brink of tears.

I wandered into the therapeutic aisle that primarily housed supports for disabled people—stuff like canes and walkers. The self-adhering ACE bandage wraps I usually bought were on the bottom shelf, so I sat on the floor with every intention of just taking them out of their packaging and putting them on right there.

Of course, I wasn't going to steal anything, I had money from tips that came from cleaning the hotel rooms and some more that was pitifully given to me by the staff. It wasn't much—just enough to buy my relief and a couple bags of chips or some microwave pasta for dinner.

I took the box of bandages from the shelf before dumping it onto the floor. And after removing my jacket, I started wrapping my left arm, the pain instantly subsiding. I reached for another package when I noticed someone else was in the aisle with me. He was tall with brown hair and a stubble beard, dressed in a long black coat that went down to his knees, and I wouldn't have paid him any mind had I not seen him watching me out of the corner of my eye.

I glanced over at him, and he looked back to the shelf in front of him, as if he had been minding his own business the whole time. *Not a good sign.* I started opening the boxes faster. I wasn't going to be able to stand back up if I didn't finish what I was doing, but panic was gradually racing through me. I looked back toward him, but he was already gone. This briefly convinced me that the danger was all in my paranoid head.

With all the wraps on, I was feeling about a million times better, so I stood and started toward the register with my pile of empty boxes.

There was no sign of the busybody from the aisle at the checkout, and luckily no one gave me any trouble on the way back to the hotel, but I still entered through the staff-only door in the back just in case. I closed the door and started up the stairs to my room. No one ever took the stairs since we had several elevators, but for someone like me whose worst nightmare is a small confined space filled with strangers, the stairs were perfect.

I was walking through the hallway to my room when a family of four passed by. "Mom, can we go get something to eat soon?" the youngest boy asked, tugging on some poor woman's shirt. She appeared absolutely exhausted.

"Later," the woman replied drowsily. "Mommy forgot your sister at the pool—again."

I was kicking myself. I was supposed to get food at the store! I blamed the man in the coat for rushing me, but no matter whose fault it was, I wasn't risking going out again. So, that meant vending machine food for dinner—again. I trudged all the way back down the stairs, dejected, but as I was about to enter the lobby, I froze in place. There he was, leaning over the front desk in a quiet conversation with the woman behind it. *The coat guy from the drugstore!*

"I'm looking for—" he started to the woman in a hushed tone before turning toward me.

We locked eyes, and after staring like a deer confronted with a pair of headlights, I bolted into the nearest elevator, frantically pushing buttons as the man advanced toward me.

Come on! I blind pushed buttons as the elevator doors slowly closed.

"Wait!" he shouted. The doors closed an inch from his face, and the elevator shot up to the... second floor. I'd clicked every button! On the second floor, I could hear someone running down the hallway toward the elevator.

He must have taken the stairs! I saw him for a split second before the doors shut once again.

He missed me on the third floor like he had the second, but eventually my luck would run out. I had to think fast. The doors opened on the fourth floor, and once again, I could hear his steps. He was going to make it into the elevator this time, and there was absolutely nowhere for me to go.

My clothes would drop to the ground, and he would know I was in here if I shifted into something smaller, but I would still lose to a gun if I shifted into something larger. I backed up to the wall as the doors opened, and he jumped inside. He leaned down and put his hands on his knees, taking a moment to catch his breath as the elevator ascended to the fifth floor. "You...," he said between breaths, "please wait—". I leaned against the back corner of the small space, grasping the handrails for dear life, absolutely terrified. There was no way out! I stared at the metal doors anxiously, ready to make a break for it the second they opened. He caught his breath. "Hey, you alright?" He sounded legitimately concerned. He reached into his pocket, and I closed my eyes as tightly as I could, preparing for the worst. "Kid," he said quietly. I opened my eyes, and

he was holding something out, offering me something. It looked like an energy bar of some sort. I didn't say a word. I didn't even move.

"I'm not a huntsman," he said.

"You're...what?"

He sighed, stepping back. His body began to glow ever so slightly until his tall human stature started slouching over into a quadruped shape. His clothes ripped from his body, unable to contain his new and very different form, and before you knew it, the stranger became a majestic-looking African spotted leopard. *Tada!* That's shapeshifting for ya, pretty cool, huh? Fortunately for you readers, the whole transformation can be translated into one verb: *shifting*. Okay, I guess that's a gerund, but you get the idea.

Relieved, I sighed loudly and slid down the wall of the elevator to sit on the ground. The doors opened for the fifth floor, but I completely missed it. "I thought I was a goner," I said, standing back up.

The large cat nodded. "But now I can't shift back," he complained, sitting down.

"How'd you know what I am?" I asked. "You know, when you saw me at the drugstore?"

"You've got Shifter's Bone," the cat said, pointing at me. "My brother had it, too. I know the condition when I see it."

I was suddenly very curious. "Wait," I said, "did your brother ever, like, get over it?"

He appeared surprised, like he expected me to be aware of something. "How long have you had it?"

"Couple years," I shrugged.

I waited for him to think of a way to answer my question gently.

"No...." he sighed. "My brother died of unrelated causes not too long ago, but he lived with the condition in his right leg most of his life."

"Alright," I replied, looking down. My reaction may not have been all that hysterical, but the news hit me like a freight train. How could I be stuck with this?

"I may be able to help with some of that pain, though," the cat continued. "Perhaps improve your quality of life. Name's Christopher."

"What do you—" I started. The elevator finally opened to the sixth floor, my floor, and I stepped out, Christopher following closely behind me.

It occurs to me that you all may be a bit confused as to how I've managed to retain all these conversations for so long, but if you're a shapeshifter, you need no reminder that our abilities depend on our memory. I'd say it's a blessing and a curse, but dwelling on things is basically a hobby of mine, and believe me, I have a lot I'd like to forget.

"We'll talk about it later," he insisted. "What's your name?"

"Chase," I replied. "This is actually pretty cool, I haven't met someone like me in years."

"I'm guessing you live alone?"

"Umm...." I approached my door, reaching into my jacket pocket for my key card. It wasn't there, and I started patting down the rest of my body. "Dang it." This had to have been the fifth time I'd locked myself out.

Christopher looked over to a housekeeping cart stationed next to the room across from mine. "See if she can let you in," he said, sitting down with his tail flicking around in an irritated fashion.

I approached the cart and pushed on the door. "Excuse me," I started shyly, walking in. I did mention that talking to strangers was not my forte.

I about blacked out when I saw the maid—face-down on the floor and motionless. I can't remember if I screamed or not, but I do recall backing up and bumping into Christopher, who I didn't realize was standing behind me.

I jumped like a startled jackrabbit. "Whoa! Just me," Christopher said, looking into the room and taking a couple steps back himself. "Oh...."

You could tell that the room had been tossed. The curtains were torn down, all the dresser drawers were pulled out, and every door had been opened, even the microwave.

"They're here," I said sadly. *Goodbye hot showers and free breakfast*, I thought.

Huntsmen don't usually kill normal people, but they are incredibly selfish. If someone gets in their way, they don't hesitate to pull a gun. Luckily, the maid was only unconscious, not dead. How did I know that this was the handiwork of a huntsman and not some petty thief? Because I'd seen it before. Shapeshifters can hide just about anywhere, it's one of our few advantages. And because of that, this is what the huntsmen do. They look anywhere and everywhere a mouse, rat, small bird, or lizard could possibly hide.

I noticed the maid's master key dangling from her neck, but my feet were frozen in place. I nudged Christopher with my leg and pointed to it. He looked up at me, then to the key before sighing. He didn't seem too keen on entering the crime scene either. He stepped timidly into the room, cautiously walking around the woman before using his paw to quickly rip the key off her neck. Yeah, I probably could have gotten it myself. But, in my defense, there could still have been someone hiding in the room.

Christopher met me back in the doorway and slid the key across the nylon carpet to my feet. I picked it up. "Least I can grab my things," I said, flipping the key card as I walked away.

"Hang on," Christopher started, following me down the hallway. "Where do you plan on going?"

"I'll figure it out," I replied. "I usually find someplace... You know, eventually."

He leapt in front of me. "Have huntsmen chased you out of every home you've had?"

I stared at him, raising an eyebrow. "If you mean those crazy people with the blow darts and guns, then yes."

"You know," he replied ever-so-casually, "you could come live with me and my family. We're in a fairly safe

area. We could protect each other." I was shocked. This guy barely knew me, and he was asking me to come live with him? He was definitely a shifter. Which, BACK THEN was a big reason for me to trust someone, and on top of that, he knew about my condition. He said he knew how to help me feel better...

It all seemed too good to be true. I didn't even know why he was at that drugstore in the first place. "Who's to say I don't have my own family who are all waiting for me right now?"

He gave me a flat look and sat down. "I'm serious. You and my daughter are probably close in age. You might make some connections with her and her friends. Seeing as you've made it out here on your own all this time, who knows? You may even teach them a thing or two."

I walked past him again, putting the sliding master key into the card reader lock above the door handle and waiting till the little blinking light turned from red to green. I then entered my hotel room for the last time. "Look, while we're here, you could go change," I said, tossing him some of the clothes I had strewn out on the bed. They were all faded and too big for either of us. Some even had holes, but it was all I could offer.

He looked down at the pile then back up at me with an unimpressed expression. I rolled my eyes and sat down on the foot of the bed to bag my things. "Come on, it's all I've got."

Moments after the cat vanished into the bathroom, a familiar dark-haired man emerged wearing the worst tie-dyed t-shirt I've ever seen, a pair of blue jeans with a hole so big the knee stuck out, and a couple of mismatched socks. "What, no shoes?" he asked.

"Sorry, last pair," I said, absentmindedly gesturing to my bright green Crocs. Only the remnants of their straps were stuck on by the black logo buttons.

Christopher laughed, sitting down next to me. "Sure you don't wanna follow me home?"

"Nope, I'm good, thanks." I zipped up my little black suitcase which held my few belongings. "But I appreciate the offer." I pushed the door to the hallway open slightly. "It was nice to meet—" I stopped talking when I saw the woman pointing a pistol at my forehead. She had a rat's nest of blond hair, was wearing a pair of khaki shorts with a white shirt, and spoke in a thick country accent.

"Gotcha now, weasel boy!" she yelled, using the pistol to ram me in the ribs. I fell down and backed up along

the ground quickly, my heart beating out of my chest. The woman aimed the gun down at me, and Christopher didn't hesitate; he smacked her in the head with a curtain rod. It was probably the only weapon he could find on short notice.

The ~~huntsman~~ ~~huntswoman~~ female huntsman was knocked out cold, the gun falling from her hand as she hit the floor. I got up from the ground slowly and looked at Christopher, who was standing over her. "So, are you coming with me or not?"

2: CHASE

Fast forward to about a week ago. I'd been living with Christopher and his kin of shapeshifters for one year, eleven months, and twenty-five days. But who's counting? And I can't say I was all that happy. Most of that time was spent staring at the wall, pacing about my "bedroom," and talking to myself. These were the most boring months/years of my life.

But as much as I'd like to sit and rant about all the torment and ridicule I put up with in that house, I think

it's better to just move on with the story. Every day was the same old limbo until the day after Christopher vanished without a trace.

McComb, Mississippi

April 2019

I ran down the hall into the living room, grabbing my backpack that was laying by the fireplace and quickly throwing it over my shoulder. That room had the strangest layout ever. There was a fireplace in the middle of one wall with a rug and an antique piano bench in front of it. Beneath the narrow doorway on the opposite wall was a small step leading down to the kitchen. In the center of the living room was the world's ugliest brown couch, facing two chairs that sat a few feet from one another. And on top of all its other faults, the room had literally no windows except a small, diamond-shaped one above the front door that you could barely see out of. It sounds hard to picture, but trust me, it's the ugliest space on the planet.

"Alex, have you seen Angela?" I asked. He was sitting in the large chair near the front door.

I stood there, waiting for an unlikely response. "What's the problem now?" he got around to replying from behind his newspaper. Occasionally, he'd utter bits and pieces of news out loud to himself. His voice was deep and hard like a prisoner's. That, or some kind of retired drill sergeant. Alex is Christopher's daughter's best friend's grandfather. Yeah, the family dynamic is a bit complicated. Bottom line: he can't stand me.

"Just never mind," I grumbled, heading down the singular step leading into the world's most disorganized kitchen, just as odd in layout. The fridge was against the wall where you enter through the living room, almost encroaching on the stair. If someone were to open one of its doors while you were trying to enter the room, your path would be blocked. There was a huge harvest table in the center of the tiny space that you had to maneuver around whenever you tried to get out the back door, one small oven on the biggest wall that only worked half the time, and dated oak cabinets surrounding— You know what? I hate this. If you're looking for the kind of book that wastes pages and pages explaining the texture and placement of every piece of furniture in the room, you might as well stop reading. No one cares about the kitchen. Moving on.

"Where ya going?" someone called from behind me as I placed my hand on the dented brass doorknob. "If you're trying to run away, I'll start the timer and see how long it takes for Grandfather to drag you back here." This would be Christopher's daughter's best friend, Osscar.

"Not running away," I replied, "going to get Angela."

"You know, maybe if you left your room every once in a while, you'd notice when this kind of stuff happens," he continued as I opened the door. "She's been gone for hours."

"You could have told me!?"

"Said I wouldn't," Osscar replied. "How about you just sit down, take a breather or something? She can handle herself."

"I can't just—" I started.

"Sorry," he cut me off, "I forgot. Who am I to take away the only sunlight you'll see for the week?"

"Hey, we were cool earlier," I said angrily. "What are you so upset about?"

"Really?" Osscar asked, pushing himself up onto the table. "Like, she invites you to come hang out with us and you blow her off, but the second you don't know where she is...." He gestured to the door.

"Look, I know you guys are friends and all, but—"

"Sure we are," he interrupted again, "but I've been giving you the benefit of the doubt since you got here."

"You know the circumstances," I replied.

"Yeah, uh huh," he scoffed. "How about this? Just this once, let Angela live her own life, since you've already decided to throw yours away."

I glared at Osscar, lacking a comeback. I slammed the door behind me and started off through the highly inconvenient grass field that spread on for miles beyond the house. It takes days to get across it on foot. Luckily, being a shapeshifter does have its occasional perks.

3: ANGELA

I'm Angela Tallon, a sixteen-year-old shapeshifter, writing this from Happy Campers Trailer Park in Louisiana. I thought I'd take Chase up on this book thing, so here we are.

I was told to include the date. It is May the 9th of 2019. I'm not exactly sure how he did his introductions, but Chase did say that he wanted me to write my own physical description.

Okay. I have brown eyes, reddish-brown hair, and before this month, I lived in the southwestern region of Mississippi in a cramped house with my father (Christopher), Chase, Alex (our...warden?), Osscar (his grandson/my best friend), my honorary sister Izzy, her "little brother" Malachi, and their grandparents, Dana and Henry. I know this is kind of an odd way to describe myself, but I'm doing my best.

Oh boy, where do I start?

Okay, my dad had just gone missing the day before. By missing, I mean we woke up and he was just gone. No note, no notice, and while I was jokingly told that it's fairly "normal" for fathers to disappear in a similar context, for whatever reason, I felt it was a good idea to wake up at sunrise and run out toward town to see if I could find him.

Back then, I didn't know what the real world was like for shifters, and while I'd been told all kinds of stories, the dangers were much vaguer in my head. I know better now, but this was only my third or fourth time venturing beyond the field since we moved to the house when I was ten, and probably the second time I'd succeeded before anyone came "chasing" after me. Alex never let us leave.

It took me hours to get across that stupid field in front of the house. Or at least it felt like hours—time and distances are hard to remember. It was like a maze. You couldn't even see where you were going the grass was so tall, itchy, and thick. But I thought that maybe my father had gone to see his half-brother Jason again? It was literally the only place I could think of that he'd go. Uncle Jason owned the local gun store in a small town a long way up the road. I'd only met him once, and once was enough. He's one of those "outspoken" types. I recall the first thing he said to my dad when he met me was, "Wow, Chris. You made that?"

I ran off in my Arctic wolf shift, so I'd be short enough to get through the grass without anyone seeing. When I finally got onto the large rock marking the end of the field and the beginning of the closest road, it was well past noon. And while that may not seem late for you, imagine walking all morning through an open field with no shade, no water, and the ever-looming possibly that you were being followed.

No one ever used this road, it was the only one to town from where we lived, but it was unpaved and bumpy, with rocks big enough to pop car tires. Straight ahead, I saw a

sign for a train station and a fork splitting the road in two: the road branching to the right was smooth and newly paved, but I was almost certain I had to keep true on the painful path forward despite the fact that the rocks were piercing deeper into my paw pads with every step.

I wasn't able to take very much with me—just an old satchel containing the only outfit I could find that I felt like destroying.

Finally, I saw a sign! A musty, dusty, broken sign:

CHATHAM CREEK TOWN: ONE MILE

I couldn't have been prouder, despite the fact that there was still a ways to go. I'd not only successfully snuck out of the house, but also made it all the way to town without a single person spotting me. As I walked closer, I began to realize that the place didn't look anything like my memory of it. It was broken down, beaten up, and empty. The streets were littered with trash, and the plants that used to surround the buildings had withered.

I wonder what happened...

I ran behind one of the old buildings. This one had clearly been vacant for a while. I shifted back to my human

form, quickly throwing on what little clothing I brought, including the horrible black funeral dress with a sewn-on lace collar that Dana purchased for me a few years before.

At first, I didn't spot anyone except the occasional old man in a porch rocker. I eventually noticed a couple Harley riders smoking in an alley, and a group of about five intoxicated teenage boys laughing it up outside what probably used to be a motel.

I already wanted to go home. My sense of achievement had worn off, and the anxiety was setting in. It felt like all eyes were on me as I made my way through the silent little ghost town, dressed like someone who could have founded it decades before I was even born. I was looking around for some kind of advertisement for my uncle's shop and found nothing, which was weird because I remembered a prominent wooden sign on top of his building.

"Hey, girl!" someone shouted from behind me. The youngest from the group of teenagers was waving me over. He looked disheveled with a gray hoodie pulled over his head and army pants so low on his waist you could see the rim of his boxers. "Need a ride?"

"N-no," I stuttered, "I'm fine."

"You sure?" he persisted, walking toward me. "You look lost!"

"No," I repeated sternly, walking faster. "Thank you."

"Whatcha got in that bag?" A couple more people broke from the group and hurried toward me.

"I don't have anything!" I shouted, turning around.

"Yeah, yeah, we'll see," he grumbled, grabbing my wrist.

I should have been smarter. I should have considered who may have been watching, but I panicked. I swung around to free myself from the boy's grip and shifted back into my wolf, growling and baring my teeth. There were no words for their horrified expressions. The guy who grabbed me fell to the ground as his buddies ran in tipsy zigzags from the scene, screaming.

"Holy crap!"

"What the hell!?"

I stood over the scumbag with my head high and watched as he scrambled to his feet before taking off after his friends.

"That's right!" I shouted, almost laughing. "Run away!" I was so confident, so stupid.

I looked back at my pile of now shredded clothing and sighed. That dress was my only outfit. I dejectedly picked up the tattered thing with my teeth, shoving it back into my bag. I couldn't walk around town as a wolf, and there was no sign of my uncle's shop anywhere.

Maybe he moved?

It didn't matter, I'd accepted defeat and was on my way back to the road when my ears picked up the slow creaking of footsteps across the wooden deck behind me. Suspiciously slow.

I froze, turning to see a man watching me. He had that uncanny look on his face—the look of someone who wanted to kill me. He was wearing a green bomber jacket, and there was a shotgun propped up against the building beside him. Both his hands had been resting on the deck railing, but when we locked eyes, he reached for the weapon. I took off running toward the road.

"Hey!" he shouted. He fired a shot at the ground next to me. "SHAPESHIFTER!"

"About time!" someone in the distance replied. A drunken woman ran out in front of me. I shoved her over.

The man from the deck grabbed me by the tail as she got up, pointing his gun at my head. I spun around, terrified.

"Guess staying out here wasn't a total waste after all!" the same woman cackled, throwing a glass bottle that barely missed me.

Heart pounding, I lunged for the man with the gun, who I could only conclude was a huntsman. He dodged me fairly easily. "Go tie the muzzle!" he ordered the woman.

"Should we just take it down here?" she suggested, laughing.

"If you weren't so wasted, we could have made twice the profit!" the huntsman scolded. "I don't think we have much of a choice," he growled, pumping his shotgun.

This was not how I was going to go out. I got ready to lunge again, but my attack was rudely intercepted. A polar bear with a backpack burst out from behind one of the buildings. Both huntsmen turned toward it.

While he had his back to me, I grabbed the man with the gun by the leg, yanking him off his feet. His head hit the ground, and he was instantly knocked unconscious. I threw his weapon away. The woman screamed loudly, running off. Upon noticing this, the bear took the unnecessary

initiative to jump on her, pinning her to the ground and ruining her potato sack of an outfit in the process.

"Please, don't hurt me!" she pleaded, half-laughing. "I wasn't going to harm the girl, I swear!"

"Sure," the bear grunted, smacking her across the head with its paw. I rolled my eyes. "I see why you wanted to leave. This place is just lovely," the animal growled, disappearing into the half-dead bushes lining the street.

"How did I just know you'd show up?" I called to him, annoyed. "You know, maybe next time I invite you to breakfast, I'll use reverse psychology, seeing as you only seem to show up when I ask you not to!"

He didn't reply. I took this opportunity to shift back to my human form. I put on the extra underwear that I'd packed in my satchel, but as I already mentioned, the only outfit I had was the stupid torn dress that was now ripped in half in the back. I was practically holding it up to my body.

Moments later, a thin, pale boy emerged from the bushes, covered in twigs and thorns. He had forest-green eyes, choppy black hair, and filthy bandages up and down his arms and legs that were hidden by jeans and a long-sleeved charcoal jacket.

"You're actually *mad* at me?" Chase grumbled, picking a thorn from his sleeve as he finished buttoning his pants. "I just saved your life!"

"Oh, sure!" I scoffed. "You knocked out an unarmed old woman. My hero!"

"That guy was about to shoot you!" he yelled. "I saw him!"

"He could just as easily have shot you!" I argued. "And—"

Chase was holding his arm weird. He'd probably hurt it either running through the field, jumping on the huntsman, or merely shifting back. He's always walked kinda funny, but he had one of his legs bent at the knee too, not stepping down on it. "Sorry. It's not that I don't appreciate the help," I said, "but I asked you not to come." I grabbed my satchel from the ground. "I wish you'd respect that, and maybe try not to be so standoffish when we do invite you to do things with us..."

"Well, *I'm* mad," he replied irritably, adjusting the straps of his backpack. "You could have been killed!"

"I had the situation under control," I growled. "Besides, there was only really one of them."

"But you can't just run off by yourself," Chase continued. "It's like you don't even care—"

"I'm starting not to!" I shouted. "This is my life, and you're making it out to be your problem! My *very existence* is your problem!"

"I miss my life!" he shouted. "I miss a lot of things... And you're—"

"Don't blame me for your personal decisions!" I snapped. "You can blame my dad, or the huntsmen if you like, but you're the one who's decided to be a recluse! You don't have to worry this much about me, especially because there's *nothing* to worry about!"

He gave me that same annoyed sideways glance. He never looked me in the eyes when we argued.

Chase came to live with us two years ago. But in all that time, by no fault of our own, my friends and I had probably spent less than a day with him at the house. We call Chase "the bodyguard," because thanks to my dad, that's what he seems to think he is to me.

The most frustrating part of the whole situation is that he's about my same age, his transfigurative abilities aren't any more impressive than mine, and he doesn't know the first thing about fighting. In fact—well, it's probably best

I stop there. Why Dad picked someone like him to be my part-time watchdog, I have no idea. I was pretty insulted when we were first introduced, and probably wasn't very nice...

"Hate to break it to ya," he said, "but you're gonna have to learn to cope with my mocking, because you'll be hearing it until the day one of us dies."

"Look, long as you're here, you could help me keep an eye out for this place," I started, secretly attempting to tie the hanging strings at the back of my dress, using the mirrored reflection of one of the store windows across the street to observe the one behind me.

"What place?"

"My uncle's store," I replied, still distracted. "I think it may be—" My attention was drawn from the conversation and my fruitless task when I noticed, out of the corner of my eye, that Chase was back in his polar bear form with a shocked look on his face. I saw his paw fly toward me, then everything went black.

I woke up on a couch—a brown couch with a musty smell and a springy, not-at-all-comfy feel to it, a couch with a large hot chocolate stain on it. It had to be our

couch... I looked around the room as my vision slowly returned to see several people staring at me. "What—?"

"You were about to be stabbed in the back," Chase said quietly from one of the chairs across the room.

"The only one stabbing backs around here is you," I retorted. "Why'd you hit me?"

"I meant literally," he murmured.

"How?" I asked, sitting up.

"I don't know." Chase was looking really upset for some reason. "A guy with a knife came out of that building behind you. I had to get you out of the way fast. I'm really sorry."

"And how did—?" I tried to ask. "How are we back here?"

Someone else in the room cleared their throat to make themselves known. It was Alex, a close family friend of my dad's, and the guy that owns the house. I'm not exactly sure how old he is and I'm too afraid to ask, but his dark brown eyes look like they've seen a lifetime of pain. His hair is mostly gray. He always looks tired, has a scarred-up human form with ashen skin, and wears muscle shirts and shorts most of the time. Probably because they're cheap, and he destroys a lot of his clothes shifting. "What were you

thinking?" he growled from the other chair. "I thought we talked about this, you—"

"I know," I interrupted. This wasn't the first time I'd heard this lecture from him.

He looked at me with eyebrows raised. "No, you don't, because your behavior has remained the same!" As many jokes as we make about Alex's deep, gravelly voice, there was nothing funny about it. "And you!" he glared at Chase. "I don't care what Chris has been telling you, you're going to come to me before leaving this house for any reason! It's twice as much work for me to have to drag both of you home, because *you* can't walk!"

Chase sank into his chair, clearly not wanting to be the focus of the conversation.

Alex rarely gets so harsh, and it was a bit upsetting to hear. He tries to be my dad way more often than he should, even when my actual father is here. "Are we clear?" he asked us both.

"Yes, sir," I found myself saying, though at the time I'd contemplated running from the room. Chase didn't reply at all, he just looked embittered as usual.

Alex sighed. "Sorry, but at this point, with another man down, we can't afford to have any *more* of us not thinking."

"Any more of us?" I asked.

Someone came from the hallway into the living room—a tall girl a little older than seventeen with long, frizzy, strawberry-blond hair, brown eyes, and lots of freckles. Her name is Isabell, but we call her Izzy. Just to recap; she and her "little brother" Malachi lived with us, along with their grandparents, Dana and Henry. Tears streamed down her face, and her blue checkered dress was stained with tomato soup.

Alex sighed again. "What happened this time?"

She looked over at me instead of answering the question. Her eyes seemed to light up. "Thank goodness!" she yelled in a relieved tone, hugging me. Izzy is a year or so older than me but treated me like her equal in the house, giving me the title of "sister" despite the fact that we're not really related. The hug turned from sweet to miserable as I felt a sharp pain in my back where she was touching some sort of wound. "Ow! Owww!" I winced, standing up.

"Oh, I'm so sorry! I didn't mean to—"

"No, no, I'm alright," I said quickly. Izzy tends to be over-apologetic, as well as easy to upset, so even if I was not alright, I would have refrained from saying as much.

But I couldn't imagine why my back hurt so much. I didn't recall injuring myself too badly. I walked over to the dusty mirror above the vanity, turned my back to the mirror, and lifted my shirt to see a few large and partially scabbed-over scratches across my back. They seemed to hurt more after I saw them. I paused, trying to imagine how something like that could have happened. There were no animals large enough in town, besides...

"Chase!" I shouted, turning to him. "You mutilated my back with your big klutzy claws!"

"Sorry, it was an accident," he mumbled, rubbing the back of his neck. I could only imagine the look on his face when he hit me. It was probably the same one he had right then—pure disregard. "Hey, no rescue's flawless."

"The 'flaw' was knocking me out in the first place," I growled.

Izzy gently tapped me on the shoulder, probably afraid she would cause more pain. I met her eyes to see how upset she looked. What on earth could have possibly happened in the one day I was gone? All of a sudden, it dawned on

me that I wasn't wearing that awful black dress anymore. I looked back at the mirror. I was wearing a different outfit!

"Hey!" I yelled, spinning around. Chase must have caught on, because he was already halfway out of the room.

"I didn't expect that dumb dress to rip in half when I knocked you down!" he yelled back from the hallway entry.

"Or when you slashed me with your claws?!" I screamed, glancing down at what I was wearing. "Oh, God," I mumbled, almost crying. I blushed with anger. I had on a dirty gray t-shirt and shorts with a worn-out jacket wrapped around the waist for a belt.

"What was I supposed to do!?" Chase yelled. "Leave you there in your underwear?! Those were the only clothes I had!"

Izzy stood there in silence, but I noticed she was biting her lip, trying not to laugh.

I heard a chuckle from across the living room. My best friend and honorary brother, Osscar, a scruffy-looking kid with dark skin and brown eyes who was wearing a green camo jacket with a hood, flung himself onto the couch. "So, what, you dressed her?" he laughed. "You know, that just gives a whole new definition to the word *bodyguard*."

Izzy couldn't stand it anymore, and she and Osscar both burst out laughing.

"That's enough!" Alex snapped.

I was usually happy to see Osscar. However, I could have choked him right then and there. I was absolutely humiliated. I could feel my face turning red as I glared at Chase. He had his hood pulled up over his head like he always did when he was embarrassed and an irritated look on his face. I ran from the room, but could hear Izzy's footsteps not far behind me. I shut the door to our bedroom and began to rapidly change clothes. In my haste, I had apparently locked her out.

"Angela?" Izzy called from behind the door. "I'm sorry, I really didn't mean to laugh, I'm so—" I opened the door again, now wearing a ripped pair of blue jeans and a blue V-neck with a fox on the front.

"It's fine. What's going on now?"

"Nothing," she said. "I just wanted to talk."

"Nothing?" I repeated, looking down at her soup-stained dress.

"I'm just clumsy," she replied, rolling her eyes. "Today was pretty stressful."

"You wanna talk here?" I asked, closing our door behind me. "Because we can go to Osscar's room. It has a window."

"Well," she sighed, "I don't think we're allowed in there anymore."

"What?" I asked. "Why?"

"I'll show you."

I followed her further down the dark hallway that made up a pretty decent percentage of our home. Our house was basically a wooden door that led into an oddly laid-out living room, with a step that went down into the world's smallest kitchen. Then, of course, was the long hallway connecting several bedrooms that were always crammed with shapeshifters. Did Chase already explain that? Sorry.

Izzy stopped at the third-to-last door in the hall. This room was Osscar's, but me and Izzy came and went as we pleased. I almost walked right past it this time. It was unrecognizable. All of Osscar's fanboy posters had been taken off the door, and his little green army men that stood guard on top of the trim of the doorway were also gone. Despite his age—sixteen—he really did enjoy

knickknacks. He was the lucky one of us that didn't have to share a room.

The only other kid who got a room all to themselves was Chase, but his was less of a room and more of a storage area with an attached water closet.

"Was Osscar planning on running away, too?" I asked, examining the barren door.

"No," Izzy said, shaking her head. "Alex says he needs this room for something. He had us clear out the storage room today."

"You guys *cleared out* the storage room!?" The storage room was practically an abyss. Whatever went in there never came back out. It was filled with old furniture, shredded clothing, and whatever you never wanted to see again. The unspoken house rule was that if you broke something, especially something of Alex's, throw it in the storage room.

"Yeah, after Alex left," she sighed. "We could have used you guys here earlier when we were moving the pipe organ."

"I'm so sorry I wasn't here," I lied.

"You really didn't want to be," she said quietly. "There was a lot of yelling."

Izzy's shyness was one of many reasons her grandparents would never let her leave the house. Another was the fact that she only knows how to shift into one, fairly "soft" animal—a rabbit. Yeah, needless to say, that form isn't really the most helpful when confronted with a huntsman. Izzy's life circumstances are a bit like Osscar's, except he ended up living with his grandfather. Truly, I've never met anyone like Alex. He's a big mystery to me—always angry, doesn't let his guard down under any circumstances, and I've never seen the guy smile, not even once.

"How does Osscar feel about all this?" I asked.

Izzy shrugged. "He got as much say as any of us would have." I nodded. "Did you find your dad?"

"Umm...."

"A question for later, perhaps?" Izzy continued, trying the locked door handle.

"Yeah, thanks," I replied.

"Well, I'm going to head onto bed." She stepped back from the now forbidden chamber. "Tomorrow will be better."

"How can you always be so optimistic?" I asked, rolling my eyes.

"I'm not, believe me," she replied. "I said that to help convince us both." There was an awkward pause when I moved to hug her before remembering the soup all over her dress. We both laughed.

"Good night," she laughed, walking back to our room. I slipped down the hall back into the living room where Alex was asleep on the sofa.

Chase was sitting on the bench, leaning over the fireplace, aimlessly stabbing its ashes with our steel fire poker. I came over and sat next to him on the bench's hand-crocheted cushion. He looked a little surprised to see me. "I figured you'd be mad at me again," he said, going back to poking around the hot ashes.

"It's useless," I sighed. "I have to live with you after all. Might as well get over it."

Chase looked at me again, but his eyes moved toward my back. "Be honest. How badly are you cut?"

"I exaggerated," I admitted, "but it does hurt."

He nodded, turning back to the fireplace and attempting to start it up this time. Good thing, too. It was our only heating for the house. I'm sure he would have already locked himself in his room, had it not been his turn to stay up and make sure the place didn't go up in flames or the

fire didn't die and leave everyone in the house to freeze. After three whole minutes of nothing but fire-crackling noises, he broke the silence by bringing up the one subject I didn't want to discuss. "So, did you find out where Chris went?"

"Nope," I replied. "But it's not like I had long in town. Honestly, though, how did you get to me so fast?"

"Well, you walked that whole way. I had to run."

"You can run?" I asked, probably a little too surprised.

He rolled his eyes. "When I have to…"

I laughed. "Sorry, but you really didn't *have to* come at all." He started shaking his head in annoyance. "Really." I stood to go.

"We can't even have one conversation," Chase huffed. "Is it always going to be this way?"

"I hope not," I shrugged. "Because I wanna leave the house *without* an escort someday."

Chase glared at the fire, probably debating whether or not to snap back at me. I walked off to bed before he could decide.

Of course, there's always a way tomorrow could be worse, even than the day that you thought would be the lowest point of the month.

The next morning, I sat up and looked at Izzy, still fast asleep in her twin bed. I hated how quiet our tiny room was. If I could, I would have gotten myself a fish tank or noise machine—something so I wasn't always sitting alone in the dark with the silence and occasional snoring across the hall.

I got up and made my way down the hall, through the living room, and into the box-like kitchen, to start scavenging for food. Only then did I realize that I'd fallen asleep in my clothes. I put my hand up the back of my shirt. The scabbed-over scratches were starting to itch, but I tried not to focus on it. I sighed, reaching for the fridge handle before I heard a loud clatter from the other room.

"Are you kidding me?" I mumbled. No morning is complete without some kind of catastrophe that will keep everyone from breakfast. "Okay, what happened?" I walked drowsily back up the step into the living room. "Hey, is everyone okay?"

That's when the large cat burst in from the hall, a broken chain around its neck and a murderous glint in its eye as it looked around wildly for someplace to go or someone to attack.

"Holy hound dogs!" I gasped, backing up slowly before tripping over the little step leading back down into the kitchen. I fell to the tile floor and the cat's head jerked toward me. I scrambled to my feet, looking around frantically for higher ground.

Nothing! We didn't have a cabinet or a chandelier, and the sloped ceiling made the top of the fridge an impossible ledge. I looked back at the cat, and it jumped right for me, missing only because I threw open the lower fridge door blocking its entry into the kitchen.

I screamed when the cougar reached its deadly paw over the door I was holding open. Running to the back of the kitchen, I hopped up onto the great harvest table, grabbing my only available weapon: our dry mop.

I'm sure you're wondering why I didn't just shift into some sort of large, predatory animal in order to fight for my life. Well, did I mention before that I tend to freeze up in the worst situations?

This happened to be one of those situations—the kind where I completely forget how to do anything useful and resort to useless household implements. Almost all shape-shifters have that problem—we can't shift when we get too

worked up, but some of us are really easy to "lock up." They call it having an "anxious delay" in shifting.

What a perfect time to enter Chase, who, while in his human form, had time to roll his eyes at my weapon of choice before shifting into his polar bear. The polar bear and gray wolf are Chase's favorite forms, probably because they're the biggest and meanest, but he can also turn himself into a weasel.

Shapeshifters don't really have a fixed set of animals they can change into—you can always learn to shift into other things, but it takes work, a lot of concentration, and, in our house, a lot of coaching by Alex who believes anything is possible with a little "push."

Sometimes that "push" was scary for you, scary for your friend, or just scary in general. One time, Osscar decided he wanted to adopt a mouse lifestyle, for fun of course. Lots of shapeshifters have "phases" like that growing up. But the point is Alex got him to shift back into his human form by turning into a snake, wrapping around Osscar, and threatening to swallow him whole. Which, of course, Alex would *never* do! I hope not, anyway. But at the time, the threat was enough of a "push" for Osscar to

shift back into his human form and run naked from the room screaming. He was only eleven years old!

I remember Dad yelling at Alex for his teaching methods after that, and Alex denying that he did anything wrong in the grandparenting department by making "a few idle threats for the boy's own good."

I personally can shift into a pretty good line-up of animals. A white Arctic wolf, a field mouse, and, my personal favorite, a brown mustang-looking horse. I don't enjoy shifting if I don't *need* to, but half the time I can't shift when I *do* need to, so...you know.

I was taken from my thoughts when a skinny polar bear crashed into the table leg underneath me and snapped it in half. I rolled onto the tile floor, scrambling to hide under the half-broken table. Small sunrays escaped through the veiled kitchen windows projecting the cat and bear's clashing shadows onto the wall in front of me. Then, I heard a roar so loud it shook the room. I turned to see a monstrous black bear charge into the kitchen. It pinned the feral cat to the ground, allowing Chase to escape to the living room. The brawl after that was short-lived—the black bear rolled the mountain lion, bashed its head to the ground with its huge paw, and everything was quiet.

I came out from behind the broken table and faced the bear that slowly shifted back into Alex, who grabbed the red curtain off the nearest window and wrapped it around his body before turning around. "Put the broom down," he ordered in his most serious tone. I hadn't even realized I was still holding it, especially after I fell. It wasn't a broom, but I wouldn't dare point out his mistake. "Hey!" he yelled angrily out of the room. "You're not absolved of this, get back in here!"

Chase came back into the kitchen doorway as a human with a sizeable bleeding gash on his chest, and a towel around his waist. His arms and legs would probably have been cut up too if not for his bandages.

I suppose I should explain those. He doesn't wear the bandages because he's always cut up. We didn't used to get injured too often.

Chase has a rare medical condition called Morph-Bone, or "Shifter's Bone," which means some of his bones are permanently fused with some belonging to one of his animal forms. He claims he doesn't even know which one, but the condition is caused by something going wrong with a shift. I recall my dad telling me that his older brother contracted Shifter's Bone by being shot in the leg by a

huntsman when they were kids. He permanently had bob-cat bones fused to his fibula after that.

Chase wears the bandages to keep his bones and muscles from displacing. They enable him to walk and use his arms normally, as Shifter's Bone is supposed to be an incredibly painful condition that makes even the simplest tasks, like picking up a glass of water, next to impossible.

He seems to get by pretty well when he has his bandages on, even with his elbows and knees exposed. Those are the only parts of his arms and legs I've seen. His condition could have been worse, I suppose. At least his joints still move normally. When he shifts, the bones of the unknown animal are still fused to whatever form he takes, so basically, he can't change his circumstances no matter what he does. It sucks, really.

The bandages also follow him to his animal forms, and they don't rip like normal clothes would. They were designed for my late Uncle Dustin, to fit tightly around his morphed leg in any form he took.

None of us knows what they're made of. They look like cloth, but are far too thick and durable. You would assume that the bandages would fall off when Chase tries

to shift into much smaller animals, but they compress for his weasel somehow.

"Chase, you—" Alex started. And I'll stop right there, considering the next few things he said were not necessarily appropriate for all readers. "What did we talk about?!" he yelled "You should have gotten me before running down here by yourself to try and take on a problem you don't understand!"

"Angela was with me!" Chase shouted defensively, gesturing to me. Alex turned to me, and I quickly dropped the mop. As it clattered to the floor, he ran his hands through his hair in exasperation. "What's there not to understand?" Chase asked angrily.

"Yeah, Alex, how on earth did Malachi get out?" I added. Oh, yeah, one more thing. Izzy's little brother. He's not human-born. Why Dana and Henry kept him around for so long, no one knows. Izzy still loved him, though. Probably similar to the way one would love a pet, but the situation was what it was.

"It's probably my fault," Alex admitted. "I don't remember locking the cellar doors last night, but you two knew better." Chase was about to pipe up again when Alex

caught him. "I know, I just don't wanna hear it," he said sternly. "Betadine's in the closet. Go clean yourself up."

Chase shut up, looking at his feet as Alex walked back up the step into the living room.

I would have left, too, had I not noticed his cut was bleeding pretty badly. "Hey, your—" I started.

"I'm fine, Angie," Chase said, wrapping his arm around his raw-boned chest self-consciously. "Just, why don't you go check on Izzy or, something?"

I rolled my eyes as he left the room. I should have known better than to poke Chase after he'd just been scolded, but to be fair, Alex did yell at both of us. Clearly, that day was already off to a great start.

4: CHASE

Could I do nothing right? *Stay with Angela! Don't stay with Angela! Help! Don't help! Come back! Get out!* It frustrated me more and more each day.

I was instructed to get the Betadine out of "the closet." Now, most would consider those directions pretty vague, but we only had two closets in the house, and I lived in one of them. I grabbed the opaque orange bottle from the medical supply closet on the wall just outside the girls' bedroom before heading further down the hall.

IN CASE WE'RE MADE INTO COATS

I opened the door to my room and stepped into the dark space, reaching around in front of me for the string I'd attached to the pull-cord light on the ceiling. I pulled it, and there was a quick flash of sparks followed by a *zap*. "You've got to be kidding me."

That was the fourth time in a week that the light bulb shorted out. I grabbed the hand-powered flashlight I kept on the floor and used it to light my way to the "bathroom." Which luckily had a light switch. Don't ask me why. There was a toilet, a rusted bathtub, and a single wall-mounted cast-iron sink with a clouded mirror above it, that I did my best to shine up to the point of functionality. I placed the Betadine on the edge of the sink and glanced in the mirror at the scratch across my chest. It looked a lot better than I thought it would. It was really big on my polar bear, but I guess when my skin shrank back up, or something... I don't know, I'll text someone who can explain it later.

You'd think I'd know more about this shapeshifter biology stuff, seeing as I am one, but, in my defense, I don't shift very often. In fact, I'm really not supposed to. I've learned the hard way that Morph-Bone can always get worse.

I looked around for something I could use to apply the disinfectant and the best I found was a sock. I didn't have too many things. In fact, I pretty much consider my most treasured possession to be the tetanus immunity I gained from the TDAP vaccine I remember receiving at some point in my life.

Which I'm not saying to make people feel bad!

Shapeshifters are lucky to get any vaccinations, considering that a good deal of them have to be "modified" in order to be safe for us, and we avoid the government like the plague. Which means no doctors. We'll touch more on that later.

"Because I wanna leave the house without an escort someday," I said into the mirror in a high-pitched impersonation of Angela's voice. I poured the Betadine liquid onto the white sock, staining it orange.

Clearly my priorities were in line that day, but you know that nagging feeling after you lose an argument with someone? The feeling that causes you to spend, like, the next three days replaying said argument in your mind going *that's what I should have said*? That can't just apply to me.

I held the sock to my body and looked back in the mirror.

Yikes...

I don't even remember what I looked like four years ago, but it had to be better than this. I didn't cut my own hair back then, for starters, and I didn't have to wear the same shabby bandage wraps around on my arms and legs every day. I try so, so hard to clean them, but at this point they look so horrible that there really isn't anything I can do but throw on some long pants and a jacket and pretend they aren't there.

I left the bathroom, walking over to my bed. Which—don't even get me started. There was a dim lamp that I was able to turn on in order to find the half-empty package of lightbulbs in the side-table drawer. I pulled out over the stepladder that I kept up against the burnt spot on the wall and used it to change out the blackened bulb for a new one. The room was then as illuminated as it was ever going to be.

I sighed, sitting on the bed and removing the bloody sock from my chest. Something had to change. Something had to break this limbo—and preferably before I was out of light bulbs. I had to get out of that house.

"Chase!" Alex called from the other room. "Get your ass in here!" There was barely a pause. "Now!"

I grabbed a sweatshirt off the ground and slid it on. "This week," I said to myself. "I'm leaving this week."

5: ANGELA

When I returned to the kitchen, everyone was in a huddle around the unconscious mountain lion. Of course, Izzy was crying at the sight of her brother on the ground. Chase was sitting on the stove eating crackers from a leftover Lunchable, and Osscar was playing with the "toe beans" of the immobilized animal, all while Alex pondered what to do as he looked down at the beast.

"We have to put him outside," he said at last.

"No!" Izzy wailed. "What if he runs off!?"

"We don't have the supplies to contain him indoors, Isabell!" Alex snapped. "He could injure someone." He then glared over at Chase, who was now wearing a baggy navy-blue sweatshirt to cover up his scratch. He put down the Lunchable and stared at the floor.

"And already has," Alex sighed. "We tried keeping him in. We have to put him outside," he concluded.

"But—" Izzy sniffled.

He gave her that same harsh look me and Chase got earlier, and she too looked down at her feet.

Man, we were like dogs in a pack, bowing to our alpha when he growled at us. It almost made me angry, but Alex had a point. If Malachi could break out of chains and a locked door, what else could we possibly do to keep him inside?

Izzy ran from the room in tears, and Alex stormed out shortly after that. Which left me, Osscar, and Chase to deal with this big predacious problem on our own.

"Not sure how to feel, to be honest," Osscar said, standing up.

"Yeah," I replied. "Any ideas on what we're supposed to do with him now?"

Chase got off the stovetop. "I'm sure Alex expects us to secure ~~him~~ it outside somehow."

We all stared down at the predator's head. Visions of its teeth, I'm sure, were flashing through more minds than just mine.

"Not it!" I declared.

"Not it!" Osscar called seconds later, offering me a fist bump that I couldn't refuse. We both turned to poor Chase who couldn't have looked more depressed if he was soaking wet, or at least that's what I thought until he picked up the head of the cat and somehow looked even sadder.

I grabbed its front legs, and Osscar rolled his eyes. "Step aside," he said confidently before shifting into a great white rhino, crushing the rest of our poor broken table and taking up all the space left in the kitchen. Me and Chase had to back up against the oven to avoid getting crushed.

Osscar used his horn to scoop the animal off the ground. It slid to the base of his horn and lay there unconscious like a rag doll.

"Well that's one way to do it, but how are ya getting out of the kitchen now, genius?" Chase laughed.

Osscar's eyes ~~shifted~~ wandered around the room as he realized how trapped he was.

Chase offered me a fist bump as Osscar shifted back into his human form, this time with a giant cat draped over his back instead of hanging off his horn. His clothes had been ripped to shreds, but the cat across his back almost acted like a fur coat.

Osscar grunted, wobbling from the weight on his way out the kitchen door. Being the kind and caring friends that we are, me and Chase followed the poor guy outside, first to make sure he didn't fall over, second to make sure no one saw him without any pants, and third, of course, to mock the heck out of him. Osscar has a pretty cool lineup of shifts if you ask me. Aside from his white rhino and human forms, he also has a grizzly bear and a gray house mouse. Osscar and I have always wanted bird shifts, but neither of us could ever seem to get it, and we weren't about to ask Alex for help!

Once around to the front of the house, Osscar threw the mountain lion off his shoulders and into the yard. "Whew!" he yelled, stretching. "You guys, that hurt, and you both owe me."

I shielded my eyes and couldn't help but chuckle at his misfortune.

"I don't," Chase replied, throwing Osscar his second set of spare clothes for the day. "We'll call it even for making me help you move all your things into the storage room, because you were—" he made gesture quotations with his fingers—"mourning a great loss."

"Aww, come on," Osscar said, "you know that even ripped to shreds that pillow is still the best in the house."

Chase shrugged. "You're not wrong."

I looked down at the cat, and my smile slowly faded. "Boys, what are we doing here? We have to remember this is Izzy's little brother. We can't be too rough."

"We wouldn't be rough on a real mountain lion either," Osscar said.

"Oh, of course not," I confirmed. "My point is, she'll kill us if we injure him, even if—" I sighed, not sure how to finish that sentence.

"Even if her little brother is trying to take our arms off?" Osscar finished, nodding in agreement. "So, what's the plan?" He slid into his new gray t-shirt.

"Chase?" I asked.

He looked at me like I was crazy and proceeded to tally the things we didn't have on his fingers. "We've got no

ropes, no cage, no post. Izzy was right, I don't think we can keep him here," he shrugged.

"Okay, you're not helpful," I concluded.

Suddenly, something moved swiftly in the grass field behind us. All three of us jerked around faster than you could say *What was that?*

Osscar jumped up, grabbing the nearest tree branch. He leaped onto it and out of the way of Chase, who was drawing a knife from his back pocket. Once he was high enough to see over the field, he started looking for anything that moved. Osscar dosen't exactly have an eagle eye, but it's not like Chase could've gotten up that high. His bandages do what he needs them to, but they're so restrictive that they can make agility a weakness.

I stepped forward cautiously, peering at the front lines of the field. A little beige fox burst through the grass, its uncommonly large ears tilting and twitching in all directions to get a better picture of its surroundings. Chase's look of panic began to vanish, and Osscar jumped from the tree and leaned up against it lazily, almost like he'd been looking forward to a good fight and was let down. The fox dragged a leather bag bigger than its whole body out of the grass by a strap in its teeth.

"That's not native," I said.

"Hello?" Chase cautiously asked the animal.

"Hello," it replied.

We all jumped back a little, shocked. Running into other shapeshifters was unheard of! And we figured the odds of a chance encounter were little to none considering the ones we did know, were located in places similar to where we lived—isolated, hidden, and without Wi-Fi.

"You're like us!" I yelped excitedly.

"I surely hope so," the fox said, sitting down. Its tail swirled to the front of its body.

"Wow," was all Chase had to say.

"What's your name?" I asked.

"My name is Liles Willis," the fox replied. "I'm looking for my grandfather."

Me and Chase glanced at each other, then back to Osscar, who looked like he was about to throw up. "Liles?" he asked with a shocked look on his face. "But—"

The little fox stood up, shifting into a tall, hand-some-looking guy with dark skin and a buzz cut. The most notable thing about him was his eyes. They were light brown, almost yellow. As for the rest of him, luckily the grass was tall enough to hide everything below his chest.

"Are you my little brother?" Liles asked, approaching Osscar. "Man, I... don't even recognize you."

Me and Chase looked at each other again. "What will we tell Alex?" I mumbled.

I didn't know much about Liles, only that he went missing a long time ago. But every time I imagined what a reunion between Osscar and his long-lost brother would be like, it was usually emotional and involved crying, laughing, or some sort of mutual excitement to see one another. This was not the case at all.

After Chase gave Liles his last spare pieces of clothing—a black t-shirt and a pair of bleached jeans—the walk back to the house was silent. Liles seemed indifferent to the events unfolding, following us calmly toward the house, and Osscar still looked like he was going to be sick every time I turned around to check on him.

Chase put his hand on the rusty kitchen doorknob and turned it slowly until the door opened, so our entrance would be as quiet as possible. We could have gone through the front door, but we knew Alex would be sitting right there in his chair in the living room, and for whatever reason, dragging this out seemed like the right thing to do at the time.

"Hey, Alex?" Chase called.

"If one of you is about to ask me if you can go hiking again, the answer is still—" Alex shouted from the living room. He was suddenly out of words, looking at us.

Me and Chase moved away from Osscar and Liles, who now stood facing Alex. Liles waved, stepping gingerly up from the kitchen into the living room. "I'm assuming you're my grandfather?" he asked. Alex blinked, then looked at Osscar, who didn't move a muscle. "It's good to see you again," Liles said, drawing his grandfather in for the world's most cringe-worthy hug. Alex barely moved. He touched Liles' back and that was about it. Liles released him, walking back to Osscar, who looked him up and down for the second time, as if he was playing at something.

"I'm gonna need some answers," Alex said finally. The only thing obvious about the looming conversation was where everyone would be sitting. Me and Chase sat on the bench directly across from the fireplace, Alex took his chair a few feet from us, and Osscar and Liles took the couch to face their grandfather. This type of arrangement was usually the kind you would sit in when you were about to lay down some serious news impacting the person in the

middle. In this case, the one in the middle was Alex. "So, are they—?" Alex asked, trying to find the words.

"Well," Liles started with a more serious look, "yes and no." I saw no emotion cross Alex's face. It was like the spectacular and horrific news of "yes and no" both hit him at just the right time to trigger absolutely nothing. "Our mom," Liles continued, looking over at Osscar, "well, your daughter..." We stared at Alex, whose eyes were wide open with terribly sad anticipation. "She's alive," Liles said finally.

Alex buried his face in his hands and exhaled loudly. We turned to Osscar, who looked no different than he had outside, just shocked. "My mom's alive," Osscar said at last. He smiled a little.

"She's alive," Alex said, nodding.

And, just when I thought I would see the man finally smile, Liles had to say, "But..."

Alex took the news after that a lot worse than the first bit, and there were a few holes in the wall to prove it. The minute Liles said the word "dead," I could have sworn Alex was about to fall down and die himself. He stood right up and took his anger and sadness out on the wall before storming out of the house, slamming the door behind him

hard enough to knock it off its hinges. We assumed he ran from the house in one of his animal forms, due to the loud and painful roar from the field.

We sat in silence for a moment to take in the damage to the house. It would require all the money we had to fix, so I knew that, most likely, the holes would be left, and the door frame would stay cracked.

Liles looked around stunned. "I didn't mean to—"

"We know," I said, interrupting him.

"It's not your fault," Chase said.

Liles nodded and turned to Osscar, who was staring down at the door. "Sorry about your—our—grandmother," he said.

Osscar wasn't paying attention. He just wanted more answers. "What about my dad?" he asked.

"He's alive too," Liles replied, "confined to a cell at a huntsman base, but alive."

Osscar ran his fingers through his short stubs of hair. "Cool."

"Who's alive?" Izzy asked as she came in. That's when I finally realized what had been playing on my mind while the dramatic conversation was unfolding.

Chase looked at me and then Izzy before having the same realization. "Oh, crap," he sighed. I took a nervous glance out the door to see what I didn't want to see.

"Okay, Izzy," I started. "Please, just try not to be too upset..."

"You...*what!* He's gone!" Izzy wailed. "He's really gone!"

"Look, we're really sorry!" Chase said in a panic.

"Sorry!?" Izzy cried. "My little brother is gone! Lost in the forest, with no way to tell him from any other wild, aggressive cougar in the world!"

"Okay! Okay! We messed up!" I yelled. "We really did! But there has to be some way to fix this!"

"How?" Izzy sobbed. "Just, how?"

"Well..." I hesitated.

"We can't," Chase said flatly. "Honestly, we can't help your dad either, Angie. We can't even help ourselves. We failed Malachi, and Alex isn't going to be any help when and if he comes ba—"

"We can't help anyone as long as we're stuck in this house," I finished for him.

"Yeah, I know..."

"This is my fault," Liles offered. "Is there anything I can do to help?"

"Yeah, hang tight for a second," Chase replied, starting down the hallway. "We're going to fix everything."

Izzy and I followed him. "Where are we going?" I asked.

"Come on, Angie. I'm assuming we have just enough time to pack and get the heck out of here before Alex comes back," Chase stated ever-so-confidently. "We're going to save your dad, find Malachi, and rescue Osscar's parents."

"Rescue Oss—" I changed to a whisper so the people in the living room wouldn't hear me. "Rescue Osscar's parents?"

"This is the only chance we have to leave," he replied. "While the old man is gone, we have to go."

"Wait just a minute!" I shouted. "You were furious when I left yesterday. Now you *want* me to leave?"

"No, I want you to come with me," Chase corrected. "That way, we can protect each other."

I rolled my eyes. "Oh, I see what this is," I scoffed. "You're trying to weasel your way out of the house."

"What do you say?" he repeated, ignoring my last comment.

"Wait, *leave*?" Izzy said in a panic. "Like, run away?"

"We aren't going anywhere," I said, crossing my arms. "Chase just wants time out of the house. He's only inviting us to keep tabs on me."

"I don't understand," Izzy mumbled.

"That's not true." Chase said defensively.

"Promise?" I asked. This was the only way I could tell if Chase was lying. He's so good at it. Promises in our house were almost sacred. You don't break a promise.

Chase just sighed. "Look—" he started.

"No!" I laughed. "You are such a—"

"Angela," Izzy said shyly, "maybe we could... consider the idea?"

"Are you crazy?" I asked. "Osscar's parents are being kept at a *huntsman base*!"

The base wasn't something we needed Liles to explain. Alex used scare tactics to keep us in the house. When his old ones no longer proved effective, we were told about the huntsman base, a horrible place where shapeshifters were held prisoner. The ones that they let live, anyway. Even the censored description we got from Alex reminded me of

what little I've been told about concentration camps, and definitely worked to keep us indoors for a few months at least.

"Chris might be there too," Chase pointed out.

I bit my lip. "I know, but—"

"We can protect each other," he said again.

"We have no idea what to expect," I countered.

"We can ask Osscar's brother?" Izzy suggested.

"He's been missing for *six years*," I reminded her. "What if *we* get stuck there?"

"We've fought off huntsmen before," Chase said. "Besides, if you really wanna prove to your dad that you don't need me around, this would be the perfect opportunity."

He was right. I stood frozen for a moment. I knew I should have said no. "Okay," I replied. "I'll go."

"For freedom," Chase said, smiling.

"For freedom," I sighed. I was still wary of the plan, but I had to get my dad home, and I knew how badly Chase wanted to leave. Maybe if we pulled this off, everyone would be happier.

Izzy was twirling her hair nervously between her fingers. "Alright," she said.

"Okay, great! You're both on board!" Chase said, clapping his hands together. "Pack some Pop-Tarts, say your goodbyes, and let's get outta here!"

"No way!" Osscar shouted as we ran from room to room gathering supplies. "You guys are absolutely *not* leaving without me!"

"Look, I've thought it through, and it's for the best that *you* stay," Chase declared from his room.

"What, why?"

"Because you're the only one in the house Alex actually gives a crap about," Chase replied, opening the hall closet.

Osscar glanced up at Liles who was standing rather uncomfortably beside him. "Uhhh, but where do you even plan on looking?" he shouted at us. "You guys don't even know where to start!"

"I might have an idea," Liles offered. Everyone stopped in the hall to listen. He sighed. "I've obviously been to the closest base. I'm sure I could find it again."

"Well, I'm not leaving if Osscar can't," I said. "It's not fair that one of us should have to stay and explain this whole mess to Alex."

"Course not..." Chase grumbled. "I guess that means everyone's coming then?"

"Yup," I said, smiling. "That's not going to impinge on any other plans, is it, Chase?"

"No," he replied, crossing his arms, "but Alex is gonna freak."

"True," I said, nodding. "Osscar, how long has it been since you've left the house?"

"Are we talking years?" he asked. "Because, I've lost count."

"Wait a second," Liles started. "Are you guys *forced* to stay here?"

Osscar: "Kind of?"

Izzy: "Well, not really..."

Chase: "Yes."

"It's complicated," I said.

"Why are you surprised?" Osscar asked Liles. "It's still Grandfather."

"I didn't know him all too well," Liles admitted. "That's crazy, but who exactly are all of you?"

"We can talk about it on the road," Chase said. "We have to hurry."

"Understood," Liles replied. "Any idea how many huntsmen we can expect if we go west?"

"Is the base west?" I asked.

"Yes."

"Then, shouldn't you know?"

"Nope, flew here."

"You have a bird shift?" Osscar said, shocked. "But you're only—"

"Eighteen," Liles continued with a flat expression.

"Oh…" Osscar mumbled. He looked surprised.

"Umm…no, we don't really know what to expect if we go any direction," I said awkwardly, in an attempt to refocus the subject.

"Do you at least know what kind of huntsmen—" Liles tried to continue.

"We don't know anything," Chase butted in. "I'm not even from this city."

"So, we're running blind?" Liles asked. "Are any of you guys experienced?" *Experienced* was a word you would use for a shapeshifter with a wide range of shifts—typically over ten with at least one flying and one aquatic.

"Nope," I replied.

"Should I even keep asking?" Liles grumbled.

"Nope."

"Alright, well, where can I get some clothes?" he asked, looking down the hall. "Do I still have any possessions?" I

turned to Osscar, who gave me a look. He had absolutely no idea. "Man, why did we move here?" Liles asked more quietly, examining the rotted wall.

"I ask myself that question every day," Chase added, clearing out the contents of our medical supply cabinet.

"Umm... I'm not sure about your clothes," I murmured, "but you can borrow some of my dad's. His room's at the end of the hall."

"Thank you," Liles said, walking past us.

I looked at Osscar. I still couldn't tell how he was feeling and figured it was time to ask. "Osscar, are you okay with all of—"

"Hey, keep packing," Chase said, interrupting me with a shooing gesture. "We gotta go."

"Oh, don't get your bandages in a bunch," I retorted, walking away.

Once in my bedroom, I pulled a small black duffle from the top of the wardrobe. It was already packed with a one-week supply of everything a shapeshifter would need on the run. Alex had us keep stuff like this in case a day came where huntsmen attacked the house and we were forced to abandon ship. We never refer to huntsmen as "hunters," though it would be much easier to say. It's too

confusing in the bigger picture. Because, like, what *actual* hunter refers to himself as a huntsman? None of them, they would call themselves hunters. Then again, what do I know? I've lived in social isolation most of my life.

Huntsmen kill shifters for what Alex calls "reasons that I don't care to discuss with minors." That's right. At the time, I didn't even know why our kind is hunted. I don't think any of us did, and my dad agreed with Alex. He wouldn't talk about it either.

I looked around our bedroom for anything else we might need. Nothing seemed to come to mind, aside from the repeating phrase, *how did I get talked into this?*

I had to go find Liles again. We'd only just met the guy, and we were already going to let him lead us off to a huntsman base located who knows where? I mean, yeah, he was Osscar's brother, and there's no one I trust more than him, but other than that, I knew absolutely nothing about Liles.

I walked into the storage room, which had become Osscar's new residence after he was evicted from his old bedroom. It was small and dusty with a large double window that illuminated a small, elongated table of plants beneath it. Across from that table by the doorway, was a writing desk that sat up against the wall, accompanied by a

plastic chair. It wasn't as big as Osscar's old bedroom, nor as nice, but there was one thing that compensated for that. Taking up almost a whole wall was a queen-sized, antique bed with a carved scene of wolves running across the wood, chasing horses. The bed probably used to be Alex's before he got married decades ago, but, man, what an upgrade for Osscar, who used to sleep on the bottom of a slim bunk-bed. In fact, that antique was probably one of the biggest and nicest beds in the house. On seeing that Osscar got it, admittedly I was a little envious.

The only bed worse than mine was Chase's, which was basically two mattresses stacked on a piece of plywood. Well, never mind, I guess Izzy's and mine were similar enough to say we both had the second-worst beds in the house. Off-topic, my apologies. I'm still salty about how long that thing sat in storage while someone could have been using it.

Liles was sitting at the desk with the executive lamp turned on. He was sorting through an old doctor's bag, the same one we saw him holding out in the field. There were a bunch of little glass vials strewn about the desk that he was delicately placing into the bag with some sort of clampy thing. Not touching a single one. The tool he was

using was about the size of an eyelash curler and resembled one of those things that metal workers use to remove rods from molten ash. Now that I think about it, I've also seen fireplace tools that looked a bit like it. He was shaking slightly as he used the odd tool to lower each vial into its own little leather holder within the bag.

"What are those?" I couldn't help but ask as I inspected the colored fluids inside the vials.

He jumped and about broke one when I asked. He must not have heard me come in and fumbled around with the grabber thing before securing the vial he was holding between its little clamps. "How long have you been standing there?"

I'd really spooked him. "Sorry," I laughed, "I should have knocked."

"These are remedies," he informed me. "Well, most of them. Some are ingredients, and some are—"

"Where'd you get them?" I asked, walking further into the room.

"Umm...it's a long story."

I took a closer look at the worn leather bag. "It says Property of Alexander. Was this Alex's bag?"

"Are we related?" he asked.

"Oh, no, sorry," I replied, "I just live here."

"The bag and book were both my great grandfather's," he said, placing the vial he was holding with the tool into one of the leather pockets.

"Book? Wait, Alex's father?"

"Maybe? I believe so, yes," he replied irritably, putting the clamp down and rushing the remaining vials into their leather holders with his fingers. Which made me wonder what the tool was for in the first place.

I inspected the bag for a leather stamp or some other form of identification and found no such thing. But the idea of this belonging to Osscar's great grandfather was really interesting to me. Alex never talked about his parents, ever. "What do they do?" I asked, looking down at the bag full of vials. Even the word *remedies* was intriguing. There was something unique about each one, and every bottle had a small off-white sticker on the front with a handwritten label. "Do they work?"

"I'm sure they do," he said, "but..."

"But?"

"But huntsmen are notorious for adding a few *extra* ingredients to stuff like this. So, I will not be sampling any," Liles concluded, shutting the bag.

I now know what he meant, unfortunately. If huntsmen really did make those elixirs, there was bound to be some sickening stuff in them that no shifter should ever be forced to stomach. Heck, the spleen of one of my ancestors could have been in one of those concoctions!

Liles opened the door, letting me lead him out. Chase had changed into a gray t-shirt and the same dumb jacket he wore all the time. He had a black duffle bag identical to mine over his shoulder and one foot already out the doorway, ready to make a break for it the second he had the all clear.

Izzy seemed to be ready to go as well. She was sitting on the sofa with her duffle. Her hair was back in a loose braid, and she clutched a large drawstring bag between her legs.

"I guess that's it," Chase said. I could tell he was trying not to smile.

"I'll do my best to recall how exactly I got here from the base," Liles said, walking past me and into the living room. "But, and correct me if I'm wrong, it seems like the current goal is to get as far away from the house as possible?"

"Correct," Chase replied, impatiently sticking his head out the door, looking around the house.

I rolled my eyes.

6: ANGELA

We didn't discuss much after that. Everyone walked out at once, over the broken door and toward the grass. There was no way around it. It was either through the grass or through the woods behind the house, and because Liles said the base was west of us, we headed that way. Besides, we never would have made it through the forest with all the bags. We would have gotten snagged on branches or cut by fallen trees. In hindsight, though,

perhaps we should have reconsidered how much we actually needed to take with us.

Not that it mattered in the end.

This is why bird shifts are helpful—to avoid walking through tall, itchy grass that's cutting your arms on contact. Chase and Liles were ahead of us with a couple pairs of hedge sheers that we'd found leaning against the house, but they didn't help much.

I'm sure you're wondering why we didn't shift into some animals with fur and thicker skin. For one, we had bags that we couldn't carry if we shifted, and we weren't going to make one person the pack mule of the gang, giving them all the bags just because they could shift into something large enough to carry them. Plus, we had to stick together. We even agreed to it out loud.

"Alex is going to be so pissed," Chase said.

Izzy chuckled. "Yup."

"You sound happy about that," I laughed.

"Well, I mean," she started, "it is kind of funny, we just... left!"

"Oh, we should have left a note," I sighed.

We continued to trudge through that grass for what seemed like an hour, maybe longer, and it was absolutely

miserable. The longer we walked, the heavier our bags became. By around nine o'clock, Liles was still going strong, but Chase looked like he was ready to fall over. Me and Osscar were also about to hit the literal hay. Or grass, if you will. And Izzy stayed behind us all. She hadn't talked since we left.

I stood on my toes, looking over the horizon in an attempt to see the end of the field, but we weren't even close. Everything was the same as the last time I'd checked. There were still miles of grass in front of us, and the sun was no lower in the sky, its heat beating down on our backs.

Chase was finally forced to take his jacket off, which I hadn't seen him do in about six months. Those bandages just looked worse every time I saw them. Liles scrutinized Chase's arms with a bewildered look on his face. Chase plainly chose to ignore it. He never talks about his condition, even on the days when it's hurting. Nobody knows what happened. We all asked when he first moved in, and he would just reply with "I don't know."

I turned to look at Izzy, but she didn't see me. She was off studying some of the patches of forest around us, probably thinking about Malachi and wondering if he could be in any of them. But after however long we had walked, the

house was completely out of view, along with the forest behind it, which I assumed Malachi would have run off to, but how could I remind her of that right then? I'm sure she knew.

Then a noise boomed through the air. It was the loudest, angriest sound I'd ever heard. A roar, from some sort of beast and it came from miles behind us, from the direction the house.

All of us turned around. "That's Alex..." Izzy said quietly.

"Sounds like he's home," I gulped.

"Run," Liles said, bolting off.

With all the shifts he possessed, we knew that Alex could track us for miles without stopping and at any speed he wanted. If we didn't hurry, he could catch us and drag our butts back to the house before we even got through the field. "I knew this was a bad idea!" Osscar yelled, running through the grass.

"We should have known we couldn't get far enough on foot!" Izzy cried.

"We still can't!" I said, stopping and dropping my bag of clothes. "Leave whatever you can't carry, and shift into something faster!"

I could have picked my horse, but then I'd be leaving the others in my dust. So I shifted into my Arctic wolf, the clothes on my back ripping to ribbons.

Chase looked at me like I must have been joking but went ahead and dropped everything but a first aid kit that he'd pulled from his duffle bag. He used the pocketknife he kept in his jacket to cut a thin strap off the bag and tie the medical kit loosely around his neck like a noose. He then shifted into his gray wolf. His clothes ripped but the strap necklace with the medical kit was secured perfectly around his fluffy wolf neck like a choker. Of course, that kit didn't really have medical supplies in it. I knew Chase kept one of those foldable backpacks, his wallet, and some survival stuff in that little plastic box—stuff like granola bars and a miniature flashlight.

Izzy and Osscar were a bit late to the party. "It's not smart to leave all our clothes behind if we're destroying the ones we're wearing!" Osscar yelled. Liles shifted into some sort of owl. His pants and underwear dropped from the sky onto Osscar's head. Swooping down, Liles the owl lifted his doctor's bag up into the air. "Does that bag have clothes in it?" Osscar shouted up at him.

"Nope!" Liles replied, flying forward.

Osscar seemed more frustrated than ever as he and Izzy fell so far behind that they could barely see the rest of us. "Fine!" he yelled in exasperation. "But when we can't shift back because no one has any clothes, let the record show that it was not my fault!" He shifted into his grizzly bear, grabbing one of his bags of clothes in his mouth and proceeding to run after Liles and the rest of us.

Izzy, of course, didn't want to be alone and shifted into her rabbit, leaving all her things behind. She could carry none of them in her pint-sized form. And so, looking like the oddest pack of animals you've ever seen, we bounded and flew across the grass, covering tons more ground than we had before.

We'd been told time and time again never to shift unless it's necessary, so being able to run recklessly out into the open with our animal forms was a whole new deal. Of course we played around with our shifts when we were younger, but when Osscar, Izzy, and I got older and more anxious to get out into the world, Dad and Alex both thought it was best that we start seeing our abilities for what they were—not toys or gifts, but curses that constantly attracted people who wanted to kill us.

After about half an hour we had slowed down, a lot.

"Almost...out of the grass now," Osscar coughed, his speed-walking progressively turning to trudging his paws across the field.

"Yeah, sure..." Chase panted. He too began to slow to a crawl.

"Wait!" I looked in front of me to see the end of the field marked by a large boulder shaped like a headstone. Just ahead of it was a dusty, rock-paved road. "We made it!" I laughed.

"Great! Can we," Osscar said through heavy panting, "take a rest now?"

Chase was done. He collapsed into the grass before a vote could be taken.

"Apparently we have to," I said, laying down. There were a few minutes of silence as we all attempted to catch our breath.

"Seeing as no one else is going to ask," I sighed, "do we have *any* clothes?"

Liles shook his head. Chase wouldn't reply, and no one could even hear Izzy's voice as it was even smaller than usual in her rabbit form, but she clearly wasn't carrying anything.

Osscar raised his big furry bear paw. "I have all my clothes," he said hesitantly. Everyone perked up and ran over to him, eager to see what was in his bag. "But!" he continued. "I only brought four outfits! And, they're not the most...feminine." He fished out a pair of shorts and a worn t-shirt from the bag with his paw.

"Ehhh..." I said.

"Or clean," he added.

Chase rolled his eyes. "Great. Now what?"

"We find someone who can help us," I replied. "One of us can go to town." Everyone looked at me, even Izzy, who had to stand up on her hind legs.

"You want to go back there?" Chase said. "Literally yesterday, Angie."

"Yeah, but like you said, it's safer to go in a group," I argued.

"You literally just said *one of us*," he reminded me.

"Look, hear me out," I started. "It normally takes a whole day to get this far out, and we basically cut the journey in half by running. Town is just down the road."

"So, by one of us, you mean me, right?" Osscar asked.

"You're the only one with clothes," Chase panted.

"Alright," Osscar sighed, "but where would I even go?"

"Angela's Uncle Jason," Chase replied. "He could seriously hook us up. Not only with some clothes, but with some fire power."

"If we can find him this time," I grumbled.

Osscar's eyes widened. "Guns?" he shouted. "We aren't even old enough to carry! We can't break the law now, too."

"Oh, come on, we're always outside the laws," Chase replied.

"Fine," Osscar sighed again, "but even if that road does lead to town, it's still a good hour away."

"And that's with no setbacks," I added.

"Can you guys honestly wait here in this heat for that long just for pants?" Osscar finished. We all looked around at each other miserably.

"Well, if you were to pick up some ice cream while you're there..." Chase mumbled.

"Now, I could wait for *that*," Liles laughed.

"Come on, I'm serious!" Osscar said.

"I have an idea," I sighed, standing up. "But I'm gonna need a minute."

I was already exhausted. Why on earth I would even suggest something so draining, I still don't know, but I

somehow found myself galloping Osscar down a dusty pebble-paved road as a majestic brown mustang.

"You okay?" Osscar shouted as we ran. It had been about ten minutes, and there was no town in sight, but I was apparently looking tired enough for him to ask if I was okay.

"Fine!" I replied. Between the roaring wind and the flying rocks on the path I was mowing over, it was hard to hear much without yelling.

"You don't sound fine!" Osscar yelled back. "WATCH!" I lifted my head almost as soon as he screamed, and just barely avoided a stop sign I was about to hit as I had drifted off the road. "You are *so* not fine!"

"Sorry!" I screamed.

"You're gonna exhaust yourself, then we'll have to walk a mile back to the others and drag you home from there!" Osscar yelled. "Do you want that!?"

"No!" I laughed. "Don't worry, I've been here before!" We passed the first entrance to town.

Osscar looked back behind us. "Hey, um, I think you missed it!"

"There were huntsmen by that entrance yesterday!" I shouted. "We're just taking precautions! Plus, I didn't see my uncle's shop before, so it has to be on the other side!"

"If he didn't move!" Osscar reminded me.

"I don't recall him being the moving type!"

"You're just lucky Chase lost the argument back there!" Osscar continued. "He really didn't want you coming here without him!"

"Yup!" I laughed. "He probably thinks I only offered to come along to look for my dad!"

"Wait—did you?"

"Well—" I started. I began slowing to a stop when I heard a faint sound behind us.

"What's up?"

"Turn around, is there anything there?" I asked nervously. "If no, then great. If yes, well, I don't know."

Osscar turned around slowly and then sighed in relief. "Nothing here, Ang—" He faced forward again and went speechless. I'm sure he noticed the large man holding the pistol between my eyes. I don't know how I didn't see him sneak up on me. One minute I was looking down, exhausted, the next, I was at the mercy of his trigger-finger. I said nothing. I couldn't see anything in front of me, apart from

the man's face, but could feel the weapon touching my head. Why do my eyes have to be so far apart in that form?

"Now, don't do anything stupid," the huntsman said, looking up at Osscar. "I know this horse isn't just your ride here."

He raised his hands, slowly climbing off of me. The huntsman merely gestured for him to walk, keeping the gun to my head. I could see Osscar, shaking as he made his way down the road.

"You, walk," he said, pushing the weapon's barrel further into my head as he shuffled me into a trot alongside my friend.

"I'm so sorry," I whispered. "It was my idea to come."

The huntsman poked the gun at my rib. "No talking," he threatened. I kept my mouth shut and continued down the road.

"Where did he come from?" Osscar whispered. I merely shook my head. I wasn't going to risk talking again, but honestly, how could I have known?

The back entrance to the town was coming into view. If I'd only been a little faster, we could have skipped this whole mess and been at Uncle Jason's before noon, which I know sounds like an irrelevant goal, but that way we

would be guaranteed to make it back to the others before nightfall, even with a few setbacks.

This side of town was different. It was small and dusty like something from an old Western movie crossed with a rest stop, and much more remote. It practically had my Uncle Jason written all over it. I was now frantic, looking for anything that screamed his name, in other words, something with a gun. We approached the back of a large pickup with a cover over the top of it. Large, but clearly not big enough to fit a horse.

"In the back?" I asked nervously.

The huntsman pointed the gun at my cheek again. "Go on," he said. "Better not make a scene of it, or I shoot."

I definitely wasn't getting into that truck as a naked human, but I couldn't fit as a horse, so that meant I needed to shift into something more compact, like my mouse. However, when the idea hit me, once again, my exhaustion and the stress of the gun against my skull rendered me useless.

"Shifter," the huntsman continued irritably, "go."

He cocked his pistol, and we heard a blast.

I opened my eyes just in time to see the huntsman fall to the ground. The shot rang through the whole town, but

no one else was around to hear it. Except, of course, the man who fired it.

Uncle Jason stepped out from behind an empty market stand and looked at me and Osscar, who I'm sure appeared just as frozen as the dead man in front of us. I honestly couldn't believe what had just happened.

"Well," Uncle Jason sighed, "this oughta be good."

I'm not sure how I didn't spot my uncle's place earlier. It was probably the most eye-catching building in town. Which did not mean it was the prettiest.

The store was called Jason's Firearms, clearly advertised in big wooden letters on the roof of the dusty little building. The whole structure looked like it was hand-built with reclaimed wood, and it had to have been a painted white at least forty years earlier, seeing as it appeared about thirty years overdue for a repaint. The letters on Jason's roof probably used to be red, but who could tell, because they were in the same condition as the rest of the building? In fact, I'd argue that the entire town was reduced to darkened spruce boards with small, grayish-white paint chips on them.

"Go get something on," Uncle Jason said, throwing what appeared to be an oversized shirt at my face, "then come meet us inside."

"What about—?" Osscar started.

"You, come with me," Jason interrupted. "You two need to tell me how you plan on getting out of this hell-hole, now that you're here."

Osscar turned to me nervously, and I gestured for him to go on. I didn't blame him for not wanting to follow the guy who'd just shot a man dead in front of us, but it seemed like a better idea than staying out here, waiting for more huntsmen. Apparently, they were all over the place.

My outfits just got worse and worse, I swear. I was walking back around the shop to the door in a long men's flannel that I was going to call a dress, and feeling really self-conscious about it.

"Understood?" I heard my uncle ask Osscar as I came through the crooked plywood-and-chicken-wire-lined door.

"I guess so," Osscar replied, looking skeptical. I didn't think much of it then, but that was a conversation I would regret not being present for.

Jason turned to me. "Glad it fits." I looked down at my outfit, disagreeing completely. "I knew my brother'd

cracked long ago, but I never thought he'd let you two leave the house alone."

"Well," I started, "he doesn't really know we're—" I stopped to look around the room.

I'd never been inside Uncle Jason's shop. I was kind of glad I hadn't. The place was musty, disorganized, with all kinds of weapons hanging from the ceiling and mounted to the wall. All the handmade discount signs in the place were covered in cobwebs and long expired.

Seriously, I don't know how else to describe how rundown the place looked. There was a large front desk on the right side of the room lined with cardboard bins filled with all sorts of junk, including such pocket-sized souvenirs as bulky twig pencils, hillbilly keychains, lucky rabbits' feet, tiny flashlights, and those big, carabiner linking-clips that you see hanging off people's backpacks in all different colors.

"What about old Alex?" Jason asked, leaning to get a beer from a mini fridge behind the front counter. "I doubt he'd let you two leave on his watch." He sat down in the worn leather desk chair next to him.

Osscar looked at me for a reply, but I had no answer.

"Hmm... Since you're quiet, I'm gonna take a stab in the dark and say y'all left when the old man had his back turned," Jason continued, popping the cap off his beer and taking a loud sip.

"Yeah, my grandfather was gone," Osscar admitted, "but we aren't the only ones who left."

Uncle Jason sat up straight and took a good long look at Osscar. "Wait a minute," he said, pointing. "So, you're Alex's grandson?"

Osscar nodded. "I know, we look nothing alike." He rolled his eyes.

"Now, that's where you're wrong," Jason replied, slouching down into his chair.

Osscar looked up, a bit confused. "What do you mean?"

"Look, kid, just because your pigment is different than his, and your face isn't as aged, doesn't mean you look nothing alike. Your nose is just like his, and I bet you're going to be just as tall." Once again, I couldn't tell how Osscar felt. He sort of kept nodding, like he didn't know if being told he bore a resemblance to Alex was a compliment or an insult.

"Do you know how that huntsman found us?" I asked, changing the subject.

Jason looked at me with an eyebrow raised. "There's a reason you're supposed to stay at home, kid, and you say you left with more people? You shouldn't have branched off from them. There's safety in numbers."

"We are—" I attempted to explain, but apparently my uncle wasn't finished.

"Those guys lie on every corner," he warned, pointing to a window across from the desk with cracked blinds over it. "I think they're onto me, but I ain't moving. This is my shop and my house."

"So, they're all here because of you?" I asked.

"Pfft... If they were, I'd be long gone," Jason scoffed. "Dana and Henry come through here all the time, and the huntsmen never give 'em any trouble. You know why?"

"Why?" I sighed. This was starting to sound oddly similar to how my dad would start a lecture.

"They don't let their animal forms be seen, for start-ers," Jason said. "They don't act so nervous either."

"We didn't act nervous," Osscar mumbled.

"Yeah, well, children ridin' in on horseback is not a normal sight in most places," Jason countered, taking another sip of beer.

"Have you seen Dana and Henry recently?" I asked.

"Nah, they've been shoppin' the town south of here down the fresh road. I don't blame 'em, this place sure ain't what it was," Jason shrugged. "Since the grocery across the street closed, I've been needin' to head out there myself, but I can't just take a weekend away with all these crazy people outside watchin' me. They'd ransack the shop."

"What about my dad?" I asked. "Did he come by here at any point this week?"

"Nope," Jason said, putting his feet up on the minifridge.

"You didn't see Dad at all?"

"No, why are ya surprised?" he asked. "He hasn't come'n seen me in over a year. In his defense, without some sorta communication, it is difficult to make arrangements. Speakin' of, did Henry relay to Chris that I needed him to check on the status of that nail gun I let him borrow?"

"He and Dana aren't back yet," Osscar replied.

Jason sat up. "You actually left when there were still people gone? That's really bone-headed."

"Well, what were we supposed to do?" I started irritably. "You don't get this kind of golden opportunity every day—a time when there aren't any adults in the house to hold you back."

"Now, wait just a minute!" Jason shouted, standing. "Are you meanin' to tell me that my idiot brother left you at the house with no supervision!? And he has the nerve to preach to me about family always comin' first! Meanwhile, he—"

"Wait!" I yelled. It probably wasn't the best idea to cut him off. "It's really not like that."

He rolled his eyes. "There's no excuse. Whatever the problem was, Chris knows better than to put his emotions before the well-being of his kids. Next I see the guy, Imma kill him." He sat back down.

"Do you have *any* idea where he may have gone yesterday?" I was already sure of the answer.

"Who says he gotta come see me every time he visits town? May have been down by the northern entrance."

"No," I sighed. "We looked there, almost everything was closed and—"

"Why'd y'all come here?" Uncle Jason asked, confused.

From the look on Osscar's face, I don't think he knew the full story of what we saw in town the other day. "Well, we didn't all come at the same time," I started to explain. "Dad was missing, and I came out to find him, but—"

"I'm not following you, kid," Jason said, shaking his head. "You and who?"

"Oh, me and Chase."

"Is that the kid Chris took in with the Shifter's Bone?" he asked.

"Yeah," Osscar replied.

"Been wantin' to meet him," Jason said, taking a gulp of beer.

"You won't get him to talk about it," I added, "or anything, for that matter."

"What, he shy or somethin'?" Jason asked.

"Or somethin'," Osscar replied.

"Hmm... Back to my brother. Where's he now?"

"We don't know."

"He went missing Friday," Osscar said. "Like, no note or anything."

"Missing?" Jason asked, setting down his beer. He paused. "That's just great," he said, shaking his head.

"I'm sorry..."

Osscar nodded again, then stared at me with eyebrows raised as if to ask, *What now?*

Jason leaned back in his chair, pondering the circumstances. "What's Alex's excuse leaving y'all alone at the house?"

"Umm, he was told that Grandmother wouldn't be coming home," Osscar said, rubbing his arm.

"I see," Jason replied. "I reckon he didn't take it so well?"

"That's a bit of an understatement," Osscar added.

"Poor guy was bound to find out one day. I'm surprised he held out hope for this long."

Apart from the humming lights, the whole room went silent. "Well, as much as I would like to keep catching up," I said awkwardly, "we've got to get some clothes and meet up with everyone as soon as possible."

"Right," Jason mumbled, scratching his head. "Well, I'm not sure if I have what you're lookin' for. Try the outfitters across the street. With all their customers spooked, the owners may give y'all some discounts."

"Okay, see you later then," Osscar said, quickly following me to the door.

"Now wait just a minute," Jason snapped. "Just what do you think you're doing, goin' out there without some heat in this weather?"

I had absolutely no idea what he meant. I'm pretty sure Osscar didn't either. That is, until Uncle Jason handed him a rifle with a short barrel and a pack of ammunition.

"Oh no, no!" Osscar said frantically. "I can't shoot."

"Yeah, and I don't think the weather's bad enough for us to need to learn now," I said, reaching for the door handle.

Uncle Jason was faster and put his hand on the handle first. "I don't care whose fault it is that you guys went out unprepared the first time around," he said, "but it's not going to happen again on my watch."

I watched him walk back over to his desk, grab one of the empty beer cans off the counter, and place it on the third row of one of the shelving units lining the back wall of the shop. "You," he started, gesturing to me, "are going to shoot"—he pointed to the can—"that." I looked over at the rifle that Osscar had in his hands and felt my stomach turn upside down. I'd never even touched a gun, though I'd seen several, most of which had been aimed at me. "Come on now, you can do it," Jason said, taking the

gun from Osscar and placing it into my trembling hands. "You'll need to focus," he continued. "And, for God's sake, stop shaking. This is a tool, nothing more. Your enemies commonly use this tool against you because it is effective, but you can easily show them you're smarter by making better use of it, and—"

I heard very little of my uncle's spiel after that. I was preoccupied with my own thoughts. *Did he just up and give me, a child, a weapon? I'm only sixteen!* I was starting to realize why the guy didn't have any kids of his own! Then I heard a bang and jumped backward, almost dropping the rifle. Uncle Jason had fired his own pistol at the can, sending it flying off the shelf.

"See?" he asked, nudging me.

"Umm...No, I mean, I didn't," I said, putting the rifle down. I was still shaken. *That sound...*

"Hey!" Jason shouted at Osscar. "You paying attention?"

"What?" Osscar replied, setting down the lucky rabbit's foot keychain that he'd been disconcertedly examining during my uncle's brief demonstration.

Jason had declared us a lost cause. "Clearly the lessons aren't possible if no one's listening. How about you take

one of these, and go learn on the job?" He handed me his pistol, which I immediately passed to Osscar like a hot potato. "And stay away from that pub across the street!" he added, vanishing through the door across from the left side of his desk, as Osscar nervously set the gun on the front counter.

I assume Uncle Jason lived back there or something, because I saw a large fridge and a worn-out couch covered in clothes and beer cans through the doorway as he entered the room. I put my hand back on the door handle, pretty sure that he wouldn't be coming back out to say goodbye.

"Angela?" Osscar said as we left. "I think your uncle has a drinking problem."

"Among other things," I sighed. The town looked the same as before, but I cringed at the sight of the fallen huntsman.

"Poor guy," Osscar said quietly, staring down at the body.

I nodded. I felt horrible. I don't know why, but I did. And not just scared, but genuinely sorry for the man. *How could my uncle do something like this?*

"Well, not poor as in he didn't deserve it, but," Osscar rambled on, "you know."

"Yeah," I mumbled, looking away from the dead man before I cried. "Let's go...."

7: CHASE

I was impatient, tired, hungry, and anxious. Angela and Osscar had been gone over two hours, meanwhile, the rest of us had just been sitting in the field doing absolutely nothing. I couldn't believe I let her leave. No one said a word for most of the time we waited. Which wouldn't be unusual for a group of teenagers with phones, laptops, or video games, but we had nothing of the sort.

Liles was reading some sort of medical book that he pulled from his bag shortly after Osscar and Angela took

off, and Izzy went from messing with her hair to staring off into space.

I was the only one who didn't shift back when Liles admitted he had a couple outfits in his bag. I said it was because I didn't want to, but the truth was far more pathetic. I was so exhausted I could barely stand. The muscles in my legs were hurting so badly that hiding it was becoming more difficult by the minute. I'd already run the field the day before, and that was literally the most strenuous activity I'd attempted in years. To have to do it again...

It's a good thing I'd thrown my knife away, because I probably would have considered stabbing myself. I'm kidding, obviously, but the pain stopped me from fighting Angela when she declared that she and Osscar were going to town without me. They both started yelling, and after a while I was too tired to yell back.

Great, more arguments to reminisce about...

By the way, if you're curious on how exactly me and Angela ended up back at the house after I knocked her out, too bad, because I don't wanna talk about it. But I will say this: it involved Alex, a blanket, and very little assistance on my part. He found me trying to drag her home in my

polar bear form, legs burning and two seconds from surrendering to the circling vultures.

And this stays between us, but the truth is, that "huntsman" who came out of the building behind her ended up being armed with little more than a milkshake.

Yeah, I lied about the knife, but what was I supposed to tell her? Sorry, Angie, I misjudged the situation and knocked you out for no reason? I'm sure that would have gone over nicely!

"So," Izzy said at last, "they've been gone awhile..."

"Yeah, I'm worried," I sighed.

Liles turned a page. "We'll go look for them if it gets dark, but this early, anything could be holding them up. You said Angela has family in town." He looked up from his book. "They're probably just caught in a long conversation."

"Guess you're right," I replied, laying down.

"What about Alex?" Izzy asked. "We're basically *waiting* for him if we stay here."

"I suppose we should keep moving," Liles sighed, closing his book.

"Keep moving?" I said, getting back up. "We can't just leave them."

"We'll head in their direction," Liles replied, standing up. "Honestly though, I'm not sure if you can tell, but I was really hoping to be able to rest when I got back home."

"Tell me about it," I sighed.

"Well, we could just...take a nap?" Izzy suggested.

"Good idea," Liles said before I could. We sat down.

"And, hey," he continued, reclining with his hands behind his neck. "If they're both captured and made into vests, we can all share the guilt."

There was a pause. Izzy looked over at me, confused.

"What?" I asked him.

8: ANGELA

As we walked out onto the road, I noticed the sun was lower in the sky. Luckily, it wasn't long before we spotted the outfitters a couple buildings down. It was big and painted light pink with blue rosette decals stuck onto the white door. It wasn't as gaudy as Uncle Jason's shop with its giant letters on the roof. It had a circular, projected sign hanging a few inches above the door, and every letter of text was written in the fanciest combination of cursive and strategically placed swirls.

The sign read:

A&A'S CLOTHING (UPCYCLED FASHION FOR THE TRENDIEST OF TRENDSETTERS)

"They're trying too hard," Osscar said, reading the sign. We both stepped onto the deck. "Did you hear your uncle?" he asked. "Me, tall?"

I smiled, placing my hand on the shop's shiny silver doorknob. "I mean, you never know."

"I just turned sixteen," He reminded me. "I'm pretty sure that ship has sailed."

We both started laughing as I twisted the doorknob. I almost instantly regretted that decision. A screaming woman flung the door open, clearly ready for a fight. There was no time to back up; she swung her arm out before even looking at us, inches from tasing me with whatever she had in her other hand. It looked like an electrified walking cane. It was long and black with a thin, hammer-like handle.

I ducked with my hands over my head. Osscar stumbled back, almost falling off the deck.

"Children?" the woman cried in a heavy southern accent. She had light brown hair which appeared to have once been up in a bun, based on the ties hanging from it, but was now dangling about her face crazily. "What are you kids doing here? You'll draw those strange people into our shop!"

Osscar stared at the woman, then at me, as if to ask *should we run?*

I was breathing heavily from the scare, unsure of how to reply. Neither of us moved from our frozen positions on the porch, waiting to see what the excitable woman's intentions were. She rolled her bright blue eyes and stormed back into the outfitters before glancing back at us. "Oh, get up," she snapped. "This place is crawling with those who kill your kind."

"Great, another person who knows who we are," I said, helping myself up using the railing.

"Should we go?" Osscar suggested. "She could be trying to trick us."

I looked back at the road. Someone was leaving one of the local bars. He was dressed in a desert camo t-shirt, black jeans, and a baseball cap. Perfectly normal until

you noticed his tool belt of unidentifiable weaponry. He turned toward us.

"You know," I said, pushing Osscar inside the shop with me, "I vote we give her the benefit of the doubt!"

The shop was, well, the only metaphor I think of is an adorable disaster. There was a huge mess of clothing all over the floor, and the walls were covered in fuzzy floral grid wallpaper and posters of bikini-top girls and smoldering boys all in spiffy outfits.

"So, how did you guys know we were..." Osscar started, trying his best to lie, "farm-hands?"

"Darlin', please, you guys aren't a bunch of myths anymore," the woman said. "No normal children come around here, not lookin' like you. You shouldn't be here. Those freaks have been tryin' to recruit people to their murderous mission all week."

"Recruit *you*?" I asked.

"Yes, pay attention," she huffed. "They don't value anyone or anything. Why would I join something like that?" She started mumbling. "Even if they do pay ninety thousand a year..."

"Ninety!?" Me and Osscar both shouted in disbelief.

"I know!" she yelled eccentrically. "It's a chunk of change! But I want no part of it!"

"No wonder there are so many huntsmen," I groaned.

Another woman then entered from the room marked

STAFF ONLY.

She was tall and younger-looking with dark skin and curly hair loosely down to her shoulders.

"Amy, I don't want to ask you again. What did you do with my button-up leg warmers?" she asked the woman we were talking to.

"Shh, Adaline, we have guests," the woman, apparently called Amy, whispered to her colleague.

Adaline turned to Osscar and me, her face lighting up. "Customers!" she said, running up to us. "Here, what can we help you with?"

"Well, actually, we're looking for some clothes," I replied as Adaline began to wrap my waist in a long measuring tape.

"Hold it, Addie!" Amy snapped. "These two are shapeshifters..."

Adaline gasped and stepped back from us, a look of extreme worry and sadness in her eyes. "The poor babies!!"

she cried, hugging us both tighter than a boa would wrap its prey.

We both winced, but I was deeply moved by the sympathy.

"Bless your hearts," she continued pitifully. "No child should have to live such a life. Here, take whatever you'd like. Anything you need."

Amy's eyes opened wide at that statement. "Addie!" she screamed. "We can't afford to go giving away our inventory! With all these weirdos scaring the customers off, we won't even be able to pay the water bill!"

Adaline looked at Amy with disgust. "These children!" she said, hugging us tighter. "*These children* are killed on sight to appease horrible humans who show them not a shred of sympathy! Doomed to live their short lives in fear! And *you* would deny them clothing?!"

Osscar and I glanced at each other in confusion. This lady knew more about shapeshifters than either of us expected from a normal human. I was starting to wonder if my Uncle Jason was really as private as we had believed him to be.

Amy sighed. "Fine...take what you want." In normal circumstances, I probably would have declined the offer to

be polite, but my spirits were finally lifted. This would fix everything!

"You mean, for free?" Osscar confirmed hesitantly.

Amy nodded slowly. "Just gather up what all you need before I change ma' mind."

At that, we both started running around the racks of hanging clothes, sorting through the piles on the floor, and immediately seeking out anything denim.

"See, Aims? Feels good to do the right thing," Adaline said, nudging Amy.

"Mhm," Amy hummed, "just don't pin it on me when we don't have hot water next month."

I had already found seven pairs of shorts, one bleached denim jacket, two pairs of stretchy blue jeans, a gray sweatshirt, a short yellow dress with a honeycomb pattern, and a black t-shirt with a horse silhouette. Things were going well.

A half hour later, Osscar and I each had a large bag with just enough clothes for ourselves and everyone back in the field to last about three days, but I knew even that was too much for us to carry all the way back, and Amy and Adaline were starting to look nervous. Probably

because of how much of their inventory we were about to walk away with for free.

Osscar looked as guilty as I did. I put down my bag of clothes by the register. "This is very generous of you guys to let us take whatever we want, but I insist you give us some kind of bill, I'm sure our family could pay you back, you know, some day."

"Oh," Amy sighed. "Don't worry about us, hun, it's just..." Adaline put her hand on her friend's shoulder. "We knew someone like you guys."

"Another one?" I asked, confused. "But I thought shifters were on the verge of extinction?"

Osscar must have overheard, because he came up with his clothes and dropped his pile next to mine. "Are we not?" he asked. "Could someone please explain what's going on?"

"All those people outside," Adaline said, gesturing to the window, "they're here because of a girl we met about a month ago."

I was relieved to hear that they weren't actually here for Uncle Jason. I guess he was right, if they really had known he was a shifter they would have just gotten a team

together and kicked his old, chicken-wire door in. "What happened to her?" I asked.

"Nothing good, I'm sure," Amy said quietly. "She stayed with us for a while, before she was taken."

"Taken by huntsmen?" Osscar asked.

"Yes," Amy confirmed, "more specifically, that wicked blond woman." The shopkeeper's expression grew bitter. "She barged in here like she owned the place and took Maggie at gunpoint."

"There was nothing we could do," Adaline added sadly.

"Wicked blond woman?" I asked. I didn't even need to ask. Little did I know, this woman they were talking about would become the very reason we're stuck where we are right now.

"We don't know her name," Amy replied, "but she's truly evil. She wears one of those—"

"Shhh..." Adaline whispered harshly to her colleague, "I'm sure they know what you mean."

We didn't have a clue. "Umm, we don't, actually," Osscar said.

They both looked stunned. "Forget it," Amy insisted. "I-I'm so sorry I said anything."

"Wait," I said, "please tell us."

"No, sweetie. It's best you—"

"Please," I begged, "if there's anything we should know, it's better to find out now."

The shopkeepers turned to each other, a deep sadness reflecting in their eyes. Amy eventually sighed. "When we met her, she was wearing this... cloak," she started hesitantly. "It fascinated us because it wasn't made from typical furbearers like mink or fox. The fur was beautiful, a black wolf's no doubt, and the underside of it—"

Adaline butted in. "The underside of it was not velvet-lined like most fur clothing. It was exposed original pelt, and as she walked about, the leather began to glow..."

Amy cut her off. "And then the fur of her cloak shrank, and it faded to a different color, from the wolfy black to a foxy red."

"Then," Adaline continued, "the long, full-body cloak looked more like a—cropped jacket." They paused to look at us. Our expressions had to have looked blank. Neither of us was getting it.

"And, once it was fully transformed, the skin underneath stopped glowing," Amy finished.

I thought about it for a minute and as the information began to sink in, I suddenly didn't feel so well. "Wait...."

Osscar turned to me confused. "What?" he asked. "Angela?"

I put my bag down and leaned against a nearby hat rack. "Think about it, Osscar," I said, shaking my head. "The coat's shape...shifted."

His eyes widened. He put his bag down and sat in the decorative salon chair behind him. "That's just wrong," he said at last.

"I'm so sorry..." Adaline said.

"No, we needed to know that," I said somewhat bitterly. "We needed to know that a long time ago."

I stood up straight and grabbed my bag of clothes. "Come on," I said to Osscar. "We've got to get back to the others."

"No kidding," he scoffed, grabbing his bag as well.

"Wait!" Adaline shouted. "Amy?" Amy looked at her. "May they have the stick?"

"Oh, come now, really?" Amy groaned. "We're already letting them take a quarter of our shop."

"They need it! All you use it for is dress-up!"

"Fine," Amy sighed. She pulled from her boot the long electric stick that she had used to nearly tase me on the porch. Adaline took it from her, pressing a button on its

handle. The top half of the stick sparked to life with small, zapping bolts of electricity.

"Oh, we're okay!" I said, waving my hands. "I don't think a taser will be of much—"

Adaline slowly pushed the sliding dial up the handle of the strange electric stick until the small zaps of electricity I was almost struck with became large, deadly blue bolts, surging through the stick like a wave. I jumped back from the object in terror. "What the heck!?"

"That's enough to kill someone!" Osscar shouted. "Like, instantly!"

"Yup," Amy said. "We got it from the blond, she dropped it when she stormed the place."

"That's a huntsman weapon?" I shouted. "Y-You almost hit us with that!"

"It was on the lowest setting!" Amy countered.

Adaline pressed the button on the handle of the stick to turn it off before offering it to me. I took it cautiously while Osscar started out the door with our bags. "Good luck," Adaline said as her colleague waved.

"Thanks," I replied, walking out. "We're gonna need it."

I shut the door behind us, and Osscar yanked me to the left, behind one of the pillars supporting the shop's large metal awning.

"Hey, I—"

"Shhhh!" Osscar said, pointing. "Look."

I looked out at the road. There were at least ten people gathered around the man my uncle had shot, like a murder of crows. "Okay, how are we getting ourselves and these bags past all those guys?" I asked. "We can't carry these as mice." Osscar must have spotted something because I could see his eyes light up as he glanced left. "The last time you had that look, we ended up having to pull the lawn mower out of a tree," I said.

Osscar led me off the porch and into the alley between the clothing shop and another market, where something was laying on the ground with a tarp over it. I looked down and noticed what he must have seen from the porch—a handle of some sort sticking out of the tarp.

"Oh, no," I sighed.

"Yeah, but this alley's a dead end," he whispered.

I looked back toward the people surrounding the body. They were definitely huntsmen. The weapons prominently

displayed against their bodies, and the deranged look on their faces were my primary clues.

"I know," I lifted the tarp. "Who's driving?"

Osscar propped the motorcycle up against a building and attempted to climb onto it. The bike was dirty, scratched up, and had obviously seen better days. "Are we sure it's even going to turn on?" I asked.

"Well..." Osscar started, positioning himself at the front of the bike. Then, it roared to life, vibrating like crazy. Of course, that caught the attention of everyone in the silent town! Dropping everything, I flung myself at Osscar and onto the bike as four people started running at us, two men and two women, all with weapons at the ready. "It won't move!" Osscar yelled, twisting the handle.

"Pedal!" I yelled.

He smashed his foot against the bike pedal, and we almost flew straight into the air. The bike bounced and swerved out of the alley and onto the dirt road. A cloud of dust followed us, filling the lungs of the huntsmen who were already on our tails.

I closed my eyes, holding onto Osscar for dear life. There was no way to see behind us with all the dust, but we didn't need to look back to know we were in trouble.

A gunshot rang through the air, and I felt a pulse run through the bike and bounce me up.

"Osscar!" I yelled.

"Just the tire!" he yelled back.

"Just!?"

The bike started slowing down, and the cloud of dust consumed us. I couldn't see; I couldn't think straight. I felt Osscar jump off the bike, and I started rubbing my eyes.

"Angela!" a familiar voice called out.

"Stop!" another, deeper voice shouted.

"I see one!" A girl's voice this time.

"Osscar!" I yelled, jumping off the bike. I felt someone push me over, and another person grab my arm and pull it violently along with them as they ran. I dug my feet into the ground in resistance, until I could finally see who it was.

"We got 'em now!" the deep voice called again.

Osscar and I ran as fast as we could, the huntsman hoard behind us gaining fast.

"Why don't they just shoot?" Osscar yelled.

"I don't know!" I coughed. "You heard the girls at the shop, maybe they don't want to damage our—"

I had inhaled so much dust that I was having a coughing fit as we ran out of the cloud of chaos, which was not the wisest idea, considering it revealed our location.

I couldn't see, my eyes were swollen, and rubbing them was pointless, but all my other senses still worked. I could hear Osscar breathing hard in front of me, as well as the sounds of the twenty people racing behind us.

"We're gonna die," Osscar wheezed. I could feel him slowing down, and the voices behind us getting louder.

"Can you shift?" I asked.

"No! I'm—" he started coughing, too.

"Please try!" I yelled. I attempted to shift, but failed. I was exhausted, and the situation was far too heated.

There was nothing more we could do. The huntsmen began to circle us, and I collapsed to my knees coughing. Osscar was done, too. I felt him pull my arm one last time before getting down with me.

"Well, you gave it your best shot," a tall bleach-blond woman in a cropped, brown fur jacket muttered as she approached us. Her amber eyes glared down at me like I was some sort of trophy fish she'd just reeled in. She had a belt of weapons unlike any I'd ever seen. One of the few I recognized was an electric stick exactly like the one the

shopkeepers gave us. I really wish I'd held onto that one. "Hmm...." she said, smiling.

"What?" I coughed.

"You don't look related. Most of the kids I catch in pairs are usually siblings," she replied, squinting as she circled us.

"We're as close as siblings," I said, looking over to Osscar. That was my way of reminding him how much he meant to me, fearing this could be the end our lives. Despite the circumstances, he managed to smile at me, nodding slightly.

"There must be more of you, then," she concluded. She spoke assertively, as if letting her teammates know that she was comfortable with this kind of confrontation.

"No, our parents died years ago," Osscar blurted out. "We found each other."

"Yeah, sure. I'll make you a deal—you tell me where your families are, and I'll let one of you go, the one who talks first."

"The big rock," Osscar said without hesitation.

"Osscar!" I yelled.

"The big rock at the edge of the grass valley up ahead," he coughed.

I looked at him with the most betrayal I'd ever felt, the most distrust. He turned to me. "I'm sorry," he muttered.

"Fine, if they're there, you go free. Load 'em into the carriage. I don't think our van guy is going to show."

9: CHASE

"You're telling me we're gonna get skinned?!" I yelled.

"Hypothetically!" Liles shouted. "Honestly, what rock have you all been living under? What did you think the huntsmen wanted, indentured servants?"

"What's an indentured servant?" Izzy asked with a shaking voice, still in shock.

"Well, that part was irrelevant, but it means you're forced to work for someone under contract," Liles

explained, wracking his mental dictionary for the most cumbersome definition possible. "It's a—form of unfree labor, usually involving multiple parties."

I couldn't think of a better way to describe my situation if I tried. Bodyguard? *Puh*-lease! That was just another one of Chris's sugarcoats for my captive circumstances. "Are you serious?" I asked. "That's what I am!"

"How so?" Liles asked, confused.

"They're going to wear us," Izzy mumbled like she was about to cry.

"I signed a contract, and now I'm stuck living in that stupid house with your grandfather!" I shouted. It's hard to make unintentional dramatic gestures in a canine form, so there was a lot of head shaking on my part.

"That makes literally no sense," Liles said. "Just... leave?"

"He thinks he can't," Izzy replied.

"Look, it may be hard to believe," I continued, "but I'm stuck there until Angela's father tells me I can go."

"You signed your life away to someone?" Liles asked. "Why would you do that!?"

"I-I don't know,"

"Yes, you do," Izzy said accusingly. "Your bandages."

"Bandages?" Liles scoffed. "You can get those at any store, you know? I have some in this bag."

Izzy crossed her arms, looked at me, and gestured to Liles like I needed to tell him something. I didn't have to tell anyone anything. "The ones you're wearing?" Liles asked. "Come on, you must be joking. Those are rags." There was another brief silence. "Wait, how are you still wearing those?"

"They're special," Izzy insisted.

"They shift with you?" Liles said. "How is that possible?"

"No idea," I replied hastily, wishing I could put my jacket back on. "Can we get moving?"

"But I thought you wanted to rest?" Izzy reminded me.

"Yeah, well, I didn't know about the whole hunts-men-make-shapeshifters-into-clothing thing until now," I said, grabbing the strap tied around my first aid kit off the ground with my teeth. The sound of footsteps coming from the pebble-paved road ahead caused me to freeze. Liles and Izzy stood up.

"What do we do?" Izzy whispered. There was a subtle panic in her voice.

"Hide," Liles said before shifting into his fennec fox and leaping off into the grass, leaving all of his things, including clothes, behind. The fox's fur was almost the same color as the grass—it was the perfect camouflage.

Izzy shifted into her rabbit, following Liles, and then there was me. I just couldn't do it. Everything was still sore, I was still tired, it was still hot. I got down as low as I could and crept through the grass away from the road. The problem with this plan: You can't tell where you're going when you can't see or smell anything but grass. I smacked right into something with my head and looked up to see a large scruffy man wearing leather hiking boots and a gray Coca-Cola t-shirt. He was holding two large plastic bags and there was a pistol sticking out of his pants pocket. I began backing up slowly.

"Don't panic, kid," the man said, setting the bags down. "I'm Christopher's brother."

"Prove it," I growled, stepping back.

"What, I don't bear a resemblance?"

"No," I said cautiously.

Which wasn't a lie—this guy was short, blond, and had an unkempt appearance and a thick southern Mississippi

accent. Probably the exact opposite of Angela and her father.

"I'll take that as a compliment," the man laughed. "Are you the only one out here?" he asked, taking the pistol from his pocket.

Without a second thought, I darted through the grass back toward where Liles and Izzy left their things. I didn't care if that guy really was Angela's uncle, who in their right mind just pulls a gun out in the middle of a conversation?

"Hey!" he shouted as I fled.

I tripped over something in the grass. Izzy shrieked out in pain, and I heard Liles make a loud "Shh!"

I was practically crawling along the ground, heart racing, thinking about all that Liles had told us and imagining myself being shot by that pistol and carried off to have the skin torn from my deformed skeleton.

"Alright!" the man shouted irritably. "How about you kids come out now? I ain't gonna shoot ya. If I wanted to, I woulda done it long by now."

"Who is that?" Liles whispered. I couldn't see him; he was so well camouflaged, but he sounded close by.

"He's claiming to be Angela's uncle," I said quietly.

"Well, is he?"

"I dunno," I replied. "He doesn't look like—"

"You better quit fooling around," the man started again. "Your friends've been taken by the huntsmen, who are on their way here now."

"What do we do?" Izzy cried.

"No," I said out loud.

If this guy was lying, coming out was a death sentence, if he wasn't and Angela was really taken by huntsmen, well... My stomach was in knots, and my legs were trembling like leaves.

"Don't fall for it," Liles whispered. "If he was a shapeshifter, he would prove it."

"I've got two bags of clothes and a plan for everyone who doesn't wanna join 'em," the man continued.

"Is he armed?" Liles asked me. "Chase?"

I was speechless. The stranger couldn't be lying. If he knew we were missing two people and that we were all shapeshifters, it didn't matter if he was a huntsman or not. Something had to have happened to Osscar and Angela.

I stood up.

"What are you doing?" Liles shouted in a panicked whisper.

I walked toward the man slowly and sat down in front of him with my head held high and a cross expression on my face. "Well, hello again," the man said, looking down at me.

"What's the plan?" I asked.

"You must be Chase," he said. "Nice to meet ya." He glanced down at my bandaged legs. "Man, you've got it real bad."

Oh, we were already off on the wrong foot.

10: ANGELA

Two men held us at gunpoint, walking Osscar and me slowly to the door of a wagon-looking thing pulled by four horses of assorted sizes and colorations. I was forced to sit next to Osscar on a long bench that stretched across the interior wall of the "carriage." Which I don't think that is an accurate word to describe it. *Carriage* sounds so fancy. This was a beat-up wooden box filled with cobwebs and claw marks. Even the bench we were sitting on had shredded upholstery. A guard sat on the bench at the opposite end of the space with a shotgun, probably to make sure we didn't "try anything." Once the carriage started moving, I scooted away from Osscar and faced the wall closest to me.

"Angela," he started, "I can—"

"Oh, drop dead," I murmured. Okay, it was harsh, but at the time, the comment felt justified. He gave me up, he gave our friends up. He may even have given Alex up if the huntsmen had continued on through the field. The ride took around half an hour, but it felt like a minute. The images spinning in my head of me and my loved ones being skinned alive made the ride short and miserable. I felt the carriage stop, and I took a deep breath. Our guard held his gun up and led us out the door. I closed my eyes and walked alongside Osscar in shame.

The woman in furs marched us down to the big rock with only two escorts. Probably so there wasn't much risk of anyone spotting a group of huntsmen and running for the hills. This wasn't their first rodeo. The escorts were holding both of us by the arms at gunpoint. Neither of us knew the first thing about fighting, and I'm pretty sure the blond woman could tell. She began treating us with complete and total nonchalance after we stepped out of the carriage. She rolled her eyes and said something along the lines of, "What, you didn't even try?"

Anxiety built up inside me as the big rock came into view, but to my surprise, when I opened my eyes no one was there. I let out a huge sigh of relief. Thank God!

"They're around here," Osscar said in a panic, "I swear."

"I know," the woman in furs replied flatly, walking on. How did she know?

After a good ten minutes of walking through the field and around the big rock, the woman, who I could only assume was the captain of the team, turned back to us. "Alright, well, seeing as no one is here," she scoffed, "you must have tipped them off somehow."

"Or he lied to you?" I suggested.

"No," she insisted. "But I have places to be in twenty minutes." I gulped, looking at her jacket. With no dust obscuring her, it was now clear exactly what it was. The coat was made of beaver pelts—multiple beaver pelts that had been sewn into sleeves, pockets, and a whole jacket. "Just as well, I wasn't going to let you go anyway."

My stare didn't break from her outfit. I had to see for myself what Amy and Adaline had been talking about, and sure enough, the underside of her jacket started glowing an all-too-familiar glow and the fur began to fade from

brown to yellow-tan. A lion skin cloak—made of multiple lion pelts.

I gasped. The woman turned to me, but pointed her gun at Osscar. "Just noticed, did ya?" she asked. "Yeah, it's made of your kind, around three or four of 'em."

"How'd you find that many shapeshifters?" I asked, shaking. "I thought we—"

"When you bond multiple pelts, they shift in unison, resulting in a morphing coat. I had to work very hard to make this one." She pridefully modeled the getup for us, walking slowly back and forth past our escorts. "It can take years, depending on the complexity of the project. This one took about a decade."

"A *decade*?" Osscar asked. "It took you that long to find that many shapeshifters?"

The woman crossed her arms. "Oh, come on now, you guys really think you're still a unicorn species?" she laughed. "No, sweetheart, our facility alone has over a hundred and sixty shapeshifters in it." We said nothing, but this was definitely news to me. She stopped her runway walk. "The time-consuming part of making these coats is making all the shifters we catch able to transform into the same set of animals."

"You forced them to learn new shifts?" I asked. "How?"

She looked at me like I was joking. "You should be able to figure that one out on your own. There are very few ways to get someone to dig their own grave."

"You tortured them..." Osscar concluded.

The woman nodded. "So, we can't kill you yet." She turned to me. "But we can use similar tactics to get the information we need."

From her belt, she pulled out a club-like weapon with parallel lines of short, rounded spikes sticking out of its bulbous end and a dial at the bottom of its thin handle. I stared at it, still shaking like a chihuahua. It felt like my insides had turned to mush. The stick was the most pain-ful-looking thing I'd ever seen. It resembled the electric one that Amy and Adaline had, but shorter and more like a weapon. Of course, it only got scarier. She pushed a but-ton at the end of the handle and the spikes began to glow red with heat.

Osscar struggled against the grip of his escort who was working hard to restrain him. I froze with fear. *Why? Why would our families keep all this from us?* I wasn't sure about everyone else, but if I had gotten *any* of this information

before we ran away, I would never have let Chase convince me to leave the house. When it finished heating up, the red-hot spikes were glowing bright orange.

"If you have any knowledge of where your family may or may not have gone," the woman started, "now's the time."

"We don't!" I declared. Of course I did. The house was only a few miles away.

"Now, that's a lie," she said, pulling the torture device back.

I closed my eyes as she swung the hot weapon toward me, but I felt nothing but a warm breeze. She yelled out in pain. And I opened my eyes to see a gray, furry body with bandaged legs standing in front of me, the weapon's handle in its mouth. I was so relieved. Had it been anyone else, I may have cried. I took a breath. "Thanks."

The thin, gray wolf looked back at me and smiled slightly, still holding the hot weapon.

"The family's here," the woman in furs mumbled. She turned her hand around to see the burn marks Chase left on her palm when he took the stick from her. "I NEED BACKUP!" she shouted in the direction of the carriage. She pulled out another strange-looking weapon from her

belt, but it was taken away from her almost as quickly as she unsheathed it. Liles flew away with the object and tossed it into the grass. I heard a gunshot in the distance. Chase and I ducked.

Looking back at how the first half of this confrontation went down, honestly, I was pretty useless. All of this was so much worse than anything we could have imagined. None of us knew how to fight. Heck, we weren't even sure exactly who we were fighting.

Out of the corner of my eye, I saw Osscar running from the scene. I was so mad at him I didn't even care. First, he gives us away, then he just runs off?

"Who has the darts?" the woman in furs yelled to her team that was nowhere in sight. "I don't want to put a bunch of holes in these guys!" There was a lot of commotion coming from the direction of the carriage. We couldn't see what was happening, but in addition to the gunshots, there was yelling, screaming, horses whinnying.

"Seriously?" the woman in furs shouted in exasperation. She patted herself down. "I need a gun!"

I'd had enough of watching my friends fight my battles. I shifted into my Arctic wolf, leapt over Chase, and lunged at the woman in furs, grabbing her belt of weapons

and ripping it off her hips. Chase followed my lead, standing guard over the belt to keep her from retrieving it. Somewhere in the middle of this, I felt a sharp prick in my right hind leg.

Moments after realizing her predicament, the woman in furs ran toward the road. Me and chase jumped the same way. We had her cornered at the big rock, and she was all out of ammo. We thought we'd won. Then, a sudden and unexplainable fatigue overtook me. I started stumbling. I felt Chase crash into me and heard another series of loud gunshots in the distance, before everything went black.

11: CHASE

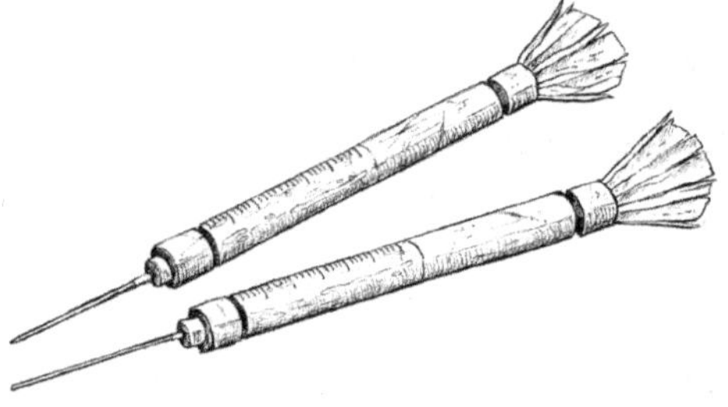

Thankfully, I rarely have dreams about things that have actually happened. When I do, they'll be of random and somewhat forgettable moments. This one was no exception, but I'm going to write it in third person because the "dream" was more of a recollection, where I was only observing my choices as a naïve twelve-year-old who didn't think twice about the consequences of wrapping half his body in duct tape because it worked as a temporary solution for pain he didn't know how to deal with yet.

Jackson, Mississippi

July 2014

A kid walked down a long hospital hallway. The sounds of phones ringing and people crying set the dismal mood of the place. The boy had makeshift stick splints duct- taped to his arms. His face was red from crying, and, despite the fact that he couldn't have looked more like a patient, he was only there to speak to someone.

The boy approached an older woman behind a tall, white desk, her glasses halfway down her nose shielding her blank, bored eyes. "Excuse me," he murmured.

The woman looked over the desk and sighed. "Do you have an appointment?"

"No...," the boy replied, looking at the ground. "I'm looking for a Doctor Pulse. Is he here?"

The woman slowly turned to her computer, clicking around a bit. "We have no Doctor Pulse here."

"What?" the boy said with a break in his voice. "Can you check again?"

"Who are you looking for, dear?" someone asked in a soft voice from across the room. She appeared even older than the woman at the desk and was holding a clipboard close to her frail body. When he told her who he was looking for, her concerned expression changed to disgust. "I'm afraid Doctor Pulse is no longer with us," she said sternly.

"He—he died?" the boy asked.

"No." The woman rolled her eyes. "He is no longer affiliated with this hospital and hasn't been since losing his license many years ago." The boy was incredulous. He looked around the waiting room, unsure what to do. "I don't know who sent you here," she continued, "and I truly don't want to. But do not seek that man out. He lost his right to practice for a good reason."

"What did he do?"

"What is your name, dear?" she asked.

"Chase," the boy shyly replied.

The old woman sighed. "He was caught performing illegal, unauthorized, and untested experiments." She paused. "On children."

When I opened my eyes, a good five seconds passed where I literally had no idea where I was. I was in my wolf form, and it was definitely not morning. The sky was dark and the chirps of cicadas and crickets filled the air, but that wasn't the weirdest thing. I wasn't in my bed or even in the house. I was laying in the middle of an itchy grass field. I attempted to stand and ended up stepping on something—a furry, squishy thing. I looked down and noticed the white wolf collapsed next to me. "Oh no," I said, stepping back. "Angie?" I poked her nervously with my paw, and she let out a groan. I sighed in relief, sitting down painfully. "Alright, you're alive."

"Chase?"

"Yeah…"

"Where are…" She started looking around. "Never mind."

"How long have we been here?" I asked, stretching.

"My back hurts," she said, ignoring my question.

"Yeah, mine too." I could tell Angela was attempting to shift back into her human form, but to no avail. "No use trying. Did we go down at the same time?" I asked her.

"I think so. The last thing I remember is you falling on me."

I felt a sharp pain in my leg again. My back really did hurt, but in an unfamiliar, itchy sort of way. I tried to scratch the pain off and felt a hard, plastic thing with a fuzzy top sticking out of the back of my neck. "Hey, Angie," I said uncomfortably, "there's a... thing sticking out of my neck."

She just gave me a disgusted look with her muzzle all scrunched up. "Excuse me?"

"Multiple things, actually." I scratched around in my fur. "They feel like needles."

Angela rolled her eyes and gave me a head gesture that said, *Turn around.*

I got up and turned my back to her. She began investigating the plastic needle things all over my back.

"Oh, no," she groaned.

"Oh no? What do you mean *oh no*?"

"I think those are sleeping darts." Angela winced. "Could you, like, check to see if I have any?" I nodded, looking over her head at her back. I could already see several gray, fuzzy dart tops sticking out of her fur.

"Sadly, we both have 'em," I said, attempting to scratch mine off with my back foot.

"Great," she snapped. "Well, I am *not* touching your butt with my mouth, so we're going to have to shift back somehow." (I laugh now writing this, but it was sooo *not* funny then.)

"Wait," I started, "if we were tranquilized, why weren't we captured? Or, like, put in a cage or something?"

"I was wondering the same thing," Angela said, scratching her darts. "If someone got so far as to knock us out, why didn't they take us?"

"Dumb luck, that's how," a deep, raspy voice from the distance replied.

"Uncle Jason?" Angela called out.

"I understand why mummy arms here would be surprised to see me, considering he didn't pay a damn bit of attention when we met earlier, but, Angela, you just came to visit." Jason came into view from behind the large rock at the end of the field.

I looked down at my bandages and rolled my eyes. "Where are the others?"

"Osscar..." Angela said bitterly, as if recalling something unpleasant.

"Broke off from me during the fight," Jason replied. "I woulda gone lookin' for 'em, had I not been worried

someone was gonna come haul you two off while I was gone."

"Fight?"

"Yup. It coulda been avoided, had someone not jumped the gun," he growled, looking over at me.

"Y-you were gonna let it hit her!" I shouted, standing up.

"I was gonna take out the blond!" Jason argued. "She would be dead on the ground right now had you not intervened!"

"Angela could've been—"

"Shut up!" he yelled.

I was looking him dead in the eyes, but I could feel my tail tuck between my legs. I hated myself for that, almost as much as I hated him.

"What happened to her?" Angela asked calmly. "The woman in furs?"

"Got away," Jason grumbled. "All of 'em—her, the captain, and a couple others."

I looked around and noticed that the hot weapon I took from the huntsman Angela referred to as "the woman in furs" had disappeared, along with her belt of arsenal.

"Was she not the captain?" Angela asked.

"No," Jason replied. "She didn't have a single lethal weapon on her; the captain always has one. There were only three folks who did, and two of them were takin' orders."

"She sure acted like she was running things," Angela grumbled, scratching at her darts again.

I didn't feel like talking anymore. I didn't want to go back to the house, but I didn't wanna be in that itchy field with Angela's hick uncle anymore either. Yeah, yeah, I'm mean. There was a moment of silence—more like a stare-down between me and Jason. Luckily, Angela decided to keep talking. "Hey, we might want to remove these darts," she said, nudging me. "Any ideas?"

Jason looked away, shaking his head. "Just shift back," he said, walking off. "You both should know how to do that by now." And he should have known why we couldn't. It's probably one of the most basic shapeshifter-specific inconveniences on the planet. You can't shift with—dang it! Liles had some fancy word for it. I may remember later, but basically, you can't shift with anything inside you. Okay, not like *anything*, but any kind of piercing or implant. You can try, but it just won't work.

I really don't need to explain why. If you shift into a mouse when there's a metal piercing in your tongue that's gonna be bigger than your head, there's no sugar-coating it—you're gonna die. Luckily, we don't have to worry about it because our bodies just don't allow it. But it's a little scary when you can't shift for some unknown reason before you realize you still have gum in your mouth. I guess darts counted as—foreign bodies! That was the word he used, but Jason should have known that.

I fumbled around, attempting to reach the darts on my back, spinning like a dog after its own tail.

"Give it up," Angela sighed. "I'll help." I looked to the ground and let her remove the darts with her teeth. There wasn't too much pain involved, but it was very awkward— for both of us. "Just so you know, I'm expecting you to do the same for me," she said, pulling another dart from my skin.

"Right," I replied, wincing. When the last dart was removed, I turned around to look at them in the grass. "Eight?" I sighed. "That's *so* overkill."

"You're lucky it didn't *actually* kill you," Angela added.

"Guess you'd like some help now?"

"Yes," she mumbled, "but we're never speaking of this again, you hear me?"

"Agreed."

Once I was done removing all of Angela's darts, we decided to go search for the others, seeing as how neither of us was tired after sleeping practically half the day. As the sky got darker, the noises from nearby insects grew louder. For me, those were the most comforting sounds in the world. They reminded me of the best parts of my childhood and spared me of the worst ones. Not even the loud crunching of my paws in the dry grass could drown them out. I turned to Angela, whose head was hanging low with her eyes half open. "Something on your mind?" I asked. "I don't blame ya if you don't feel like sharing, but if I can help, or..."

She sighed, sitting down in her tracks. "Several things, actually." I sat down. "I'm not sure if you already know, but—" I tilted my head as if asking her to continue. "Maybe I shouldn't say anything," she mumbled.

"Maybe you shouldn't," I replied. "I learned something pretty disturbing already today."

"What was it?" Angela asked. "Maybe we're talking about the same thing?"

"I don't think so. Liles told me and Izzy while you were gone."

"If Izzy can handle it, so can I," she laughed. "We can say our things at the same time, if you want?"

"Okay."

"Three...Two...."

Angela: "Huntsmen make shapeshifters into coats."

Me: "Huntsmen kill shapeshifters for their pelts."

Angela: "Yup, that's, umm, that's what I was gonna—"

Me: "Yeah, that's what I meant to—"

Both of us sighed.

"Welp," she laughed.

"It's pretty morbid," I said, nodding.

"No kidding. No one ever told you either?"

"No," I replied, shaking my head. But I wasn't too upset about it. I'm still not sure if I'm thankful for that information now. When Liles explained it to me, it felt like someone was describing exactly how I was going to die.

"Well," she said, "I guess we're just gonna have to be more careful."

"So, we're still aiming for the base?" I asked.

"I can't just leave my dad."

"You're sure he was captured?"

"Jason hasn't seen him, and we didn't find him in town," she continued. "It's the only explanation."

"And he's never left the house before?"

"No," she replied, "not without telling us."

"Then maybe he's up to something."

"Up to something?" she repeated. "What are you suggesting?"

"Well, it's not like he could have been captured at the house," I pointed out. "Chris had to have left at some point. So, why wouldn't he have left a note, unless he didn't want us knowing where he—"

"Just stop there," she snapped. "How on earth can you suggest something like that?"

"Look—" I tried to start again.

"You've been living with us for *how* long now?" Angela interrupted. "My dad gave you a home, an aid for your condition, a family, and you *still* don't trust him?"

"*Home* is a bit of a stretch," I mumbled.

"Seriously?" she scoffed. "You were right, we can't have one conversation."

"I'm sorry," I said. "Really, I didn't mean to upset you again. I guess I don't know how to say anything comforting..."

Cricket noises.

"Well, we should keep looking for the others," I said.

"I'm not sure what I'm going to say to Osscar if we find him," she said.

"Did something—" I didn't even need to ask; she was already working on a rant.

"He betrayed us!" she snorted, still fuming. "He gave away where you guys were without a moment of hesitation." The flames in her eyes were noticeable, but I still wasn't sure why she was upset.

"Wasn't that part of the plan?" I asked cautiously.

"Plan?"

"Yeah, we didn't just invite your uncle over for tea," I said. "There was a plan. He told me, you knew?"

"What plan?" she asked again, a little frustrated.

"Jason dropped off clothes and told us you guys were captured by huntsmen that were on their way here," I explained. "We were supposed to stay out of sight until he shot the woman in the fur coat." Angela still looked confused. I kept talking. "But I sort of wrecked the plan when I saw that she was about to hit you with that club thing. Which explains half the reason why your uncle's mad at me."

"How does that have anything to do with Osscar?"

"Well, Jason said he asked Osscar to tell the huntsmen to come here if you two were captured," I replied. "Honestly, I thought you knew." Her eyes went wide and her body was stiff as a board. "You alright?" I asked, tilting my head.

"We have to find Osscar," she declared, "right now." The moment she got up, her pace had changed drastically from when we started searching. Apparently, Jason's plan was news to her, but even then, I wondered what the big hurry was for. She was practically running through the grass. We would have called out names, but we were still concerned that Alex might hear us. We knew that he'd still be looking throughout the night.

That's when the hard reality hit that as soon as we found the others, we'd have to get moving again.

A soft, sad noise filled the air, and we knew Izzy had to be close. Angela's ears perked up, and I put my nose to the ground in an attempt to sniff her out. It's odd going back to my human form from my wolf considering just how much more "defined" my sense of smell is as a canine. And it's the same with my polar bear, it always feels like

something's wrong with my nose when I shift back and it isn't as powerful.

Soon enough, we spotted her laying in the grass. Izzy was sobbing into the ground. Her clothes were covered in soil, and her leg was cut and scraped.

"Hey!" Angela shouted, leaping past me and over to her. She kneeled down on all four paws. "Are you hurt?"

Izzy looked up from her wall of (normally) light orange-blond hair. Her freckled face was (probably) red and clothes were covered in tears and dirt. That's another difference between my human and animal forms. The way I see color changes pretty significantly when I shift. I'm barely aware of it anymore, so it can be difficult to remember when writing stuff like this. Notice how a lot of our clothes are "gray"? Maybe they were, maybe they weren't, but we barely hold onto an outfit more than two hours anyway, so what's the point in remembering?

"Angela!" she cried, throwing her arms around her furry white neck.

"It's nice to see you too," I joked, rolling my eyes.

Izzy sat up, turned to me, and smiled. "Hi Chase, it really is so so good to see both of you."

"What's up with your leg?"

"I don't even know... I was running away from the fight and tripped over something."

"That's a little lame," I replied thoughtlessly.

Angela shot me an angry look that said *are you serious?* and I knew I'd messed up.

"I-I didn't mean it like—" I stammered.

"You're one to talk about lame," Angela snapped back at me.

I kinda deserved that one...

"He's okay," Izzy sighed. "It is pretty lame. I was just afraid to go looking for you guys after I heard all those gunshots. I guess I was expecting to find the worst...."

Angela hugged her again with her front paws. "I understand, really I do. But we have to keep looking for the others."

I nodded, trying to make eye contact with Izzy through her hair. "And we don't wanna leave you here, so will you come with us?"

She pulled her hair back and nodded. Her eyes were still red but she was done crying, which was a relief. Izzy has always been extremely sensitive. I heard her cry outside my door almost every day. Which sucks because whenever someone else is upset, she seems to find a way to lift their

spirits, but the second the roles are reversed, no one has a clue what to say.

"Slow down!" Izzy yelled.

I looked up to see Angela running. Toward what, I didn't know. I picked up the pace as well. Angela stopped to admire the newly constructed tent a few feet from the headstone marking the end of the field. It had a rock-ring firepit and a bunch of beds on the inside. It looked cozy and sturdy, and, based on the heavenly smell in the air, there was food in it.

"Chase, you're drooling," she said, nudging me.

"Sorry, Angie, canine forms aren't really the most dignified," I replied. "Besides, I'm starved."

"Your clothes are in the tent," Jason shouted from a few feet away, walking toward us. "You guys picked up a lot more than I thought you would. Those two townies don't usually sell for cheap."

"Are you talking about Amy and Adaline?" Angela asked. "They were more than generous with us."

Jason raised an eyebrow. "All that was *free?*"

Angela nodded. "They pitied us more than anything."

"You told them you were shifters?" I was angry now.

"Not exactly," Angela sighed. "They kind of... knew?"

I rolled my eyes and started toward the tent. "Get back here, bandage butt, no one's storming off," Jason demanded.

I was done with the ridicule, and, in a spontaneous act of stupidity, I decided that it was going to stop there. Clearly I'd been in my wolf form for too long that day. The instincts were getting to my brain, and I really, really wish someone had stopped me from myself.

Now, I'd never have the guts to do something like this with Alex, but from the information I gathered that afternoon, I'd learned something about Jason I don't think anyone else had figured out. Something that for whatever reason, made me believe that I had an advantage over him.

I didn't mean to "challenge" his authority. I just wanted him to leave me alone. I swirled around with teeth bared and growled as loudly as I could. My eyes locked with Jason's, able to see his anger plainly. I surprised the girls, that's for sure. They both froze in place, like they couldn't believe what I'd just done.

Have you ever replied to an adult "I *WILL* hurt you"? And with a completely straight face? Yeah, that's basically what I did, and I *don't* recommend it, because just as I was

about to walk away with my pride intact, Jason did something so painful, I'm not sure I can describe it.

He grabbed my front leg, held it up, and ripped the bandages off. There wasn't a second for me to react before he twisted it backward. "YELP!" I could feel the horrible snap when he broke it. What *it* was, I still have no idea, but the pain shot through my leg and up my spine like a tremor. I fell to the ground whimpering and screaming. I couldn't even see the others, but I could hear their collective gasps.

"Uncle Jason!" Angela screamed.

"He deserved it!" Jason yelled, looking down at me, disgust in his voice. "Remember this the next time you think you're in charge, kid! You're burning your bridges faster than they can be built, and you've no idea just how vulnerable a wolf is without a pack!"

I couldn't stand, I was going to need to shift back into my human form to walk, but I was in absolute shock. How did he know how to do that!?

"Wh-what do we do!?" Angela stammered as Jason walked off toward the tent. Once I was sure he'd left, I turned and looked at my ~~arm~~ leg. It hurt even more when I could see it. Broken, twisted, uncovered, and I couldn't

even tell what color it was through my fur, but I imagine it wasn't good. He got my leg unwrapped in a matter of seconds, like a magic act. I still couldn't get my mind around it.

Angela ran over and stared at me like I was some poor dog who'd just been hit by a car. She started panicking, certain that there was nothing she could do to help. "Can you—" she started.

"No," I said, blinking back tears. My breathing quickened, but I was not going to cry, no matter how badly it hurt.

"Oh, my gosh," she murmured fearfully, looking down at my arm.

"Oh, that is so not helpful," I winced. My voice was already cracking.

"Sorry!" she yelled. "It looks real bad!"

Liles casually walked up behind Angela and Izzy, like he'd been there the whole time. "I can help," he said. "But—"

"Liles!?" Izzy shouted excitedly. "Where on earth were you?"

I looked up. "But what?"

Liles picked up his large brown doctor's bag. "What is that?" I asked nervously. He dug around in the bag and found a small glass vial filled with a dark red liquid with chunks of brown stuff floating around in it. Its label was too small to read. "No way." I lay my head back down in the grass.

"You have Morph-Bone, don't you?" he asked. I looked back up, but said nothing. "I don't know how badly you have it, but morphed bones don't heal normally," he continued. "You could lose the function of your arm. This may save it." He rolled the vial toward me.

"What's in—"

"Don't ask," Angela replied before I could finish.

Liles came over and popped the cork off the vial. It steamed for a moment, then stopped. The smell was awful. I didn't think about it and snatched the vial with my jaws. I tilted my head back and drank it as fast as I could, but the taste was so bad my eyes watered. When the vial was empty, I threw it away, coughing.

"That was difficult to watch," Angela said, sounding like she was going to be sick.

I could not have felt worse. Now, a million more things hurt, but after about ten minutes of whining and

Liles trying to calm everyone down, I could feel something happening to my ~~arm~~ front leg. I watched in horror and yelled out in pain as it appeared to "reset" all on its own. When it finally stopped hurting, it looked the way it normally would, but unbandaged. Which probably wasn't any less disturbing to the girls.

Izzy, Liles, and Angela were all still staring at me, silent as the grave. I attempted to stand and luckily succeeded, but I could tell the remedy didn't do anything to amend my usual handicap. "Can someone get me those?" I coughed, gesturing over to my bandage wraps a couple feet away.

Liles nodded and walked off to fetch them.

"Chase, I'm so sorry," Angela said. "I didn't know my uncle was so—"

Liles came back with the bandages, and I took them in my mouth. "I'm going to go try to shift back to put these on," I said, clearing my throat.

"You still don't sound okay, though," Izzy said. "Maybe we could... help you put them on?"

"You guys don't know how," I said unequivocally. "You'd most likely hurt me trying." Izzy nodded, stepping back. "I can't walk, so could you guys just, um, leave for a second?"

Angela and Izzy obliged and started walking away, but before Liles joined them, he dropped a pile of clothes at my paws. "You'll want these," he said.

"Thanks," I replied.

I was really dreading having to shift back. I knew it would hurt. But it was nice to be able to walk on two legs again, and to have new clothes. I definitely approved of what Liles picked out for me: a black t-shirt, a pair of jeans with some tears in the knees, a pair of tennis shoes a lot nicer than the ones I had on when we first left the house, and a black beanie. Which he didn't have to include, but I appreciated it.

I would look for a jacket later, but first had to get my wraps back on and find my bearings. I extended my left arm and wrapped the bandages tightly, so that my elbow was exposed, but any other bare skin was covered. Oh man, it made the pain go away almost instantly. I let my arm drop carelessly to my side.

Everything seemed okay now, except my stomach was really beginning to bother me. Whatever was in that remedy made me feel nauseous and tired. I decided to keep walking in hopes of riding those sensations out. Of course, I didn't regret taking it. Liles clearly knew more about

medical stuff than me. I was sure he was right about me possibly losing my arm.

I saw the big rock and camp ahead and was sure the others were there, but Jason would be too. So, I sat down in the grass for a minute, a million things running through my mind. Number one being *why did we even leave in the first place?* I know it was my idea, but why did I think it was a good one?

I intended to sneak into the tent after everyone had already gone to sleep, so there wouldn't be a scene, but after about twenty minutes, despite the circumstances, I laid down in the grass and fell asleep.

12: CHASE

"Hey, wake up." Izzy was poking me. I sat up drowsily. "We're leaving."

"Leaving?" It was still dark. How could it already be time to leave?

"Yeah, Liles flew over the field and said he saw people coming. We have to go," she explained, helping me up.

"Crap," I said, rubbing my eyes. "Where are the others?"

"They're at camp packing. I came to find you. Oh, and I found your first aid kit." She held the little white box out in front of me.

"Oh, thanks," I mumbled.

"Hurry up."

When she left, I opened the box, removed my dark gray foldable backpack, and shook it out. It looked all wrinkled, but it would do. I figured it was about time I had something I could wear when I shifted. That's the great thing about backpacks—adjustable straps.

I was about to close the kit, when my eye caught one of the granola bars inside. I picked it up and examined it. I remembered being hungry that last night, but for whatever reason the food just didn't look appetizing. I placed the bar in the pocket of the backpack so I could reach it later and threw the kit inside. I tossed it over my shoulder and rushed after Izzy.

I could see Angela sitting by the big rock stuffing clothes into some kind of tote and Liles packing up his doctor's bag. Just seeing that thing made me sick all over again. They both stood up. Angela's face was red from crying. This was weird for her, because unlike Izzy, she doesn't cry often. It surprised me a little. "Angie, what happ—" I started to ask.

She simply pushed past me and Izzy, heading toward the road.

"Don't take it personally," Izzy whispered. "She looked for Osscar all night. He's gone."

I sighed and started toward Angela when I heard a loud, obnoxious voice behind me.

"Okay, is that everything?" the voice asked. My eyes narrowed—it was Jason walking right toward me. Now that I was back in my human form, I noticed that his gray t-shirt was actually a faded red color. He stopped, studying me with a raised eyebrow. He spoke softly. "Are you okay?" That really surprised me. Why would he care? He was the one that broke my arm in the first place! "I didn't mean to hurt'cha badly as I did," he admitted. "That said, I hope you know your place now."

I hated that I did what he wanted. I remembered the pain—it was fast but horrible, and I remembered everything that followed: the remedy, the sick feeling that still lingered, and the image of my arm twisting back into place from the mangled position that it was put in.

I broke eye contact and looked at the ground as he left. Izzy must have seen what happened because she came and hugged me, but it hurt my pride even more. I shook her off and walked on.

We trudged out of the field onto the road, trying to stay in the wooded areas and out of plain sight. This went on for an hour or two. Walking and walking in silence. What was weird was that we weren't walking back to the house, just straight out of the field toward the fork in the road leading from the rocky path onto a much newer looking one.

I started convincing myself that my initial conclusion about Jason was wrong, and that he was shapeshifter after all. Because despite all evidence to the contrary, flying here seemed to be the only explanation for how he got to the field so fast after Angela and Osscar were captured. I considered taking off on my own a few times. It could have been a nice journey, had we been able to just enjoy each other's company, but Izzy was too busy moping. Liles was reading, and of course Angela, once again, was mad at me.

So, we'll just skip to when things started getting crazy again. I never saw the huntsman. I'd fallen too far behind, wandering slowly with my head someplace else, but out of the blue I heard Jason yell, "Run! Get out of here!"

I froze. Looking left, I saw Liles and Angela running along the side of the road. I started after them when I heard a scream behind me from deep in the woods. I still

couldn't see anything through the trees, but it sounded like Izzy.

Angela and Liles must have heard it too, because when I turned back to them, they were running toward me. Liles grabbed my shoulder. "You two, go find someplace to hide!" he ordered, shoving Angela at me. I stumbled back, watching him run off toward the scream.

"Hey!" I replied. "What about you?"

"If everyone gets captured, we're better off having people to get help!" he yelled back. "Now, get out of here!" I pulled Angela out of the woods and onto the road, running as fast as I could and looking for someplace to hide.

"We're just running away?" Angela yelled angrily.

"You heard Liles!"

"You're just afraid!" she snapped.

No cars came, but we couldn't stay out in the open like that—someone was bound to see us. I ran off the road and onto a grass patch leading down to a ravine.

Apparently, we were going too fast downhill, because the next thing I knew, we were both *ROLLING* into the ravine. I crashed sideways into a tree trunk, which knocked the wind right out of my lungs. I had only just reoriented when Angela tumbled into me.

"Great," she huffed, sitting up. "I hit at least five rocks on the way down." Once the world stopped spinning, I got to my feet, looking up the hill at the road. Angela was still on the ground. "Way to go!"

"Sorry," I mumbled painfully, offering her my hand. "We gotta keep moving."

Angela smacked my hand away, and once she helped herself up, we headed further into the wood patch at the bottom of the ravine. I realized that I'd lost my beanie when we fell. My hair was a mess, my ripped clothing was grass-stained, and I was covered in scratches. Just like old times, I was rocking the crazy homeless look.

"I hope everyone's alright," she said, still sounding upset.

"Me too," I replied.

Silence.

"Have you eaten anything today?" she asked. "Or yesterday?"

"I planned on eating dinner yesterday," I said, shrugging.

"You never came back to camp, though."

"Well, I didn't want to see your uncle," I replied honestly.

"That's understandable, but why didn't you get breakfast this morning?"

"I got up late," I replied. "Why are you asking me all these questions?"

"I'm a little worried about you. Will you eat dinner with us tonight?" *Worried about me? Since when?* I could think of about a million times when I would honestly have expected her to worry about me, and this wouldn't even compare.

"We may not get to," I reasoned. "The others might have been captured. Why are you worried, anyways?"

"Because there's a granola bar sticking out of your backpack and you haven't eaten since we left the house," Angela said. "We must have burned a million calories since then."

"I just don't feel like it," I said defensively. "I swear, you look for things to fight about."

"You should, though," she replied. "You said you were starving yesterday, and now you have food, and you've shown absolutely no interest in it."

I stopped and faced her. "Okay, what are you *really* worried about?" I asked. "It's only been a day, Angela. I'm not going to starve to death."

"Liles just scared me a little, that's all," she said, getting a bit defensive herself. "Apparently, that medicine you took can have some side effects..."

"What kinds of side effects?"

"A few," she mumbled. "Some sounded pretty serious."

I sighed. "I appreciate the concern, but of all the things to worry about, my eating habits are last on the list."

"Will you at least *talk* to Liles about it?"

"Fine. Now, can we please change the subject?"

I heard sticks snapping behind us and looked at her. We were about to take off running again when we heard the unmistakable voice of Izzy. "Guys!" she yelled.

We ran back toward the hill to find her.

"Thank God," Angela sighed. We saw Izzy slowly making her way toward the edge of the hill. She was dragging something in front of her that we couldn't see.

"What happened back there?" Angela called.

We finally saw that what Izzy was dragging was a sizable gray lynx, and she could barely carry it on her own. We didn't know he had a shift like that, but it had to be Liles because she was holding his old doctor's bag under her arm.

"Oh my gosh," Angela gasped.

"I think he's okay," Izzy said, out of breath. "But he got knocked out somehow."

"What about the huntsmen?" I asked.

"Jason stayed behind to fight, but I didn't see what happened," Izzy said weakly before dropping Liles like a sack of potatoes. "We've got to get out of the area."

"Ugh... why is this our lives?" Angela groaned, leaning her head back.

"Let's go find someplace with more people," I suggested, rubbing my back. I was still a little sore from hitting the tree.

"*More* people?" Izzy asked.

"It's harder to find a four-leaf in a field of clovers than singled out among daisies," I replied almost subconsciously.

"That's a lovely analogy," Angela said, nearly laughing. "Where did that come from?"

"I think my dad said that once," I replied, shrugging.

"Alright, but where do you think we should go?"

"How about a hotel?" Izzy suggested.

"No!" I replied instantly.

"Why not?" Angela asked. "That sounds like a great idea."

"Hotels have beds," Izzy said, smiling.

"And free breakfast," Angela added.

"Guys," I said seriously. "Hotels can be really dangerous—limited exits, elevators."

"Come on, Chase. Where else can we get a bed?" Angela asked. "Jason took our tent."

"Seriously," I continued. "Bad idea."

"Too bad, you're outvoted," Angela declared.

Izzy gestured for me to hand over my backpack, and I did so reluctantly. She put it on and adjusted Liles' old bag in her hand. "I'll carry these," she said. "You get Liles."

"You know, he's a lot heavier than those..." I muttered.

Izzy and Angela started back up the hill toward the road while I struggled to lift Liles off the ground.

Once up, I followed them, knowing good and well that it would only end badly. I did my time at hotels and was more than over it. Sure, it's fun at first, but eventually you learn that it's the first place they look for you—a convenient shelter from the rain for a relatively small price with free food and tiny shampoo bottles. But the girls were headed into the death trap with or without me, and we really didn't have anywhere else to go.

We headed down the smooth road branching off from the fork. It had to be the same one Izzy's grandparents

took to get supplies from the store. It led to a handful of gas stations, rest stops, and inevitably, hotels, motels, and B&Bs.

"Which one are we going with?" Izzy asked. "There's so many."

"Well, Chase wanted lots of people, so we'll honor his wishes and pick the place that's the most crowded," Angela declared.

"I appreciate the compromise," I said sarcastically, attempting to haul Liles' body up onto my shoulder. For someone like me, carrying anyone is difficult. Especially Liles, who even in his cat form, probably weighed about as much as I did. The girls had to have known this.

"You're welcome," Izzy laughed.

"That one it is," Angela said, excitedly pointing to a small hotel in the distance. "It's packed."

"Would you two stop being so loud? Someone could hear us."

"You worry too much," Angela said, waving her hand back at me.

"I worry too much?" I disputed. "Not ten minutes ago, you were lecturing me about how I need to eat more."

Angela rolled her eyes. "Look, we didn't just stick Liles on you to be rude."

"Though it is nice not having to carry him," Izzy admitted.

Angela laughed too. "You'd better be hungry when we get to the hotel, or something is definitely wrong with you," she declared. "And you better talk to Liles when he wakes up."

"Lots of people have days where they don't eat," I argued. "You agreed to change the subject." Honestly, I didn't feel like eating. I'd been through a lot that week and had convinced myself it was merely a stress thing, but now Angela had me paranoid.

"Fine, fine," Angela said. "Consider it changed. Izzy, where did Uncle Jason say he was going?"

"He didn't," Izzy replied, "but in his defense, that moment was pretty heated."

Angela nodded. "I hope he got away, but now we're really in trouble."

"What do you mean?" Izzy asked.

"Well, we're without our weapons expert now," Angela replied. "How are we going to defend ourselves?"

"You're kidding, right?" I asked. "We're shifters, Angie, we have built-in weapons."

"Well," Izzy mumbled, "I don't exactly have the most useful set of weapons, then."

"You can learn to get better ones," I said weakly. I had to put Liles down and pick him up again.

"Yeah, Izzy," Angela added. "I love your shifts, but I'm sure deep down, there's a predator in you."

Izzy chuckled slightly. "Thanks, I'll work on it."

The town was much livelier than the one I ran to earlier that week. For starters, there were people. But also superstores, gas stations, marketplaces, and freshly paved roads. It was no wonder the place me and Angela had visited was so desolate. If I had to take my pick between the two, there wouldn't be a debate.

Soon enough, we were standing in the parking lot of the small hotel the girls had selected. Almost every parking spot was full, and there were folks walking all around with suitcases and duffle bags.

"We're here," Angela said, still smiling the way she had been the whole walk. She ran through the door past a family of six, and Izzy followed right behind her. I was about to apologize to the kids' parents when I locked eyes with

one of the younger boys in the group. He was looking at me with either extreme confusion or hatred, I couldn't tell. I watched the family walk away, but the boy kept looking back. He appeared to be examining me. I really needed to find myself a jacket. Of course people would start giving the guy that looks like he broke both his arms some odd stares.

My gosh, am I actually that self-centered? It's literally just now dawning on me that they were probably looking at Liles. The DEAD ANIMAL I was casually dragging around.

"Chase, come on!" Angela shouted. She was gesturing me through the automatic doors.

"Got us some rooms," Izzy said, walking away from the busy front desk.

"Rooms?" I asked.

"Yeah, you and Liles are getting your own room," Angela said.

"So we're splitting up now?" I asked. "What if one room gets attacked, and we have to let the others know?"

"We'll be right across the hall from you guys," she replied.

"You're underestimating the probability," I argued.

"Live a little," Angela said, slapping a keycard into my free hand.

I flipped the card over and read three-digit number. "One two six."

"We're one two three," Izzy said pridefully. She took my backpack off and handed it to Angela, who hung one of the straps around my neck since I was out of hands. Could neither of them see that I was already trying not to fall over?

"Wait a minute," I started. "How did you pay for these?"

"Well, I knew there was a wallet in your kit thing," Izzy replied shyly.

"Seriously?"

"Hey, my dad gave you that money for stuff like this," Angela reminded me. "We're spending it as intended."

"Besides, they were only two hundred total," Izzy added.

"Fine," I sighed. I'd been holding on to that money for years, but Angela was right. Chris gave me the wallet in case of emergency, like if we needed food or a place to stay. This was exactly how it was intended to be spent.

"It'll be fine, and remember to talk to Liles," Angela said. "When he wakes up, of course."

"Where are you guys going?" I asked. "Our rooms are upstairs."

"Snacks, silly," Angela said like it was obvious. "You're welcome to join us, but you might want to go put Liles in bed first," she laughed. "He looks heavy."

I limped over to the familiar metal doors as the girls ran off toward the vending machines, and when the elevator opened, it was empty, lucky for me. I took this opportunity to put Liles down for a moment. My back and shoulders were horribly sore from carrying him all that way.

"Owww," Liles groaned.

"Oh, good, you're awake," I said, stretching. I really didn't want to have to drag him past all the people in the hallway.

"Why is the ground moving?" he asked, putting a paw against the wall of the elevator in an attempt to get his bearings.

"We're in an elevator," I replied, removing the backpack from around my neck. "It was the girls' idea to stay at a hotel." I rolled my eyes. "Believe me, I know the risks."

"Oh, man," he grumbled, sitting up. "I got knocked out?" I nodded. "I forgot what that feels like. Did anyone get hurt during the attack?"

"Besides you, I don't think so," I yawned. "But Jason stayed behind."

Liles put his paw to his head. "I remember..." I got some clothes out of my backpack and threw them at him as he shifted back to his human form. Once he was dressed, I helped him up and he thanked me with a nod. "Where are the girls?"

"Went to get snacks," I replied. "Oh, and that reminds me, we have to talk." The elevator opened onto a hallway packed with people. Our room was at the end of the hall and close to an exit, so I suppose that was a good thing, but I kept my guard up. It all felt so enclosed, and some of these people had to be wolves in sheep's clothing (for lack of a better metaphor). "We'll talk about it later," I said, exiting the elevator.

Liles followed me down the hall to our room, where I slid the keycard into the reader. The light beneath the handle flashed green and the door latch unlocked.

So far, so good....

The room was fairly nice. It had two good-sized beds, a flat-screen television atop a dresser, and one window on the back wall overlooking the street and a Love's gas station.

Liles immediately flopped onto the bed furthest from the door. But soon after doing so, he noticed something was off. "Wait, where's my bag?" he asked, sitting up in a panic.

"Izzy has it," I said. "Don't worry, she won't let anything happen to it."

Liles put his hand on his heart and let out a sigh of relief. "She's very kind," he nodded.

"Yeah, she is," I replied, sitting down on my bed, "but she did make me carry you all the way here, so... she has her days."

He chuckled, leaning against his headboard. "Where's the remote?" he asked. "I haven't watched television since I was, like, twelve."

"Really?" I asked, picking it up off the table between the beds. "Me neither."

I tossed the remote over. Liles caught it and turned on the TV. It was already on one of those detective shows that people watch late at night, the ones where they investigate

real crimes. "I've never been the biggest fan of these," I said. "I've got my own problems. I don't need to get depressed watching someone else's."

"I actually used to enjoy them," he laughed. "Reminded me that other people have crosses to bear."

"You can leave it on if ya want," I shrugged. "I don't really care."

"I said used to." He changed the channel. "I've seen enough death. I need a pick-me-up."

"Thank God," I mumbled. A loud noise shook the room, and my attention turned to the window. "Thunderstorm," I said, nodding. "Now those, I like."

"You like thunderstorms?" he asked skeptically.

"Yeah, they make me thankful for a roof over my head."

"What if you're outside?" he joked.

"In that case, they make me wet."

"Oh man," Liles laughed again, looking up at the ceiling. "I'm in a *bed* right now."

"Yup," I said, smiling, "a real bed."

The window rumbled from the wind, and the lights in the room flickered. I got up and turned off the main light, so we only had the side table lamps to worry about shorting out.

"I honestly never thought—" his stare never broke from the sky "—I never thought I would get out of there."

"How long did you stay at the base?" I asked, returning to my bed.

"Six years," he sighed. "We never had beds."

"Honestly?" I asked. "That's insane. Where did you sleep?"

"On the ground, on other shapeshifters. Someone was always sleeping in the shower; it was the most coveted spot."

"Why?" I asked. "That sounds horrible."

"No cameras in the shower. Not that it mattered. They didn't give us any clothes."

"Man," I sighed. "I'm sorry." I felt horrible for pitying myself for even five seconds. I *did* have a bed at the house. It was small and hard, but it was a bed. I had clothes, too. They were worn out and never fit right, but they were clothes.

"It's okay," he reassured me. "My friends got me through it."

"What's gonna happen to them?" I asked.

"I don't know," he replied with a dispirited tone. "I left." Clearly, it was a sore topic. I of all people could

understand that. I didn't ask any more questions. There was a pause. "You said you needed to talk to me earlier?"

"Oh," I said, "yeah, Angela kind of got me paranoid." He looked at me, waiting. "She said something about side effects? Of that medicine you gave me."

"Do you feel okay?" he asked.

"I think so? Angie was concerned about me not being hungry. I guess it's kind of a stupid thing to worry about."

"Well," he said, "it's not stupid—that can happen."

"*What* can happen?" I asked. "Please, try to be as specific as possible."

"You see," he started, taking a breath. "The particular remedy you drank contains a few mild toxins meant to counteract a couple problems presented by the chemical compounds that triggered the internal shift, which caused the bones in your arm to move back into position without causing serious nerve damage. And I suppose it's possible that these toxins could have either messed with some of your normal bacteria, or maybe they simply pumped you with some extra adrenalin, slowing your metabolism. That said, there are more serious side effects that we would have to test to see what you are experiencing. For example, your loss of appetite could mean that one of the ingredients in

the remedy caused some sort of allergic reaction, or coated your stomach, resulting in some kind of—"

"STOP!" I yelled.

He looked a little stunned. "You said—"

"I know, I know! I'm sorry!" I shouted. "But you're freaking me out! Why didn't you mention any of that before I—"

"That's understandable," Liles replied, butting in. "You do have some cause for alarm, but it's only been a day." I put my head in my hands, trying to process what he was saying. "I didn't mean to upset you."

"I know," I replied.

"Chase, with your condition, in all likelihood you could have lost function of your arm. It was absolutely vital you take that."

"I know," I said again.

"You should try to eat something, though. If you can."

"If I can?" I asked. "What else should I know? And this time, go easy on me."

"Well, depending on the circumstances, it could cause you pain."

I sighed and turned off the lamp between us. "Thanks," I said. And I meant it.

"Anytime," he replied. "Let me know if things get worse. I may be able to help."

"I blame Angela for all this," I said, rolling my eyes. "I'm probably fine, she just has this way of getting to me."

"Funny," he yawned. "She said the same thing about you."

I rolled over. "Said what?"

"She said you always know what to say to get to her, no joke."

"When did she say that?"

"At dinner last night. She was concerned for you and started asking me about the side effects. I probably worried her."

"That's nice of her," I mumbled. "I thought she hated me."

"No, but she is her own person," he continued. "You're going to have to let her lead the way more often."

"I signed a contract," I grumbled, rolling over. "If something happens to her, pretty sure there are consequences for us both."

Liles paused to think about that. "What?"

I pretended to be asleep.

The next morning, we attempted to visit the girls' room, but were greeted with a lovely "Go away!" Apparently, they were enjoying themselves, because after that came a lot of whispering and laughing.

"Breakfast, then?" Liles asked.

"Sure," I replied.

Not even a minute later, the girls' door swung open. Angela and Izzy ran down the hall, both still in their pajamas, their hair a couple of big, matted messes.

Liles looked over at me. I shrugged and walked after them. It was good to see the girls were doing alright. We couldn't assume the worst about Osscar just yet, but Angela was pretty distraught about him going missing yesterday. Izzy probably worked her cheering-up magic.

The lobby/breakfast room was jammed with people. There were screaming babies, laughing toddlers, and couples arguing, all the typical crowded room noises.

Oh, by the way, shapeshifters should never be taken to all-you-can-eat buffets. I doubt the hotel had enough food for the rest of its guests when Liles and the girls were done piling their plates high with at least two of everything in sight. I still wasn't hungry. At this point, I knew something was truly wrong, and I probably wouldn't have

put anything on my plate at all, had Angela not turned around. It was too early for a public argument.

"Let's go eat upstairs," Izzy suggested joyfully, stepping into the elevator.

"Yeah, in the boys' room. Our place is in no condition to entertain," Angela said, trying to sound sophisticated as she followed her inside.

"What did you do to that room?" I asked as the doors closed behind the four of us. "You were only there one night."

The girls just kept on laughing.

Once back on the second floor, Liles took the key from my pocket and opened our door. We all sat down on the nylon carpet in a messy circle, setting our paper plates down in front of us.

"You'd think Alex would have found us by now," Angela said quietly.

"We did stay in that field for an awful long time," Izzy said.

She looked over at Liles, who raised his finger to say he needed a second to swallow before providing conversational input. He ate so fast, like the food in front of him

was about to up and vanish. "True, but he could have followed your and Osscar's scent to town and lost you there."

"It's possible," Angela said somberly.

"We're gonna find him," Izzy said, hugging her. "And your dad, and my brother."

"We keep saying that," Angela sighed, "but the list is just growing longer. Think about it—we left with only a couple people missing, and now Osscar's gone too." Malachi didn't necessarily fit into the category of "people," but whatever.

"I'll admit my plan to go off on our own was a bad one," I said with guilt. "It's just, that house is like a prison. I thought I missed—" I wasn't sure how to finish that.

"It's okay, we all know it," Izzy replied, "but it's safe."

"It's not like we didn't know we'd be attacked when we left," Angela added. "This was anticipated."

"Yeah," I agreed, "it's a lot easier to picture yourself succeeding than failing when you don't know what you're up against."

"I can relate," Liles added.

Izzy shoved a pancake into her mouth before nudging Angela and pointing around, which was some secret girl way of asking her to ask Liles something.

"Why aren't you more upset?" Angela asked. "I mean, I know everyone grieves differently, but you know…"

"I'm assuming you're talking about Osscar?" he wanted to know. Angela nodded. "Well, I know the base, and if we move quickly, we can probably get him out before he even starts his stages."

Liles must have grabbed an extra cup of water at the breakfast bar. He placed it in front of me and tapped the side. I figured he expected me to drink some of it.

"His stages?" Angela asked.

"The process of harvesting shifter pelts is…complicated," Liles said awkwardly. "They only start torturing you after you get to know your cellmates. They want all of you to be able to shift into the same things."

"So, you were tortured?" Angela stuffed a piece of a giant waffle in her mouth.

"Yeah, I mean, we all were," he said. "Their methods can be pretty painful, but I didn't have it so bad."

I took a sip of water cautiously and nothing seemed to happen, so I drank the rest of it.

"How come?" Izzy asked.

"I'm good at learning new shifts," Liles explained. "The pressure doesn't really get to me. There were a few of

us with anxious delays, though." He was clearly recalling something unpleasant. "They were barely able to stand when they came back."

"Came back from wh—" Izzy started.

Angela looked horrified. "Did anyone die?"

"Only a few people. In my cell, anyway," he continued. "This guy named Jake was killed by one of my friends over a chicken leg. The other was a girl named Cindy, she umm... she got stepped on."

"Ouch," I winced.

"Your friend *killed* someone over a piece of food!?" Angela shouted.

"Yup," Liles replied. "Fights broke out all the time, usually in the cell across from ours."

"I'm so sorry," Izzy mumbled sadly. She either dropped or forgot her previous question.

"It's alright," he reassured her. "Scars fade. But it'll be hard to go back to that place."

"We won't make you talk about it anymore," I insisted.

"Wait, but how did you escape?" Angela asked. "I mean, you were there for a really long time."

Liles sighed. "If you don't mind, that story is one I'd like to wait on. One day, though."

Angela nodded respectfully and began poking at her last pancake, probably debating whether she could finish it. When she looked up at me, her expression changed to anger.

"What?" I asked. "What have I done this time?"

Angela sternly gestured at my untouched plate. "Chase?" she said irritably. "What is going on with you?"

"This again?" I snapped. "I'm fine."

Liles leaned his head against his hand, probably preparing for what he knew was coming next.

"Liles, did he talk to you?" Angela asked.

"Yes."

Angela glared at me. "What aren't you telling me? Why would you even get all that food if you weren't going to eat it?"

"I'm sorry, what's going on?" Izzy asked.

"Apparently, Angela thinks I'm dying?" I scoffed. "I don't know, I thought I would try and—"

"Oh my gosh, are you dying?" Izzy asked.

"No!" I yelled, standing up. "And this is stupid."

"Liles, what's wrong with him?" Angela asked as I grabbed my backpack off the bed.

"I don't know," Liles huffed. "Can we please *not* do this?"

"Where are you going?" she demanded.

"I'm going for a walk," I replied.

"Oh, so now it's okay to split up?"

I swung my backpack over my shoulder. I couldn't have been more ready to leave, but the second I opened the door, I immediately regretted the decision.

"Alex," I gulped. His eyes pierced into my soul. There was so much anger behind them, so much hatred.

"Move," he growled, shoving me aside.

I stood by the doorway, wide-eyed and confused. "We're going home," he told Angela. "Right now."

"What? No, we can't!" she said, frantically standing up. "We still have to find Osscar, and—"

"Osscar is gone! Captured!" Alex shouted furiously, gesturing over to me like it was my fault. I stood frozen.

Angela looked at the ground as if watching her thoughts that had just spilled out onto the floor. She took a few steps back. "Maybe, but we—we don't know for sure!"

Alex stared down at Izzy, who was already a big, teary mess. "You knew better than to follow them. I assure you, Osscar is not coming back."

I remained motionless as he ushered the others out the door. Liles turned to me in confusion, before glancing back at Alex. "Go with them," Alex growled. Liles didn't look like he'd fully submitted the way the girls had, but he complied anyway.

Alex slammed the door behind them and marched up to me. I had my back up against the window by the time he even spoke. "I know it was your idea to leave," he said resentfully. "Don't you dare come back. You're no longer welcome in my house."

I struggled to find the words. "Alex—"

"Quiet!" he yelled, turning around. "Thanks to you, now my grandson—one of the few things I had left—is missing!"

My eyes widened. "You just said he was captured!"

"He's as good as captured out here on his own!" he snapped back; his voice filled with pain. "You kids just don't get it!" I broke eye contact. He wasn't done. "This bone-headed move could have gotten you all killed! It was only a matter of time before someone found you here, and you all actually believed you could just walk into a huntsman base and leave with your freedom?" He didn't even finish, just shook his head.

And at that, my head was bowed. I have no idea how Alex knew what we were planning, but the answer probably wasn't going to help my case. "What about Angela?" I asked.

"You were foolish enough to put your life on that dotted line," he huffed. "The consequences are yours. Maybe you should have thought about that beforehand."

"You know it wasn't my fault," I replied, staring at the ground.

Alex put his hand on the door handle. He glanced back at me but walked out without a word.

13: ANGELA

"We're leaving him?" I shouted, trying to keep up with Alex, who was walking with an unbroken stride of vexation. He was leading me, Liles, and Izzy through two automatic doors that led out to the parking lot of a little hotel I can't remember the name of, after leaving Chase behind.

"Wait, why?" Izzy asked.

"He almost got you all killed," Alex huffed. "He got my grandson killed."

I held myself. I knew Alex was angry, but *I* felt responsible for Osscar getting captured. How could it be Chase's fault? Just by leading us out of the house?

"This isn't right," I heard Liles mumble.

"No, it's not," I said irritably. "I'm going back."

Just as I turned around, Alex grabbed my wrist and pulled me in front of him. "Angela," he said sternly. "With your father gone, Chase's contract is terminated. I'm sorry to have to tell you, but he asked to stay."

I didn't know how to process that. Alex said he was sorry, but his venomous tone reflected the exact opposite. Regardless of how it was relayed, the news felt like a knife to the chest.

He continued past me. "If you need to see him," he went on, "make it quick, we have a train to catch."

I stood still for a moment. Izzy ran up and hugged me. Everything was going wrong, everyone was leaving. I glared back at the hotel one last time before walking on.

Liles remained quiet the entire walk to the train station, but I could see his mouth moving sometimes, as if he was reciting what he planned to say out loud.

It was an outdoor train station, and to my surprise, Alex already had tickets for everyone. When he pulled

them out, I noticed he hadn't even bothered to get one for Chase, which made me suspicious. If Chase had asked to stay, why wouldn't Alex have bought a ticket for him initially? I wanted to point that out, I wanted to question Alex a bit more, but every time he looked back at us, the cold and enraged glare in his eyes forced my words back down my throat.

Who knows what all the man was doing while we were running around, but he was angry, and not his normal kind of angry. He had a look of pure disdain burned into his face, one that wouldn't fade.

The train blasted its whistle as we walked aboard from the wooden station base. I barely knew where I was supposed to go; I was in a haze. Could Osscar really be gone forever? How did Alex know for sure he was captured? Did he see him dragged off?

Izzy led me into a private train cabin and shut the door, waiting until Alex and Liles passed by before sitting on one of the two large benches lining the cabin walls. I sat on the opposite bench to face her. Then a loud noise shook the train car. I looked out the window on the wall between us. It was starting to rain.

"Thunderstorm," Izzy said. "There was one last night too."

I turned to her. "I don't know what to say."

Izzy looked down. "I'm so sorry about Osscar."

"Yeah, me too. Izzy, the last thing I said to him was *drop dead.*"

Izzy took a deep breath and looked out the window. "Yeah, that's bad...."

"I know," I replied.

Izzy swapped benches and scooted closer to me. "He had to have known you didn't mean it. You didn't know about the plan."

I leaned onto the window ledge. "How could he want to stay there alone?"

"Chase?" Izzy replied, confused.

"Where will he go?" I asked. "He has no family, no connections."

"He lived by himself for a long time before we came along. I guess he'll just do what he did before?"

The cabin door swung open. Liles was standing in the doorway. He looked frazzled. "Now, I may be speculating," he started in a hushed tone, "but I think my grandfather is lying to you."

Izzy scooted over to face Liles, who had his arms rest-ing on his knees. I'd suspected something was up when I saw the number of train tickets, but I didn't want to make a fool of myself with the suggestion. Liles pulled Chase's small leather wallet from his pocket; it was worn and dirty like most things Chase owned, but filled to the brim with cash.

"I guess we forgot to give that back," I sighed.

"How are you going to stay in a hotel, or anywhere for that matter, without any money?" Liles asked us.

I sat up, taking the wallet from him, but my high hopes faded when I opened it and pulled out the remaining cash. "He *does* have money," I said quietly, closing the wallet. "My dad gave him five hundred dollars."

"We spent two on the hotel rooms?" Izzy reminded me.

"I know, but there's only a hundred in here," I coun-tered, handing Liles the wallet back. "In a cheaper room, Chase has plenty of time to decide where he wants to go next."

Liles took it from me and flopped back onto the bench. "I'm sorry," he started, "I didn't mean to—" There was a brief pause before he rolled his eyes and sighed.

"Hey," I said. Liles glanced at me. "It's okay." I said with half a smile. "Scars fade, right?"

He nodded. "But not quickly."

The rest of the journey was silent, and I stared out the window for most of it. I could see the grass valley zoom past us in a matter of minutes, and it was hard to believe it took us a whole day of running to get through it. I would be coming home to a house with only half the people I was used to being there. This reality was crushing me. Then the train stopped.

We all sat up and looked out the window as the whistle blew. The station was just outside the woods on the other side of the house. The woods that hid it so well, but expanded on for miles. I thought I couldn't be more disheartened, but when I realized there would be a lot more walking in our future, I almost cried. Alex opened our cabin door and gestured us out, his face still cross, but drowsy now. He'd probably fallen asleep during the ride.

Izzy, Liles, and I walked out onto yet another wooden outdoor station. I stared down the dirt path we would have to follow around the woods to the house and sighed. I didn't know what time it was, but the sky was pitch black and the only light came from the train and the moon. We

would have to walk all night just to get back to the house by morning.

Izzy was about to step off the wooden base when Alex stopped her with his arm. "I've arranged us a ride," he said without affect.

We were all confused. We hadn't ridden in a car for years. My dad said it was because he didn't want to risk huntsmen tracking us with one.

"But Alex?" Izzy started.

He didn't respond. But soon after, a car approached the opposite side of the train station. It was an older, black S.U.V. Uncle Jason was in the driver's seat. Alex walked over to the back door, opened it, and gestured us inside. I entered first and slid over. Izzy took the middle, probably to be next to me, and Liles came in last.

Alex shut the door and headed to the passenger's seat. Once again, silence.

It took almost an hour for Uncle Jason to find the clearing in the forest that led straight to the house. Which I didn't even know was there, but its existence only proved that there had *always* been a way to drive cars in and out, and that Alex—and maybe my father—just didn't want us to leave. If only we had known about the clearing before

we went off through the miles and miles of grass. We may have actually gotten enough distance between ourselves and the house so Alex couldn't have caught up to us.

If only.

The car slowed as we turned into the property. But as eager as I was to reunite with my bed, something was off. The lights in the house were on—not all of them, but the ones in the kitchen and the living room. Liles had the best view from where he was sitting, so we all leaned toward him.

"Stay here," Alex said, getting out of the car. He slammed the door behind him and approached the house slowly.

"Someone fixed our door?" Izzy said, confused.

"You're right," I whispered.

Alex was about to twist the doorknob, but someone opened it first. I sighed a deep breath of relief, leaning back in my seat. Dana and Henry were alive—alive and uncaptured. I figured Izzy would be thankful, but I heard her grumble. Alex turned toward the car and waved for us to get out.

Izzy stepped over Liles and exited the car. We watched as she vanished into the house with her grandparents.

"You two best get out," Uncle Jason called back to Liles and me. Liles jumped out of the car, but before I could do the same, Jason stopped me. "Hey." I placed my hand on the latch of the open door. "You holding up okay?" he asked. I nodded slightly, stepping one foot out. "You're a lot like your dad," he continued with a sigh, "but you don't have to go it alone either." I turned back to him, unsure of how to respond. "Get out."

The house felt empty, despite the six people in it. The hallway was darker than usual, with half the doors closed and no light shining under them. I immediately went to my room, not bothering to wait for Izzy, who was probably being lectured by her grandparents. It was hours before my restless brain would let me sleep, and even then, that brief snooze ended just before two in the morning.

With your father gone, his contract is terminated.

"Is it though?" I said out loud, sitting up. I turned to Izzy who was sound asleep in the matching wrought-iron bed parallel to mine. "*Psst*, Izzy," I started in a half-hearted attempt to wake her.

Silence.

This was going to bug me all night. I eventually reasoned that I might as well go check for myself. That way,

I would know for sure and could start working on letting sleeping dogs lie. I got up from bed and stepped into the hallway. *Where would Dad have put it?*

I wandered down the hall to my father's room and slowly pushed the door open. It was dark, and I could barely see, but I eventually found his old desk. There were no words to describe how horribly sad that cluttered little room made me feel now that it was vacant. I turned on the standing lamp. Piles of paper and envelopes were stacked on top of each other, so that even the slightest disturbance would send them all falling onto the floor.

"Seriously, Dad," I mumbled, rolling my eyes. This would have taken hours to sort through, but me being me, I jumped the gun. I took my arm and swiped it across the desk, sending everything flying. I frantically opened every desk compartment until I got to the middle one. I pulled the drawer out so fast it fell to the floor, and sure enough, there it was. The glittering gold signatures at the bottom of its last paragraph were unmistakable. I picked up the piece of paper and read it, my eyes widening on the sentence I was hoping to see.

This document cannot be terminated by any other means than that of the mutual agreement between the writer and the signer. The signer must agree to these terms.

I shook my head. Of course Alex lied. That's a shape-shifter for you, a professional prevaricator.

I dropped the paper and ran down the hall and out the door, my pajamas ripping from my body as I shifted into my Arctic wolf. I bounded toward the newly discovered clearing in the woods, the quickest way to the train station. It wasn't long before I heard the inevitable howl echo through the trees. There was a large black wolf quite literally on my tail.

"Angela!" he barked. I tried not to acknowledge him, but he was quickly outrunning me. The wolf stopped when it was in front of me, snarling in my face.

"Out of my way," I growled.

"Where do you think you're going?" Alex threatened.

"You know where I'm going!" I snapped. "You lied to me, and you left my—" I couldn't think of another word— "friend alone to be captured!"

"It was for your own good!" he yelled.

"It wasn't his fault Osscar was captured!" I snapped. "And while the trip may have been his idea, we all agreed to go!"

Alex stood with paws spread out. "You'll die out there alone."

"Normally, someone would be forced to go with me," I replied, standing up higher.

We stared each other down for a few more seconds before Alex closed his eyes and stepped aside. "The train coming west has a car in the back with a door missing," he said quietly. "Jump for it."

Wait, I won? I thought. "Thank you," I replied, running past him into the clearing.

14: CHASE

I left the hotel later that evening after room service informed me that my stay was up. I searched my backpack, only to find I had no cash to renew it. The girls must have forgotten to give my wallet back, and I was sunk. It wouldn't stop raining either, but wet clothes were the least of my worries. No one came back. And maybe it would have been for the best, but deep down, I was really hoping someone would dispute leaving me there.

I walked along the dirt road from the hotel, wondering if there was any way I would be able to get home on my own. I was a walking target.

"You've no idea just how vulnerable a wolf is without a pack."

I didn't know what Alex told the others, but if they all truly believed I was the reason Osscar was captured, they wouldn't miss me.

Lightning flashed above, and I noticed the ravine up ahead where me and Angela had fallen. My heart sank as I toured it from above, but I was quickly snapped from my nostalgia when I noticed someone at the bottom, and they looked up at me. I took off down the wet, dirt road with mud splashing up behind me. I turned around, and whoever it was had begun running after me.

If I shifted, I'd be throwing away my only pair of shoes, and possibly everything in my backpack. It wasn't like I had any money in there, but there was water, food, more clothes! I couldn't lose my resources now.

"Hey!" the person behind me yelled.

I stopped in my tracks and turned around. I knew this voice. They approached slowly and stopped about five feet from me.

"Osscar?" I asked, stepping toward him in the dark.

"Yeah," he panted, "you're fast for someone with—"

"Where on earth have you been?"

"I umm... I've been around," he sighed.

"You knew we were looking for you?"

"Umm, yeah...."

"Osscar, Angela was devastated!" I shouted. "She—"

"I know," he said, interrupting me, "but I know where I have to go, and I don't want anyone to get hurt."

That sounded like a quote from some cliché drama film. It was one of the stupidest things I'd ever heard. "You're going to the base *by yourself*?" Osscar sort of looked around, like he wasn't sure what to say. "That's suicide!" I yelled.

"No, I have a plan!"

"What were you doing in that ravine?" I asked, quickly losing patience.

"I, umm," he stammered, "it's complicated."

"Complicated?" I crossed my arms. "Try me."

"I...can't say," he replied.

"Then why would you bother running after me?" I asked.

"I've been out here alone, okay?" he mumbled. "I guess I just wanted to see a familiar face."

"I don't understand," I continued. "You ran away from us—intentionally?"

"Yes. But I promise there's a good excuse."

"Well, let's hear it," I shrugged.

"The only reason we were going to that base was for my parents," he started, "and after all we've learned, I would never forgive myself if any of you guys were murdered trying to—"

"Hang on just a minute," I snapped. "We were never going just for you. Those are Liles' parents too, and Angela's dad—"

"Isn't there," Osscar said quietly.

"What do you mean?" I asked.

He took a deep breath. "Yes, I know where Chris went, but he made me swear not to say."

"You knew this whole time!?" I yelled, shocked. "Then why did you let us leave?!"

"Well, we were going to find Malachi, and I was worried about Izzy's grandparents. There were other reasons for leaving the house, but the base is a different story."

"Where's Chris?" I demanded.

"Honestly, I can't say," Osscar mumbled. "They told me not to tell any of you."

"And why do *you* get to know?" I asked angrily. "What about Angela? He's her father, wouldn't she get— Wait, *they*?"

"My grandfather and Chris."

"Alex knew!?" I shouted. "What are you going to tell me next!? Liles knew!?"

"No!" Osscar yelled. "He had no idea, neither did anyone else."

I backed away from him. "You're really not gonna tell me what any of this is about?" I asked.

"I can't," he repeated. "I'm so sorry I even approached you."

"Yeah, me too."

There was a pause. "Please don't tell Angela you saw me," he begged. "She'll be so hurt."

"You'll be lucky if I don't," I growled. "You're something else."

"Please! Just this once, look past your pride and think of other people."

"Think of other people?" I was appalled. "*I'm* not the one keeping secrets!"

"You know," Osscar countered, "I think that's the biggest lie I've heard out of you yet." I looked away from him.

"Why do you care anyway? You never planned on going to the base, you probably didn't even plan on looking for Chris and Malachi either." He either felt bad or realized I wasn't going to reply, because after about a minute, he changed the subject. "Where is everyone anyway?"

"I'm sure they're on their way home," I replied, walking off.

"You aren't with them? Then where are you going?"

"I dunno!" I snapped. "But who says I'd tell you if I did!" Unbelievable. We all felt terrible that Osscar was captured, me especially, because I actually thought it was my fault! Oh! And not to mention, *he* got me kicked out of the house—for no reason!

Dang it! Shoulda brought that up! I totally could have won the argument.

The point is—meanwhile, he's wandering around with a handful of secrets and lies, intentionally avoiding us? I kicked a rock down the road in frustration. It rolled a few feet and then splashed into a puddle. Everything was still wet from the storms.

Alex knew...the whole time?

Nothing was adding up, but I told myself I had to be right. Why else would Chris want to leave without us knowing? *He was working for the huntsmen.*

I know, it's a pretty big accusation, and I don't have a whole lot of evidence. But it just makes sense. I've suspected that there was something odd about him since the day I met him. Then what about Alex? He lied to all of us—did that mean he was in on it too? I had to get back to the house, I had to warn everyone.

"There!" someone yelled from behind me. "I told you!"

I turned around and saw a group of people with flashlights staring at me, about five of them. Their reflective orange vests glowed in the dark, and the man in the middle of the group was pointing at me. "Don't move!" he shouted with his hand outstretched. I bolted. If a bunch of strangers in the middle of the night asked you to do something, would you obey? "Kid, stop!" the man in the middle yelled in a panic. I slipped and fell on the muddy road and looked up to see a creature staring down at me. Its narrowing eyes glowed bright red like the taillights of a car. And when they locked with my own, I was paralyzed with fear.

The monster's thick fur blew about in a strange black mist that encircled the ground in front of it. And the long, tusk-like canine teeth extending from its mouth pointed down at me like daggers. I would have screamed had my voice been able to escape me. "Kid!" the same man screamed in the distance.

I backed up, attempting to stand, but the creature placed a paw on my chest, and I was trapped between it and the road. My blood ran cold. The dark mist surrounding it grew thicker. I could hear it whispering like something out of a nightmare. No, it was less whisper and more drawn-out exhale. It was the same prolonged word over and over again, but I couldn't make out what it was.

I tried to look the creature in the face again. I could barely see beyond the bright glow of its supernatural eyes, and its death-dealing fangs were all I could focus on.

Horrified at all the possible outcomes of my current situation, I closed my eyes, and a second after, I heard a gunshot. The monster leapt off me, dragging its cold, black mist along with it, and once the shock left my system, I sat up to see another group of people on the opposite side of the road. These guys, I knew.

"Grab the cat!" a man leading the second group yelled.

A familiar woman jumped from the group and charged the red-eyed creature with a long black object surging with electricity. There was barely a delay before the creature spun around and snapped at her. It was the same woman who had led the assault on us in the grass field! Her long blond hair and shapeshifter-pelt coat were unmistakable.

"Who are you people!?" one of the men with the flashlights shouted to the newcomers.

I attempted to get off the road and out of the middle of the incomprehensible mess, but was stopped by someone from the second group. He wrapped one hand violently around my neck and pulled me to my feet by my backpack. "I recognize this one!" he called out. It was clear to me now if not sooner, that the second group was made up entirely of huntsmen, and that I was in serious trouble.

"What are you all doing with that animal?" the man in the middle of the flashlight group shouted angrily. When he came closer, I noticed that the shield-shaped badge on his shirt read: *CONSERVATION LAW ENFORCEMENT.*

Another huntsman pulled out a gun, took a shot at the creature, and missed. This outraged the woman in furs. "You moron!" she screamed. "Anyone shoots my Exotic, they're dead!"

"*Your* Exotic?" the man leading the huntsman team shouted. "Know your rank, woman! You still answer to me!"

The conservation officer pulled out a radio transmitter. "Poachers have moved in on the subject!" he shouted. "They are armed. Requesting—"

The leader of the huntsman team pointed his pistol at the officer from across the road and shot him dead. Screams and cries from the other officers filled the air as I struggled to break free of my choke hold, but the person restraining me only tightened his grip.

"REQUESTING BACKUP!"

"LIAM!"

"CALL NINE-ONE-ONE!"

"ASPEN, NO!"

"RUN!"

The huntsmen began firing shots at the remaining flashlight men, most of whom fled in fear. A few stopped to yell, others to fight back. Some were armed, but they were outnumbered. In the end, the officers had no choice but to run.

That's when I learned that it wasn't just us. These huntsmen weren't just in the business of killing shapeshifters;

they were in the business of killing anyone who got in their way.

"Drop the kid!" the woman in furs shouted in my direction. "Get over here and help us!"

"He's a shifter!" the man holding me argued.

I continued to struggle, trying desperately to shift into anything, but I was too worked up. It felt like I was about to pass out.

"Then get him in the truck!" the woman in furs screamed before being struck down by a large paw belonging to the red-eyed creature.

"No!" the leader of the huntsman team yelled. "Kill the kid while we have him; we can use the pelt for a smaller project!"

My heart skipped a beat, and I screamed. I knew no one was coming, but the possibility of dying right there and then compelled me to try anything I could. The man holding me drew a pistol from his belt and pointed it at my head. My eyes watered and my breaths became short and quick.

Jason's pontifical words would have been the last thing I thought of before I died. I had no pack. I couldn't run, couldn't shift, and was going to die alone in the middle of

the road. I heard the cock of the gun and closed my eyes once again. Not a second too soon, a fluffy white animal knocked both me and my executioner onto the ground. I rolled across the road and hit several rocks, but I was alive! I coughed and gasped for air, not realizing just how tight of a grip the huntsman had my neck until I was free. I couldn't stop hyperventilating, but the tears forming in my eyes were those of relief. Or, you know, physiological shock....

I heard a horrible scream, looked up, and saw the red-eyed creature shaking one of the huntsmen like a ragdoll, its teeth embedded in his neck. It was a horribly violent thing to witness, but at the time, all I could focus on was my timely rescue. The white wolf was standing over the huntsman who nearly murdered me, with no clear intention of hurting him, despite having pinned his arms to the road. My eyes widened with terror when I realized who it was.

"Angie!?" I coughed. "No! Get out of here!"

"There's another!" the woman in furs announced, getting up from the ground. The cat creature must have gotten away from her.

The white wolf leapt off the huntsman she was holding down, turning to the woman in furs with a foaming mouth full of canine teeth. I'd never seen that side of Angela before. I was both shaken and overcome with a strange admiration.

When I finally spotted the red-eyed cat again, it was running into the woods, limping on its back leg.

"Go get the Exotic!" the woman in furs yelled, gesturing to the man who ordered my death. "I'll take the wolf."

Another huntsman came running toward me, and I jumped out of the way. Then, *BANG!*

"ANGELA!" I screamed.

With a shriek, the white wolf fell to the ground. The woman in furs marched triumphantly over to Angela, stomping on her body. She uttered something to her victim while aiming her pistol down to finish the job, but I couldn't hear a thing through my own panic.

This was no time to panic, no time to rest either, but if ever there was an emergency that warranted me putting my health at risk, this was it.

I shifted into my polar bear, jumped over to the woman in furs, and full-body slammed her off of Angela.

She tumbled into the ravine just off the road, and that's when the one remaining huntsman began advancing toward us. I hadn't really been paying attention to the red-eyed creature, but it had somehow taken out the rest of them all on its own. The only two left were the man who almost killed me, who for simplicity's sake I'm going to call Zack, and the leader of the team.

I'm sorry, but I'm going to briefly interrupt this very suspenseful moment to preface something;

You're unfortunately going to see a few lines in the upcoming paragraphs that are sort of worded a bit like, "Blah, blah blah, I killed someone." Like it was no big deal to me, or something I do every day. I promise that's not the case. This event is difficult to relive, and the last thing I want to do is describe images I wish so badly to put behind me. Believe me when I say I felt horrible. Admittedly, less now than when this happened.

But no matter how terrible the person was, the murder ~~made~~ makes me feel like I'm no better than them. All that being said, when you're in this kind of situation, you really only have two choices—fight or run away. And running would have meant leaving Angela to die, which wasn't an option.

The creature intercepted their charge, taking Zack as its latest victim, which left the leader of the team, who already had a gun pointed at me and Angela. I blindly launched myself at him before he could shoot, attempting to pin him to the ground, but he reached for his belt with his free arm.

There was a brief moment of panic when I heard the cock of whatever weapon he'd gotten ahold of. He was right under me, all he had to do was pull the trigger. Maybe I had a choice, maybe I didn't, but I was scared. Everything was happening so fast, and I didn't wanna die.

I closed my eyes, threw my head down, and bit the leader of the huntsman team as hard as I could around the throat. When I let go, I looked down at the man—of course he was dead. My eyes welled up again, and I sat with my mouth hanging open, disgusted by the nauseating taste.

Needless to say, I was upset. Really, really, upset. Something inside me was slowly breaking free from a mental barrier I subconsciously put up years ago. This whole disaster reminded me of the day I sustained Morph-Bone, the day I lost everything.

Suppressing the memory, I looked up to see the cat creature staring at me from across the road, its beaming-red eyes dimming fainter.

I expected it to speak, but it only lowered its head and limped off into the woods. I paid it little mind after that and ran over to Angela. It was too dark to see if she was still breathing, so I lay down on the ground, placing my polar bear head against her chest. I had no idea where she had been shot and was anticipating the worst.

For a while, I heard nothing but my own heart pounding a million beats per minute. Then, I felt Angela take a breath in. I sighed, collapsing down next to her.

"Chase," she whispered.

"Yeah," I choked.

"It hurts so bad," she cried.

"I—I'm sorry," I stammered.

"Are you okay?" she asked, sniffling.

"No."

"Wh-what happened?"

"I don't know," I said with a break in my voice.

"I can't walk," she cried. "How are we gonna get home?"

I'd forgotten all about Chris and Alex until she said that. What was I supposed to say? I feared I was about to collapse. "We can take a minute," I decided.

The moments that followed were pathetic. We both just laid there. Angela was in shambles from the pain, and I was wallowing in self-pity trying to come up with a plan. I didn't know how badly she was hurt. I didn't know whether to say anything about Osscar. I didn't even know what time it was.

After about seven minutes, Angela was done crying. "We have to get up," she sniffled. "I need to shift back."

"Yeah." I stood up.

"You're not hurt, are you?" she asked.

"No."

"Okay, do, um, do we have any clothes?" Despite her circumstances, she was more clear-headed than me.

I helped her up and noticed the white fur on her lower back and left leg was blood-stained. It was pretty apparent that she wouldn't be walking home.

"I have spare clothes in my bag someplace," I said, "if I can find it."

"Please hurry, before anyone shows up."

I walked over to the side of the road where I saw my bag near the ravine. I picked it up with my teeth and looked over the edge. The woman in furs was gone.

"Yeah, we gotta go," I mumbled, dumping the bag onto the road. My old hotel keycard, a granola bar, and a small pile of clothes spilled out. *Okay okay okay*, I thought, still trying to calm down. I picked up the pile of clothes in my mouth and walked them to Angela who was barely standing.

"What was that thing.?" she asked. "That monster?"

"I have no idea."

"Do we have any shoes?"

"No," I said. "My old ones might be around here some-where." Angela nodded. "I'll be back." I grabbed some clothes for myself and shifted back into my human form behind the bushes, quickly getting dressed.

Ugh, the horrible blood taste was soooo much worse in human form. I spat into the grass and licked the collar of my shirt trying to get rid of it. I sat down, burying my

face in my hands. What was I going to say? How much was I going to tell her?

After everything, I didn't want Angela taking Liles and running off in search of Osscar to a huntsman base. We barely survived a fight against a small group of huntsmen, going into a whole building full of them? We'd all be captured or killed the second we stepped onto the property. Alex was right about me and my reckless planning, but I wasn't going to make the same mistake again. I didn't care if I stayed in that horrible house for the rest of my life... This could not happen again.

Onto problem number two—Angela would be furious if I kept pushing the idea that her dad was working against us, but it all made sense. Then again, how was I going to prove to her that Chris wasn't really captured if I didn't tell her about Osscar?

Problem three: Alex. He knew where Chris went, but I didn't think I'd ever be in any kind of position to interrogate him, if he even let me back in the house. Did I even want to go back there? I swear I thought he was gonna murder me at the hotel, and, based on what Osscar said, he's in on whatever Chris is doing behind our backs.

Problem four: I killed someone.

So, after evaluating my circumstances, what did I elect to tell Angela?

Nothing.

Meeting up with her didn't ease my panic. The blood from Angela's gunshot wound had already soaked through her clothes, and she couldn't have had them on for more than five minutes.

"Yikes," I whispered.

She was standing, but barely, with her hand covering her leg wound. "It really hurts."

I sighed. "Maybe I shouldn't have shifted back, I could have carried you."

"No—no," she replied. "We had to shift back, so we wouldn't attract attention at the train station. An injured girl riding on a polar bear would definitely cause a scene."

"Train station?"

"Yup," she sighed. "Down the road from the hotel."

"We have to walk all the way back there?" I asked dejectedly.

"Afraid so."

I sighed again and stepped over to her, putting her arm around my neck so I could walk for her bad leg. "I was

really hoping I wouldn't have to drag you another mile so soon."

"Sorry," she said with a rueful smile.

"Oh, it's no problem," I replied sarcastically. "It's not like I was just thrown across a dirt road after being re-strained, choked, and chased. I have all the energy in the world to walk you barefoot to a train station."

"You're milking it now," she said, almost laughing. "I just got shot!"

"Not to mention," I continued, picking up my empty backpack, "abandoned by my friends, broken by your Uncle Jason, forced to ingest poison, and knocked to the ground by a monster-sized feline."

"Hmm," Angela mumbled. "Maybe you win."

That's when we heard the sirens and noticed the dark, rocky path behind us light up with red and blue reflecting in the puddles. There were two ambulances, five police cruisers, and a firetruck, but I doubt there was anything any of them could do to help the people still left on the road.

We looked back at the scene. But I kept walking, try-ing to keep the subject rolling and my brain distracted.

"I don't know about that," I said, propping her arm further up onto my shoulder. "You lost your dad, your best friend, and, since you're here, I'm going to assume the trust of your family."

"Actually," she started, "Alex let me leave."

"Really?"

"Yeah," she continued. "I think he realized that I'll never change."

"Hmm?"

"You know, like, I'll never stop doing the stupid things I do." She sighed angrily. "He knows I need you." She uttered that sentence so bitterly, as if accepting some kind of unfair defeat. Pride fell with every word. I never thought I'd be so sad to hear her say that she needed me. Especially because I could tell she didn't mean it. Needing me only made her feel pathetic.

But if there was anything I could say to get my sparring partner back into high spirits, I was gonna say it. Even if it meant giving up my first win.

"Well, as much as I'd love to agree," I sighed, "you don't need me. You kicked butt out there, and I'm no more experienced than you."

"I appreciate you admitting that," she coughed, almost laughing.

"Besides, it was really *you* that did the saving this time," I reminded her.

"True," she said, a little more calmly. "You still saved me after that, though."

"Well, yeah," I panted. "I sort of have to, remember?" She started laughing out of nowhere, which made it harder to keep balance for us. "What?" I asked.

"You would be dead if it wasn't for me." *She's back...*

The sun was coming up in the east as we approached the train station. My feet were sore from walking on rocks, and I was beyond exhausted. I think Angela was starting to pick up on that, because I could feel some of the weight taken off my left side.

"Hey, don't try to walk," I protested.

"You're going to pass out."

"I'm fine," I replied.

"You are not, you're fatigued," she insisted.

"I'm not the one who's lost a pint of blood," I argued.

"How can you say that? You look like a mess!"

"What happened?" I asked foolishly.

"You tell me. What, did you get punched in the face or something?"

"I don't—"

"Don't say you don't know. You say that all the time." There was a pause. "Forget it, I won't argue with you," she continued. "It's just going to make you worse."

"Thank you," I said between breaths.

I stepped onto the platform of the outdoor train station, pulling Angela up with me. The train wasn't there yet, and the ticket both was vacant, so I sat us both down on a nearby bench.

"Once we get on the train," she started, "I have to talk to you."

"About what?" I asked.

"Well, I guess we can talk here," she sighed. "I let Alex leave you behind because—"

"Hey, you don't have to tell me," I said, waving my hands, "as much as I would love to know."

"No, I—I let him leave you because he told me you *wanted* to stay."

I rolled my eyes. Course he did...*Come on, stupid!* I thought. *She needs to know what's going on, just tell her.*

"I know he lied," Angela continued, "but he mentioned that with my dad gone, your contract would be terminated."

"I hadn't even thought of that..."

"Chase?"

"Yeah?"

"If you had, would you have left?" she asked.

"N-no." She didn't say another word. I probably wouldn't have left, but I think my hesitation hurt her feelings. I just hadn't thought about it. If her father was really gone, did that mean I was free to go whenever I wanted?

We could hear the train from a mile away, chugging and screeching the whole way toward us. Angela looked behind our bench at the ticket booth, which was still empty.

"Is no one coming?" I asked.

"No," she replied.

Now I could tell she was angry, but what was I supposed to say? I could try and reassure her that I really did mean what I said, but it wouldn't erase my reaction in the moment. I guess I would've been angry too. She came all the way back out there to get me, even getting shot in the process. "Angie," I started.

"Please don't," she said, shaking her head.

The train pulled in slowly. It took a minute for it to stop, and still no one was at the ticket booth. I was starting to worry. The doors slid open, and people started walking onto the platform. I got up and stepped in front of Angela. We didn't need anyone seeing her injury. Not super helpful, now that I'm thinking about it. I was the one with the face full of blood. She stood up on her own and moved away from me. I turned to her with concern, but she refused to acknowledge it.

Once all the passengers had gotten off the train, the conductor stepped out to talk to us.

"Sorry, you two," he said. "We're closin' for the night. They're just about to take ole' Cola back to the northern station where she'll retire until—"

"Wait," I interjected, "can we hitch a ride one stop north?"

"It would be on the way," Angela begged.

The conductor looked back at the engineer who was shaking his head. "Look," he said, "you kids are better off just takin' a bus. The ticket prices are lower, and we don't have any more stops scheduled."

A bus was already out of the question, but we couldn't force this guy to let us on. We watched as the engineer walked to the empty ticket booth, closing the window in front of it.

We looked at each other sadly as he boarded the train once again. "We aren't going to make it home. What now?" Angela asked. "We bleed to death trying to walk there?"

"Hey, no one's bleeding to death."

"Better hope not," she scoffed.

I turned around. "Then, the contract isn't—?"

"Terminated?" Angela asked sarcastically. "No, I reviewed it. The only way to terminate it is by mutual agreement between the writer and the signer. So, you and Dad."

Of course she reviewed it. "So, you *did* believe Alex?"

"I did, but I didn't want to. So I looked for a reason not to, and I found one."

"You're always saying you don't want me around. Why bother looking for a reason to come back and get me?" I asked.

"I *never* said I didn't want you around, I just don't want you running after me like you don't trust me to take care of myself!" She let her head fall into her hands.

"Ugh! We have this same fight all the time, why can't you understand?"

As usual, I wasn't sure what to say. I still didn't feel like she understood where I was coming from either.

The train's whistle blew, and the arguing had to stop. The long line of passenger cars began slogging forward. Our only way home would soon be out of sight. Angela sat down, clutching her injured leg, and I paced anxiously across the platform. It had to have been causing her a lot more pain than she was letting on. We had to do something.

I finally mustered up enough energy to shift into my gray wolf. I ran up to her. Luckily my backpack stayed on. It trapped my shredded shirt between it and my back.

"What? Why did you shift!? Aren't we out of clothing? Now we can't even take the bus!"

"No, but the bus was never an option! It's too far, and you're hurt! That's a gunshot wound. What if someone were to call the cops on us?"

"What are you thinking?" she asked from the ground.

"Can you shift into your mouse?"

She looked up at me like I was crazy. "You couldn't catch a train if you tried!"

"We *have* to try," I insisted. "The train isn't even close to full speed; we have to go now. Can you shift or not?"

(Dear Me of the Past, You are an idiot!)

Angela took a deep breath, shaking her head. I knew she had that anxious delay thing, but this wasn't the time. I'm not one for pep talks, but I gave it my best shot. "You've got this." I tried to sound as calm as possible. "And once we're back home, I promise I'll never, ever ask you to do anything like this again."

Angela shifted into her mouse, leaving her blood-soaked clothing behind. The train whistle blew loudly from a few yards away. Some of its cars were still moving past us.

"Okay, umm." I lay down. "Maybe you could climb up those backpack straps?"

"I can't even walk," she replied in her tiny voice.

I rested my head on the platform. "Step up onto my paw," I ordered, "then my nose."

"This is so stupid." She limped onto my paw, then my muzzle, and from there, she climbed over my head onto my back. The last train car zoomed past us. It had a missing door. "Go!" she shouted from my back.

I took off, running down the tracks toward the last car with Angela holding on for dear life. It hadn't even been a minute, and the train already seemed a million miles away. My heart was pounding. I had decent night vision in my wolf form, but the wind was so strong I had to close my eyes.

"Look!" she yelled.

I opened my eyes to see two bright lights ahead of us. They were foggy and blurred. The train's whistle blew loudly for the third time, and the sound was so close it shook us. I was looking right at the safety lights at the back of the last car. We were only a couple feet away!

I sped up, but so did the train.

"You've got this!" she yelled ecstatically.

I knew I didn't. I was giving it all I had, and the distance between us and the car was only growing.

Now, for a healthy and unimpaired shapeshifter, maybe this plan would have worked, but my legs were already burning. It felt like my heart was about to explode, it was beating so fast.

A sudden feeling of hollowness overcame me. Like my whole body was empty.

"Chase!?" Angela called.

I didn't get the chance to warn her, or even slow down. I began swaying back and forth as I careened forward before my legs gave out and we crashed onto the tracks. I watched the lights of the last train car fade off into the distance as I closed my eyes.

15: ANGELA

I was thrown from Chase's back as he went down, and, for once, I shifted back at just the right time. If I had hit the ground as my mouse, I'd have bigger problems to worry about, worse even than a gunshot wound. Unfortunately, I couldn't seem to avoid landing on my injured leg. It really hurt. I remember hissing in pain, pulling my leg out from under me, and turning to Chase, who was unconscious in his wolf form with a backpack twisted around his neck, laying on the old wooden train tracks like roadkill.

"Hey!" I called, crawling over to him. As uncomfortable as this felt without clothes on, it's not like I could wait til I was dressed to check if he was okay. I shook his canine body violently, but he wasn't waking up. The train's whistle blew from about half a mile away. I was ready to give up. Things couldn't have been worse. I detangled his legs from his backpack and put on the remaining clothes that were inside it. Of course, they weren't women's clothes, but what else is new?

I buried my head in my friend's fur. It looked like there was no way either of us was ever getting home. It wouldn't be long before the morning train started coming south. I had to get him off the tracks somehow, but I could hardly walk. I looked around. There was no shelter anywhere, only a couple of dead trees, some grass patches, and a pile of junk over by a broken telephone pole. Help wouldn't be coming by happy coincidence. Or so I thought.

That's when I spotted something driving alongside the track toward us. Coming from the north was a beat-up old SUV caked in mud with a cloud of dirt behind it.

"Great," I sighed.

Uncle Jason pulled up to the tracks, rolling his passenger-side window down. He looked at me with a perplexed expression.

"How did you know we—" I started to ask.

"Alex asked me to scout the trail coming home," he replied flatly. "Case you two tried somethin' stupid."

"Oh," I mumbled.

"Get in," he demanded, getting out of the car.

I attempted to stand one last time, and my hip made a terrible clicking noise. I sat back down next to Chase, hanging my head in shame.

"You let yourself get shot?" Jason yelled.

I said nothing. I felt bad enough as it was, but I think my uncle pitied me because he just offered me his hand. I let him help me up into the passenger seat. He shut the door once I was inside and went back to grab Chase, who was apparently pretty heavy in his wolf form because I could hear a lot of grunting and cursing.

I watched them in the side mirror, Chase's skinny canine body dangling from Uncle Jason's arms like a rag-dog. He was tossed into the back seat, and Jason joined me up front, reaching into the car's console to give me a towel that had probably been there for years. "Try not to bleed on

the seats, please." I took the towel and wrapped it around my leg. The blood had only just begun to soak through my "new" pair of black jeans. "Do I wanna know what happened?" he asked, his sunglasses hiding his expression.

"Probably not," I replied.

"Alright, Imma ask," Jason decided. "What happened?"

"Well, we were trying to catch the train, and—"

"I meant to *you*," he cut me off.

"Oh, yeah, I got shot," I said. "There were a bunch of huntsmen, a very large cat, and we almost died."

"Man," he mumbled. "Glad ya made it out alive."

Uncle Jason started the car, and there were several questions playing on my mind. I normally didn't see the guy very often, so I figured I'd better ask while I had him there. "Hey," I started, "can I ask you something?" He nodded and kept on driving. "What can you tell me about Uncle Dustin?"

"I changed ma' mind," he retorted. "You may *not* ask me somethin.'"

"I'm serious," I snapped.

He sighed. "We don't talk about Dustin much. He had what your friend has. He exploited his condition to manipulate people. Used it like a crutch, and he only had

it in parta one leg. That's all I wanna say on the matter. The man was truly crazy."

"That's absolutely no reason to take it out on Chase," I fumed. "He's nothing like that."

"That ain't why I gave your friend a hard time. He thinks he's got everything figured out. It's gonna get him killed someday."

"*You* almost caused him to lose his arm," I muttered.

He turned to me sternly. "He challenged me, I won. It's simple as that."

I shouldn't have asked. The rest of the car ride was long and miserable. Three hours of driving along another dirt path that went around the grass field. Nothing to see for miles but clouds of dust and, of course, plenty of grass.

We hit a large rock in the road and everyone jolted forward. Including Chase, who spilled onto the floor of the back seat with a thud.

I looked back to check on him. "He'll be fine," Uncle Jason said.

"It was so weird...He just collapsed."

"Probably just out of steam."

I thought about it for a second. "He still isn't eating..."

"Still?"

"Never mind," I grumbled, crossing my arms and slumping back in my chair.

"Alex wanted this boy gone badly," Jason started again. "It surprised me when he called and said—"

"You have a phone!?" I shouted excitedly, sitting up.

"Damn it," he groaned.

"May I see it?" I begged.

"It's just a flip phone, kid." Uncle Jason reached into his pocket. "It don't do anything fancy."

He dropped the little silver phone into my hand, and I studied it carefully, opening the lid and touching every button. "Did my dad have one of these?"

"You're already talking about him like he's gone," he sighed.

"Oh, sorry," I mumbled. "It's just, after seeing what it's like out here...."

"I get it. We didn't think our parents were coming back either."

"Dad never talks about you guys' parents," I said quietly.

"In his defense, there ain't much to say. Nothing good, anyway."

"What happened?"

"Blood issues," he replied, shrugging. "You know how it is."

Chase said the exact same thing two years ago when we asked him why he didn't have any family. Shapeshifters and lineage... Hopefully, we won't get into that mess for a while.

"Chris was lost for a long time before he met your mother," Jason continued, changing the subject. "You look so much like her, it's crazy. You look like 'em both."

I looked out the window and noticed we were coming to the end of the grass valley. My heart sank. "I didn't think I would live in that house my whole life," I said dolefully, "but I can't do this again."

Uncle Jason slowed the car a bit. "Now, don't you go letting Alex convince you that the world is cruel, because it ain't. You just haven't found your place yet, and maybe this town isn't where you oughta be looking."

"You're saying I should leave?" I asked.

"No," he replied, "but I *am* sayin" that you should start considerin' what you want most and chase that, instead of followin' in the footsteps of someone who's walkin' in circles."

"Alex?" I asked.

"That man's lost a lot," my uncle sighed. "He's just try-na hide what he's got left."

"How do you—"

"I've been around the block. But I'm not tellin' ya to run off with your friends again either. I'm askin' ya to be smart, because this really was stupid."

"We just want our freedom," I said, looking into the rearview mirror to check on Chase on the floor of the backseat.

"I know," Jason replied. "Don't we all?"

After a brief trip through the clearing in the woods and around the property, Jason stopped the car. "Alright," he sighed, getting out. I watched him walk up to the house and knock on the front door, which was opened soon after by Alex, who had a cigar in his mouth and an annoyed expression on his face.

Alex rarely smoked—only when he was really, really stressed out. He looked at me, and I sunk down in my chair. *We're doomed…*

16: CHASE

Once again, there was a brief moment when I had no idea where or what I was. Waking up on the rug by the fireplace, I had mixed feelings. On the one hand, *Yay, I'm alive.* On the other hand, *Alex...*

I glanced around. The living room didn't look any different than it had before we left, except for the front door, which was back on its hinges. But I was alone. Which was odd, considering the space was almost always occupied by at least three people. I was just about to start calling out names, when I heard footsteps coming from the kitchen. I

spotted Izzy coming up the stair. She smiled when she saw me and rushed into the room. "Angela!" she called. "Chase is awake!"

I looked out the window of the door at the darkened sky. "How long was I out?"

Izzy walked over to the couch and ripped a blanket off Angela, who had been curled up asleep. Her leg wound was covered in cotton with an elastic bandage, and there was a pillow propping her foot up. "Probably shouldn't wake her," Izzy sighed, tossing the blanket back over Angela. "She's been waiting all day for you to wake up, though."

"All *day*?" I asked.

"Yeah," Izzy replied. "She said you passed out from exhaustion on the train tracks last night."

I sighed, rubbing my eye with my paw. Even after shutting down for a whole day, I was tired. "How'd we get back here?"

"Jason brought you two back early this morning," she told me. "You're probably glad you were unconscious. Alex had a lot to say about Angela getting shot."

I was sure I'd get an earful about that soon enough. "Yeah, I let her down," I mumbled.

"She isn't angry with you," Izzy assured me.

"I would be," I said, pushing myself up to sit. "Course I couldn't catch a train."

"She said you almost did though!" Izzy laughed. "Don't beat yourself up. You're both home and safe now."

"Jason took us here?" I asked for confirmation.

"Yeah," she repeated. "He drove in and—"

"He has a car!?"

Jason's all-too-timely appearance in the field was starting to make perfect sense. He had a car! A car that he didn't want us knowing about.

"I know, right!?" Izzy shouted, sitting down on the floor next to me. "We were all pretty surprised."

I laid back down, placing my head on my paw weakly. "I should probably get some more rest...."

"But you just woke up," she said, confused. "Is something else wrong?" I glanced at her before turning back to the fireplace. "You still aren't eating, are you?"

I didn't reply. As odd as it sounds, the last thing in the world I wanted was food. The very thought of it upset me.

"Chase..."

"Please, go away," I said. Sometimes I forget how sensitive Izzy is. She got up and left the room, sniffling with her arm over her face. I instantly regretted my words. "Wait," I

sighed, standing up. "Izzy," I started down the hall after her when I saw his feet. I looked up to see the angriest pair of eyes on the planet, and slowly started backing up. I turned around just as he called me.

"Chase," Alex grumbled.

I stood frozen with my tail tucked between my legs. "Yeah," I replied, rolling my eyes.

He walked into the living room and sat down in his chair—the one across from the couch where Angela was laying. He was smoking some kind of hand-rolled cigar that created a strong odor, impossible for me to ignore in the form I was in. I approached him, sitting with my back to the couch.

"I would prefer to speak to you in—"

"I'm sorry, I don't have the energy to shift back right now," I interjected.

He just stared at me like I was wasting his time. I looked over my shoulder at Angela. Though I was glad she was finally getting some rest, I wished she would wake up. There was so much we needed to talk about. I glanced down at her leg.

"It was a decent grazing," Alex said.

"Grazing?" I asked.

"You both got lucky," he grumbled. "Had she been shot through her femoral artery, she could have bled to death." This is how it always starts: a passive information packet of words before the inevitable rant and rave. "That doesn't mean it won't still be painful." He drew the cigar back up to his lips. He took a breath in. "For a while," he added, exhaling the smoke.

"Yeah," I said, looking down.

"But this is my fault," he said. I looked up, confused. I was half-expecting him to start yelling at me right about then. Especially after what Izzy told me. "I overreacted," he said. "I shouldn't have left you." I wasn't sure whether to be content or concerned with this sudden change of character. "I wasn't myself."

As nice as it was to be pardoned for the first time in the two years I'd known the guy, I was still angry with him. For lying to everyone; for keeping secrets. But then again, how was I any better?

"I'm sorry," I sighed, "about Osscar, and...everything else." Yeah, I knew Osscar was alive and uncaptured, but I also knew how long that would last if he went through with the suicide mission he had vaguely talked about.

Alex gave me an odd look. He had to have seen the stained fur around my muzzle. "You bit someone?"

"I don't—" I was going to start being honest. All the lies, all the secrets. They were eating me alive. "I killed someone."

"Did you have to?" he asked without hesitation. He didn't seem fazed in the slightest.

"I think so," I replied, hanging my head low.

"Long as you were thinking," he said, taking another puff of his cigar.

"Not a big deal?" I asked. He was acting so nonchalant about this, it almost made me upset. *Did you hear me, old man? I...KILLED...SOMEONE!*

"It'll be a big deal later. If you ever need one of these," he raised the cigar, "let me know."

I was shocked. This unprincipled offer coming from the guy who literally made me sleep outside for three days one time because I was "too young" to say even a mild curse word that I'm gonna refer to as *crap* spelled with an S. Am I not "too young" to smoke?

"Now, take care of Angela." He stood up and exited the room.

What on earth just happened?

After shifting back, the rest of the night was spent taking a shower, trying to clean the blood off the stupid bandages, and brushing my teeth about a hundred times.

The next morning, I woke up in my own bed. Which for once I could be thankful for.

I hobbled down the hall to the living room to look for Angela, but she must have moved late at night. The couch, along with the rest of the room, was empty again. Probably for the best, considering I didn't have the energy to talk to anyone. I couldn't even change out of my pajamas. But the main thing I noticed was my heart. It was beating really quickly, like it was struggling to keep up with no fuel. I was gonna have to try and eat something, whether I wanted to or not.

I heard footsteps and turned to see Liles walking down the hall in a silk bathrobe. No idea where he got that. He looked up from the newspaper he was reading. "Oh," he said. "Morning." I nodded, raising my hand slightly to wave. "Just, seeing what all I've missed," he explained, gesturing to his outdated paper. I can't remember what I said next. I felt terrible. "I went to bed early last night," he continued. "It's good to see you awake and conscious again...though I can't say you look all that rested?"

I sat down on the bench by the fireplace. "I'm sure I've slept all I can," I sighed. "I just haven't eaten."

"Wait a minute," he said. "Have you eaten since we last talked?"

I shook my head. "I know I should try. But, it's weird, the very thought of eating anything makes me sick."

"You tried to catch a train without—"

"I know, I know," I interrupted, rolling my eyes.

"Well, it takes the average human your age about a month to starve to death, but with all the stuff you've been doing, you can get your organs into some serious trouble."

"Just go get me a banana or something?" I asked.

Liles went into the kitchen and came back with a glass of milk. "That's not a banana." I said, unimpressed.

"It's really best to start off with a liquid form of nutrition," he replied, handing me the glass.

I took it from him. Just looking at it made me nauseous. I refocused my eyes to the ground. "I should know better than to accept drinks from you by now," I grumbled.

"I promise it's not going to taste anything like the remedy," he assured me.

"I don't trust you,"

"You're stalling..."

I took a small sip of milk and quickly set the glass on the floor. My emotions were conflicted. I couldn't tell if I felt better or not. "Are you okay?" he asked.

I put my head in my hands. "I guess," I coughed.

"Don't throw up," he ordered, "or pass out again."

I definitely felt worse. It felt like my insides, starting with my stomach, were progressively being lit on fire. All of my paranoia was definitely warranted. "What the heck did you do to me?" I choked.

"You're in pain?"

"Yeah, I'm in pain!"

"Your arm still works, though!"

"You're right," I mumbled.

"It'll wear off," he said, rubbing the back of his neck. Another shock of pain raced through me. I clutched my stomach and glared up at him furiously. "Eventually...."

We heard voices from the hall, and Angela limped into the living room with Izzy helping her walk. Angela's weary expression seemed to light up when she saw us. "You're awake," she said, smiling. I winced when she hugged me, but smiled anyway. I think that was the first time she actually acted happy to see me.

"Angela," Liles started hesitantly.

"She's fine," I said weakly.

She sat down next to me, and Izzy leaned up against the arm of the couch.

"Do we have some Advil or something?" I asked.

"What's wrong?" Angela asked.

"That's really unwise," Liles replied.

"Again, what are we talking about?" Izzy asked.

Everyone started laughing.

"Seriously, guys," Angela started. "What are we doing? We can't just act like everything's back to normal."

"Things are going to be very different around here without Osscar," Izzy sighed.

"I miss him," Angela said quietly. "I never got to tell him just how much he meant to me, what a great brother he was." The guilt was almost more painful than my stomachache. I looked down. If I tried to tell them that Osscar was alive, where would I even start? What would I leave out? "I guess we'll just have to hope he dies in the most humane way possible," Angela continued with a sigh that I should have realized was exaggerated.

"I suppose so," Liles replied. "But the cruelty of the huntsmen knows no bounds."

"We'll never know," Izzy fretted, putting her head in her hands.

"He's not captured," I said at last, cringing.

"Ugh, finally!" Angela shouted, throwing her arms up. Izzy and Liles high-fived each other.

"Now, where is he?" Angela yelled, shaking my shoulders. I was stunned. "You—"

"You were talking in your sleep!" she laughed.

I looked around at everyone. None of them looked angry, but I was shaking. "Wha-what did I say?" I stammered. "You guys came into my room?"

"Nah, this was yesterday," Liles replied, "when you were passed out in here."

"You were, like, having a conversation with yourself," Angela explained.

"Osscar!?" Izzy mocked. "How could you!"

"That's suicide!" Angela joined in a similar mocking tone. They broke out in laughter, and I let out a small sigh of relief. I can't believe I said any of that, but at least I didn't go on about her father.

"So, where is he?" Angela asked again.

"You're not mad?"

"Oh, we're furious!" Izzy laughed.

"So, you planned to *guilt* me into admitting it?" I asked.

"And it worked!" Angela laughed evilly.

"I'm not doing this again," I said quietly. "We're not leaving."

"Come on, Chase!" Angela said, punching me gently in the shoulder. "What happened to freedom?"

I stood up. "No!" I snapped. "I'm exhausted, I'm sick, and, Angie, you got shot!"

"I have a remedy that can fix that bullet hole," Liles added. "Or kill you—one of the two."

The laughter carried on. "No!" I yelled again. "No more remedies, no more getting hurt, no more leaving." Angela pushed herself up to look me in the face. "I-I'm sorry. I know you miss your dad, but they *skin* shapeshifters." I searched my food-deprived mind for a metaphor and came up emptyhanded. "Like, an *animal* that gets... skinned."

"We aren't just running away again," she reassured me. "This will take some planning—a lot of planning, and it will give us plenty of time to recover both mentally and physically."

"But we need you to tell us where Osscar's headed," Liles continued.

"The base," I said reluctantly. "He said he has a plan, but he's going alone."

Everyone's spirits seem to deflate, like someone just dumped a gallon of water on each of their heads.

"We can't wait, then," Angela mumbled.

"We have to," I replied. "If we go at all, we go with your plan."

"You're right," she sighed, dejected. "How far could he get on his own in a week?"

"No clue," Liles replied. "That depends on whether or not he knows where he's going."

"It's gonna be hard to make a plan when there are this many 'what ifs,'" Izzy said, nervously twirling her hair around her finger.

I sat back down on the bench. None of this would be happening if I'd kept my mouth shut. Then again, how could I help it? I was asleep. I'm just now realizing how much trouble the whole sleep-talking thing could get me into later on.

"What would you prefer we say to my grandfather?" Liles asked.

The room went silent, and *I* sure wasn't going to say anything. To my limited understanding of our conversation, me and Alex had reached a truce. Or... something like that.

"We'll tell him the truth," Angela declared. "Maybe we can get him to train us."

Izzy looked shocked. "Have you seen Alex *teach*?" she shouted.

"He is pretty... forthright," Liles added. "If he decides he doesn't want you all going, he won't let you."

"Guys," I butted in. "If Alex thinks I told you all this, which I did, I'll get kicked out of the house again." There was a pause. I don't think anyone knew how to respond. I glanced down the hallway to make sure no one else was listening. "Me and Angie saw something weird the other night, and I can't get it out of my head," I whispered.

"Are you talking about that monster?" Angela asked.

"What monster?" Liles asked.

"It was a huge cat with pointed fangs," I replied, "like a saber-toothed tiger, but with glowing red eyes."

Liles and Izzy looked at each other, as if they were checking to make sure they both knew I was crazy.

"Well, *Smilodon* are very much extinct," Liles said awkwardly

"Smile-odon?" Izzy asked.

"Saber-toothed tigers, I mean," he replied, rolling his eyes.

"I saw it, too," Angela added. "I don't think it could've been anything else."

"I've never heard of an animal with glowing eyes," Izzy added.

"It's possible you guys just saw the effects of the *tapetum lucidum*," Liles started, "a reflective surface in the eyes of a good number of animals, including cats, that makes their eyes appear to glow in the dark."

"No, no," I replied. "They were glowing, *really* glowing. Like the headlights of a car, and bright red."

"Again, I saw it too," Angela murmured.

They didn't say anything else, but it was clear by their expressions that they still didn't believe us.

"Where are your grandparents?" Liles asked Izzy, changing the subject.

"They left," she replied.

"What?" Angela asked. "Where did they go?"

"I don't know," Izzy said. "They were talking to Alex outside last night, woke up early this morning, and left." She shrugged, looking a little bitter about the whole thing. Things were just getting worse. I had it in my head that we were being rounded up like cattle, and soon enough Alex was just going to mysteriously "disappear" too. Then, the huntsmen would come take us away. I had to say something. "Is nobody else finding any of this odd?"

"Any of what?" Angela asked.

"The adults," I replied. "They're clearly keeping secrets from us."

"They're always keeping secrets," she grumbled.

"Do I fit into the 'adult' category?" Liles asked.

"Depends, keeping secrets?" I asked.

"A few," he admitted, nodding.

"Then yes," I replied flatly.

"If we can't even trust each other, how can we possibly expect to be able to work as a team?" Angela asked. There was an intensely awkward pause. I avoided looking at anyone, especially Liles. I hadn't quite come up with a theory for his timely arrival after Chris's disappearance, but I knew something was off.

Liles broke the silence. "In my defense, I just met you people," he said, shrugging.

"You know, Liles," Angela started. "You aren't how I pictured you would be."

"I hope that's not a bad thing," he replied.

"It's not," she insisted. "I just assumed you would be like Osscar, you know, in a way?"

"I don't know what he's like anymore," Liles said, shaking his head. "But I know I'm not the same person I was six years ago."

"You seem nice," Izzy chimed in.

"Thank you," he said, smiling ruefully. "It's nice to get a fresh start, but, I'm sorry to say, if we'd met at the base, your impression of me would probably be very different."

"How come?" Angela asked. "If you don't mind me asking, of course."

"We're talking about a place where people get killed over chicken legs," Liles replied. "It was survival of the fittest."

"You said you were friends with the guy who did that?" Izzy asked. "What did you do?"

"Umm," he started with a sigh. "We shared that chicken leg."

"Man," Angela said quietly. "I definitely can't picture that..."

"Oh, really?" Liles asked, crossing his arms. "And why's that?"

"Don't get me wrong! You look the part, tall and athletic and such," she said. "But you say stuff like, I don't know, that eye thing you just told us about, *Tapetum luci*—something? What is that, Latin?"

"Angela!" Izzy chuckled.

"Hey, *fittest* can mean a multitude of things," Liles laughed. "Superior language actually helped my status. Not to mention, I was one of very few who could translate the only book in our cell."

"Is that the book you carry around?" Angela asked.

"Nah," he said, waving it off. "That's just a collection of old remedy formulas. The book I'm talking about was *The Shapeshifters Encyclopedia*, written in Elizabethan English."

Oh, where was I during this conversation? Rocking back and forth on the bench, holding my knees and trying not to throw up. In case you were wondering.

"I didn't even know that was a thing," Angela replied. "How'd you get it?"

"A girl I met had it on her when she was captured," Liles explained. "They didn't search her well, and she gave me the book for saving her life," he sighed. "I worked very hard to keep that bothersome thing from being stolen."

"What kind of stuff was in it?" Angela asked.

"A bit of everything, I suppose, half the book contained medical information," he replied. "A lot of the practices in it were outdated, but I learned about a wide range of shapeshifter ailments from that. The other half was useless—fictitious legends, purebred propaganda, terms we were already familiar with."

"Right, right," Angela said.

"I'm sorry to change the subject," Izzy interrupted. "But you guys should know—my grandparents didn't come back with anything."

"What!?" Angela shouted surprised. "Then what were they doing the whole time they were gone!?"

"I don't know that either," Izzy mumbled. "But we're completely out of food and shampoo."

"Seriously?" Angela asked. "What does Alex expect us to do?"

"He hasn't woken up yet," Izzy replied.

"Hang on," Liles said. "Who makes the money here? Who supports everyone?"

"Our families each pay for their own expenses," Izzy explained. "My grandparents, my brother, and I all live off my parents' retirement savings. They were fairly wealthy when they were alive."

"I'm sorry to hear about them," Liles replied. "Does the money belong to you and your brother now?"

You know what? I don't think anyone's told Liles about Malachi yet. Oh well, he'll figure it out eventually.

"They never wrote a will," Izzy continued, "and there was no trustee because they were shapeshifters. The money may have gone to us, but since I was underage, my grandparents sort of—" she rolled her eyes, "stepped in."

"So, there's no income stream?" Liles asked.

"No," Angela confirmed, shaking her head. "Dad sold our house shortly after my mom died, and we came to live here. We still have some money from the sale."

"I'm sorry to hear about your mother as well," Liles said. "How did my grandfather know your dad?"

"You know," Angela laughed, "that's kind of a funny story. Alex and my dad were supposedly really close friends, but I literally met him and Osscar the day we moved here."

"And my grandparents were actually her babysitters," Izzy added, gesturing to Angela. "When her dad told them he was moving here to save money, they sold our house and jumped on the bandwagon."

"I see," Liles said, nodding. "So, what about you?" He nudged me.

"Umm," I sighed.

"My dad took him in," Angela replied for me. "We pay for his expenses, too."

What "expenses"? The less than a tenth I contribute to the water bill?

"Yes, I have that much figured out," Liles replied. "I'm not sure I fully understand the whole contract thing, though?"

"We don't either, so..." I rolled my eyes.

Everyone went quiet.

"Well, I'm gonna go find something to drink," Izzy sighed after about a minute of silence, walking off toward the kitchen. "I think there's still some milk left in the fridge."

"Hey," Liles whispered to me, pointing to the glass of milk on the floor, "you gonna drink the rest of that?" I

shook my head violently. He picked it up. "Nope, we're out!" he called Izzy before taking a gulp from my glass.

"Hey!" Angela laughed.

"Survival of the fittest," Liles said, standing up. He headed down the hallway with the glass, most likely on his way to Osscar's new room that he'd temporarily taken over. I'd contemplated going back to bed myself. I couldn't seem to shake the tired feeling... but me and Angela were alone, and I didn't want to seem tactless.

"I'm not in denial," Angela started to me. "I know it's suspicious. This whole thing with my dad, with Dana and Henry coming home emptyhanded...." She just shook her head. I was afraid to say anything that would set her off, but I really hoped she was coming to the same conclusion I had. "I know we're being lied to." She crossed her arms.

I wanted to roll my eyes and say something sarcastic along the lines of *Oh, really! You don't say!* But after seeing how upset she looked, I decided to try and be a decent friend instead. I put my arm around her, pulling her close in a sorry attempt to comfort her.

"Um..., yeah. I know you're trying to make me feel better," she said awkwardly, throwing my arm off. "But you really don't have to console me. I can handle it." She paused

for a moment, scooting away from me. "Why is your heart beating so fast?"

Yeah, I'm a little out of practice when it comes to friendships. "Okay, well, I feel bad." I was ignoring the thing about my heartbeat. "Besides, you've had a bad week."

"So have you, though," she sighed, "I wish you'd eat. I know I can't make you."

We heard footsteps down the hall, too loud to be anyone but Alex. He walked into the room wearing a cut gray muscle shirt and a pair of pleated shorts. His gray hair was messed up, and his eyes were dark, most likely from lack of sleep. "Have you at least had anything to drink?" she asked me, ignoring Alex.

"Technically?" I replied, needing to think about the question. "Water at the hotel. Some milk, I guess?"

"You're going to kill yourself," she snapped. She looked at Alex and then at me with this evil glint in her eye, and I instantly knew what she was thinking. "*I*...can't make you," she started, "but...."

"Angie, no!" I pleaded quietly. She ignored me, turning back to Alex, who sat down in his chair with a newspaper he had tucked under his arm.

"Hey, Alex," Angela started with a very innocent-sounding voice.

"Angela!" I whispered.

"Chase hasn't eaten in days," she continued.

I covered my face with both hands, anger boiling up inside of me. "I'm fine."

"His heart rate is up and everything," Angela persisted, this time throwing in some false pity.

Alex looked up from his paper for a moment. "And what am I supposed to do about that?" He flipped the newspaper back up over his face.

"Huh," Angela mumbled, "that worked once. Almost five years ago, Osscar wouldn't eat anything but Twinkies for three days because I dared him to."

"Yeah, well, you're forgetting," I replied. "Nobody here really cares what's going on with me."

"What do you mean?" she asked. "Of course we—"

"I sleep on two rock-hard twin mattresses in the drafty back room," I started. "Eat whatever's left in the cabinet at the end of the day, and wear anything your dad or Osscar don't want anymore. I mean, I know you guys invite me to do stuff when you see me. But you don't *really* want me there." It definitely wasn't the ideal time to uncork two

years of bottled-up bitterness, and if it wasn't for my fasting, I probably never would have. "Like, Osscar's old room is right next to mine. You think I don't hear all the things you guys say about me behind my back?"

I swear, I wasn't looking for an explanation. I was just in the mood to complain. But, judging by her body language, I'd clearly made her uncomfortable. "I'm sorry," I sighed. "I didn't mean to go off like that, probably just—lack of calories or something."

"It's okay," she said quietly. I zipped up my jacket. What was I thinking?

"Liles!" Alex called, standing up. "I need your help with something."

Now what is he doing? I'd completely forgotten Alex was even in the room. I figured it was best to just head back to bed. Before I said anything else I'd later regret. I pulled my hood up over my head, starting toward the hall. I was accidentally blocked by Liles in the entry.

"Don't let Chase leave!" Alex yelled from the kitchen again.

Now my heart really *was* racing. Liles and I looked at each other, confused. "Umm, why did you need me?" Liles shouted back to the kitchen.

"Do you have a catheter in that bag?" Alex asked.

I about fainted. "A what?" I asked.

Angela got up, limped over to the front door, and leaned up against it. "Good luck!" she laughed at me. I was beginning to catch on.

"No, I don't," Liles said. "What's the problem?"

"Never mind," said Alex. "I found something."

I looked around for an exit, but every door was blocked. I heard Alex coming up from the kitchen; he had both hands behind his back. "Sit down," he snapped, gesturing to the bench. He had his usual indignant look on his face. I didn't know what to do, but found myself slowly lowering down onto the bench. He was holding a small glass of what looked like sparkling water. I didn't even know we bought stuff like that. "Drink this," he threatened, "and we won't have to make you."

"Grandfather?" Liles said. "This is premature. I'm looking into Chase's symptoms as we speak, so could we please not—"

"Shut up," Alex ordered, which stopped his fast talking. "What will it be?" He looked right at me.

"I really didn't mean for you to hear any of that," I said quietly to Alex. "I—"

"I don't care," he interrupted. "These are the same gestures of compassion I show my own grandkids. You wanted it, you got it."

"Grandfather—" Liles tried to intervene again.

"I said, shut up!" Alex was raising his voice. "We wouldn't want Chase to feel like he's being treated unfairly in the house we let him stay at for free."

Angela stepped away from the front door. She had to have figured out this was nothing but a power trip. "Alex, I'm sorry," she said. "Can we please just forget about this?"

"Last chance," he warned, ignoring her.

I took the glass and apprehensively drank what tasted like ginger ale. I set down the empty cup. Alex then re-vealed his other hand, which, as I had expected, contained absolutely nothing. "I hope you feel compensated," he de-rided, walking back to his chair.

Angela limped to the couch. She didn't look happy with the outcome of things, especially when she saw how angry everyone had become. She looked at Liles and me sympathetically, like she was saying sorry for starting anything in the first place. I wasn't in any more physical pain, but once again I was the focus of the room, with everyone staring at me while I got punished for not being

grateful for the undeserved privilege of getting to live in that crappy house with a bunch of people who couldn't give a flying foxtail about me. I dug my nails into the bench like a stress ball as the room fell into an awkward silence. I was probably still glaring at him, because after about three seconds, Alex looked up from his paper again. "Still have a problem?" he asked.

I wasn't going to take this. I jumped up from the bench and stormed down the hallway, slamming my bedroom door behind me.

17: ANGELA

Watching Chase run from the room, I couldn't have felt worse.

"He's sick, you know," Liles said, breaking the silence. "It's a remedy side effect. It hurts him to have calories. A lot, apparently."

I slumped down in my seat. "I feel terrible," I groaned. "How come no one ever tells me these things?"

"Well, it wasn't exactly your business," Liles grumbled.

"Yup," Alex said, standing up. He clearly felt absolved of any wrongdoing.

"Hey," I called. "Please wait, I need to talk to you." He slowly sat back down, gesturing for me to go on. "First, I want you to know that we know what the huntsmen do to us now. You don't have to hide it anymore."

"I'm sorry, I wish you didn't," Alex replied. "But it's probably best you know your enemy."

"Yeah," I sighed, "but that's not what I was going to ask. Chase and I saw this, like, monster that they were after. They wanted it pretty badly, and—this is gonna sound crazy—but it had glowing red eyes." Alex suddenly looked incredibly interested in the conversation. He leaned over with his arms on his knees to better hear me. "It was a big cat with long, pointed fangs," I continued. "And—"

"Did they catch it?" he asked impatiently.

"No," I replied. "It got away." He nodded slowly, lacing his fingers together. "Do you have any idea what it might have been?"

"Yes," Alex admitted after a minute. "But I've never seen one in person." Liles came and sat down on the couch next to me. If he was still irritated, I couldn't tell. "There

have been cases," Alex started with a sigh, "of shapeshifters who were able to shift into extinct species."

"How long ago?" Liles asked, sounding surprised. "I've never heard of anything like that."

"They became extremely valuable among huntsmen," Alex continued. "They were, and probably still are, the ultimate trophy."

"How can you tell which—" Liles tried to ask.

"How many times am I going to have to ask you to be quiet?" Alex growled. I was too engrossed in the subject to focus on how harsh he was being. "They were referred to as 'exotic shapeshifters,' once they had an extinct animal shift." He turned back to me. "And their primary characteristics were their glowing red eyes."

"How'd they get shifts like that?" I asked. "It's not possible."

"You're right," he replied. "You normally can only shift into animals still left in nature. But the old legends say that the shifters who had the unique ability to take the form of an extinct animal were in a position of great peril. Something so awful, their bodies searched desperately for anything that could save them. Their glowing red eyes serve as a symbol that they are reaching beyond the grave

to take the form of an animal no longer of this earth." That was the most I'd ever heard him speak. I took a moment to let that sink in. "But believe me when I say that's bull," he huffed. "The exotics don't last five minutes due to the odds being so stacked against 'em. Their stories don't get a chance to be told."

"That's horrible," I said quietly.

"It's a shame, too. Exotic status is impossibly hard to achieve," Alex ranted. "Even before the huntsmen, they were extremely rare."

"You've tried?" Liles asked.

"No," he snapped. "Nobody wants that. But it almost happened to me."

My eyes widened. "Almost?"

"*Happened* to you?" Liles asked.

Alex stood up. "Good thing it didn't," he said. "The exotics are a doomed class. That one that you saw probably isn't long for this world."

"But can't you hide it?" I asked.

"Hiding only works for so long," Alex replied, starting to leave. "It doesn't matter what kind of shapeshifter you are."

"Wait!" I called.

He turned around from the hall entry.

"Dana and Henry didn't come back with anything," I said. "What do you want us to do?"

He sighed, rubbing his hand across his face. "Just hang tight. I'll figure something out."

"Okay..." I mumbled.

Liles scoffed, muttering something under his breath. I made out a couple of curse words.

"What's the matter?"

"Really?" he asked, turning to me. "You can't see what he's trying to do?"

"No," I replied honestly.

"He's trying to dominate me," Liles said bitterly. "It's not going to work."

"Dominate you?" I asked.

"Trying to get me to submit to his authority," Liles continued. "Assimilate me into the house under his rule. It doesn't surprise me that you can't see it."

"I've always seen it..."

"Then why put up with it?" he asked.

"What choice do we have?"

Liles shrugged. "I don't know, but I don't blame Chase for wanting to leave this place so badly. From the look of things, he's let himself become the pack omega."

"You're talking about all of us like we're—"

"Animals?" he said. "It's true, but not because your shapeshifters. Even normal humans turn into animals when you lock them in a cage." I was at a loss for words. "Sorry, I only speak from experience." He raised his hands in surrender. "But the way I see it, it's not so different here from the base—a small space with scarce resources, lots of people, and no way out."

BANG!

Me and Liles looked at each other fearfully. He helped me up, and we both rushed over to the door window.

18: CHASE

I sat on my bedroom floor, leaning against the wall. I couldn't be on the bed. For some reason, it made me even more nauseous. I was irritated with everyone in the house, mainly Angela and Liles. Don't get me wrong, Alex was certainly on the list, but Liles was the one who poisoned me in the first place, and Angela only tried to make it worse.

I'd never admit that the ginger ale actually made me feel a tiny bit better. My heart rate was slowing too. I looked around the dark room. *How did I end up back here? How was being stuck in that room any different than sitting in a cell for the rest of my life?* There was nowhere to go, nothing to look forward to, and, either way, I was waiting alone to die.

I remember thinking at that moment that it didn't matter what they tried to convince me, this place would never be my home, these people would never be my family. Another shock of pain raced through me. I winced and tried to stand up, but something happened and the attempt caused one of the haphazard bones in my leg to move. "Ow!" I screamed, falling back down. "Ow! Ow! Ow!" I could get the bandage wraps off only so fast. This kind of thing rarely happens, but when it does, there's not much I can do. It's a bit like pulling a hamstring, but much more painful.

I took the bandages off my leg, trying to rehabilitate it. Which is kinda hard to describe. But basically, I'm squeezing and extending out my leg until it feels like the bone or whatever has moved back to a position where it won't hinder my ability to walk.

Yeah, it's just as weird as it sounds, but honestly, I can't guarantee anything I just wrote isn't complete baloney. It's funny, *after* I let him drive me out to the middle of nowhere and signed his subjugating paperwork, Chris ended up knowing about as much about Morph-Bone as I did. Jack-squat!

Some X-rays might be helpful, but, like I said earlier, no doctors.

"Who is that!?" I heard Izzy ask, from outside my closed door.

This can't be good. I wrapped the bandages back around my leg and stood up.

"Hey, Alex!" Angela shouted.

"What's going on?" I called, opening my door. I headed down the hall to the living room, where everyone was gathered around the diamond-shaped door-window looking out at the grass field.

"Oh, my gosh!" Izzy mumbled.

"How many?" I heard Liles ask nervously.

I pushed past them to get a glance at what everyone was gawking at. At first, it only looked like a couple of people, but it quickly changed to something from a horror movie. They were coming in a mass, armed with guns and

privately engineered sticks of heat and pain. The huntsmen had found us. *We're dead.*

"Wh-what do we do?" Angela stammered, stepping away from the window.

"Alex!" Izzy shouted again.

"No!" I snapped. "Don't call him!"

"What?"

It didn't matter what I said. Alex must have heard the commotion from down the hall because before I even noticed, he was behind us looking out. "Move!" he barked. We all backed away toward the hallway as he evaluated the situation.

"What do we do?" Izzy cried.

"Grab the emergency bags and shift into the fastest thing you've got," Alex replied quickly. "I want you all headed out the kitchen to the backyard. We'll run for the clearing in the woods."

I had no idea what he was talking about. No one told me about any "clearing in the woods," but that would have been nice to know about sooner! We froze at the mention of the emergency bags, looking and gesturing to each other, trying to pass off the blame like toddlers who'd just

broken something. "We lost those," Liles confessed on our behalf.

Alex turned sternly back to us. "Get your clothes, then. Now!"

Everything was in total disarray. There was no food to pack, barely any clothes, either. I ran back to my bedroom and began picking up any clothes I found on the floor and shoving them into my backpack. I didn't know what to do. I needed another plan, one that didn't involve following Alex into a potential trap. He could have been running us right into some kind of—

Wait a minute!

Angela had a busted-up leg! How was she *running* anywhere? I flung my backpack over my shoulder and was on my way back to the living room when Alex blocked my path. I tried to go the opposite direction when he shoved a small, black briefcase at me.

"What?" I asked, confused. I was forced to take it.

"Important paperwork," he replied, pointing to the case. "*Don't* lose that."

"Wait." He ignored me and walked into the living room. I followed him. Everyone else was still in the hall. "Alex, what about—"

He opened a drawer from the lamp side table in the living room, pulling out a matchbox filled with cigars and then walked right past me. My blood was boiling. This was the same crap I'd dealt with every day. It didn't matter that lives were at stake, he still refused to acknowledge me with anything but contempt.

I'd finally lost it.

"HEY!" I screamed. Alex froze, glaring at me with narrowed eyes. "I don't care how much you hate me!" I dropped the briefcase. "You can kick me out, yell at me, force me to drink things, wha-whatever! Later! Angela can't walk, and what do I do!?"

Angela came in from the hall, limping for the kitchen. She looked almost as angry as I was. Liles jumped out into the room as well, but as a lynx with his doctor's bag of remedies and a half-filled garbage bag of clothes tied to opposite sides of his body. The demands from the huntsmen outside became louder.

"Liles," Alex called, "have any sedatives in that bag?"

"Um, I have some huntsman darts," Liles replied. "I think they're some kind of modified Midazolam."

"Perfect," Alex said. "Get those out."

Liles nodded and started working to unfasten the garbage bag from his side.

Alex turned back to me. "You," he said, pointing, "you wanna live? Get that smartass look off your face, and go make sure Angela doesn't leave this house." That wasn't an inconsequential ultimatum. I didn't fully understand the plan, and I was still fuming, but I started toward the kitchen anyway. We were running out of time.

"Angie!" I called, stepping down into the room. She already had her hand on the back doorknob, looking agitated. "Don't open that!"

"Where are Alex and Liles?" she asked in a panic. "There's no way we can make it out of here, we have to go now!"

"We can't!" I insisted. "Just wait, please!"

BANG!

BANG!

The huntsmen were coming closer and closer. Angela swung the door open in defiance. What was I supposed to do? I didn't trust Alex in the slightest, but I didn't have a better idea. After the incident on the road, the last thing I wanted was to convince Angela that I only cared about myself by stopping her from leaving once again, but asking

wasn't working. So, I referred back to my directive. Maybe I'd gone into the job without an ounce of training, but over the years, whether I acknowledged it or not, "bodyguarding" was becoming intuitive. I quickly shifted into my wolf, blocking Angela as she approached the door.

"Are you for real?" she asked.

"You can barely walk!" I snapped. "Alex has a plan!"

"Oh, now you trust him? Chase, we're going to die!" She tried to move around me. I kept maneuvering in front of her. "Would you move!" she yelled. "I'm going—"

"You're not going anywhere," I growled.

Angela looked shocked. "Is that so?" she asked, almost laughing. "Watch me."

She reached over me and grabbed the doorknob. I tried to push her away from it with my front paws and accidently knocked her to the ground. "I'm sorry!" I felt horrible, but I figured for a second that maybe I'd done the right thing. I was foolish enough to think Angela wouldn't be able to get up quickly with her injured leg.

"Oh, you will never change!" she shouted from ground. She shifted into her white wolf, standing now despite her injury, with one back leg lifted off the ground. "Get away from the—"

BANG!

BANG!

BANG!

Angela froze after each gunshot. She stopped fighting with me and leapt with three legs up the step into the living room, headed for the front door.

I ran after her, blocking her escape path once again.

"You'll kill both of us!" I yelled.

"No, the huntsmen will!" she countered.

"Chase!" Izzy called from the kitchen. Her voice was much smaller than usual. She had to be in her rabbit form. "Come on!"

"Get her to shift!" Liles yelled from behind Angela. "Something smaller!"

It was about time!

"You need to shift into—!" I tried to say before Angela grabbed hold of my ear, pulling it toward her.

That's not civilized behavior at all, by the way! Two human-born shapeshifters getting into a physical fight is just as frowned upon as two normal humans going at it. However, that's never seemed to stop Angela when she's mad.

"Oww, oww, oww!" I said, shaking my head. She wasn't trying to hurt me, just direct me away from the door. It only hurt because I wouldn't budge.

"Not helping!" Liles shouted.

"Give me that thing!" Alex snapped. "You can't aim it with paws!"

Soon after that demand came a whistling noise. Next thing I knew, Angela was lying unconscious on the floor, and Alex was holding a blow gun.

"Where'd you get that!?" I asked.

"We can't carry her in this form!" Liles yelled back at Alex. "We should have waited!"

"Waited?" I scoffed. "The huntsmen are—"

BANG!

There was a glass-shattering noise from the other room, and several bullets flew through the front door, leaving some good-sized holes in the hallway entry. The house was mostly brick, so there was only a minimal chance of something shooting through the walls and killing one of us, but we all got down anyway.

"We're gonna have to leave her now!" Liles snapped.

"NO!" I yelled.

Alex picked Angela up and threw her over his shoulders, shifting into some kind of big, black horse in the process. The shift was so big it almost finished off our prehistoric couch and appeared even scarier with Angela's unconscious canine body cloaked over it.

"Go!" Alex's thundering voice yelled. "Wait! Chase, grab that!" I looked down at the black briefcase I dropped earlier, leaned down, and grabbed its handle between my teeth.

BOOM! The door fell down, and they in flooded like an angry mob.

"SHIFTERS!"

"WE GOTCHA NOW!"

"THERE!"

I ran for the kitchen and burst out the back door with Izzy and Liles. Izzy was her jackrabbit and unable to take much with her besides a locket with a chain just small enough not to slip right off her neck. Liles, on the other hand, had taken quite a few things, bound by the two large bags tied to his side with twine and a belt.

BANG!

BANG!

BANG!

We all bounded on four legs through the backyard with Alex well ahead of us, despite the fact that he was carrying Angela. The huntsmen were wrecking the house by then. I figured that the sounds of people yelling and windows shattering would be the clearest indicator of their intrusion, but I could feel the heat on my back and see the light reflecting everywhere. The house was on fire.

We all stopped and turned to see the smoke darkening the windows, the flames engulfing the back door. I can't say I was all that heartbroken, but it *was* a bit of a shock. "Stop gawking!" Alex barked.

We sped up as we neared the clearing in the woods. The huntsmen hadn't caught on to us yet, and it was looking like we may have been able to stay together, but much to our inconvenience, there was a sleek, navy blue sedan blocking our only path of escape. And lo and behold, someone was in it.

Alex barely paused in front of the car and didn't hesitate to jump right over it, denting the top and almost dropping Angela. The rest of us were stopped when someone climbed out of the driver's seat onto the top of the car. This kid definitely didn't look like a huntsman. He had brown hair, wore a bright orange t-shirt and denim shorts,

and there wasn't a piece of fur or leather on him. He was standing on the hood of the car, pointing a small rifle at us and shaking like a leaf.

"Move!" Liles shouted at him.

"No!" the kid yelled. He looked no older than thirteen. You'd think he would be an easy opponent for the three of us to take down, but he still had a gun.

"Who are you?" Izzy asked.

"Shut up!" the kid shouted. The anger in his voice surprised me. He had tears in his eyes and wouldn't stop trembling.

"Are you alright?" Liles asked. He must have noticed it too.

"I said, shut up!" he cried. "I was there when you killed him! I followed your inhuman paw prints! And now, you're gonna pay for what you did!" We all froze when the kid worked the lever, cocking his weapon. That little speech, judging by the way he said it, was clearly rehearsed.

"Wait!" I shouted. "There's a misunderstanding!"

"No, there's not!" His voice broke sharply. "You killed my dad!"

"*We* killed your dad?" Liles shouted, confused.

"He did!" the kid sobbed, pointing the gun down at me.

"I—I didn't..."

"You and your girlfriend!" the kid went on. "You murdered him on the dirt road to town!"

"You killed someone?" Liles said, turning to me.

"He tried to kill us!" I stammered.

"My father would never kill anyone!" he cried. Those words surprised me. Huntsmen killed all the time, but this kid said those words so angrily and wholeheartedly. I doubted he knew he was lying.

"I watched him!" I snapped.

"You're a liar!"

I could hear the huntsmen coming around the house, shooting and yelling victoriously like an angry mob. They must have realized by now that we'd make a run for it, but they didn't appear to have figured out where to yet.

The kid looked horrified at the group of people coming around the house and subconsciously lowered his weapon. This was our only chance. I jumped up on the car and tackled him to the ground, giving Liles and Izzy a chance to get around.

BANG!

BANG!

I got up weakly, shaking my head. I looked over at the kid. He was laying on his side next to me, unconscious.

BANG!

I picked Alex's briefcase up with my teeth and started over the car again. That's when I heard one of the huntsmen yell in the distance.

"THIS WAY! ONE OF 'EM'S DOWN!"

My heart sank. The kid wasn't with the huntsmen, and if he was, then the group chasing us didn't know it. While I could tell by his actions that he wasn't a shifter, those cold-hearted predators wouldn't hesitate to shoot a sleeping target.

Oh, I'm not one to play the hero, and the kid was still a human being. Those are hard to drag around! I looked around in a panic, trying to figure out what to do with the briefcase. Finally, I noticed the open sunroof.

I threw the case in, jumped back over the car, grabbed the kid by the shirt, and dragged him around to the passenger side of the car with my teeth, all while dodging the bullets being fired by the only huntsman who figured out where we were. No one else in the horde listened to a

word. They were screaming and still running around like chickens with their heads cut off.

Now, in normal circumstances, a car would be my last resort, but the huntsmen were too close. I couldn't outrun them. I put my front paws up on the car and pulled at the door handle with my teeth.

LOCKED!

It had started to rain, and the windshield was slick as ice, but I eventually got back up on the roof. This was probably one of the most ill-thought-out plans I'd ever attempted. I jumped down through the sunroof, unlocked the passenger door and dragged the kid up into the seat. I'd never driven before, but I know a bit about car mechanics, and even more about learning on the job. I got into the driver's seat and shifted back into my human form. Luckily there was a blanket in the car. I wrapped it around myself before pulling the gearshift into reverse and slamming on the gas.

The car shot backward into a tree and the alarm went off. Things were already off to a great start!

BEEP, BEEP, BEEP, BEEP…

All the huntsmen who hadn't been paying attention before knew exactly where I was now.

"THERE!" one of them announced.

I pushed the gearshift back up and turned the car so fast a spray of mud shot out at the approaching killers. I hit the gas again, and the car went shooting through the clearing in the woods at about a hundred miles an hour, so fast the poor kid in the passenger's seat slammed into the glove box.

BANG! A bullet flew into the car and put a nice big hole through the windshield, just missing my head. I started swerving around to try and throw off their aim, but when the next small projectile took out the rearview mirror I was using to watch the approaching mob, I found myself shrinking lower in my seat than the unconscious kid next to me. They could actually aim!

I heard another scream from outside and looked out the window at a trail of huge hoof-prints leading left. I quickly turned the car again and another bullet zoomed past my face. Goodbye, passenger-side mirror.

For a moment, I thought maybe this was all just a really bad dream. What were the chances of the huntsmen casually stumbling upon our house, which was located three miles of switchgrass beyond the sticks? Could they have

really been wandering around that field since we fought them?

I snapped back to reality when the windshield took its third hit, and no sooner did I make another turn when I saw something flash across the road. A large black horse, no longer carrying a white wolf on its back, and a lynx racing behind it.

"Alex!" I yelled, rolling down the window. The horse kept on down the road. It was almost faster than my now busted-up car, but the lynx turned around.

"Hey!" Liles called, running up to me.

I rolled down one of the broken windows in the back, shattering it completely. Liles jumped through the window frame into the back seat, all his bags still tied to him.

"Izzy went west!" he shouted. "Alex threw Angela when the huntsmen started gaining!" He paused to catch his breath. "I didn't see where she went."

"Then where is Alex going?" I asked.

"I—I don't know," he replied, shaking his head. There was nothing but silence as I drove down the road like a maniac, looking for any sign of the girls. "Who's that?" Liles asked. I looked down at the kid on the floor of the

passenger seat. "Is that the kid who tried to shoot us? Why'd you bring him!?"

"He's not with the huntsmen!" I shouted back. "They would have killed him!"

"So, he's a shifter?" he retorted.

"No," I snapped. I didn't have the energy to keep arguing. "I don't think so."

"Then why did you—?" Liles went mute when I jerked the car and he nearly crashed into the floor. I could still hear the mob. We weren't in shooting range any more, but I was worried it would only be a matter of time before they got their own car. It had been almost an hour, and It seemed like I was passing the same trees over and over with no sign of Angela or the others. I was starting to panic again. Apparently, it was obvious, judging by what Liles said next. "Hey, are you okay?" I didn't respond. I was switching my view between broken windows and mirrors. Not a paw print, not a trail, not a trace. "Well, we can't keep driving around through this clearing, we've scoured the whole thing," he said. "We're going to need to find a place to hide."

He was obviously getting frustrated. "Are you even listening?"

"No, I'm not!" I shouted, exasperated. He let me talk. "The girls are still out here. And after what you told us, dead or alive, I'm taking them with me."

I wasn't being completely straight with Liles in that moment, I knew good and well that I wouldn't be going anywhere if something had happened to Angela, and that was probably what was shaking me to the core. It was like I was running away with my body while my soul was still outside, lost and vulnerable. Let me clarify: that was not in any way some kind of lovey-dovey analogy. If you haven't already figured this out, that creepy contract between us and her father has consequences.

"I respect that," Liles said, nodding. "But I ask that you consider the possibility that Angela may not have regained consciousness soon enough to make it this far. I recommend you head back toward the house."

"Okay," I replied, turning the car.

After another hour or so heading in the opposite direction, still nothing. Liles gave me some of the clothes that he brought to put on, which made me feel better for about five seconds, before I started officially losing it. I stopped the car, laying my head down on the steering wheel. At that point, there was no sign of the huntsmen

either, which didn't make me feel any better. What if they were still chasing Alex and the girls? What if they'd already captured everyone, and we just had no idea? Angela could have been bleeding to death in the woods for all I knew. She had an injured leg. How far could she get on her own without being shot, if she even woke up?

I was losing all composure. My mind went back to the attack on the road, the petrifying creature, the man I killed. Those memories began to combine with my current location into some kind of nostalgic nightmare. Car, creature, murder....

June 2014

BANG

"ETHELIA!"

Something rushed over me that I hadn't felt in years, a cold and formidable sensation following what I can only describe as heartache. When I looked up from the steering wheel, Liles about had a heart attack. He yelled at the top of his lungs, and I snapped out of it. His shriek made me jump. "What?" I said. He was staring right at me through

the broken and dangling rearview mirror with frightened eyes. "What's going on?" I asked, looking back at him irritably.

He took a deep breath. "It was you!" he shouted, looking both shocked and confused.

"What was me?" I returned with equal confusion.

"The shapeshifter you and Angela were rambling on about!" Liles continued. "It was you!"

"What are you even talking about!?" I snapped angrily. "What did I do!?"

"You had—" he stammered. "Your eyes started glowing!" I looked at myself in the broken mirror and didn't see anything wrong. "Not anymore, stupid!"

"Glowing?"

"Glowing red!" he claimed. "Like that creature you told us about!"

"Like the cat thing!?" I asked, frightened.

"YES!" he yelled. "That thing! The exotic!"

"The what?" I replied.

"You mean you don't know?"

"No..." I was out of breath from screaming.

"So, you're telling me that you didn't just lie and make up some 'creature' to cover up your own undisclosed

identity? Because, your eyes were *literally* glowing like flashlights!"

"I didn't lie!" I replied. "I *swear* it wasn't me. You can ask Angela. We were both there with the cat, it was huge, had red eyes, and it was killing people!"

"Then there are two exotics, and one of them is *you*," Liles insisted.

"Maybe you're just seeing things."

"Listen to me, if the huntsmen find out, they are going to kill you," Liles asserted. "You can't tell *anyone* about this."

"Oh, so they're not trying to kill me right now?" I asked sarcastically, gesturing to the bullet holes in the windshield.

"They'll try harder!" Liles returned. "Alex said the huntsmen stop at nothing to find the exotics. They'd never leave you alone."

"Just because my eyes turned colors?"

"It means more than that!" he shouted. "Exotics can shift into extinct animals. That's why they want them, what were you about to—"

"Please, stop," I begged, still driving further down the road.

I'm sure many of you are wondering what the lead-up for this break-neck plot twist was, and honestly, I've got nothing. This, like so many other things, was news to me. Well, duh. Of course I'd noticed the red vision before, not recently, but I'd never thought much of it apart from the fact that it was probably part of my condition.

"Can you just promise to keep this between us?" I asked.

"I can," he replied. "However, I'm not sure it's in your best interest to hide this information from the girls. Unless, of course, you feel for some reason they can't be trusted."

"Do you promise, or not?"

"I promise," he sighed. "But I hope you know what you're doing. Omitting the truth is still lying."

What? Old habits die hard. I'm working on it, okay?

"Something must have happened for you to gain an exotic shift," Liles said. "And from what Alex said, getting frustrated in a car wouldn't do it. How long have you been able to do that?"

I took a deep breath. The "event" that I must have gained the "exotic" shift from is hard to talk about, and there's a lot I still don't know. I may have been able to trust Liles, but I wanted Angela to be the first to know what

happened "that night" four or five years ago. It's just that I knew she'd give me honest advice. Whether it was what I wanted to hear or not.

19: CHASE

"Stop!" I heard Liles shout from the back. I looked up at the road, slamming on the brakes. There was a white wolf standing on three legs only a few feet from the car. She had a nervous glint in her eye, like she was about to bolt back into the woods, but I could feel all of the panic drain from my body when I saw her.

"Wait!" I called, opening my door. Angela looked at me, and her big fluffy tail started wagging slightly. She ran up to the car. "I'm glad you're okay," I panted.

Angela was a mess. Her fur was drenched from the rain and stained brown with mud. She didn't seem nearly as happy to see me, but that's to be expected.

Izzy was back in her human form, wearing a dirty tracksuit I'd never seen before. She walked past me coldly, hopping into the back seat of the car with Liles and slamming the door behind her. That was less expected.

Angela was still looking around the woods. I could only assume she noticed we were still missing people. "Alex'll be able to find us," I said. "Don't worry."

She nodded, trudging past me to the car. She jumped through the broken window into the back with the others.

Not that my feelings mattered. But seriously? No *"Oh! Chase, thank goodness you're okay!"* or *"I'm glad to see you're still alive!"* Anything but the silent indifference I was given.

I got back into the driver's seat and shut the door. I didn't shut it very hard, but hard enough to shatter the rest of the windshield. The shards of glass fell loudly into my lap and onto the kid on the floor of the passenger's seat. I sighed, pushing the gearshift up.

"Who's that?" Angela asked nervously, peering up over the seat.

I looked at the kid. He was still unconscious, but breathing.

"I dunno," I said, rolling my eyes.

I turned the car around and drove through the clearing and out of the woods, onto the unfamiliar road. I glanced up at the dangling rearview mirror. I didn't realize that Angela was staring at it from the back. I looked away quickly when we locked eyes in the reflection.

"So, where exactly are we going?" Liles asked.

"Anywhere?" I replied. "Name a place, and we'll head there. Unless it's a hotel."

"Inconvenient parameters, considering we need someplace to stay," he sighed.

I checked the mirror again. The girls were sitting at opposite ends of the back seat, leaning toward their respective doors with Liles in the middle. Something must have happened in the woods. They both looked furious. I drove straight down the road for a while, not taking any turns since no one had a single suggestion.

"Where do you think Al—my grandfather went?" Liles asked awkwardly. I don't know what he was keeping to himself, but it sounded to me like Liles wasn't all that sure what Alex was to him.

"Umm," I started, "I think he'll come find us when he wants to."

"What?" Angela snapped. "You can't possibly expect us to believe that he wanted us to leave him here?"

"Why not?" I asked bitterly, looking back up at the broken mirror. "It's not like he explains half the stuff he normally asks us to do. I mean, why'd you guys clean out the storage room?" I held my tongue from there, continuing the list in my head. *Why didn't he tell us where Chris went?*

"Are you seriously going to leave him?" Angela asked. "You're that angry?"

Yes. "No, but I'm suspicious, okay? We don't need him anyway."

"Oh, come on," she said. "None of us are exactly equipped to protect the group all by ourselves."

That comment felt more like a personal attack than anything. I glared at her in the mirror one last time, speeding up.

"Would you two quit bickering?" Liles asked. "This doesn't get us anywhere."

"We aren't going anywhere!" I yelled. "Someone tell me where to go!"

I slammed on the brakes, and everything in the car jolted forward. Then I heard someone beside me moan.

"Ouch...."

I looked down at the floor of the passenger seat, and the kid was rubbing his head. He opened one eye to look at me and—

"AHHHHH!!"

He screamed in terror, trying desperately to open the door that was apparently stuck shut. He jumped for the window, and I pulled him back down.

"Hey!" I yelled. The kid stared at me, fear gleaming in his deep blue eyes. "We aren't going to hurt you!" I tried to assure him. "Please, don't yell, you'll attract some bad people."

His watering eyes darted around the car, frantically assessing his situation. He had a tight grip on the handle of the car door. "You killed my dad!" he wailed at last. "Let me out!" I sped down the road, so he couldn't jump out if he got the door open. It was well past midnight in the middle of nowhere. I couldn't just let him fend for himself.

"You killed his dad!?" Angela asked.

"No!" I yelled. "I mean—well..."

The kid cried, grabbing the black briefcase off the ground. I turned to him at just the wrong moment to get smacked in the face with it. The vehicle swerved around rapidly, spinning down the dirt road like a flipped beetle. The whole car went to chaos as I recovered from the hit.

The kid took hold of the steering wheel and pulled it toward him. "Chase, we're drifting off the road!" Angela shouted. I kicked him back, trying to regain control.

"Get off!" he cried, pushing my foot back.

"*AHHHHH!!!!*" Everyone in the back seat screamed as the car swerved over to the edge of a frightfully large ditch.

"Get him off the wheel!" I yelled.

Me and the kid were caught in a *VERY* dangerous game of tug of war at that point. I don't think he could see what he was doing, considering his back was to the fatal ditch. Angela jumped over Liles and grabbed the kid's shirt with her teeth, pulling him into the back seat.

I straightened out the car, violently rubbing my head where he hit me with the case. "I'm really starting to question why I brought you," I groaned.

"I will ask again, why *did* you bring him?" Liles demanded.

Angela had the kid pinned against the back of my seat with her paws.

"The huntsmen would have killed him," I replied, still rubbing my head. "They thought he was with us."

"I'm not with you!" the kid yelled from the back. He tried to pry Angela's paws off his shoulders, but she would only reposition them. "Let me go!"

"Sorry to break it to ya," I grumbled, "but you're stuck with us until we find a way to get you home."

"No!" he cried, struggling. "You—"

"Killed your father!" I yelled. "I know, I know!"

"So you admit it!" the kid sobbed.

I was overwhelmed with pain and eventually overcome by hysteria. "*Fine!*" I screamed. "I ADMIT IT! I KILLED SOMEONE!"

The whole car went silent.

"You killed someone..." Angela said quietly.

"Yes," I sighed.

"Like, on accident?" she asked.

"No," I replied.

"Murderer!" the kid screamed.

"It was self-defense!" I snapped.

"Chase, did you have to?" Angela asked.

"Yes," I said.

"Promise?" she checked.

"I promise," I replied, looking back at her. I truly believe I did. I wasn't sure at first.

"You're a liar!" the kid shouted.

"He isn't lying," Angela growled in his face.

"Get off me!" he yelled at Angela, still sobbing. "You were with them, too!"

"Them?" I asked.

"Those people you were with!" the kid screamed. "You guys shot him two nights ago!"

I tried my best to remember what exactly happened the other night on the road. Oh man, how I didn't want to...

"You shot someone?" Liles asked, confused.

"W-wait a minute," I stammered, stopping the car. "Was your dad a park officer?"

"Yeah," the kid sobbed. "And now—"

"I'm so sorry," I butted in, sighing with relief. "But you have to believe me, I *didn't* kill your father."

"But you said—" he started again.

"I know, but there's a huge misunderstanding here!" I yelled. "I *did* kill someone, but I didn't shoot them, I bit them in the neck."

"That explains some things," Angela mumbled.

"You pierced his jugular?" Liles asked.

"No," I snapped. "I just said, I bit him in the neck."

"Oh, if I had palms right now," Liles mumbled. "One of them would be smacked against my face." Apparently, he felt pretty stupid.

"Why were you there then!?" the kid yelled. "You—"

"Look, please listen, those people that killed your father... They were trying to kill us, too."

"What about the big cat?" he asked between heavy breaths. He'd clearly exhausted himself, and given up trying to fight Angela.

"We don't know them," Angela said. "But they were a shapeshifter too."

"How do you know about shapeshifters?" I asked him. "You had to have known before the incident or you wouldn't have recognized me as the wolf."

"My dad told me about them," the kid sniffled. "He said they protect the forests from evil spirits."

The whole car laughed a little.

"Sorry," I said, biting my tongue. "We mostly run around trying not to die ourselves."

The kid went quiet for a second. "So, can I get off of you now?" Angela asked. He still looked confused and a little shaken, but nodded. She removed her paws, letting him get up into a seat.

"So," he started more calmly, "the people with the guns?"

"We call 'em huntsmen," I replied.

"They want to make us into transmutable jackets," Liles continued for me.

The girls didn't find his truism very funny. Then again, even if Izzy had she wouldn't have laughed. She didn't make a sound the whole trip.

"I'm sorry I accused you," the kid said, sitting up next to Liles. Examining the vehicle's interior more closely, his eyes progressively widened with alarm. "What happened to my mom's car!?"

"Sorry, it has a few dents now," I replied.

"A few dents!?" the kid shouted. "The windshield's missing! There's bullet holes in the seats!"

"It adds character," Liles laughed.

That sounded a lot like something Osscar would have said, so much so that it made me a little sad. Not that he and I were friends or anything, but if I could see past my feelings about our last conversation on the road, I might have felt bad for him. I could tell he didn't want to be out there by himself any more than I did. Then again, that's what he gets for lying. (Still mad, if you couldn't tell.)

"Wait, where are you guys going?" the kid asked, rubbing his eyes.

"No idea," I started. "By the way, what's your name?"

"Aspen," he sniffled.

"Oh, that's nice," Angela added.

"Nice to meet ya, Aspen," I said. "I'm Chase, the wolf is Angela, the cat is Liles, and that's Izzy."

"Where's my gun?" Aspen asked.

"Oh, yeah, we left that," I replied. "We don't need any more guns to worry about."

"Hey, Chase?" Angela asked.

"Yeah?"

"How about we go find some food?"

"At two in the morning?" Liles asked, looking over at the digital clock on the dashboard.

"Hey, that's the first direction I've gotten all day. I'll take it," I said, turning left onto a slightly smoother road.

"So, you're *all* shapeshifters?" Aspen asked.

"Yup," I replied casually.

"My dad would've loved to meet you guys," he said, looking down sadly.

A full spectacle of bright headlights and reflective barrier delineators quickly came into view. We were beginning to merge onto a three-lane road. My whole body tensed up. I barely knew how to drive with one lane and no one else around!

"We may not have to wait long to meet him," Liles said. "Chase, please don't crash into anyone."

"Trying not to," I replied.

"Hey, Aspen?" Angela asked. "Is there a radio in this thing?"

"I think so," he replied.

"Seriously?" I asked.

"Music helps," Angela insisted. "Trust me."

Aspen crawled back up into the passenger seat and turned on the radio. A country jingle filled the car.

"What else is there?" Angela asked. He adjusted the radio again by twisting a few knobs. The other channels

were only static. "Go back to the working station," she said, pointing.

Aspen turned the radio knob in the opposite direction, and the static flipped back and forth between channels. It was starting to get obnoxious. I felt like I was about to have an anxiety attack. "Stop distracting me!" I yelled, "I'm trying to keep the car straight."

Truly, I wasn't as concerned with the car, but it made for a good excuse. I was upset and trying to keep from biting people's heads off, metaphorically speaking, of course. I may not have felt the hunger, but my ability to keep a level head was clearly affected by low blood sugar.

"There's no need to stress," Liles said. "Your body can't afford to anyway, and we're in far more trouble if you black out at the wheel than if you miss a turn."

Aspen turned the radio back to the country jingle and sat back down. "Thanks," I mumbled, not so sincerely.

"Feel any more relaxed?" Angela asked.

"No."

"Chase?" Aspen asked. "Why do you wear those bandages?"

"Alright, that's really... not helpful," I said, taking a slight right onto an exit ramp. Liles started stamping his

paws on the seat to the country rhythm, and, in response to this, Angela barked whenever it reached a high note. "Please, stop!" I begged. Aspen started clapping to the beat, and, just like that, the car was a big musical barn. "Okay, you said look for food!" I snapped, trying to disrupt their rhythm. "What do you guys want?"

"I don't care," Angela said. "You pick."

I suddenly felt bad for every time I ever said that to my parents.

"We can't go in anywhere looking like this," Liles reminded us.

I glanced in the broken rearview mirror at Liles and Angela. We really couldn't walk into a restaurant with two apex predators, but I was already dreading having to relay everyone's order to some poor drive-through worker over all this noise. "Fine," I said, "but when we go through the drive up, stay low."

Aspen seemed to be finding every bit of this interesting. "Why can't you guys just turn back into humans now?" he asked.

Angela sort of grumbled like she wasn't sure how to answer. "Shifters don't keep their clothes," I replied.

"Oh," Aspen said, "but I saw you as a wolf with those bandages on?"

I looked down at my arms. "Well, they're designed to shrink and expand."

"Why do—" he started again.

Angela nudged him. "Chase is irritable right now," she laughed. "You can ask me questions."

"I don't mean to backseat drive," Liles said, "but do you have any idea where we're going?"

"Not really," I replied. "I told you, I'm not from here."

"Well, then I should inform you," he continued, "there are no fast food restaurants located off any of the rural roads you're about to drive us onto."

"Okay, let's just go to the store and pick up some clothes," Angela suggested. "We can get food while we're there."

"That may have been an acceptable idea," Liles replied, "but need I remind you, it's past midnight."

HONK!

"HEY, HOW 'BOUT A TURN SIGNAL?" someone outside the car shouted.

I was shaking so much after that, it was a miracle we didn't get into an accident. I gulped, tightening my grip on the wheel.

"Yeah, you need to turn that on when you switch lanes, too," Aspen reminded me.

"How about a convenience store then?" Angela sighed.

"I've never known those to have clothes," Liles argued.

"You guys really don't have a plan, do you?" Aspen asked quietly.

"No," I replied, trying to calm down.

"We did, though," Angela added.

I hit a stop light. "What plan?" I asked.

"You're referring to the half-baked one about infiltrating the base?" Liles asked.

"Yeah," Angela replied, "but part of that plan was taking time to heal."

I looked in the rearview mirror at Izzy, who was still facing her door, not saying a word.

"Yeah, that's out the window," I sighed.

"New plan then!" Aspen declared, standing up on his knees on the passenger seat.

"Get down!" I ordered.

"Oh, calm down," Angela laughed at my frustration. "You're not going to wreck the car."

"He better not," Liles said. "We may have to sleep in here tonight."

"It's looking like that," I agreed. "It's really, really late."

"Or really early," Liles shrugged, "depending how you look at things."

I was so short-fused, all I remember thinking was *Does he just have to have the last word?*

"I totally hate this," Angela grunted. "We're always stuck in limbo."

"We're homeless," I said. "Our house *literally* caught fire. So, we're going to have to figure something out."

"Darn," she mumbled, dropping her wolf head onto the seat.

Aspen looked around at us like we were all stupid. "Just go camp out somewhere?"

"If only it were that easy," I replied. "The huntsmen are everywhere."

"They'll find us *anywhere* eventually," Angela argued, lifting up her head. "Aspen gave us a plan. Let's just try it?"

"Fine, and where do you suggest we go to buy tents?" I asked.

That's when I realized I didn't have my wallet. I took one hand off the steering wheel and gave myself a quick pat down. It was definitely gone. Of course I didn't have it, I hadn't seen it since the hotel, and these were Liles' clothes.

I was about to bring up the very unfortunate fact that we had no money when Aspen finally said something that didn't just stress me out. "No need. My dad always kept camping gear in both of our cars in case of emergency, so there should be some in the back."

Everyone seemed to perk up. "Great! We have a plan," Angela said cheerfully.

As happy as I was to know we wouldn't have to sleep in that car for God-only-knew-how-long, I could feel my fatigue coming back. Maybe I should have tag-teamed with someone in the back instead of trying to do all the driving myself. I turned onto the highway and noticed a bright green sign, indicating that we were headed toward Louisiana.

"Are we leaving the state?" Angela asked.

"I guess so," I replied. "I don't know what to expect, to be honest. I'm sure there are more huntsmen than just the ones in Mississippi."

"You have no idea," Liles added. "This isn't going to save us any trouble."

I glanced up at the mirror to see how Angela was feeling. She looked a little dejected. I couldn't blame her—she would be leaving both Osscar and her father behind. "Angie?" She looked up at the mirror. "We won't leave if you don't want to."

"No," she sighed, rolling her eyes. "I don't wanna try and bust up a huntsman base right now." She glanced down at her injured leg. "Not like I could."

"Izzy, your grandparents are here," I reminded her. "What do you think?"

Izzy sat up. "I don't care," she muttered. "What else is there to do? Go back to the burning house and look for Alex?"

"It's decided, then," I declared, flipping on the turn signal. "I don't know how I'm staying awake though."

Aspen didn't provide a vote, but it didn't matter. There was no way I was turning around, all the way across that cursed road where I almost got killed. The ride to Louisiana was about three hours. I'm sure it could have been shorter, but I was driving well under the speed limit. While I didn't get pulled over, there were a couple close

calls where someone would honk at me for breaking a traffic law, and I would have to take a completely different route in case a cop was watching.

"We should look for a trailer park," Aspen said, reaching into his back pocket.

"Know where one of those might be?" I asked sarcastically as I pulled over into an alley.

"Not yet," he replied, pulling out a flat, rectangular smartphone. Everyone in the car leaned forward to look at it.

Aspen glared at them oddly, scooting closer to his door. I glanced over at it quickly, afraid to look away from the road for too long. "You guys not have phones or something?" he asked, unlocking the device by touching his finger to the base of it.

"Wow," Angela whispered, staring at the small, glowing piece of technology.

"Nah," I replied. "We live somewhat off the grid."

"That sucks," Aspen said, clicking the search icon in the corner of the phone. "You guys can play with it once I find us a place to stay." Everyone was practically hovering over him except for Izzy. I still couldn't figure out what her

deal was. "There's a trailer park two point five miles from here," he informed us, swiping his finger across the screen.

"Great," I said quickly. "How do we get there?"

He played around for another minute and then placed it on the dashboard. "In a quarter of a mile, turn right," the phone blurted out in a robotic female voice. Everyone, including Izzy, stared at the tiny rectangular box in bewilderment.

"That's so neat!" Angela said, smiling.

"Yeah," I agreed. "Anything that can give me directions without consulting you guys is epic."

Everyone started laughing again. Aspen seemed super proud of himself, like he'd just saved the day. I looked over at him, and he smiled slightly. "You guys are so cool," he said. "I'm really sorry I tried to shoot you."

Wow, I thought, *he was quick to bury the hatchet*. Not that I'm complaining, we would've been in for a rough night had Aspen not taken my word for what happened to his father.

"Hey, don't mention it," I shrugged. "We get shot at all the time."

Liles nodded.

"Seriously, it's alright," Angela laughed.

"If you don't mind me asking," Aspen started politely, "I saw there were more of you before I passed out. What happened to the big black horse?"

"We get separated from each other a lot," I sighed. "Just, in the heat of the moment."

"We still need clothes," Angela reminded me, changing the subject.

"You guys can wear some of my mom and dad's spare camp clothes in the back," Aspen offered.

"If there aren't bullet holes in 'em," I added. "The back took some hits."

"Now I'm worried about the tents," Liles said.

"They'll probably be fine," Aspen replied as we approached the turn the phone was talking about.

I turned right and the phone screen changed. "Looks like you just keep going straight until you see the park," Aspen said, looking down at the phone.

"How come it didn't tell me that?" I asked.

"Phones can be stupid sometimes," he said, shrugging. "I probably messed it up when I reopened the window."

"What?" Angela asked.

"I'll show ya later," he laughed.

"Your destination is on the right. Happy Campers Trailer Park."

We turned into the trailer park and just past the official entrance was a sign that read: *RENT A PRIVATE CAMPSITE* with an arrow pointing left.

"Perfect," Angela said.

Following the sign, we were greeted by a happy-looking man in front of a small tollbooth holding a clipboard. He was wearing a bright orange reflective vest and large square glasses, and his light brown hair was up in a man bun.

"Hello!" he said to me cheerfully. "Did you reserve a campsite?"

"No, but we would like one," I said, clearly not reflecting the same enthusiasm.

"No problem! We have a few spaces available!" he announced loudly. "How many days will you be staying, and would you like to rent any gear!?"

"Um, no," I continued. "And we'd like to stay for three weeks."

"Three *weeks*?" he said, surprised. "I hate to break it to ya, but that would be a pretty big bill, since you pay by the day. I'm not sure we've ever had anyone stay that long."

"How much?"

"Thirty a day." He held his clipboard to his chest. "There's only one private campsite available. It has a working bathroom with a sink and toilet, but it hasn't been rented for a couple years now!"

"Now that's one thing we won't find out in the woods," Liles mumbled.

"We'll take it," I said. "How do we pay you?"

"Well, credit is preferred for longer stays. You know, so we can charge you per night. And you don't have to worry about paying a ton for only a few nights if something happens."

"What do you mean 'if something happens'?" I asked.

"Well, if Imma be frank with you, that particular site hasn't been used since a family went missing a couple summers ago," he informed us. Aspen and I glanced at each other. "The cops assumed it was a bear attack, and while we took precautions, once it hit the news, no one wanted to rent the spot." He was becoming less and less peppy.

"So," I replied, "what I'm hearing is, no one goes over there?"

"Nope. The staff stopped managing it altogether, seeing as how no one will ever be—"

"We want it," I said, smiling evilly.

The man tilted his head and looked down at his clipboard. "Hmm... Please sign this waiver." He handed me a pen and a pink piece of paper through the window frame, and after briefly skimming it, I discovered that the document was basically a big pink notice that the park wouldn't be held legally responsible if we were injured or killed during our stay. I would have signed it, but the second I clicked the base of the pen, paranoia washed over me, and I bit my lip.

"Hey," I whispered, leaning over to Aspen, "what was your dad's name?"

"Liam Green," Aspen replied quietly.

I scribbled the name onto the paper and handed it back to the park guy. "Do you have a card?" he asked, taking the paper from me. He had dropped his joyful act.

Aspen handed me a thin, blue credit card. The name *Hailey Green* was printed on it in silver lettering. "My mom's," he mumbled.

I handed the now dispirited park guy the card. He sighed before heading into in his booth to swipe it. "You may go," he muttered, handing me back the credit card along with a pamphlet containing directions to the site

and a small, green cardboard pine tree with the number *113* on it in white lettering.

"It goes on your rearview—" He took one look at our dangling, broken mirror and raised an eyebrow.

"Thanks!" I shouted cheerfully. "We'll make it work!" I quickly drove past the man and down the park road.

Angela and Liles, who were staying low in the back seat, poked their heads up.

"That was hilarious," Angela laughed.

"Yeah." I smiled. "He looked terrified."

Liles looked over at the tiny green tree in my hand. "A hundred and thirteen? As if our luck could get worse."

"Least it wasn't just thirteen," I replied.

Aspen was playing around on his phone next to me, not paying too much attention to us. "My mom'll know where I am as soon as she checks her bank statement," he said, not even looking up from the screen. "She has to know by now I took her card."

"Hopefully we'll be out of here before then," I replied.

"And if not, at least you'll get to go home," Liles added. Aspen nodded, going right back to his phone.

"Seriously, though, Chase, why did you agree to the cursed campsite?" Angela asked.

"No one will bother us. It's perfect, unless of course there really are killer bears in there."

She sighed. "I didn't even think about that."

"It'll be fine," I assured her. "Just try not to light anything on fire."

"Well, *someone*'s feeling better," she laughed.

"You're right." I paused. "I've never been camping. And I'm not at the house. Those two facts alone are enough to make me happy."

"I agree," Izzy laughed for the first time since we left.

"Where do you guys live?" Aspen asked.

"You know Alex will just drag us right back, right?" Angela said.

"Back *where*?" I scoffed. "The house is gone!"

"I wouldn't get too cocky," Angela said. "We might end up living with Uncle Jason."

My left arm started to hurt for no real reason, and my facial expression probably looked concerned. "Are you afraid of that guy?" asked Aspen. My face turned red, and I sped the car up.

"Yup," Angela snickered.

"There's nothing in my contract about living with that big, arrogant—" I suddenly realized something. I think everyone but Aspen did too.

"Wouldn't it have burned in the fire?" Liles asked.

I should have been happy, I should have felt free, but it was too good to be true. That accursed paper had to be around there somewhere.

"I guess you're off the hook then," Angela said dejectedly. Her ears were slowly lowering to the back of her head, which surprised me. I knew she hated that contract as much as I did.

"It's too easy," I started. "There's no way Alex would have—" I looked down at the floor under Aspen's feet and saw the black briefcase.

"Hey, Aspen?" Angela asked, smiling. She must have caught on. "Would you throw me that case please?" I reached for it, trying to keep one hand on the wheel, but Aspen was faster. He grabbed the case and tossed it back to her. "Thank you," she said, putting one paw on it proudly.

"Could you please give that back?" I asked. "I won't destroy it."

Angela looked surprised. "What?"

"I won't destroy it," I sighed. "Not like I could but, I just—I want to review it."

"I'd actually like to see that contract myself," Liles added.

"Please?" I begged. "You can have it back tomorrow."

"I don't believe you," she retorted. "Besides, I already reviewed it."

"Let me rephrase," I continued. "I don't *want* to destroy it."

Angela blinked a few times. "What?"

"Just give it to him," Izzy groaned, clearly sick of us.

Angela passed the case to her, and then she handed it to Aspen, who put it back on the floor of the passenger's seat.

"Thanks," I said, parking the car. I took the case and got out of the near-totaled vehicle, admiring our new campsite. It was a large, open field with a steep hill at the end, and the whole thing was surrounded by trees. There was a wooden outhouse-looking thing on the very top of the hill with a tiny sink next to it and a thin flagpole waving the American flag. There was also a firepit in the center of the site with piles of trash and cobwebs all around it. You could tell no one had cleaned the place up in a while.

IN CASE WE'RE MADE INTO COATS

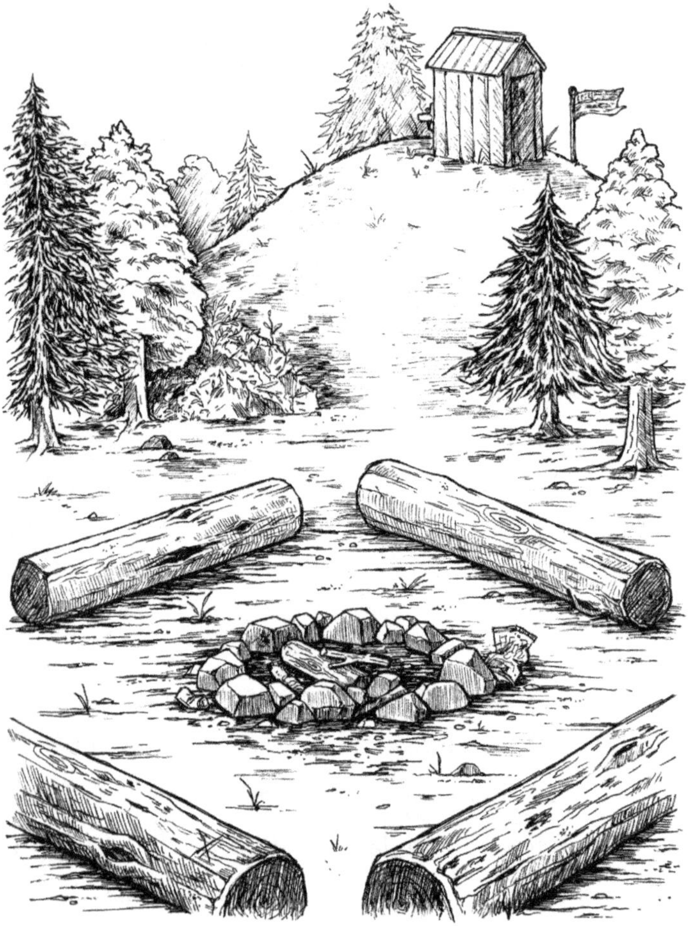

Aspen got out of the car, attempting to shut the passenger door behind him, but the frame was so dented that it just swung open further. "Home sweet home," Angela said, stepping up into the front seat and following him out on her three good legs.

"For now, anyway," Liles added, leaping out of the car through the broken window frame.

Aspen walked around to the back of the car and popped the trunk open. "Oh no," he sighed.

Izzy opened her door and started walking around the site, Angela limping behind her. I walked around to Aspen to see what the problem was. "Some of the supplies we may not be able to use," he said, rummaging through a clear Rubbermaid tub in the back of the car.

"Like what?" I asked, watching him. He pulled out a canteen and flipped it around, so I could see the three bullet holes in it.

"Do we have duct tape?" Liles asked.

"I don't know," Aspen replied, "but it won't hold much water without some."

"It's fine," I said quickly. "How about the tents?"

Aspen lifted two brightly colored cloth cylinders out of the car with some poles sticking out of them. One was dark blue, the other hot pink.

"The boys will take the blue tent," Liles declared, taking the blue cloth cylinder from Aspen with his teeth.

"*We* want the blue one," Angela said, limping over to us on three legs with Izzy at her side.

"Too bad, ours," I replied, leaning against the car.

"Um, guys?" Aspen said hesitantly. "We may want the pink one."

I waved him off. "Sorry," I continued to Angela. "First come, first serve." Angela growled, dragging the pink tent away with her teeth. I was relieved that there wasn't an argument.

Aspen rolled his eyes at us. "What?" I asked. He walked in front of us with a flatly annoyed look on his face and pointed backward to the girls in the distance, who were unsheathing their tent from the pink cover. The tent was blue.

Liles put his paw to his face. I sighed, unsheathing our tent from its blue cover to reveal its pinkness. "I mixed 'em up last summer," Aspen said. "My little cousins always want the blue one."

Angela and Liles shifted back into their human forms and put on what they could find among Aspen's parents' clothes that didn't slide right off their bodies. The girls then began building their tent up proudly while Liles, Aspen, and I grumbled around with our plastic pink poles and vague instruction manual.

"We'll take it back from them one of these days," Aspen said. "Right?"

"I suppose we could challenge them for it," Liles replied. "However—"

"It's more trouble than it's worth," I finished for him.

"Precisely," Liles sighed.

"What's in that case?" Aspen asked, pointing to Alex's black briefcase that I'd put down in the grass a few feet away.

"It's nothing," I replied, sliding a string through one of the pink plastic poles.

"He's a liar," Liles declared. "Seriously, though, when do you plan on lighting that contract on fire?"

"I don't," I mumbled.

Liles gave me a bewildered look. "Come on, really?"

"I promised I wouldn't," I said firmly, clicking two poles together. "Besides, it's not that simple."

"Are you two friends now?" Liles asked. "I have only ever seen you guys fight."

"I dunno," I replied. "She was pretty mad at me earlier."

"You bet," Liles said. "You did save her life, though."

"That means absolutely nothing to her," I told him. "She hates it when I save her."

"That doesn't make much sense," Liles started. "Then again, I know a girl with similar self-regard."

I noticed the sun coming up behind us, and the last ounce of willpower drained from my bones. We had missed a whole night of sleep, and I was feeling it. Liles connected the last of the pink poles and began trying to make them stand on their own. Aspen took the tent cover and slipped the poles through the fabric loops. I helped him position them upright and attach the corner pieces. Moments later, we had one somewhat structurally sound, hot pink tent.

Liles stood back to admire it. "It's lovely," he yawned.

I didn't have the energy to speak and just nodded. Aspen turned around and looked at the girls, who seemed all too happy with their blue tent. They were sitting in it victoriously, already covered in the blankets they'd taken from the trunk of the car.

"Don't we get one of those blankets?" Liles asked.

"We were supposed to," Aspen sighed.

"Hey," I said, still looking back at the far-more-contented campers. "Do you have, like, a spider shift or something?"

"That's an arthropod," Liles reminded me, "but I understand what you meant. I'll work on something."

"So, do we go to sleep now?" Aspen asked. "I know it's morning, but..."

"We can, but we really should wait until tonight to sleep, I'm afraid," Liles said. "We'll mess up our sleep schedules even more if we don't. However, Chase, it may be best if you at least take a nap."

"Why me?" I asked.

"Well, everyone else is probably going to eat the freeze-dried fruit and beef jerky in the back of the car, and since you won't, you will need to conserve your energy," Liles said. "There's a lot to do tomorrow, and you can't run on oxygen alone."

"Why do you talk so fast?" I sighed.

"I'm serious."

"Fine," I groaned, "but, seriously, Liles, are you working on some kind of antidote?"

"I will...try," he said hesitantly.

"Try?" I replied nervously.

"You need a real doctor, Chase," he insisted. "Or a shifter-physician, and I am neither."

"You're the closest thing I've got," I said.

"What's a shifter-physician?" Aspen asked.

"Aside from all the other shapeshifter-specific treatments they perform, they can be like pharmacists for remedies," Liles explained. "They make them, prescribe them, and try to figure out the best course of action for side effects."

"What's the worst that could happen if you get a dose wrong?" I asked.

"You die," Liles shrugged, "painfully."

"Great. Well, starving to death isn't exactly fun either," I snapped.

"Just eat despite the pain, then," Liles advised, "until you can get some help."

Aspen looked confused. "What are you two talking about?"

"Remedies contain some pretty heightened, long-established medicinal ingredients," Liles tried to explain. "They're universal cures. So, useful for us, considering that

not all human medicine is beneficial or safe for certain animal species and, therefore," Liles had to stop to yawn, "therefore not always safe for shapeshifters."

"Uh-huh," Aspen said quietly. "So, what's wrong with Chase?"

"Yeah, Liles," I said. "What's wrong with me?"

"I don't know!" he shouted. "For the last time, I'm not a doctor!"

"Is there such thing as a doctor for shapeshifters?" Aspen asked.

"Oh, yeah," Liles nodded. "But, most of them are huntsmen. It's hard for anyone else to work on shifters without the government finding out and taking their equipment."

All this talk of doctors got me thinking about the past again. Normally, I'd be able to push those thoughts aside, but I was tired, incognizant, and went a little too far back, wandering across that barrier I mentioned earlier, the invisible yellow caution tape I'd put up in my head years ago. I'm not sure if I'm going to include my momentary flashback, because even though (admittedly) writing this book is helping me feel better, I don't think I can write about this particular incident just yet.

That being said, if my sob story does somehow make it into this book, well, things must have gotten a lot worse for future me, because I don't want to have to answer a single question.

20: CHASE

JACKSON, MISSISSIPPI

JUNE 2014

A sleek black Lexus made its way down a smooth, wet road in the middle of the night. Its headlights illuminated the space in front of it. The only noticeable sounds from

inside were the windshield wipers and rain hitting the roof. The car's three passengers hadn't said a word since leaving their empty house several hours earlier. The driver, a beautiful woman with long black hair, kept a firm grip on the wheel, her brown eyes welling up with tears as she stared at the road before her.

The other two passengers were kids. One was a tall, seventeen-year-old girl whose hair and eyes were similar to the driver's. The other was a twelve-year-old boy with black hair that was short and styled into a faded mohawk. He had dark green eyes.

In the backseat, the boy was laying on his car door, looking out the window at the trees along the side of the road. The girl had headphones on and was typing on a small, purple-and-blue laptop decorated with white decals of swirls and butterflies. She looked up from it for a second at the boy. She noticed he hadn't moved since they got in the car.

"Hey," she said, pulling her headphones off. He didn't respond. "Hey," she tried again, nudging him with her hand. He sat up and faced her. "Just making sure you're alright." She paused. "You handled yourself pretty well today. Maybe too well."

"It's just—it's not a big deal," the boy replied.

"Of course it is," she insisted. "We've never moved before, and—"

"I still don't see why we have to leave," he interjected, rolling his eyes.

"Yeah." She looked up at the driver to make sure she couldn't hear them. "This is all pretty stupid, isn't it?"

"Mhm."

"I'm sorry this whole thing kind of ruined your birthday," she said, closing her laptop.

"I don't care about that," the boy replied, shaking his head.

"Then what's up?" the girl persisted. "Come on, you're never this quiet."

"It's just not fair," he said bitterly. "Mom shouldn't have to deal with any of this."

"You're upset with Dad?" she asked, confused. "How could he have known?" He leaned back against his window. The girl took a moment to think about it. "I hope I didn't cause you to think that way..." she said, tucking her laptop under the car seats.

"No," the boy mumbled. "This is all his fault."

"Well, we don't know what happened. But I understand how you feel, I mean, just because he's gone, doesn't mean he's a saint now. These past few years he's just been such a—"

"Shapeshifter," the boy finished for her.

"I don't think there's a better word," the girl chuckled, putting her headphones back on. "That was a horrible joke, though."

The car suddenly stopped. Both kids jerked forward in their seats and were caught by their safety belts. The driver of the car looked around wildly.

"What's going on?" the girl asked, removing her headphones once again.

"Ethelia, stay with your brother," the driver said to the girl in the back, opening her car door.

"Mom!?" Ethelia asked from the back. "What, where are you going?"

The boy unbuckled his seatbelt and leaned over the console in an attempt to see what the driver was looking at.

"I said, stay with your brother," the woman repeated, shutting the door.

Ethelia watched her mother walk out onto the road and turned to her brother, who was scanning the woods through the windshield. "What do you see?" she asked him.

"There's other people over there," he replied, squinting. "I'm not sure what they—"

BANG!

The sound rang through the air, and both kids froze in horror. Their attention immediately turned to the driver, who fell limp to the pavement. Ethelia shrieked, throwing her hands over her mouth. The boy's eyes were wide with shock as his mind struggled to comprehend what had just happened.

"Mom!" he screamed.

The boy tossed himself into the backseat and frantically opened the driver's side door. "CHASE!" Ethelia yelled as the boy bolted out of the car and toward the fallen woman in the road.

"Mom!" He fell to her side. Her chest was bleeding and her breathing was slow.

"No!" the woman gasped. "Go!"

"There!" someone yelled from the woods. "I told you!"

A young female huntsman with a long, blond ponytail stepped out from the forest and onto the road. She was pointing her pistol at the boy and his mother.

The boy pulled his mother's arm in a desperate attempt to lift her off the road. "No!" he cried. "Get up! Please!" She

wrapped her free arm over her gunshot wound. The boy, exhausted, collapsed down next to her. His heart ached.

"I love you, baby," his mother cried. "I love you, Chase."

"No!" the boy sobbed. He covered his eyes. "Please, no!"

"Pretty good for your first day on the job," a man said to the blond. He grabbed the pistol away from her. "But this is still my gun." He pointed the gun at the boy, who was doubled over with grief, crying into his hands. The man racked the side of his pistol just before a faint whispering wind began blowing. The whispering turned to a whoosh, and the man lowered his gun. "What the hell?" he asked, looking around.

The female huntsman turned back toward the shapeshifter she'd just shot. Her body lay lifeless on the ground. The boy, still clutching her arm, was shaking uncontrollably. A black mist started forming around his feet. The boy's mother was dead. Despair washed over him. A chill ran up his spine. A cold, consuming sensation took over his whole body, and when he opened his eyes, they glowed a horrifying red color.

"EXOTIC!" the female huntsman yelled hysterically, throwing her hands up into the air. "YES, YES, YES!!" The other huntsman raised his pistol as she spun around victoriously. Upon noticing, she pulled his arm down. "NO!" she screamed. "You can't kill it now!" The boy's body began to

glow and slowly started shifting into a large creature whose appearance was hidden by the black mist surrounding it. Its eyes, however, were more than visible in the dark. "It's mine!" she proclaimed.

Once fully shifted, the creature glared furiously at the blond from across the road. The wind that had picked up in the area concentrated on the red-eyed animal, spinning the dark mist around its paws. The whispering sound had left the air, but continued around the creature, almost like it was emanating from him now.

The animal emitted a low, loud growl as it stepped closer to its mother's killer.

The killer's eyes widened, and she took a couple steps back. "GUYS!" the other huntsman shouted into the woods. "WE'RE GONNA NEED SOME HELP!"

The creature leapt at them.

"CHASE!" A large grizzly bear shot out from the dark, grabbing the red-eyed creature by the neck and yanking it toward herself. The creature threw the bear off and viciously charged at the man holding the gun. "NO!" the bear yelled from the ground.

The female huntsman screamed, running from the scene as the creature mauled and mutilated the man with the gun in a fit of rage. "STOP!" the bear cried. "STOP IT!"

BANG!

More huntsmen burst from the forest, surrounding the large creature. Some hurled ropes around it until all four of its legs were tied up individually. The man who'd been critically injured by the red-eyed animal was wailing as he backed away on the ground with his hand over his bloody shoulder. Two other huntsmen dragged him to his feet and led him away.

The bear tried her best to intercept, but to no avail. There were huntsmen kicking her and bullets flying past her head. "Chase!" she cried one last time.

The creature resisted as long as it could before the huntsmen pulled on the ropes tangled around its legs. "WE GOT IT!" the killer shrieked. "We need the darts! Now!"

The creature crashed to the ground, its legs sprawled out and pulled in four different directions. The bear got up and began running desperately back toward the chaos. She was shot in the leg by one of the huntsmen.

The creature failed to free itself. Eventually, fear overpowered sadness. It attempted to shift back into its human form, but the huntsmen just pulled the four ropes tighter.

As it started shifting, the creature let out a horrible cry that resonated through the forest. Its legs tried to turn back into arms, but the position the ropes had put them in caused the animal's bones to fracture in the process. They shifted improperly, fusing to each other, puncturing and tearing the creature's muscles.

The coalesced creature cried out again as it finished shifting, and once back in his human form, the naked and heartbroken boy from the car laid on the ground weak and deformed. His arms and legs were burning and stabbing him from the inside as his muscles attempted to realign to his new and abnormal bone structure.

The huntsmen had no trouble dragging the boy. His eyes continued to glow red, and the whispering sounds didn't die down, but he didn't put up a fight. They tried to pull him to his feet, but he wouldn't stand, nor would he stop crying. The injured grizzly bear stood again, and with her last remnants of energy, she tackled one of the four unarmed men handling the boy. The three remaining huntsmen dropped their ropes, running back to the forest to regroup per the angry demand

of their distraught and injured leader, who was shouting his head off, begging for medical assistance.

"Chase!" the bear yelled to the poor, misshapen boy who, despite being liberated from the ropes, wouldn't move from his curled-up position on the concrete. "What did you do!?"

"I'M PARALYZED!" the boy wailed. "I'M PARALYZED!"

"No!" the bear cried in a panic. "No! We—we have to get out of here!"

"I'm paralyzed!" The boy was inconsolable.

"I don't know what to do!" the bear sobbed.

BANG!

"ETHELIA!"

"YOUR WEASEL! NOW!"

"I CAN'T!"

"CHASE!"

21: CHASE

"Hey," Aspen said, waving his hand in front of my face. "You good?" I stumbled back and vaguely remember extending my arms out as if Aspen was going to hurt me.

"Hey, you alright?" Liles asked. "You looked like you were going to pass out." He paused. "Again..."

"I'm fine," I replied, regaining my composure. But I wasn't sure if I was fine. I thought I'd put that all behind me, I thought I'd forgotten.

Aspen looked over at the girls. "I'm gonna go see what they are doing," he said, walking off. I think I may have spooked him.

"I won't ask," Liles said, crawling into our pink tent. I sighed, wandering off on my own. Just remembering that day so vividly caused my arms and legs to start hurting again. Well, that and low blood sugar.

I trudged up the hill to investigate the outhouse and look for some wood for the firepit. I knew it would eventually get cold seeing as it was early May and the weather had already been pretty unpredictable. Not to mention all of the logs we had laying out in the open had been soaked by the storms. Once I reached the top of the hill, I inspected the wooden outhouse. It had been half-eaten by termites, with a door that didn't quite line up with its frame. On the inside, there was a concrete floor and a singular cracked toilet with a pull cord flusher dangling from the side. Spider webs occupied every corner, and there was a dead mouse at the base of the toilet. But the most obscure thing about the structure was the huge pile of empty tuna and Campbell's cans laying by a small hole at the base of a rusty porcelain sink around the back of it.

I kicked one of the tuna fish cans off the pile and studied it. It didn't appear that old, and, judging by the stack, whoever it had belonged to stayed for a while. So, either the peppy guy at the gate lied about the grounds not being used for two summers, or the campsite had accommodated some squatters in the recent past.

Seeing as how there definitely wasn't any firewood up by the outhouse, I stumbled back down the hill and started thinking about what I'd tell Angela about my circumstances before I had to leave. There was no way I could stick around and put everyone in danger if I was in fact such a huge target, like Liles claimed all exotics were.

Then again, how would the huntsmen know to seek me out personally when they'd never seen my eyes glow or seen me turn into anything obscure? It's not like they could scan for exotics, right? I figured if I just kept my mouth shut and didn't do anything stupid, maybe I'd be able to stay.

When I got back to the bottom of the hill, everyone was occupied with their own endeavors, and they seemed to be having a decent time. Liles was in our tent, laying out his clothes and sorting through his old doctor's bag of ~~poisons~~ remedies, while Aspen was taking pictures of the

vials with his phone. Angela was wearing a new peasant blouse with a loose jean jacket and a pair of black leggings that had belonged to Aspen's mom. She was poking at the firepit, turning some of the logs over, and determining whether they were too wet to burn. And Izzy was straightening out the tines of a cheap plastic comb she had to have found somewhere on the campsite.

I sat down on one of the four logs surrounding the firepit, lost in thought. Angela came and sat next to me. She started laughing. "What now?" I asked.

"Well, this isn't too different from what we did at the house. Sit on a bench by a fire. Except this time we don't have a roof," she shrugged.

As much as I wanted to keep talking like nothing was wrong, I felt there were some things I had to address. "I don't think Alex will be back for a while."

"Why would you think that?" she asked. "You don't think he was—"

"Captured? No. But remember how you were saying that Chris's behavior was suspicious?" See how I completely turned that around, like *I* would never jump to such a conclusion?

"I believe that *you* suggested it first," she replied, crossing her arms.

Yeah, that didn't work. "Well, if you want my opinion," I continued, "I think Alex is in on whatever this is, too."

"You're only saying that because you don't like him."

"No, I'm saying that because—" It was so frustrating. I really wished I'd told the others exactly what Osscar had said before getting into this whole mess. But informing her at this point would make me seem like a huge liar. Which I ~~was~~ am. "It just seemed," I said, stepping around the truth, "like he knew something was going to happen."

"There's no way he could have predicted a horde of huntsmen coming to burn the house down," she replied.

"I know," I sighed. "But I have a feeling there's more than just my contract in that briefcase. It's too heavy."

"So, you think he planned on leaving us?"

I nodded, zipping up the hoodie Liles gave me. It was definitely getting colder.

"Could he have known about Osscar?" Angela asked. "If he does, he didn't hear about it from me."

"No idea," I replied. "But I think it may have something to do with your dad."

"You think Alex knows where he went?"

"He *did* know where he went," I foolishly replied.

Angela scooted away from me. "You know where he is?"

"No," I said, turning to her, "not exactly..." Why did I say that? All I knew was that he wasn't at the base! I didn't know where he was in the slightest, let alone inexactly!

"Not *exactly*!" she shouted in disbelief. "You knew where he was this whole time and didn't say anything?"

"It's not like that!" I yelled. "Osscar and Alex knew where he went, but when I asked Osscar, he told me we weren't allowed to know."

"You're telling me this *now*!?" Angela cried. "Chase, I thought we were finally getting somewhere! I should've known there was a good reason why you wanted the briefcase. You weren't going to review your contract, you just wanted to conspire against me and keep more secrets!"

"You're misreading everything I'm saying! I haven't even looked inside! I wanted to look at it with you."

"Forget it," she growled, standing up. "I don't want to know. Osscar didn't wanna tell me, you didn't wanna tell me. Neither of you were looking out for me."

"Angie, please," I said, following her. "That's not why I wanted the case, I didn't even think about—"

"Why else *wouldn't* you want that contract burned?" she asked, walking closer.

"I don't want it burned!" I continued defensively. "I already said that!"

"Why not? What did you want to review?"

"Okay, I admit it! I wanted to see what else was in the case!" I yelled. "But I never denied it. I just wanna look at it with you, because I don't wanna leave you in the—"

"Why didn't you tell me about Osscar then?"

"Because he—"

"What did Alex tell you?" she persisted.

"Would you let me talk!" I shouted. "You know what, Angie? The way I see it, the *only* reason you and I can't get along is because you never give me a chance to explain!"

"Alright, now's your chance!" she snapped. "Why are you still keeping things from me?"

"Because—" I suddenly didn't feel well. I started reaching behind me for something, anything, to support myself on. "Because... I don't want you to die?" I finally replied, trying to catch my breath.

I don't know why I said that either.

She looked furious; her eyes burned with anger. "No, Chase," she said slowly. "I'm done trying to figure out what

your deal is, but don't pretend for five seconds that you keep watch on me because you care." She stormed back to her tent, and I turned around to do the same, when I noticed Aspen and Liles standing a few feet away, staring in my direction.

Aspen looked extremely uncomfortable. He gave me an awkward little wave.

"What was that about?" Liles asked.

I groaned in frustration, shuffling past them and grabbing the briefcase I'd left by our tent. I eventually found myself back up at the outhouse. I went around it, sitting down under the tree across from the piles of tuna fish cans where no one could see me from camp. I unlocked the briefcase and as I suspected, it was full of paperwork of all different varieties.

I took a deep breath, picking up the pile of documents and setting it down on the ground. I then sifted through the papers until I found the one sheet I was nervous to even touch. It looked like any other normal contract, except it had three golden names, including my own half-legible signature, written in gold-colored ink at the bottom. I skimmed through its contents until I came upon the paragraph I'd missed the very first time I read it.

The signer of this document agrees to protect the subject of the contract with all that he has to offer her, and acknowledges that the consequence of failing to do so will be to take his last breath with her.

I bet you're wondering how I missed that, right?

McComb, Mississippi

May 2017

"Okay, Chase, please read this over," said Christopher. He was sitting on an unsightly brown couch, in a strange little living room that was the heart of the house he'd just led me into. I was seated on the ground at the opposite side of a coffee table.

He pushed a piece of paper in front of me, which I read over. Every word was written in bright blue. "I guess that's fine," I mumbled, thinking this was all pretty weird. I was told on the lengthy drive from Jackson that I would need to sign something if I wanted the perks of staying with

Christopher and his family. But I was expecting it to be some kind of agreement to uphold the household's values, not whatever this was. However, I was enticed by the promise of an easy, pain-free life with my own kind, and was willing to overlook it. "And I'll get the bandages?"

"And you will get to live here," Christopher said. He was tapping his index finger on the table.

"But, who's the subject of the contract?" I asked.

"That would be my daughter, Angela," he replied. "You'll meet her soon. You can take all the time you need to think about it," he continued, lacing his restless fingers together. "It's completely your choice." He slid a pile of clothes across the table for the wolf to put on. "You'll need to shift back to sign that, though."

"Now?" I asked with a sigh.

"Why not?" Christopher asked. "You may change in any bathroom you like. This'll be your house now."

I nodded, taking the clothes in my mouth before walking from the room down a long hallway of doors. I nudged at least three of them open before I found the only bathroom not attached to someone's bedroom. I was beginning to get a feel for the place, and it wasn't a good one... But desperation for a place to live made me ignore my bad feeling. I couldn't be

ungrateful, this was a "privilege" after all. ~~Right Alex?~~ The bedrooms I peeked into weren't so bad, and I was told that I would be getting my own.

I'm sure it'll be just fine...

My fourteen-year-old self hobbled back into the living room in my human form, wearing the "new" clothes I was given. I was barely able to stand, so I approached the coffee table slowly, wincing as I lowered myself to the floor where I had sat as the wolf.

"Perfect," Christopher said, "now, sign here." He pointed at a dotted line at the bottom of the paper.

"I don't have a pen," I said, looking around for one.

"Oh, sorry," he replied, patting himself down. "How could I forget?" He produced an average-looking, black gel pen from his coat pocket and handed it across the table.

I took the pen and signed the paper with my name.

CHASE WAGNER

The black ink began to turn gold as my signature dried. It and the other two names listed in the contract all shimmered radiantly when it became permanent.

"There," he sighed, slumping back on the couch. He sounded relieved. He took the pen back. I glanced at the contract once more as he reached over to take it, and my eye caught something new.

"W-wait," I stammered. "I didn't see that part when I read it." I pointed to the last paragraph in the paper that appeared in bright red ink.

Christopher sort of froze. He closed his eyes, placing the paper back down for me to review again. "Please don't worry about that too much," he started. "It's just a—" He rubbed his hand across his face, clearly not knowing what to say. "It's, umm...."

... failing to do so will be to take his last breath with her.

I felt a hot wave of horror wash over me. "You knew I wouldn't see this as a wolf!" I yelled, outraged. "The red looked gray and blended in with the paper!"

He winced. "I'm sorry."

"You said I needed to be the wolf so your family wouldn't think I was a huntsman!" I shouted. I'll admit I was hurt—not as hurt as I would be later, when Christopher refused to take me back to Jackson where he found me, he gave the car back to whoever he "rented" it from, or when I saw my bedroom, but hurt nonetheless. My trust in shapeshifters died that second. "You lied to me..."

"I didn't. That was true as well."

As well!?

I'd convinced myself there was no way the threat on that paper could be real. I stared at the last paragraph. My eyes began to water with fear.

"Welcome to the family, Chase," Christopher said, handing me a wad of bandages made of a special material that would shrink and expand to meet the needs of a shapeshifter with a rare skeletal condition called Morph-Bone.

22: CHASE

I could have ripped that paper in half after my brief flashback, but what good would that have done? I set it aside and continued through the pile. A lot of the other papers must have been included by accident. There were some Walmart receipts, a couple coupons, even an old newspaper. The next significant document I found was Angela's birth certificate, which I quickly glossed over. Of course it wasn't a *real* birth certificate. Shifters don't

have those, considering that their parents, if they're smart, make sure their kids aren't recognized by the state. That way they won't be tracked by huntsmen. Handmade birth certificates for posterity were not uncommon. Even *I* had one once.

> *STATE OF MISSISSIPPI*
> *January 21, 2003*
> *Female*
> *MOTHER: Bonita Rose-Tallon, 23*
> *FATHER: Christopher Tallon, 25*

I hadn't heard Angela's mom mentioned in the house too often. This was my first time learning her name. I rummaged through the last few papers in the case. More junk. *Seriously, Alex? Your home of, like, who-knows-how-many years is under attack, and this is what you think to save?* I cast it all aside. What a stupid thing to get in a fight about. Alex acted like that case was this big important thing. Was it all just to mess with me?

I heard the crunching grass of someone coming up the hill and frantically started collecting the scattered papers off the ground. I closed the briefcase just as Aspen came around the outhouse. "What are you doing?"

"Nothing," I answered, picking up the briefcase. "I'm just—"

"Sorry," he mumbled as I stood up. He looked around, rubbing his arm like he wasn't quite sure what to do with himself. It made me feel kinda bad.

"Don't be sorry," I replied, sitting back down. "I, um, I could use the company."

Aspen smiled. He was holding a little leather-bound book with a strap wrapped around it multiple times. The spine was hand-stitched, and there was a paw print stamped on the front of it.

"What's that?" I asked as he sat down next to me.

"Sketchbook. I like to draw, but I'm not very good at it."

I looked at him suspiciously, taking the book. Each page I flipped through was covered in graphite and charcoal sketches of various animals and monsters. There were headshots and creatures drawn from every angle so you could imagine them in almost any pose. "Aspen, these are great," I said, flipping through the book. I wasn't lying. The artwork was absolutely epic, but a few pages caught my attention more than others. "Is this—" I stopped at a drawing of a large leaping cat with long saber-like teeth and rings around its eyes.

"I tried to draw what I could remember. The waves around its eyes are supposed to represent the way they glowed in the dark."

It was nice to meet another eyewitness. I figured it could help me and Angela convince the others that we weren't just delusional. I looked closer at the drawing and noticed something he had drawn around the cat's leg. "What's this?" It looked like a long string with a few beads on it.

"I don't know. The beads were colorful, but I don't draw in color. Did you not see it?"

"I was a little more focused on its teeth," I replied, almost cringing.

"A bracelet, maybe?" he suggested.

"If it was a bracelet, it was stretched to the max," I mumbled, flipping the page.

The next few drawings were of a skinny gray wolf with bandaged legs. These were much more detailed. Aspen had drawn the wolf jumping, limping, even a close-up of its eye. To give you a rough idea of how debilitated I felt that week, it didn't even cross my mind that those were sketches were of me.

IN CASE WE'RE MADE INTO COATS

I turned the page and saw a graphic, full-page drawing of the same red-eyed cat from the road. Its open mouth and fangs pointed up at someone with long, light hair. Their defensive stances foreshadowed a showdown between the two. Next to that was a charcoal sketch of a white wolf. It was standing over a huntsman who was lying on the ground with a gun in his hand. All of these images started piecing together the story of my worst Wednesday to date.

The last page I saw was of a road. Long, quiet, and dark, there were dead people on it and a couple of police cruisers. The focus of the piece was a silhouette of a large man lying further down the road from the rest of the slain, like his was the only body that mattered of the group.

Yikes. I closed the little book and bit my lip, trying to find the words.

"I'm sorry," Aspen said. "I know they're pretty bad, and I didn't mean to draw you. It's just the only way I really know how to cope with it."

I remember finding that statement pretty strange. *Wouldn't it be more like reliving it?* I couldn't fathom how drawing something like that could possibly help someone cope. But I'm beginning to understand. "Aspen, stop," I

said, shaking my head. "These are great, and I can assure you they're...very accurate."

He gave another half-smile, taking the book back from me. "I woulda asked permission before I drew you, but at the time, I kinda hated you."

"Completely understandable." I paused. "They're really cool, but I really am sorry about your dad."

"Oh yeah," he sighed. "That was hard to draw, but I wanted to remember what I saw."

"Right," I replied.

"But I don't wanna draw him like that," Aspen continued, referring to the dead man at the end of the road in his drawing. "I wanna remember him when he was alive and happy. I just—"

"You just can't get the image out of your head?" I asked, looking down.

"Mhm," he replied, closing his sketchbook. I was starting to feel responsible for him losing so much, and it was probably reflected in my expression. He was just in the wrong place at the wrong time. If I was never there, maybe things would have ended differently. Then again, how could I have been responsible for that saber-toothed cat?

"It's not your fault," he said. "I know that now, but I still want justice for my dad."

"Well, if it makes you feel any better, I killed the guy who shot him," I said, shrugging. The secret was out, and it was getting easier for me to talk about it. Which may not have been such a good thing, now that I think about it...

"You did?" Aspen said, shocked.

"You must have missed the last part of the fight," I replied, "where all the huntsmen ran off, and Angela got shot in the leg?"

"Definitely missed that," he said with wide eyes. "I ran off when I saw Angela tackle that one guy."

I would have left around that time too, had I been given the choice. I'm thankful Angela showed up before I became another body along the road in Aspen's memorial drawing, but I'm still not sure why she did. All I remember was another fight.

"You really killed the guy who shot my dad?"

I sighed. "Yeah...I don't like hurting people, even if they're bad, but if it brings you some kind of—"

He hugged me. "Thanks." I didn't know what to say. I know I didn't deserve that much gratitude for such a

terrible deed. "What happened to the cat?" he asked, releasing me. "And the woman trying to catch it?"

"She got away," I replied. "But so did the cat. I don't think there's much hope for it, though."

"Why not?"

"Well, they know where it is," I shrugged. "And it's an exotic shifter; they don't get to live long, apparently..."

"Does that mean *you're* going to die earlier than the others?" Aspen asked with concern.

I stood up with wide eyes. "How do you know about that!?"

"Oh," he said quietly. "I heard you and Liles in the car, and—"

"You were awake!?" I couldn't believe it. That was supposed to be a confidential conversation, and it was already out of my hands. I didn't know how well Aspen could keep a secret, if he was even willing to try. But if the girls found out about my secret through anyone other than me, I'd never hear the end of it.

"Umm," he started, "I think I was slipping in and out of consciousness and—"

"Shh! Okay, Aspen, I don't know if you heard the last part of that conversation me and Liles had, but—"

"Nope."

"Alright, well, no one else can know about that stuff, okay?"

"Not even Angela?"

"*Especially* not her!" I whispered loudly. "Please, just promise to keep that a secret?"

"I promise. It's the least I can do."

I let out a sigh of relief. "Thank you."

"But seriously, are you gonna die?" he asked.

"I-I don't know. It's complicated."

"I can tell," he mumbled, picking up his sketchbook.

"Hey, Chase!" I heard Liles call from the bottom of the hill.

"If anyone asks, we were talking about these tuna cans," I said, pointing to the pile of containers by the sink.

"Really?" he asked.

"It's the best I've got." I quickly started down the hill again, Aspen following behind me.

"Oh, good! You found him!" Liles yelled to me. "I thought Aspen had run off."

"It's all good," I said, stumbling back to the firepit. I almost fell forward. "Everything's fine." Aspen gave me a look of pity before walking off to join the others.

"I'm starting to think the lack of calories is getting to you," Liles confided.

"You probably have grounds for that," I sighed.

"Hold down the fort," he said, walking past me. "I'm gonna find us some dinner."

"We have jerky sticks in the car?" I called, pointing back to our beat-up little blue sedan.

"That's not dinner!" Liles replied from halfway up the hill.

"You're going to go kill something?"

"Not if I can avoid it!" he shouted back.

I went into our little pink tent, shutting the flaps behind me. There were glass vials scattered in a pile, pencils lying about, and clothes everywhere. I wasn't sure what space was classified as "mine." Liles and Aspen's things were all over the place, but a nap was definitely warranted. I pushed the clutter aside and lay down in the corner. We didn't have any blankets, so I was convinced I would be up for a while, but as soon as my head hit the ground, I was out.

23: ANGELA

I sat in our tent, staring at its blue-tinted, blanket-filled interior. I was done with my pity party, but I knew that if I tried to leave, it was possible that someone would ask what happened between me and Chase a few hours earlier. Or worse, I could run into him. I was getting better at walking on my hurt leg. It was still sore whenever I stepped down on it, but it was better than the sharp, throbbing pain of a few days earlier. So, there was a chance I'd be able to trek up the hill on my own to get some time away from everyone. I crawled out the flaps of the tent, and

fortunately no one was there but Izzy, who was sitting on one of the logs by the firepit. She had a blank expression, and her eyes didn't move from the ground. I found it best not to engage her, especially after what I assume she saw in the clearing shortly before I did…

McComb, Mississippi

May 2019

I woke up in the woods all by myself, covered in mud with no idea how I ended up there. I stood up on my three good legs, trying to find a way out of the trees, which would have been difficult to navigate even with all four. I thought of calling for help. Chase was in his wolf form, last I recalled. If he hadn't shifted back, he may have heard me, but I didn't want to risk drawing the huntsmen.

Light flashed across the sky and thunder shook the ground. I turned in a panic just as a bolt of lightning struck a tree a few yards away, and in that moment, I saw that I wasn't too far from the clearing. I started running toward

it, but about a foot from the path, I noticed something that made me stop in my tracks. I closed my eyes. All I knew was that it was an animal, a large animal...

I didn't want to look. I didn't want to know. My eyes began to water. Please, God, let me be wrong. No one else was allowed to die, everything was already so horrible. There's no amount of psyching yourself up that can prepare you to face the possible body of a friend, but I took a deep breath, turned toward the animal, and opened my eyes.

A dead mountain lion. Its tawny brown fur was soaked by the rain. I couldn't determine how it died, the night was so dark, but when lightning flashed once again, I could see the animal's lifeless eyes for a split second.

Malachi...

I know I probably should have told the others. But it wasn't my news to tell. Izzy, if you're reading this: please, stop for a second. Skip the next paragraph. Trust me on this one.

While I would never have wanted to see Malachi come to any harm, I remember the overwhelming sense of relief that I felt when I encountered the body. I know, it's a

terrible thing to say, but I never really knew Izzy's brother. I mean, he was a wild animal. And on top of that, Dana and Henry had kept him locked in the cellar ever since they came to live with us. Izzy's always been bitter about that. Yeah, I'm only explaining this to defend my feelings, but if the dead animal in the road had turned out to be part of *my* family, or one of my friends, I'm not sure what I would have done. I don't know how Malachi died, but Izzy made one thing plain to me when I ran into her in the clearing, shortly before the boys found us. And that was that he'd probably still be alive had Osscar, Chase, and I just tied him up like we were supposed to.

I started up the hill toward the little outhouse, that I realized wasn't the cleanest thing in the world. I know everyone was excited about getting a camp with a working toilet, but from the look of it, the woods were a step up.

I went around to investigate the sink when I noticed a pile of soup cans stacked on top of each other into sort of a cylindrical tower shape. I picked up one of them, glancing down at a hole beneath the sink.

When I leaned closer, I could have sworn I heard nois-es coming from it. I'd just checked inside the outhouse, and after looking around, I concluded that there was

something alive under that sink. I tossed the empty tuna can down the hole, and the screams that followed scared me so badly, I fell right to the ground and scooted away from the hole as fast as possible. A rat emerged from the crevice and gave me a stare like no other animal's ever stared at me before. Just pure annoyance.

"Sorry," I mumbled, out of breath. The rat vanished back down the hole, and soon after, the tuna can I'd tossed down came shooting back up, hitting my foot. "What?" I crawled closer to the sink. The next thing I did was a little stupid, but that rat seemed far too aware of me. "Are you, by chance, a shapeshifter?" I called down the hole.

Moments later, something else came shooting out of the hole, but it wasn't a tuna can or a rat. It was a massive cloud of smoke. Despite momentarily clouding my vision, I could still hear something run around me. "Stop!" I shouted, turning around. I smacked right into the tree behind me and sat down, covering my face and trying to determine whether my nose was broken. Then I saw it. Through the smoke, something small and blurry scurried past the tree down the other side of the hill.

"Wait!" I called, standing back up. I ran around the tree and was about to start down the other side of the hill

when I looked down the mud-covered slope. It would be extremely hard to get down something like that with my injured leg without tumbling into the creek below.

"Fine!" I yelled down the hill. "But I know what you are, and I'm coming for you!" I turned around and noticed Aspen standing awkwardly by the sink. "I was just...," I started, pointing.

"I can't even go to the bathroom without spotting one of you guys doing something weird," Aspen said, turning on the sink. The water from the faucet flowed out orange and turned clear once the rust had run out of it.

"You'll get used to it," I replied, heading back down the hill to camp.

24: CHASE

I woke up to the sound of crickets, cicadas, and scream-ing. I'd apparently slept through most of the day. The tent no longer glowed the same bright pink that it had earlier, and the buzzing and chirps of the nighttime insects filled my ears. I opened my eyes slowly, and everything was peaceful...

...for a good five seconds.

There was a shrill, piercing noise from outside. I jumped and already my heart rate was back up to its

panicked pace. I got up, throwing the tent flaps open to see Izzy storming away from the tents. Angela and Aspen were standing in front of the firepit laughing and high-fiving each other. They appeared to have cleared away all the trash while I was sleeping.

"What's going on?" I asked, drowsily ducking out of the tent. "Where's Liles?"

"He's not back yet," Aspen replied, "but you just missed Izzy screaming over the jumping spider in the empty Pringles container!"

"How long has he been gone?" I grumbled.

"Don't worry," Angela said, waving it off. "I saw him down by the creek in his lynx shift. *Purr*-haps he'll bring us back some dinner." She laughed at her own pun, and Aspen rolled his eyes.

"Alright," I said. "Maybe it's best that you and Osscar are spending some time apart."

"Oh my gosh, you're right... Ugh! I used to hate those stupid jokes." It was good to see her willing to talk to me. In fact, she looked like she'd put our whole argument behind her.

Izzy walked back down the hill looking frustrated. "Pretty sure the spider's gone," Aspen laughed. Izzy ignored him, staring at me.

"What?" I asked.

"You look different," she started, looking me up and down ~~like I was somehow offensive to her.~~ "Sicker, thinner." I crossed that out because I really don't think Izzy meant to be judgy. She was probably just concerned, but I was feeling really defensive, and the comment seemed out of the blue. I thought she may have been trying to make me feel bad.

"Thanks," I replied, "I was going for that, because I'm aiming to make myself look bad so everyone else around me will know that I'm not feeling well..."

Not proud of that comeback. (Hangry past me, get a grip.)

She just looked shocked. I really, really wish someone would have told me why she was so upset.

"Sorry," I mumbled, walking past her over to the others. It was dark and getting colder. We could have used a fire. "How come we haven't lit this thing up yet?"

"We were busy," Angela replied.

Aspen came and dropped a pile of tiny sticks at my feet, some only an inch long. "Is that all we have for firewood?" I asked.

"No, those are only to start it."

"I saw a matchbox in the car," Angela said.

"Do you want to start a forest fire?" Aspen asked sarcastically. "We have to do this safely. Now, both of you, start making those sticks into a teepee-like structure."

"I'm all about safety," I said, "but this will give us, like, ten solid seconds of fire."

"Just do it," he sighed and walked off.

Me and Angela crouched down and started stacking the tiny twigs into the center of the firepit. "Doing okay?" I asked. Terrible icebreaker, by the way, I may as well have asked her what she thought of the weather. She didn't look at me—just nodded. "Look, I need to talk to you."

"If it's about our argument earlier, it's fine, just forget it."

"No, really, you should know what I found in the case."

Angela put another stick onto the teepee structure. "I don't wanna see it."

"There was nothing important. The contract and your birth certificate, but the rest was trash."

"Chase, I don't want to talk about it anymore."

"Okay, well, do you at least want the contract back?"

"Hey!" Aspen shouted from a few feet away. "Less yacking, more stacking!"

"Do what you want with it," she growled. "It doesn't matter anymore anyway."

"Alright, well, I promised I'd give it back. I don't want you thinking I'm trying to go behind your back here."

"I said I *don't* care." I reached into my pocket and handed her the paper anyway. "Chase!" she shouted. Our tiny pile of sticks fell over. She glared at me, standing up to storm off again.

I ran in front of her. "Please, hear me out, I don't want you to think I only kept the case for my own benefit," I said with haste. "I'm trying to share with you!"

"*Share* with me!?" she yelled. "You went and opened the case in secret! For all I know—"

"I swear, there was nothing in it! I wanted to open it *with* you, but you were busy throwing a fit, so—"

"So, you could have waited for me!"

"Whoa, whoa, whoa!" Aspen intervened, stepping between us with arms spread out. "What's going on?" Angela crossed her arms. I put my hands in my pockets and looked

down. "Okay...," Aspen said, slowly lowering his arms. There was a pause. "It's not my place," he continued sadly. "I'm sorry."

"It's not your fault, Aspen," Angela replied. She sighed. "It's not Chase's fault either..." I kept listening but didn't move from my stance. "I guess I'm—I'm a little frustrated with the circumstances." She uncrossed her arms. "Everyone just ran off and left us."

"Your guys' parents?" Aspen asked.

"Something like that," Angela mumbled. "My dad and the other adults who live with us."

"I'm sorry," he replied.

"It's fine," I reassured him.

Another shriek echoed through the woods, and we all turned toward the hill. Whoever it was, they were in trouble. "Where's Izzy?" Angela asked. We all started up the hill as quickly as possible.

"Slow down!" Aspen yelled from a few yards behind us. Once at the top, me and Angela ran around the outhouse and past the tree that me and Aspen were sitting under earlier. Upon reaching the cliff edge of the other side of the hill, we looked down the slope at the creek below.

We heard another shriek, and this time, we knew it *had* to be Izzy.

I successfully shifted into my weasel, which I remember being surprised about, considering how weak I felt. I started down the muddy cliffside, with Angela following me as her field mouse.

"So, I'll just wait up here then?" Aspen shouted down at us. "Great! Thanks!"

Despite its many advantages, I try to avoid shifting into my weasel as much as possible, due to the amount of horror stories you hear about shapeshifters dying tragically in smaller forms. I bounced through the mud and slid down by the creek. The mud engulfed all four of my tiny legs and plastered my fur and bandages. Angela joined me at the bottom, and we scouted the fast-moving creek for any sign of the others.

It didn't take long before we spotted Izzy and a fennec fox trudging back up the hill, soaking wet. "Hey!" I shouted, bouncing over to them through the mud. "What happened?" Izzy looked okay, despite being soaking wet, but her expression was wide-eyed and pale, like she'd just seen a ghost.

"There was another shifter," Liles said.

"Was it a rat!?" Angela asked, jumping over my head.

"Another shapeshifter?" I asked, confused. I turned to Angela. "What about a rat?"

"Well, she was a turtle first," Liles replied. "I was fishing, and—"

"Wait, *she*?" Angela asked.

"Yeah, it sounded like a girl," Izzy continued for him, wringing out her wet mop of hair. "She shifted into the rat and ran off before we could ask, but she scared me pretty badly."

"You fell into the crick?" I asked, tilting my head. I heard myself and cringed. *Please tell me no one caught that...*

"What'd you just say?" Liles asked, half-laughing.

"What did she say to you guys?" Angela continued impatiently.

"No clue," Liles replied. "She didn't speak English."
Thanks, Angie.

"Or Spanish," Izzy added, messing her hair up.

"You speak Spanish?" I asked.

"How long have you known me?" she asked.

"A year and a half?"

(Um, yeah, sorry, past me, it's more like two years.)

"My parents were from Brazil," Izzy explained.

"Then wouldn't they speak Portuguese?" Liles asked.

"Guys!" Angela yelled. "Off-topic! Where'd the rat go?"

"We didn't see," Liles said. "She was sitting on that rock as a turtle." He pointed to a rock by the edge of the creek behind us. "She was muttering to herself, and when we approached her, she yelled at us and Izzy fell into the water." Liles shook himself off, and the fur on his back fluffed up. "She splashed me in the process..."

"When we looked up, we saw a rat jumping off the same rock into the creek," Izzy added, "but we didn't see her resurface."

"Lovely," Angela sighed. "Well, I know where she lives, and she'll be back."

"You do?" I asked.

"There's a hole under the sink by that pile of tuna fish cans," Angela said. "She ran out of there."

"How come you didn't tell me?" I asked.

"Because I'm mad at you," she replied flatly. I noticed she didn't say *was*.

"Hey, um, guys!" Aspen yelled from the top of the hill. "Can we eat dinner now?"

"Remind me again why we couldn't let him go and leave us the car?" Liles asked. "He asks tiresome questions."

"I noticed that as well," Angela sighed. "He's just a kid, though."

"Hey," I started, "Aspen's been through a lot, cut him some slack."

We all headed back up the muddy hill. When we looked down at camp, there was a blazing fire in the firepit. The smell of food filled the air, drifting toward us through the smoke. "Does that answer your question?" Angela asked, nudging Liles' leg with her paw.

Liles nodded and his ears perked up. "It smells like—"

"Hot dogs!" Angela finished for him, standing up on her hind legs to take in the smell.

I turned around and spotted my pile of clothes from when I shifted. "You guys go ahead," I said.

Angela ran over to her pile of clothes not even three feet from mine. "I'm getting changed here," she declared. "Get lost."

Normally this wouldn't be a problem. I could shift into a larger animal, take my clothes, and leave. This time, however, I was so exhausted that I was pretty sure if I shifted into another animal, I'd be stuck like that for the rest of

the night. But I didn't feel like arguing with her, either. I dragged my pile of clothes across the grass to the outhouse with my teeth, which of course stained them. Nothing I wore could ever lack some kind of imperfection, and those were the only clothes I had. All of Aspen's father's clothes were way too big. It took me several attempts to shift back into my human form, and I barely made it down the hill afterwards.

When I got back to our campground, everyone was in their human form again with dry hair and new clothes. Well, for the most part. My bandage wraps still had some mud caked on them, but it was slowly sloughing off as they dried. We gathered around the four log benches surrounding the firepit, and I sat down where I normally would in the living room—on the far left. Me and Angela seemed to have the same idea and ended up sitting together on the log that, in my mind, represented the bench in front of the fireplace. Liles and Izzy chose the log representing the couch, and Aspen took the log representing the two chairs across from them, leaving one open.

"Where'd you find hot dogs?" Angela asked, leaning toward the fire where Aspen was holding out two large skewers with six impaled hot dogs.

"I brought a Yeti cooler of food when I ran away," he replied. "We have supplies for s'mores, one steak dinner, and a couple soups too."

Everyone was practically drooling over the flames as they watched the food cook. Everyone but me.

"It's probably best if everyone only eats one a day to conserve our resources," Liles said, counting the remaining beef franks in the little plastic package. "We only have twenty-four hot dogs, including the five cooking."

"We have one extra tonight, though. So—" Aspen started.

"DIBS!" Angela and Liles yelled in unison.

Izzy chuckled. "I heard Liles first!"

"Dang it!" Angela laughed.

"You can have mine," I sighed. "Can't eat it anyway."

Liles looked over at me. "I'll do what I can to help tomorrow."

I nodded, glancing back at Aspen who seemed more than exhausted. He was hanging his head low and resting his arms against his knees as he twirled the skewers. He'd stayed up for two whole nights.

"Leave mine in a little longer," Angela requested. "I like them burnt."

"I like them that way, too," I said.

"What is wrong with you guys?" Izzy laughed.

"Nah, I do the same thing," Aspen replied. "It's normal.

"It is not," Liles corrected.

"And the marshmallows," added Aspen.

"Now, we agree there," Liles said. "Those *have* to be burnt."

"You're *so* wrong," Izzy replied, shaking her head. "When they turn golden, you take 'em off."

"No, because then you don't get that nice ashy taste," I replied. Still wasn't hungry, but had to get the facts straight.

"Now I'm really starving," Angela mumbled. "Forget burnt, are those hot dogs done yet?"

Aspen lifted the skewers out of the fire. "Yup."

Everyone got one hot dog, a bun, a couple of ketchup and mustard packets that Aspen found in the console of the sedan, and, before the food was even cooled, people started shoving them into their mouths. "Thanks for sharing with us," I said.

"I'm just glad you weren't offended," Aspen replied, rubbing his eye. "I was worried that I may have seriously messed up."

"Offend us?" Angela laughed. "By making us dinner?"

"You know," he yawned. "I was afraid you guys would be, like, vegan or something."

"Why would you think that?" Liles asked through a mouthful of hot dog bun.

"Well, you can turn into animals that can be food and stuff."

"We can also turn into wolves and bears," I shrugged.

"Yeah," Aspen replied, trying to open one of the little ketchup pouches with his teeth.

"Actually, I'm vegetarian," Izzy mumbled shyly, raising her hand.

"I didn't know that," I said.

"Because you don't eat with us," Angela replied, tilting her head down in an accusatory fashion.

"Oh," Aspen said. "Sorry."

"Oh, no, it's okay!" Izzy laughed. "Are you guys okay with me having the fruit?"

"All yours," Angela declared, smiling.

Seeing the girls getting along lifted my spirits a little, but I was still tired, even after just taking a nap that took up a whole 'nother day. Aspen must have noticed because

he shot me quick a look of concern. "Hey," he said, "did ya wanna go, like, sleep or something?"

Liles looked over at me. "Yeah, Chase, you should go."

"No, I'll go to bed with everyone else. You guys have stayed up for two nights in a row, and I took a nap."

Aspen pulled out a bag of marshmallows and started skewering those. "You guys can have chocolate, right?" he asked.

"Yup," Angela replied. "That's an odd question."

"Sorry, I know my dog can't have it," he said quietly. "I didn't wanna kill you."

"We're all human-born shapeshifters," Liles informed him, finishing off his hot dog.

"Human-born?" Aspen asked.

I groaned.

"There are millions of kinds of shapeshifters," Liles explained. "But in a lot of people's eyes, there are only two—human-born, and animal-born."

"What's the difference?" Aspen asked.

"Do we have to explain all of this now?" I asked.

"Yeah, Liles, I beg you to keep it short," Angela said.

"Fine," he said. "I'll sum it up. Human-born shapeshifters maintain our human intelligence and sentient

disposition no matter what animal form we take, as well as our ability to make human vocalizations, digest human food, and display normal, physical responses to human emotion. So, things like crying, laughing, and so on."

"Can you still make animal noises?" Aspen asked.

"Yes," Angela replied.

"We can't understand what we're saying, though," Liles added. "If I'm in my owl form, I can make all kinds of vocalizations, but I could be swearing like a sailor in owl language and never know it."

"Can the animal-born shapeshifters still turn into humans?"

"Yes, but they won't understand what they're saying in our language—if they're saying anything at all," Liles continued. "They also maintain their animal intelligence in their human forms, so it does look a bit...strange?"

"Maybe an example would help speed this up?" Angela suggested.

"Alright, let's say there was a ferret-born shapeshifter," Liles sighed, "it would maintain its *mustelid* intelligence, still be capable of ferret vocalizations, and be able to digest its same obligate carnivore diet, in any form it took."

"Cool. So what do—"

"Sorry, Aspen," Liles yawned, interrupting him. "I know you're curious, but this topic could literally go on all night until we get to controversial topics like hybrids and purebreds."

Aspen nodded, pulling the marshmallow skewer from the fire. "Sorry," he mumbled.

Izzy was looking more and more upset by the minute. I still didn't understand why, but was afraid that it may have been my fault for how I reacted when she told me I was looking unwell.

"Hey," I asked her, "everything alright?" Angela stamped on my foot, and I was oblivious enough to brush it off like it was an accident. Izzy looked up at me, her eyes already misty. "I'm sorry for what I said earlier," I continued. "Just not feeling great right now. Is there something—" Angela punched me in the arm this time, which I'm sure wasn't intended to hurt as badly as it did. It shut me up, though, which was probably for the best.

Aspen took two graham crackers and a piece of chocolate from the pile of wrappers by his feet, made a s'more out of the least burnt marshmallow on the skewer, and handed it to Izzy on a paper plate.

"Thank you," she said.

He handed me two more plates with two blackened marshmallows to give to Angela and Liles. We all sat in silence. I squished an uncooked marshmallow around in my hand and sipped from the thermos of water Liles got me while the others finished eating.

"My dad would be happy to know his emergency camping supplies were finally being used," Aspen said, twirling his charred hot dog skewer around.

"I would think you guys used it often," Liles replied. "If it's always on hand, wouldn't it be fairly easy to take trips like this?"

"Nah, my mom hates camping," Aspen shrugged. "I went once a year with Dad and sometimes my cousins, but the stuff in this car never gets used."

"How old are those jerky sticks then?" I asked.

"Old," he laughed.

"So where are we going after this?" Angela asked. "We can't pay for this place forever."

"Maybe we can," I said.

"What are you suggesting?" Liles asked.

"You heard the guy at the gate. They thought the family who last camped here was eaten by bears, and after that,

no one wanted to come back," I reminded them. "Not even the staff clean the place."

"I think I know where you're going with this," Angela mumbled, "and I don't like it."

"We could fake our own bear attack," I continued. "Then we can stay here, and no one will bother us."

"There is so much that could go wrong with that," Liles replied. "What if they hire people to come kill the bears? Or there are traps set?"

"We could make them think it was a monster?" Aspen suggested.

"We can't shift into monsters," Angela countered.

Liles shot me a quick and possibly unintentional look. I glared at him then rolled my eyes.

"You guys could use a bunch of animals to make it look like there was a monster, though," Aspen said.

"How would we avoid detection for so long?" Angela asked.

"We could all shift into something smaller and—" I started.

"*Ahem*," Aspen coughed.

"Right, never mind."

"We'll worry about it later," Angela insisted. "It's only been a day, and we have three weeks here."

"Or as long as it takes for my mom to cancel her credit card," Aspen mumbled.

All of a sudden, Izzy burst into tears, and everyone looked at her. She buried her hands in her face and started absolutely wailing. I was wondering how long it would take for that to happen. Izzy is many things, but emotionally guarded isn't one of them.

"We should—" Angela got up, "we should go to bed." She helped Izzy up, and they ~~walked~~ limped back to the blue tent. You could still hear the muffled crying after they closed the flaps.

That left Aspen, Liles, and me on separate logs around the fire, staring awkwardly at the ground.

"That tent is cramped," Aspen said as if nothing had happened. "I think I'll sleep out here."

"I was about to suggest the same thing," I yawned.

"I wasn't," Liles laughed, standing up. "With all these storms? You two have fun, but I'm staying dry."

"G'night, then," I mumbled. He ducked into our little pink tent and closed the flaps behind him.

"Great," Aspen sighed. "I can't even go to sleep till this fire is out."

"Hey," I said, "I already took a nap, let me stay up. You go to bed."

"You sure?" he asked. "I'm sure you're still tired."

"Yeah," I nodded. "You should sleep, but good luck out here with no blankets."

"One second," he yawned, getting up and walking to the sedan.

He returned with a couple rolled up sleeping bags. "I didn't know we had those?" I said.

"I didn't want the girls to take them," Aspen said, tossing me one that almost fell into the fire. An hour later, he passed out on the other side of one of the logs facing the pink tent. And the fire was still crackling, which meant I was still awake. The smoke was starting to bother my eyes, but the coals were almost dead. It could have been completely out in a matter of minutes if I'd only had some water. However, the closest water source was the sink up the hill, and it was frightfully dark out. Not to mention there was no way I could climb that steep hill again when I barely had the energy to stand.

This gave me another moment to think about how exactly I would leave. But why did I need to go anywhere? I could have asked Liles more about what Alex said about the exotic shifters, but what difference would that have made? I was dead either way. If I stayed, in theory, the huntsmen would eventually find me at the camp. If I left, I'd be alone again. It took me this long to realize that was the last thing I wanted...

"You've no idea just how vulnerable a wolf is without a pack."

Then there was Angela—I had to talk to her before I made any serious decision, but how would I justify putting her and everyone else in danger just because I was afraid to leave? All the hypotheticals were driving me crazy. I lay down on the log I was sitting on and watched the fire die, its light fading as I closed my eyes.

The next morning, I awoke to what sounded like an alarm. It was subtle, but enough to get me up. The wind must have changed direction or something that night, because my eyes were almost swollen shut and my clothes reeked of smoke. I followed the noise which led me to Aspen, who was sleeping soundly, despite the obnoxious blaring right next to his ear.

Angela emerged from her tent, like me, still wearing the same clothes as yesterday. Her eyes looked heavy, and her hair was a tangled mess. "What happened to you?" I asked. I started shaking Aspen. "Hey, get up."

"Me?" Angela said. "What happened to *you*?" Aspen sat up and rubbed his eyes. He picked up his phone.

A light above its camera was flashing, and the alarm was definitely coming from it. "Is it ringing?" Angela asked.

"It shouldn't be," Aspen mumbled, barely awake. "I blocked all my contacts." He looked at the phone and squinted painfully at the bright light before lying back down. "It's just an Amber Alert, it'll go away," he yawned. I picked up the phone and investigated the message flashing across the screen.

"What's an Amber Alert?" Angela asked.

"It's for abducted people," Aspen replied drowsily. "The phone sends you Amber Alerts so you can, like, look out for the missing person and call the cops."

"Aspen," I said, "I think it's about you."

"What?" He sat up and took the phone from me.

EA: [AMBER Alert, MS LIC/ : a long list of numbers I can't remember: (MS) Navy-Blue Sedan.]

Aspen stared at the message on the screen, then swiped it right. From a dropdown list, he selected some sort of news app. It wasn't long before he found the story. "Aspen Green, age twelve, last seen in Pike County, Mississippi, with stolen navy-blue sedan," he read out.

"Does your mom think you were abducted?" Angela asked.

"I don't know," he replied. "I didn't leave a note or anything, so maybe?"

"Great," I grumbled. "Now we're gonna have to disguise the car somehow."

"It—it's already busted to scrap!" Aspen shouted.

"Yeah, we might have to paint it," Angela agreed. "It's still a navy-blue sedan."

Aspen sighed, sitting up on the log he'd been lying next to. I turned to Angela. "What should I say?" I whispered.

"I spent all night comforting Izzy," she muttered, "you're on your own with this one." She patted me on the shoulder, starting up the hill to the outhouse.

I sat down with Aspen. "Sorry." It was all I could think to say.

"It's fine," he said, rubbing the tired from his eyes. "I just feel a little guilty. I'll bet my mom's really worried."

"We'll get you home as soon as we can," I assured him.

"Right," he sighed. "It's just—I really don't want to go home."

"What?" Now, the way I said that, it may have been taken the wrong way, but I just couldn't imagine anyone wanting to stay with us after everything that had already happened. "If it's the car, I think your mom will just be happy to have you back."

"Never mind," he mumbled. "I, well... there's this—" He took a moment. "There isn't really much to do at home, and you guys are really cool."

Liles came out of the tent, stretching his arms up above his head. He was also wearing the same clothes from yesterday, but despite his exhausted appearance, he had a glint of crazed energy in his eyes, like he just drank a hundred cups of coffee.

"Chase," he started triumphantly, "I think I've finally found a formula for a successful antidote!"

"Wait, really?" I asked excitedly.

"Yes!" he said, clapping his hands together. "But we're missing a couple ingredients."

"Name 'em!" I said, standing up. "I'll find them, right now."

"We need flowers from a plant called a Phlox, and—" He pulled out his small, ancient-looking book. It was black with a strange medical caduceus on the front cover and binding that was visible through its bent leather spine.

"Where'd you get that?" I asked. Looking back on it, I'm pretty sure that it was the same book he was reading out in the field. One more blank-out to credit to my half-starved brain.

"It was my great-grandfather's," he replied, flipping the pages. "It took me long enough to translate his handwriting. It was tucked in one of the pocket things inside this bag when I found it."

"Go on," I said.

"One teaspoon of honey, and a diluted form of bismuth subsalicylate."

"Where are we gonna get all that?" I asked.

"The drug store?" he suggested. "Bismuth subsalicylate is basically Pepto Bismol. I'll probably need to get Kaopectate, though, since it says in the book that it needs to be a dog-safe amount, and I've heard veterinarians more commonly use that one. Meaning, it will be easier to find the dose on Aspen's Internet."

"No, it's not *my* Internet," Aspen corrected. "I mean, it's my phone and my data, but—" He gave up. "Never mind."

"Then why all the extra honey and flowers and stuff?" I asked. "Also, even I know about the Internet, Liles. Where were you living before—"

"Before imprisonment?" he asked. "With my family, which is also Alex's family, if that tells you anything. In regard to your original question, one, because you're a shapeshifter, and, two, because you have Morph-Bone."

"Who was your great-grandfather?" I asked. "This is some pretty advanced stuff."

"Well, the book says *Property of Dr. Alexander*. It's a family name. It's my middle name, too."

"What was your great-grandfather's last name?" I asked.

"Um," he paused, turning to the last page of the book. "It doesn't say."

"Well, what's Alex's last name?"

"Good question," he mumbled.

"You don't know?" I said, confused. "He's your grandfather!"

"I got captured when I was twelve," he said defensively. "And we never visited him when I was around."

"You never heard anyone mention it?"

"What's going on?" Angela asked, walking over to us. She had new clothes, brushed hair, and fresh breath, but she still looked tired.

"Do you know Alex's last name?" I asked.

"Willis?" she offered.

"That's my dad's last name," Liles sighed, still reading.

"Wait, you don't know?" Angela asked him.

"Hey, you've lived with him longer than me," he replied, turning a page.

"Oh, wait!" Angela shouted, snapping her fingers. "Pierce."

"Pierce?" I asked. "Are you sure?" Liles looked up from his book. He seemed skeptical.

"Positive," she replied. There were a few voices missing. I turned around and noticed Aspen was gone.

"Oh, no," I grumbled, turning around.

"What's the matter?" Liles asked.

"I've gotta go find Aspen," I sighed.

"Hang on, I'm going to need some help with this," Liles said, gesturing to his book.

"Later," I replied, "I'm sorry." I started up the hill toward the outhouse, leaving Liles and Angela to talk (let's face it) gossip.

"You know, the longer you delay this, the fewer ketone bodies your brain has to live off of!" Liles shouted at me when I was about halfway to the top. "If you've any left at all!"

I searched in the outhouse, over by the tuna cans and around the tree, but Aspen wasn't there. I must have upset him. I didn't really act all that excited when he said he wanted to stay. I quickly turned to face the back of the outhouse, and that's where I found him sitting in the grass drawing in his sketchbook while Izzy attempted to tie his layered hair into tiny braids.

"Hi," Izzy said, looking up.

"What are you guys doing?" I asked.

"You guys were just arguing with each other, as usual, while Aspen was forced to sit and listen. So, I brought him up here," she sighed, frustrated with us, or at least me.

"Oh," I mumbled, looking down.

Aspen seemed pretty transfixed on his paper and pencil, probably unaware that Izzy was styling his hair. "Come sit with us," Izzy insisted, patting the ground next to her.

I walked over and sat down awkwardly. There had to have been some leftover tension from our little confrontation. There's no way she just brushed it off. Then again, I may only have that impression drilled in my mind from all my fights with Angela, who never lets anything slide. "What were you all talking about anyway?" she asked me.

"Besides the fact that my life revolves around medical problems," I sighed. "Nothing much."

She simply nodded. "I didn't hear much. Something about Alex…"

This caught Aspen's attention, and he looked up from his paper. "Who's Alex?"

"We were just trying to remember his last name," I replied.

"I don't think I know it," Izzy shrugged. "Alex keeps a lot of secrets. So do my grandparents, they waited years to tell me they knew my parents were dead."

"Sorry."

"It's fine." She finally completed one mini-braid in Aspen's hair.

My words felt meaningless, like I had been treating everyone's problems the same. Man, I wish there was another word out there besides "sorry."

"It felt good to share with Angela last night," Izzy continued. "I thought I could keep to myself just this once." She paused for a moment. "Speaking of, I'm sorry for what I said yesterday. But you were right to be upset, I was just calling attention to myself..." I know she didn't mean it like that. Why would she own it?

"No, I should be the one apologizing," I insisted. "I've been a jerk, and I know you weren't trying to feel, I mean, trying to make *me* feel—" I couldn't even finish the sentence. I was out of breath, out of energy. "What I mean is, keeping secrets can come back to bite you. Like with Angela, I should have just told her what Osscar said about Chris as soon as I saw her."

How was that even relevant? I was supposed to be apologizing. Luckily Izzy just went with it. "Yeah, but she's like you. She doesn't share with anyone."

"Are we thinking of the same Angela?" I couldn't think of anyone more outspoken if I tried. She doesn't seem to have any trouble sharing her grievances with me.

"She's just lost her father and one of her best friends in a single month, and she's barely shed a tear," Izzy said. "I swear, you're so oblivious sometimes."

"That's fair, but in my defense, no one's telling me anything."

"Now you know how it feels," she mumbled. "You keep secrets, too." I wasn't sure what to say to that. "You don't have to, you know. We all care about you."

I just didn't buy it. "I guess." There was a long silence as I thought it through. "Sorry, some things are just hard to share."

"I can understand that." Another pause.

"Is something else wrong?" I asked. "I mean, you're usually more—happier?" Nice grammar, I know. But I specifically remember saying that.

"Nobody told you?" she asked. I shook my head, and she turned back to Aspen. "My brother didn't survive that attack on the house…"

"I'm so sorry." It's occurring to me now, like so many other things, that I didn't really write all that much about Malachi. But what's there to say? None of us ever saw him, not even Izzy. The cellar was strictly off-limits, mostly because the entire basement level was also Alex's bedroom.

"I'll change the subject," she said after yet another long pause in our conversation. "Why did you and Angela get in another fight back at the house?"

"Come on, you have to know why. I couldn't just let her run out injured."

"She seems to think you were only looking after your own skin."

"I thought you said she didn't share," I grumbled.

"She does sometimes," Izzy laughed.

Aspen closed his sketchbook and tied the little leather strings back around it. "Could you guys tell me more?" he asked, turning around. "I know it's annoying when I ask so many questions, but it's no fun being lost." It's possible Aspen heard what Liles said up on the hill the night before. But it was more likely that my attitude during the whole shapeshifter conversation was what led him to feel like a burden. I was surprised he wanted to stay after that. I needed to do something to make it up to him.

"Any question you ask, I'll answer it," I said. "I promise."

Izzy glanced at me, shocked. She smiled like she was proud of me and hugged Aspen. Then she started back down toward camp. Aspen now had a couple of insubstantial braids at the base of his hair. Izzy did her best with hair as short as his. They didn't look half-bad.

"Izzy's really nice," Aspen said, twiddling his pencil around.

"Yeah, she is," I mumbled, already questioning why I'd agreed to tell him anything.

"Who was your sister?" he asked.

"Wait. What?" I was horribly confused. *Not once did I mention—*

"You talk in your sleep."

"What?" I crossed my arms.

"You said *any question,*" he reminded me.

"My sister's name was Ethelia." I think that was the first time I'd said her name in almost five years. I choked on it. But seriously, if I'm just *blurting out* random personal facts in my sleep, how do I have anything to hide?

"Who's Osscar?"

"Osscar is Liles' brother. He went missing a little while ago."

"Why do you wear those bandages around your arms?"

I wear long pants all the time, so it's not surprising that Aspen didn't know my legs are also wrapped up. "I have a medical condition called Morph-Bone," I replied. "My bones are fused with one of my animal forms."

"What animal?" he asked.

"I don't know."

"That's all," he said.

"Good," I sighed.

He still looked like he was holding something back. "What? Come on, something's still bothering you."

"Do you want me to go home?" he asked.

"Yes," I replied quickly and honestly. "I enjoy your company, and I wish you could stay. But I don't want you to get hurt. It would be my fault for not taking you home when I should've."

He nodded. "Now that's all." The questions were less explicit than I expected. It made me wonder if he knew more than we thought he did about shapeshifters, or if he was just afraid to ask anything more than the basics about me.

25: ANGELA

Liles didn't seem as annoyed as I was when Chase excused himself from the conversation. I had to ask myself why I cared—probably because I was used to it from him. "Why does he just run off like that all the time?" I wondered. "We get to a point where we require his input, and suddenly he has an excuse to leave."

"You're joking, right?" Liles asked. "You both do it."

"I do not."

"Three times just yesterday."

"Pfft. Well—"

"You have no excuse," he continued.

"What was he blabbering on about anyway?" I asked, getting flustered. "Just Alex's last name?"

"Don't change the subject. See? You're doing it right now."

"That's not the same."

"Sure it is," he replied.

"I think you like confrontation," I laughed.

"I do, occasionally. After spending years in a box where you're forced to co-exist with a bunch of other people twenty-four seven, what would *you* wanna do when you got out?"

"Punch somebody," I replied, nodding.

"Exactly."

"I guess I do have a tendency to...avoid certain conversations," I mumbled. Liles nodded. "We should probably go see where everyone went."

"You go ahead and do that, but I have to go to the store," he said, leaning over to tie his shoe.

"The store?" I asked excitedly. I *never* got to go shopping, no matter how much I begged Dana and Henry to let me come with them to get supplies.

"Yeah. I saw a drugstore a ways past the camp entrance. I'm headed over there to get stuff for Chase."

"Can I come? Please? It's safer to take someone with you."

"That would mean we are leaving Chase and Izzy to watch Aspen."

"They'll be fine," I said, waving it off. "Please let me come?"

Liles sighed. "Do you have any kind of bird shift?"

I bit my lip. "No. But you could carry me there as your owl, right? If I was a mouse?"

"Okay." He paused, looking at my leg. "I don't want to hurt you, though."

"How would you hurt me?"

"I don't know....owl instincts, sharp talons, small rodent."

"Oh, come on, it'll be fine." I shifted into my field mouse, my clothes dropping onto my head. As fun as it is being small, it never ceases to be scary. Imagine suddenly being smaller than the bottom of someone's shoe.

He rolled his eyes. "Another thing you and Chase have in common—you both tend to jump the gun."

"I know," I said proudly. My voice was much higher in this form. Liles walked over to our busted car and grabbed some clothes from it, stuffing them into a garbage bag. He picked up the straps of the bag, pulling them around his arms like a backpack, and used his belt to fasten it to his torso. "Good idea," I squeaked. He wrote something on a small piece of paper from his pocket and rested it on the top of the boys' pink tent. It was most likely a note for the others. *Finally, someone thinks to write one!*

"Ready?"

"I'm ready!" I said, hyping myself up.

He ran across the campgrounds and shifted into his eagle owl. He used his beak to tighten the belt strap holding the garbage bag of clothes to his body and lifted straight up into the air. I looked up to see the owl diving toward me. Every instinct in my little mouse body was telling me to run away as fast as I could to the safest hole I could find, but I closed my eyes tightly, trusting Liles and bracing myself for impact.

SNATCH!

I was hoisted into the air, resting in Liles' talons as if they were a cage. It was terrifying when I opened my eyes to see just how high up I was, and I'm sure I screamed like

a tiny banshee. I'd never flown before, not even in an airplane. Neither Alex nor my dad would ever let me.

Treetops zoomed by below us, and I watched our campgrounds fade from view. I smiled as we flew over one of many suburban lakes in the area, and before I even noticed, a large Louisiana heron was soaring alongside us. The beautiful tricolored bird was so close its wing and Liles' almost touched. The wind in my fur felt amazing, and the relaxing sound of the small manmade fountain at the center of the lake made me confident enough to uncurl my tail, letting it flop around in the breeze. Now I really understand the expression "free as a bird." It was the most liberating experience ever. Sadly, it ended as quickly as it began.

I felt Liles start to descend and turn left. I held on tightly as he took us over the road leading out from the trailer park. He jerked right, and when I looked down, we were hovering over a gas station. His wings flapped rapidly as the ground slowly approached me once again. He carefully dropped me on the pavement behind a large dumpster, shortly before landing. I was still trying to take in everything that had just happened, when I looked up at the sky and saw the same heron from earlier fly over

us, slowly shrinking into the distance. My ears drooped. I would have loved to continue across the sky with it. I realized that I could someday, and for the first time in years, I didn't feel like being a shapeshifter was such a curse after all.

When I turned around, Liles was already in his human form, halfway dressed. He slipped his shirt on, stuffed the empty garbage bag into his pants pocket, and fastened his belt back on his waist before offering me his hand to jump on.

"I'm not shifting back?" I asked.

"It's much easier if we just go in, get the stuff, and come back," he replied. "I didn't injure you, did I?"

"No!" I shouted. "That was really—it was really fun!"

I jumped onto his hand, and he put me into his t-shirt pocket. "Try to stay low," he said quietly. "I don't want to scare anyone." I poked my head out of the small pocket and watched as Liles walked past the gas station and onto the sidewalk. This side of town looked safe enough, but I was still worried for him. A field mouse truly isn't the best backup if you're confronted with a strange character.

We approached a tan building that I assumed was the drugstore. The sign was too high on the roof for me to see.

Liles entered through a pair of automatic doors and went to an aisle that smelled heavily of cookies and crackers. He picked up a package of Oreos and tucked it under his arm.

"Wait, how are we going to pay for those?" I asked quietly. "Or, any of this stuff, for that matter?" He reached into his back pocket and pulled out a wallet stuffed with cash. "Is that Chase's wallet?"

"His medicine, his money," Liles whispered. "Plus, he owes me for making the trip down here. So, cookies."

I laughed. "Good idea, pick up a gallon of milk while you're at it."

He wandered over to a shelf of jars and canned goods, grabbed a bottle of honey shaped like a bear, then walked down another aisle lined with shelves stocked with over-the-counter medications.

"Can't get milk, it's too heavy to fly back," he whispered. "That would be nice, though."

He scanned the tiny boxes and bottles of meds, grabbing two: Kaopectate and Advil.

"Why do we need painkillers?" I asked.

Liles sighed. "Just in case."

I didn't like the sound of that. He continued on through the store, grabbing a bottle of chocolate syrup next to where he got the honey. "Just in case again?"

"It will make this concoction of crap taste better," he mumbled, scanning the remaining aisles.

"How bad could it be? Honey, flavored medicine, and flowers?"

"Are only three of the ingredients," he added. "I had most of the others already."

"Oh," I sighed. He grabbed one last thing as we approached the register. "A pencil sharpener?" I asked.

"For Aspen." He dropped all the stuff onto the counter. "I noticed he didn't have one."

"Does he write?"

"He draws. He's even drawn you a couple times," he whispered as a woman approached the counter.

"Did you find everything you were looking for today?" she asked as she scanned the items.

"Yes, can you please put those in one triple bag?" Liles requested.

"Alright," she replied suspiciously. "It will be pretty heavy. Are you sure?"

"I'm sure."

I watched a man behind the woman checking us out. He was a big guy with a scruffy walrus moustache, khaki pants, and a button on his checkered shirt that said *Manager*. I noticed him squinting at us, and hoped it was just my paranoia, but I could hear Liles gulp nervously. I tucked my head further into his shirt pocket to avoid being seen.

"Twenty-three forty-one," the cashier said quickly.

Liles handed her a twenty and a five. "Keep the change," he said, taking our bag of things. By the acceleration of his heart rate, I could tell he was just as eager to leave as I was. But as we turned to approach the automatic exit doors, the manager stopped us.

"Where ya headed?" he asked.

"Back to my hotel." Liles was a much better liar than Osscar, but that's not saying much.

"Alright, well, you kids stay safe," the manager said as we exited the building.

Liles stopped in his tracks as the door closed behind us. "Did he just say—"

BANG!

Something small flew past us, hitting the base of the telephone pole a few feet away. Liles started running, and

I feared we were done for. I looked around his shoulder and spotted the manager holding a BB gun that was still halfway in its packaging. He must have just grabbed it off the shelf, and while it wasn't enough to kill us, or at least Liles, it would really hurt.

"Shifters!" he yelled, chasing us.

BANG!

A ~~bullet~~ pellet from the gun hit Liles in the arm, but it didn't seem to faze him one bit.

"Are you okay!?" I shouted.

He didn't respond, but the manager was gaining on us.

BANG!

BANG!

BANG!

I wasn't just going to sit by and watch my friend get mauled. This guy already knew what we were. I could do this without freezing up. I jumped from the shirt pocket and shifted into my horse, stopping only to let Liles climb onto me.

BANG!

I felt the BB hit me in my bad leg. I winced and shook it off. He was only about a foot away by the time Liles and the bag of groceries were on me.

"Go!" Liles yelled.

I took off running almost as soon as the manager grabbed for my tail. We went around the lake and through the wooded areas, trying to lose him in the trees. But he was persistent and kept up until we leapt into the bicycle lane along the road. Cars swerved and people pointed as I continued toward the trailer park.

The manager jumped out into the lane as well. We were saved when he was hit by a rather unfortunate motorcyclist that wasn't able to stop fast enough. I was recently informed by Aspen that riding a motorized vehicle in the bike lane is illegal, so I guess this is why. There was a huge crash followed by some screaming and honking. The motorcycle, its rider, and the manager of the drugstore all tumbled down the road, and we kept on.

I took the turn before the one I was supposed to—just in case the manager somehow walked away from that crash and saw us—and cut through the woods to the Happy Campers Trailer Park entrance shortly after. The gatekeeper wasn't there, so I jumped the car blocker. When we finally spotted the windshield-less navy-blue sedan guarding the entrance to our site, my heart was beating out of

my chest. I let Liles off, but didn't have enough energy to shift back. We both collapsed, me on my three good legs.

I saw Chase and Aspen running over to us. Aspen was holding a bunch of purple flowers.

"Hey, where'd you guys go?" Chase asked. "What happened?" He looked over at me, and his tone changed drastically.

"There were huntsmen at the drugstore," Liles groaned, sitting up.

"You guys alright?" Aspen asked.

"We sustained some minor injuries," Liles sighed, looking over at the back of his arm, which had two small red holes in it. They weren't bleeding too badly.

"You guys got shot?" Chase said, panicked.

"With a BB," Liles grumbled. "But, yeah. I got two in the arm, one in the leg."

"I also got one in the leg," I said, looking back at my left leg. I must have been extremely sensitive near my injury because the pellet hadn't even penetrated my skin.

Aspen dropped the flowers and ran over to the sedan. He came back with a small white box decorated with a red cross, pulling out some Betadine and Neosporin and gesturing for Liles to extend his arm out. Liles didn't strike

me as the type to accept medical assistance, but he went ahead and let Aspen pour the Betadine on his arm.

Izzy ran over from the firepit. She took one look at us before coming to hug me around the neck.

"I'm fine," I assured her. "Really."

Chase stood frozen for a moment, zipping up his jacket.

"You think you can shift back?" Izzy asked me quietly. Having calmed down, I nodded and stood up, letting Izzy lead me away behind our tent.

26: CHASE

I had watched the girls leave, racked with guilt. I couldn't help feeling like it was partially my fault. I was the whole reason they went to the store in the first place. Even if they weren't injured too badly, Liles and Angela seemed rattled. I stared at the ground as Aspen helped Liles to his feet and remained silent.

Liles walked over, placing a hand on my shoulder. "Don't worry," he said. "We'll walk it off." I nodded and he started up the hill to the outhouse.

Aspen was picking the contents of the first aid kit off the ground and looked over to me. "I'll get us a fire here in a few minutes," he said, standing up. "You can go rest if you want."

"I'm perfectly fine," I grumbled. "*They're* the ones who are hurt."

"You say that, but you look like death." I looked at him, confused. "Just saying. You have, like, dark circles under your eyes."

I shrugged off the comment and made my way up the hill where I saw Liles washing up in the sink. He seemed a lot calmer. He wiped his face with his sleeve and turned to me.

"Is there anything I can do to help?" I asked.

"You can help me make this remedy," Liles suggested.

"No, I mean help *you*," I replied.

"That *would* help me," he countered. "Chase, what happened was not your fault, and I'm fine." I looked over at the two red holes in his arm. The surrounding skin was darker from the orange colored Betadine. "It was just a

BB," he laughed. "It's more of a toy than a gun. I'm sure Angela's fine too—it was only a little stressful."

I nodded. "Well, I'm still sorry it happened."

He waved it off. "Don't be, we got everything we needed, including some cookies. Besides, Angela seemed to have a good time on the way there." That put me at ease. "Now, will you come help me get you better, or not?"

"Yeah, but I want to check on her first," I replied.

"Fine by me. Later I'll attempt to make that Advil we bought safer for her and me to take," he continued. "It will stop inflammation in her leg and hopefully reduce the pain."

"Never mind, let's make that now," I said.

"We probably won't get your antidote done by the end of the day then."

"That's fine," I replied. "It'll make me feel better, you know, mentally."

"Alright," he shrugged, "let's get started on that, but *I* will feel better when you're healthy."

"I'm afraid neither of us will live to see that day," I replied, almost laughing.

"Okay, healthy-*er*," he corrected. "I just have to fix the parts of you I broke, so I don't have guilt. The rest of your

problems are on you." We headed back down the hill to our pink tent with the bag from the drugstore and, once inside, spilled its contents onto the floor. We sat across from each other with the pile of purchases between us. He took a box of Advil from the pile and opened his doctor's bag.

"Chocolate syrup?" I asked, holding up the tall brown bottle.

"Yours," Liles replied. "It will help your antidote go down easier." That's not exactly the kind of thing you wanna hear when your jailbird friend is making you experimental drugs from a little pink tent in the woods. He pulled out a small mortar and pestle from his doctor's bag and started crushing the Advil tablets. "We don't have an exact weight on myself or Angela, so I'll have to dull the dose a bit."

"You should do this for a living," I said. "You're really good at this doctor stuff."

"I'm just reading the notes in my great-grandfather's book; the legible ones, at least."

He pulled a couple of plastic syringes from the bag and popped the needles off. "We only have Luer Lok syringes," he sighed. "I knew I was forgetting something at the store."

I looked back down at the pile of stuff. "How did you buy all this? Did Aspen lend you his mom's credit card or something?" He reached into his back pocket. "You took my wallet?" I flipped through what little cash was left inside.

"Yeah," he replied. "This was your stuff, after all."

"Fair point," I mumbled, closing the leather thing. "It's seriously nice to know I still have this though."

"Apologies for not giving it back sooner. I brought it accidentally with my clothes when we fled the house," he said, adding the substances from a few vials and the crushed-up Advil to a paper bowl in front of him.

"I... guess it's fine," I sighed, pocketing the wallet.

"So, are we going to talk about what happened in the car yesterday?" Liles asked. I knew he was referring to the whole glowing eyes thing I'd been hopelessly trying to forget.

"Um," I started, rubbing my neck. "You know, I really don't want to."

"Well, it's kind of a big deal." He opened a tiny box containing a small, dead plant. "Has that kind of thing ever happened before?"

"I think so, but I always thought the red, saturated vision was a Morph-Bone symptom."

"Pfft, no," Liles laughed, ripping the withered leaves off the box plant. I felt like an idiot at that point, in part because I had absolutely no idea what he was doing. "So, what's your extinct animal shift?" he asked, crushing the tiny leaves with the mortar and pestle.

"I don't know."

"Angela told me that whenever you say that, it's likely a lie."

"I still don't know what an exotic shapeshifter even is," I argued. "Maybe you could elebrate on that?"

"Well, assuming you mean *elaborate*, Alex told us this creepy legend. Or—my grandfather, whatever I'm supposed to call him. Anyway, it was some hokey thing about positions of great peril and bodies reaching beyond the grave."

"What?"

"Yeah, so I'm curious about that." He dumped the ground-up leaves into his paper bowl. "I'm also curious about what exactly those bandages are made of."

"I really don't know," I grumbled.

"I might believe ya on that one," he laughed. "Those things are sorely in need of replacement."

"Hey, they're all I've got."

"You've seriously been wearing those same ones for two solid years?" he asked. "That's actually disgusting." And everyone wonders why I don't share? You'd think eventually those kinds of comments would stop hurting my feelings, but no. Not to mention, people tend to lean toward commenting on things I can do absolutely nothing about. "I'm starting to warm up to Aspen," he said, changing the subject. "He's very resourceful."

"Me too," I sighed. I still had some guilt from earlier. I meant what I said to Aspen about enjoying his company. He's a good kid, but he has to go home. He can't shift. How would he defend himself if someone attacked the camp?

Liles mixed up the contents of the tiny paper bowl with what looked like a little blown-glass spoon and used the two non-idyllic syringes to suck up the liquid concoction of Advil until one was filled to the 10mL mark and the other to the 9mL mark. "Since I couldn't get a weight, I calculated by age," he said, handing me the 9mL syringe. "That's for Angela." He stuck the 10mL syringe into his mouth and squirted it down. "Well, that tastes horrid," he

coughed, shaking his head. "Better go, um, give that to her, and bring me those flowers you and Aspen had on your way back."

The girls weren't hard to find. They were sitting with Aspen, trying to build the fire back up. Angela was back in her human form with new clothes. She had her auburn hair tied into a twisted braid, with her side bangs still flowing loose. Izzy had to have done that, considering I've never seen Angela style her hair even once. Izzy also taught me those substandard hair terms. Against my will, I might add.

I walked over and sat down with them. "Hey," Angela said, smiling. She truly looked very nice. I wanted to compliment her, but for whatever reason, I hesitated. Maybe I felt like it would just make things awkward?

"Liles made you some painkillers," I said, handing her the little syringe with gray liquid Advil inside.

"I feel much better," she replied, stacking twigs onto the firepit, "but I appreciate it." She held it up. "Wait, what's in this?"

"No clue."

She shrugged, squirting the syringe into her mouth and handing it back to me.

"Will you help us?" Izzy asked. She did her own hair as well. It was pinned up, leaving a few loose curls dangling in front of her face. I complied.

"We're having steak for dinner," Aspen said. "We have to eat the meat before it all goes bad. Out of dessert, though."

"That's alright," Angela replied. "We'll manage."

"Liles bought Oreos," I said quietly.

Everyone turned to me like I'd just blurted out the answer to an unsolvable problem that would save the world.

"Oreos!" Aspen smiled.

"Oh, that's right!" Angela said. "I almost forgot.

"Do we have to wait until dinner?" Izzy asked.

Aspen nodded. "Did you get the ones with the pop rocks?"

Angela turned to him. "They make those?"

"Only around the Fourth of July, but they're really good."

"I like the vanilla golden ones," said Izzy.

"You would," Angela chuckled. They all started laughing.

"Chase, do you have a favorite?" Aspen asked.

The thought of food still made me sick. I couldn't recall ever liking anything enough to eat it, let alone having a favorite. "Not sure."

He looked down at the pile of sticks. "Okay, everyone, step back, I think we can light it now." He pulled out a butane lighter and ignited the twigs. The irony of the youngest kid carrying out this task wasn't lost on anyone. The fire burst into brilliant orange and yellow flames. He threw in some dry leaves, slowly building up the smaller engulfed sticks with larger logs.

Angela stared at the fire and smiled. Something about her had changed. She looked invigorated. "I wanna talk to you about something," she said as she sat down on our log. I joined her without the energy to speak. Every now and then the lack of nutrients would catch up with me, usually when I got off my feet. I rested my head against my hand. I could have dozed off, had she stopped talking for a few minutes. "Liles took me flying today. It was the most amazing feeling in the world." She continued passionately. "Even though I wasn't in control, I've never felt so free."

"That sounds... really cool," I replied listlessly. "I'm glad you had a good time."

"Will you help me get a bird shift?" she asked. "Please?"

"Angie, I don't have one of those—"

"I know, but maybe you can help me get one. You don't have to be the kind of coach Alex was, but if you were, I wouldn't mind."

"You want me to scare you?" I asked, sitting up.

She laughed. "Only if you have to—but yes."

"When?" I had an idea. This was almost the perfect opportunity for me to tell Angela about my extinct animal exotic thing. We would be alone. I just had to come up with a plan to stall until I knew what to say.

"Now?" she suggested, looking up at the hill.

"Race ya," I said, standing up.

"No you don't!" Liles yelled from our stupid pink tent. "You're going to burn your heart out before I even finish this antidote!" Angela looked over at the tent annoyed. "You can walk!" I sighed, slowly starting up the hill, but we secretly picked up the pace halfway to the top. My heart was pounding, but this time, I don't think it had anything to do with not eating.

Angela ran out to the big open space near the outhouse and stood ready. "Hit me!"

"With what?" I tried my best to remember exactly what Alex used to do to get someone to shift. It usually

started with making the person believe they were in a safe scenario, then pulling the rug out from under them. I could do that. "Okay, close your eyes."

"What?" She closed her eyes and I put my hands on her shoulders, walking her backwards over to the edge of the top of the hill, the side opposite the creek. "Oh, dear," she mumbled. "Where are we going?" I spun her around a few times so she couldn't picture where she was. "Whoa, okay," she laughed, stumbling over.

"Trust fall," I said, letting her go.

"Um, no, you made me dizzy. I won't be able to catch myself?"

"That's the point," I replied, walking behind her. "You *have* to trust me."

"I don't know... You can literally turn into a weasel at any point."

"Now!" I shouted.

Angela let herself fall halfway backward, but attempted to stand straight up on her own. The act of pulling herself forward caused her to tumble over the edge off the hill and hit a bush. I looked down the hill and almost laughed as she emerged from the plants. Her styled hair was now messed up, and she was pretty mad. "I trusted you!"

"No, you didn't," I insisted. "I would have caught you. I was standing right below you, but you tried to catch yourself and got off balance."

"So you let me tumble down the hill? I'm sorry, how is this helpful?"

"Because I need you to trust me before I try and scare you."

"I *do* trust you," she argued.

"Then what was that?" I asked, gesturing to the bush.

"Look, Chase," she sighed. "I don't want you to take this the wrong way, but—" She paused and looked around. "It's not that I don't trust *you*, but you *are*...physically impaired. And I really don't want to have a situation where I fall backward, you try to catch me, and—" I waited. "And we both end up having to take whatever medicine Liles gave you back in the field."

"Part of trusting me is trusting my body," I replied.

"Do *you* even—"

"No," I interrupted, "but I don't trust my mind either, so between the two of us, you've made more headway. You're already halfway there."

Angela laughed. "Fine, let's just try again."

"Alright," I replied, walking just below the edge of the hill. "Stand above me and fall backwards."

"I'm going to hurt myself," she muttered, closing her eyes. She started falling but panicked again. This time she had enough balance to fall on her butt in front of me. I looked down at her with eyebrows raised. "Again," she said, more determined. She stood back up.

"Eventually, we'll do this over the creek," I said, crossing my arms.

"I could die if I hit one of those rocks."

I shrugged. "Then I'd die too, so, you know, we'll save that until you know you can trust me."

She got up, brushed the dirt off her knees, and stood over the hill again. I got under her when she started leaning back. "Hold your arms!"

"Seriously?" she asked.

Suddenly, the smell of smoke and meat filled the air again. "We'll try again later," I said. "The others are probably waiting on us."

"Fine, but I'll trust you next time."

"Sure you will," I said. We both ran down the hill to see Aspen and Izzy spinning two small skewers over the firepit, each impaling two large steaks.

"Everyone gets a T-bone!" Aspen called. Angela stared at the steaks with wide eyes. "You guys can have these two if you want."

"I'll pass," I mumbled, looking away from the food.

"You may change your mind in a minute," Liles said, walking over to us.

"Wait," I started. "Did you—?"

He held a small vial filled with a green and brown liquid in front of my eyes. "I had to go get the flowers myself, but this is it."

"Possible side effects?" Angela asked, examining the vial.

"None," he replied confidently. "It either works, or it doesn't." He put the remedy in my hand. "I should warn you—it's probably going to be very painful at first."

I studied the little glass vial. Angela sat down on our log and gestured for me to scoot over. I sat with her, and Liles took the log parallel to ours, watching me closely to see if his antidote would work. "What's that?" Aspen asked, looking up from the steaks.

I mustered up the courage to uncork the little vial, and the smell alone made me want to throw it right into the

fire. Angela took it from me, putting the cork back on. "Wait until you're ready," she said calmly.

"What? No!" Liles shouted. "I lost sleep over that." I took the remedy back from Angela, uncorked it, and gulped it down. "It will most likely take a few moments for the pain to—"

Then, it hit me all at once. The familiar burning sensation spread from my stomach to all of my insides like someone had just lit me on fire from the inside out, but it was worse now than ever. The room started to spin, and I clutched my stomach in agony. I closed my eyes tightly, waiting for it to stop. Then I felt that same cold and consuming sensation I'd experienced in the car with Liles. But it wasn't caused by any grief this time, just good old physical pain...

"Never mind," Liles said.

"Chase?" Angela asked. I looked up, and everyone gasped in horror. Angela stood up and stepped away from me. "What's wrong with his eyes!?" she screamed at Liles.

"Oh, no," I heard Liles mutter. "Chase, you're going to be alright, but you might wanna close your eyes!"

I knew what was happening. My vision went red, like I was wearing a pair of super-saturated, red-tinted glasses.

This had *definitely* happened before; I could just never explain it.

"Wow!" Aspen gasped.

Angela was freaking out. "What did you do!?"

"*I* didn't do anything!" Liles shouted defensively. "He's just in pain."

"Pain makes your eyes glow like a monster!?" she shrieked.

"What's happening?" I heard Izzy cry. I kept my eyes closed, as pain zapped through me, along with that weird feeling that caused tremors throughout my whole body.

"Chase, you aren't in danger," Liles said calmly. "It will stop."

"*How* is that helping!?" Angela yelled.

"Because this isn't my fault!" he snapped.

"How is this not your fault!?"

I took a few deep breaths and unexplainable waves of cold slowly left me. The pain also started to die down enough for me to let go of myself and sit up. I opened my eyes, and everyone was staring at me. "How come he's normal now?" Angela shouted. "That was like the—" She stopped herself, looking over at Liles. She must have figured out what was happening. Liles simply nodded.

Angela turned back to me, her eyes full of fear, but in a different way this time. I didn't have the words. I should have told her earlier, but she didn't look angry, she looked terrified.

"I'm sorry, what's going on?" Izzy asked, a little frustrated. She seemed to be the only one still confused.

"Hey..." Liles said. I looked over at him. "You snapped out of it. But that aside, how do you feel?" My stomach growled loudly, and I pulled my jacket hood over my head in embarrassment. "That answers that question," he concluded. "I'm a genius. I fixed you, that's that."

"Thanks," I muttered.

Angela wouldn't stop staring at me like I was someone else, like I was deformed. *Sigh.* Bad analogy. Liles must have noticed, too, because he walked over and stood between us, breaking her stare.

She sat back down, much further from me this time. I turned away and looked down. I didn't expect her to react so brutally. Not only did that hurt, but I really was starting to feel like I was starving to death. I felt empty, like there was nothing inside me but hollow space and my heart that wouldn't stop racing.

Liles shot Angela an angry glare. I could tell they were having a conversation about me without words.

"Steaks are done," Aspen said awkwardly, "all of them."

Aspen gave Liles a steak on a paper plate. It was grilled to a charcoal texture on the outside, but the blood inside it pooled around the meat. Its smell filled my nose, and I could barely resist the urge to grab the plate right out of his hand. He offered it, and I cautiously accepted. I was still worried I would get hurt eating it, and then not be able to stop the red eyes a second time. But with my heart continuing to pound like it was about to quit on me, I had to try. "I'm really convinced the antidote worked," Liles said. "You can eat that, if you're hungry."

I ripped a piece of steak off the T-bone and ate it. I didn't feel the slightest bit of pain, and my heart rate slowed almost immediately. I actually wanted to finish the rest of the food. "Yeah, I'm fine," I said, "thank you."

"No problem," he replied. "Glad to see you're all better."

"I'm not so sure of that," Angela added. I couldn't tell what she was thinking, but she looked furious. "They're going to slaughter you!" she shouted. "Once they find out what you are, we'll *never* be safe!"

"We'll worry about it later," Liles insisted, glaring at her to drop it.

"You knew!" Angela yelled, standing up. "Alex told you all about what comes with being one of those—*things*!" She said that like I wasn't even a shapeshifter anymore, but some sort of cannibalistic creature that couldn't be controlled.

"Excuse me?" I snapped.

"Stop being so loud!" Liles whispered. "You never know who's listening!"

"Exactly!" she continued. "I bet you found out when the house went up! What if one of the huntsmen from the clearing had seen his eyes glow like that? We wouldn't have gotten away!"

"You don't know that!" he snapped back.

"What did he turn into?"

"He didn't, he just—" Liles started.

"Hey!" I shouted, standing up. "I'm right here! You can ask *me*, not Liles. He was just looking out for me."

Angela turned to me, her eyes filled with tears. "We'll die if—"

"No," I interrupted. "You're not gonna die because *I'm leaving*. I planned to as soon as I got better." Angela was

speechless. "Besides," I snapped, "you won't die if I do, you know the contract doesn't work that way." No one said a word after that. I turned around and started toward my tent. It was late anyway, and I was sick of the names, the accusations, the yelling. I put my hunger aside and went to bed.

The next morning, I woke up to Aspen and Liles playing a game of cards in our tent a few feet away from me. I sat up drowsily. Aspen turned around and waved. "Morning."

"How are you feeling?" Liles asked.

"Um," I said, rubbing my eyes, "hungry."

"Good," Liles smiled, drawing a card from one of the decks in front of him.

"Go fish," Aspen called, triumphantly laying a card down.

"Wait, I thought we were playing Rummy?" Liles said, confused.

"Got bored of that," Aspen replied. "We can put multicolored dots on the cards and play Go Fish." He pulled out his little blue case of colored pencils and began drawing red dots on all the Kings.

Liles rolled his eyes and looked back at me. "We'll cook breakfast here in a minute."

"I thought we were only doing one cooked meal a day?" Aspen argued.

"Well, Chase needs it, and I want hash browns."

"Yesterday sucked," I groaned.

"Yes, it did," Liles said, "but now we need to move on, and focus on getting you back to normal."

"I am back to normal," I replied, stretching.

He grabbed Aspen's phone off the floor, opening the camera app before handing it to me. My eyes widened as I looked at myself on the screen. My skin was a sickly greenish-white color and my eyes had big dark circles under them. My lips lacked color, and I'd definitely lost weight. "Told ya so," Aspen said. "You look like death."

"My point is made," Liles declared, taking Aspen's phone back. "You need food, you need rest, and you need fluids. You do not need to go back out there and fight with Angela some more. Though I'm sure you two could do that all day long."

"She thinks I'm a monster," I mumbled, lying back down.

"She's just worried about you," Liles insisted. "It's a lot to take in."

"She's right, though, I need to get away from you guys as soon as possible."

"Oh, please," he said. "You can't go out there by yourself."

"I've *been* out there by myself," I sighed. "Besides, even if we do somehow meet up with Alex and find someplace permanent to stay... If he found out what I am, I'd be kicked to the curb or killed for good measure. And you know it."

"Then I'll go with you," Aspen shrugged. "I'm not a shapeshifter, so I should be fine."

"They would kill you, Aspen," Liles replied. "If the huntsmen caught us."

"That's the thing," I argued, sitting back up. "Those people on the road were willing to kill me and Angela right there and then to make sure that saber-toothed cat didn't get away. What's to stop them from doing the same thing to get to me, and killing all of you on the spot?"

Liles rubbed the back of his neck. "Good point. But they don't know right now, and you can control it."

"Pfft." I crossed my arms. "My eyes started glowing after one stupid stomachache. I can't control anything."

"Well, in your defense—"

"No," I interrupted. "There is no reason I should be selfish and stick around."

"To save your own life?" he suggested.

"Liles," I started, "if Angela dies, I die. Leaving is my safest bet, and hers too."

"You truly think that contract is something to be concerned about?" he asked. I didn't have a reply, at least, not a believable one, but Liles seemed to be a master of sore subjects himself. "When will you leave?"

"Tomorrow?" I suggested. "I promise I'll take food."

"You aren't ready for that."

"They'll get me one of these days," I said irritably.

"Well," he sighed, "if you do get captured, a little word of advice, I—wouldn't mention my name."

"How come?" I asked. "What'd you do?"

"I broke a promise," Liles replied. "A pretty big one."

"Thanks for the warning. Hopefully, I'll never have to worry about it." Aspen hugged me and let go. "Thanks," I said, half-smiling. I turned to Liles. "Don't tell the girls, alright? They won't let me leave."

"I won't."

I looked back at Aspen. "I won't either," he mumbled.

"Promise?" I asked him.

"I promise," he replied, rolling his eyes. We all exited our pink tent and walked over to the firepit. "Guess I'll work on getting the fire back up," Aspen sighed.

"I'll help," Liles said, putting his foot up on one of the log benches to tie his shoe.

The girls had to have already been awake and up at the outhouse, because their tent flaps were wide open. Or, at least that's what I thought before I felt someone tap my shoulder. I spun around to see Izzy, who seemed uneasy. "I need your help," she said in a nervous tone.

"How can I—" I started to ask.

"Just follow me." She headed up the hill to the outhouse. I was hesitant at first, since I still didn't know where Angela was, but when I looked back at the guys, they both gestured for me to go on.

Izzy led me to the hole at the base of the sink next to the giant pile of tuna cans. "Angela went down that hole about ten minutes ago," Izzy said quietly. "She hasn't come back up."

"And you let her!?" I shouted.

"I'm sorry," she whimpered. "My rabbit won't fit. Can you go see if she's okay?"

"Sure, if she's not *dead*." I was about to shift into my weasel when a cloud of smoke erupted from the hole in the sink and a little brown field mouse came running out. It coughed, rubbing its eyes rapidly.

"Oh, thank goodness!" Izzy said, putting her hand over her heart.

"Izzy, I can't see!" Angela shouted. She covered her eyes with her mouse paws.

"One second!" Izzy told me before scooping up Angela and running into the outhouse.

Moments later they came back out, this time both as humans. Angela was wearing a loose yellow dress and was holding a wet T-shirt to her eyes, which (I could see when she uncovered them for a second) were bloodshot and swollen. "There were at least three of them," she said to Izzy. They slowly made their way back around the outhouse. Angela removed the T-shirt from her face for a moment to look up at me and stopped in her tracks. "Izzy, can you give us a minute?"

"I'm sorry," Angela told me, "for how I reacted last night. I'm sure this is all pretty hard on you."

"I really did mean to tell you," I replied.

"I believe you, but you aren't really leaving, are you?"

"Later t-today," I sighed. My decision was made. Why drag it out?

She looked stunned. "Where will you go?"

"Not sure," I replied, "but it's safer that way, for both of us."

Angela looked down. I don't think she knew what to say. "I'll miss you," she said finally.

Oh, okay... "I'll miss you too."

We stood there for a moment, neither of us sure of what to do. She eventually elected to hug me. It was quick, awkward, and made me a little sad. "Thanks," she continued, "for everything you've done for me."

"You too," I mumbled. *Wow, I guess I really am leaving.*

She stepped back. "But how will I know you're okay?"

"I'm gonna try and get a phone with my remaining money," I said. "I'll call Aspen's number. I promise to answer it."

"And if one day you don't?"

I wasn't sure how to respond. "I, um, I should keep packing," I said, pointing down the hill. "But, just so we don't end things on a bad note, I know you can protect

yourself and always have." I paused. "I just—didn't know how well you could protect us both. But things have changed, I've changed. And, I guess what I'm really trying to say is... I trust you."

Her eyes were misty. I couldn't tell whether it was because she was sad, or because they were still inflamed. "Chase, I didn't mean to—"

I really didn't want the conversation to go on. She'd given her opinion, and that's all I needed to hear. "I'm gonna go," I mumbled, waiting for her nod of confirmation, that there was nothing more to say, before starting back down to the tents.

Liles and Aspen had the fire back up and they were making hash browns on a grill engineered from a couple of hot dog skewers linked together and propped up by two sticks over the firepit.

"Hey," I said to Liles. He walked over to me. "I've changed my mind. I'm gonna leave now."

"What?" he asked. "Why?"

"Just—before I make the wrong decision. What do I need to take?"

He looked over at our tent and gestured for me to follow him. We both entered the little pink thing and sat down. "You talked to Angela?"

"Yeah," I replied, looking down, "she understands why I have to go."

"She didn't try to stop you?" he asked, rooting around in his doctor's bag.

"No."

Liles didn't ask any more questions. He pulled out a couple glass vials and a Sharpie. "I'll write the function of each of these on the back of the labels," he said. "Just, if you get into trouble."

I nodded. "Thanks."

"Here's the mild pain medication," he started, giving me a grayish vial. "Only drink to the line each time you take it." He drew little Sharpie lines on the sides of the remedy.

"Right," I replied.

"This can help heal bullet wounds," he continued, handing me a pinkish remedy. "Only use it if you really have to. The side effects, I don't have a cure for. But you'll need to remove the bullet yourself before you ingest it, unless you have an exit wound." I took it, and let it all sink in.

Persuaded by my own pride, I was headed out into a state I'd never been to, that we already knew was crawling with huntsmen. "And, um, you know what this one does." He gave me a reddish looking vial with a chunky brown film at the top.

"Yup," I replied, nervously taking it. "I'll be half-paralyzed before I take this again."

"Antidote," Liles said, handing me one last vial. "Just in case." I stuffed all the remedies in one of the plastic drugstore bags. He then shoved a stack of clothes at me. "Sorry, two outfits is all I can surrender. None of the clothes in the trunk fit me either."

"That's more than generous," I replied. "Seriously, thank you."

"Anytime," he said, ducking out of the pink tent. I followed him out. "Just take care of yourself."

I nodded, turning to Aspen who was handing me a black backpack. "Thanks," I said, smiling. "Where'd ya get this?"

"It was mine," he replied, shrugging. "I put some food in it." I put the drugstore bag with the vials and clothes into the backpack and slid it on.

Aspen had his hands in his pockets and didn't seem all that interested in what was going on. "Is it okay if I call your number to talk to everyone?" I asked.

"You're getting a phone?"

"Yeah," I replied, "if I can."

Aspen ran over to the blue sedan and came back with something that he was clutching tightly in his hands like a lucky charm. I looked down at it. "It was my dad's," he said, handing the clearly treasured object to me. "It already has my number in the contacts." I looked down at the sleek black phone and rubbed my finger across the screen. "It never had a password on it. You deserve it for avenging him."

"Oh, man," I mumbled, pushing the small round button at the base of the phone to turn it on. The screen displayed a younger picture of Aspen holding up a large fish by a pole. There was a small beagle puppy in the background of the picture and a woman that I could only assume was his mother. She looked so much like him, except her eyes were hazel. She appeared to be holding the dog back from the fish. The corner of the photo was obstructed by someone's thumb. "Seriously, thank you," I said, pocketing the phone.

Aside from the excitement of having a phone for the first time, I remember thinking something along the lines of: *Crap, it's glass! What the heck am I going to say if when I break this?*

Izzy emerged from her tent. "What's going on?" she asked, looking around at us. She figured it out moments later. "Wait a minute, Chase? Are you actually leaving?"

"Yeah," I said. "I'm sorry, Izzy."

"What about Angela?" she asked. "Does she know your leaving!?"

"Yes."

"And she didn't try to stop you?" Izzy shouted. Liles glared at her as if telling her to drop it. She looked up at him, then back over to me sadly. "Be careful."

I nodded, walking past the navy-blue sedan. "Thanks for everything, guys." I turned around and everyone was standing a few feet away. Everyone but Angela, who was nowhere to be found. It was probably best that I didn't go looking for her.

I kept on past the exit of the campgrounds, heading out toward the road.

Well, I guess that sort of leads up to now? It took me a good three days to write all of that down, but I can already tell this whole thing is going to need some very extensive editing, and that I don't even have half the story with only my account of what happened. That said, I've decided to include one more entry, featuring an event that took place just a couple days ago. You're welcome.

27: CHASE

WOODWORTH, LOUISIANA

MAY 2019

I had gotten, in total, about twelve minutes of sleep that night. Probably because I decided to start writing a book at midnight, due to the overwhelming amount of insomnia that comes with being alone as a shapeshifter in an unguarded place, especially when it's pitch black outside. It was six in the morning, and I was lying on a bench outside at one of those rest areas off the interstate. I wasn't quite sure if I was allowed to be there, but nobody came and said anything, so I just kept writing until the sun came up.

I purchased the notebook and pen as a set from the Late Night Rest-Stop Shop the morning before, and I was initially going to use the notebook paper as kindling for a fire, but quickly realized when I opened my wallet to pay for said notebook, that I didn't even have enough for a bus

ticket to get me to a place where I could legally camp out, let alone start a fire.

I was keeping track of all we had purchased, and, as far as I could remember, the two hotel rooms were our only big expense. It was about two hundred dollars for both. The cookies, syrup bottles, and over-the-counter meds combined wouldn't even make fifty bucks. So, either those rooms were two hundred a piece, and I just misunderstood, or someone decided to pickpocket a couple hundred bucks off me.

Nevertheless, the sun was coming up and the hard reality hit that I would soon have to abandon any hope of sleep, get off the bench, and find someplace to hide out for the day. Why did I think this would be anything like it was when I was thirteen? Huntsmen weren't as common back then, and Jackson was so familiar. I almost always had someplace I could go that I knew would be safe, or at the very least have a bed.

I dejectedly reached around in my backpack for one of the beef jerky sticks Aspen had packed for me when my hand grazed the cold, ceramic screen of the phone. Suddenly, things weren't so bleak. I sat up, fished the phone out of the bag, and clicked the round button on the

base of it. The screen illuminated almost instantly to reveal Aspen's family fishing photo.

I wanted to call the others that very minute. I didn't even think about how early it was. The only problem was I didn't know the first thing about smart phones. I tapped on the little green app at the bottom of the screen that clearly had a phone in the center. It pulled up a keyboard of just digits to type in.

I didn't know Aspen's phone number, but he told me it was in "the contacts." I wasn't sure how to get to that either, so I attempted to go back to the home screen by clicking the round button at the base of the phone again. And all of a sudden, it started talking. "Hello, Lone Ranger, how may I help you?" the robotic female voice of the phone said, following a small beeping noise.

Lone Ranger?

"Um," I started hesitantly.

"I'm sorry. I didn't get that. How may I help you?"

"Call Aspen?" I said, unsure.

"Calling-Aspen-Green."

I couldn't believe that worked! I was so excited it was almost pathetic. I literally just saw them the day before—that yesterday. The phone started ringing, and I was

476

racking my brain for what exactly to say. *What happens if they don't pick up? What if everyone is still asleep?*

After about fifty seconds, the phone was still ringing. Maybe Aspen didn't unblock—"CHASE!" someone on the other side of the phone squealed. I fumbled around with the phone and just about broke it. Well, they weren't asleep.

"H-hey Izzy," I said, smiling.

"Oh my gosh, where are you?" she asked.

"Umm..." I mumbled, looking around the rest stop. "I'm—"

"Hey," another voice called.

"Hi, Aspen," I replied. "Where'd Izzy go?"

"Oh, she and the others are fighting over the phone. I think Angela's winning. She was moping about you all night." I couldn't help but laugh.

"I was not!" a voice called from the distance.

"Hi, Angie!" I shouted into the phone.

"Chase says hi," Aspen relayed to the others. "Guys, there's such thing as speakerphone."

From the sound of things, moments later, everyone was huddled around the phone.

"How are you?" Angela asked.

"I'm alright," I said. "Kinda tired."

"Where'd you even sleep?" Aspen asked.

"Bench," I replied. "Okay, I *tried* to sleep on the bench, that plan—didn't really work out."

"Did you find any hardy form of sustenance?" Liles asked.

"Any what?" Aspen asked.

To say yes would be an understatement. Just after leaving the campgrounds, I spotted the happy-go-lucky gatekeeper holding a cappuccino, and I'd never been more inclined to mug someone in my life, despite the fact that I'm pretty sure I hate coffee. I had to shake the thought and remind myself of the food in my backpack. I wanted to focus on finding a safe place to stay before dark, but the second I walked onto the sidewalk, the smell from the fast food restaurants near the entrance of the camp caused me to cave. Which probably heavily contributed to why I don't have enough money for a bus ticket right now. "Um," I said, looking down at the two empty Happy Meal boxes by the base of the bench. "Yup, I feel much better."

"You sound it," Liles replied. "I hope you went easy on yourself. Any huntsmen?"

"None so far, I—"

"What have you been doing?" Aspen interrupted.

"Writing," I replied honestly. "I started writing a book."

"What, why?" Angela asked.

"Just in case I don't come back or something," I explained. "Or, in case I do and want to remember what happened to us."

"Why on earth would you want to remember any of this?" Angela laughed.

"Well, you know," I mumbled, "to show other people someday."

"No, I don't know," she countered. "All of this has been a total nightmare."

"I agree," Izzy chimed in.

"Hey, people love tragedies," Liles told the girls.

"Is it gonna be published?" Aspen asked.

"Course not," Liles answered for me. "Getting books published is an incredibly difficult and time-consuming process."

"Well," I continued shyly, "that was the plan. I was also kind of hoping Angela would help me with a few pages."

"Wait, you're serious about this?" she asked.

"Yeah," I replied, "it wouldn't take too long, and I can edit your sections if you don't want to."

"What would you even call the book?" Izzy asked.

"You know what, I never thought about that," I said, lying down on the bench.

"You could name the book after yourself?" Aspen suggested.

"I guess," I replied, shrugging.

"I don't know," Liles started. "Then he would just be another kid with black hair, green eyes, and a book named after him." Everyone on the other side of the phone started laughing. I just rolled my eyes.

"Okay, you guys pick the title then," I said, reaching into my backpack for the jerky stick I gave up on earlier.

"No offense to you," Liles continued, "but your name isn't all that sing-songy."

"Sing-songy?" I said, confused. "You just mean cool, right?"

"Yes," he confirmed.

"Angela's name is cool," Aspen added.

"Thank you, Aspen," Angela said cheerfully. "Sorry, Chase."

"Hey," I butted in, trapping the phone between my ear and my shoulder, freeing my hands to unwrap the beef jerky. "How is her name better than mine?"

"I can see it now," Izzy chuckled. "Angela Tallon, the book."

"Okay, okay," I said. "The book is gonna be about all of us. It's a 'just in case' book for us to show other people."

"In case of what?" Liles asked.

"In case we're made into coats," Angela laughed.

"Perfect," I laughed, sitting up. "That's what I'm calling it."

"No, I was kidding," she told me. "That's terrible."

"Actually, it might appeal to people who like suspense," Liles argued.

"It appeals to me," I said. "I'm keeping it." The other end of the phone went silent. "You guys still there?"

"Um, yeah," Angela replied, distracted. "Chase, we're gonna have to call you back."

"Oh, okay," I replied, "I hope everything's—"

The phone disconnected before I could finish. I sighed, picking up my notebook and pen off the concrete. It was pretty generic-looking with its spiral-coil spine and solid light-brown color, but I figured now was as good

a time as any to dub it. I pulled the pen cap off with my teeth and proceeded to write on the front cover of the book.

IN CASE WE'RE MADE INTO COATS

THE END

For all the latest news about the In Case We're Made Into Coats series and other books, join our newsletter:

emerald-design.co/newsletter

Find out more online:

incaseweremadeintocoats.com

www.ingramcontent.com/pod-product-compliance
Lightning Source LLC
Chambersburg PA
CBHW070812190726
48292CB00006B/1978